THEATER
PEOPLE

Also by Marc Acito

How I Paid for College

ATTACK of the THEATER PEOPLE

MARC ACITO

Broadway Books
New York

PUBLISHED BY BROADWAY BOOKS

Copyright © 2008 by Marc Acito

Published in the United States by Broadway Books, an imprint of
The Doubleday Broadway Publishing Group, a division of
Random House, Inc., New York.
www.broadwaybooks.com
BROADWAY BOOKS and its logo, a letter B bisected on the diagonal,
are trademarks of Random House, Inc.

This book is a work of fiction. Names, characters, businesses,
organizations, places, events, and incidents either are the product
of the author's imagination or are used fictitiously. Any resemblance
to actual persons, living or dead, events, or locales is entirely
coincidental, with the exception of Marian Seldes, whose lifelong
dedication to the craft of acting defines the term *theater person.*

Book design by Gretchen Achilles

Library of Congress Cataloging-in-Publication Data
Acito, Marc
Attack of the theater people : a novel / by Marc Acito. — 1st ed.
p. cm.
1. Actors—Fiction. 2. New York (N.Y.)—Fiction, I. Title.

PS3601.C53A88 2008
813'.6—dc22
2007041077

ISBN 978-0-7679-2773-4

1 3 5 7 9 10 8 6 4 2

First Edition

For Floyd,

Because no one laughs louder

ATTACK

of the

THEATER
PEOPLE

One

If you think about it (which I try not to), the very term is absurd: *acting school*. Like Juilliard were some kind of substitute filling in for the real thing, as in "acting president" or "acting chairman."

At least, that's what I tell myself as I pace around the fountain at Lincoln Center, my heart throbbing like Vesuvius about to blow. The May sky may be as blue as Frank Sinatra's eyes, but I'm equipped with my own personal rain cloud. Dread has its own ecosystem.

I look at the genuine fake Swatch I bought on the street—3:21 EST (Edward Standard Time)—which means it's 3:10, because I set it eleven minutes fast. I don't know why I bother, because I automatically make the necessary eleven-minute adjustment, which means I'm still always late, plus have to do math.

Adhering to the Italian-Catholic tradition of optional piety, I make a silent prayer to the patron saint of lost causes, whose name escapes me, take one last gulp of spring air, then stalk around the corner with the grim, determined footfall of a condemned man hoping for a reprieve. As I pass through the glass doors leading into the finest drama school in the country, I glance at my reflection, only to see a pallid, hollow-eyed stranger, a faded copy of the Technicolor person I used to be. His face has the haggard, undernourished look of someone who has subsisted solely on a diet of criticism and sheer panic.

That's what two years in acting school can do to you.

As I turn away from the ghost in the glass, I console myself with the knowledge that, unlike my life, at least my hair is under control. Years from now, if anyone asks me which technological advance of the mid-1980s most impacted my life, I won't say personal computers or video-cassette recorders. No, I will extol the miraculous properties of Beautonics® Ready-Set-Go Spray Mousse.

Straight-haired people living in dry environments have no idea of the immense challenges facing curly-haired residents of the New York tristate area. Forget the cat-sized super rats that stalk the sewers and have been known to creep into tenements and carry off infants. Disregard the legions of shaggy mental patients the Reagan administration has unleashed onto the city streets. No, for curly, coarse-haired Mediterraneans like myself, nothing compares to the indignity of having steamy, urban humidity transform your head into a privet hedge.

But then, this past New Year's Eve, while getting ready to ring in 1986, my roommate Paula sprayed a handful of foam into my palm and, with one swoop across my scalp, ended twenty Bad Hair years.

I take a disproportionate amount of solace in the fact that, no matter how muggy it is outside (or inside my personal ecosystem), no matter what occurs, even if the unthinkable, the unmentionable, happens today, my hair will remain rigid, steadfast, and true.

But I still must wait to learn my fate. Even at 3:47 EST,

the door to Marian Seldes's classroom is closed, which means that the grande dame of the Juilliard drama department hasn't finished with Willow.

Willow.

From the moment I heard her name—Willow Branch—I knew I wanted to be her friend. What kind of parents name their kid Willow Branch? (Hippie parents, as it turned out.) She asked obtuse questions during orientation, always in sentence fragments you had to piece together like a puzzle: "Is Juilliard doing anything—because Manhattan was stolen from the Native American people—well, they paid, but not a fair price—and Lincoln Center is funded by the city—at least, I assume it is—so don't you think we should be doing something to compensate the native people?" Everyone else rolled their eyes, the faculty included, but I found her fascinating. Willow has an ethereal, Ophelia's-mad-scene quality about her, like she's listening to music no one else hears.

We met in the cafeteria. She was seated alone at the next table, moving a saltshaker along a subway map. I didn't realize she was talking to me because she just sighed and said, "I feel sorry for Fiftieth Street."

I looked up from my copy of *Much Ado About Nothing* to see her freckled face peering at me, her skin like a speckled egg, her frizzy ginger hair growing every which way, as if it couldn't be bothered to coordinate the effort.

"Excuse me?"

"The Fiftieth Street station," she said. "It has no identity. It makes me—well, just look—Fifty-ninth Street is Columbus Circle and Sixty-sixth is Lincoln Center. Then, to the south, there's Forty-second Street, Times Square, and Thirty-fourth Street, Penn Station. But Fiftieth—nothing. Just a number. It's the neglected middle child of the

Seventh Avenue line." She looked at me, her eyes glassy and fragile, as if this mattered a great deal. "What would you name it?"

"I don't know. Gershwin Theater? Circle in the Square?"

She frowned. "I'd like to name it Nowhere. That way, when you got off, you could say you went Nowhere: 'Where ya' goin'?' 'Nowhere.'"

"The existential subway station."

Willow clutched her hand to her chest. "Oh! That's so— it makes me—you have no idea." She advanced on me, her hands flying a few inches away from my body, as if she were molding me in clay. "I just love that you used the word *existential* in a sentence," she said, practically crying. "Let's be friends."

We have been ever since. Hanging out with Willow makes me feel grown-up and responsible because she's apt to do things like lose her shoes at a party or try to hug a police horse.

The door to the studio swings open and out she wafts with the vague, contented expression of Blanche DuBois after a couple of spiked lemon Cokes and a nooner with the delivery boy. Unlike me, Willow's not in any danger. She has no trouble being "publicly private" or "emotionally transparent" in acting class. All she has to worry about is not taking the wrong subway and ending up in the Bronx.

Behind her I see the whippet-thin silhouette of Marian Seldes, her regal profile like something you'd find on an Etruscan coin. She turns and extends an oh-so-graceful arm.

"Ah, my little bird, come in."

Seldes calls all of us her little birds, with great affection, but I can't help wondering whether it's her way of protecting herself emotionally. Much in the way farmers don't name the animals they're going to slaughter, or the Pilgrims didn't name their children until they survived infancy, perhaps Seldes doesn't address us individually until she's certain we're going to last.

After a semester on probation, today's the day I find out. Probation. As if bad acting were a crime. I pass Willow, who crosses her fingers, then her eyes, which makes me smile. I love it when beautiful women cross their eyes. It's subversive.

Marian Seldes gestures to a chair, a Park Avenue hostess inviting me to tea. "Do sit down, Edmund."

"Edward."

"Oh, I'm so sorry. We were just discussing *Long Day's Journey into Night.*"

Undoubtedly imagining Willow's future triumph as the dazed morphine addict Mary Tyrone.

I smooth my dingy black jeans, which I washed in the tub with shampoo because I can't afford the Laundromat, then pull my navy blue T-shirt away from my belly. It's the same shirt I wore when I played Jesus in my high school production of *Godspell,* but I've turned it inside out to hide the Superman decal, which now sticks to my chest. I don't really like wearing black and blue together, as if I were a bruise, but there's an unspoken competition in the drama department to see who can look the most ragged. Mention that you only slept four hours last night and someone will nod and say they only slept three. Back in high school I treated every day as a costume drama; but anyone who spiffs themselves up here isn't taken seriously.

And I seriously need to be taken seriously.

Marian Seldes folds one attenuated leg over another

like a cricket about to commence a solo. "Dirge for a Drama Student."

"Tell me, my little bird," she murmurs, "how do you feel you're doing in your studies?"

Truthfully? For two years, I've been lost in a Freudian bog without a map. Improvising as ourselves, without a character to hide behind, is supposed to free us from self-consciousness and fear, but the exercises only make me more self-conscious and fearful: three minutes alone in your room waking up; three minutes alone in your room getting dressed; three minutes alone in your room reading a letter.

In the words of Sally Bowles, "What good is sitting alone in your room?"

Acting class doesn't feel anything like doing a show. No backstage buzz. No spotlight. No applause. What's more, we're never supposed to penetrate the invisible "fourth wall" between us and the audience, never "perform." I feel like someone's cut off my arms and legs.

The actors who succeed here are the ones who are emotionally available, like Willow. Press a button and out come tears. I don't know how she does it. She's a human spigot. I'm more like Morales in *A Chorus Line*. I dig right down to the bottom of my soul and I feel nothing.

How am I doing?

"Okay."

Marian Seldes fixes her eagle eyes on me, radiating the same steely resolve that landed her in *The Guinness Book of World Records* for performing five years on Broadway in *Deathtrap* without missing a performance—all while teaching. Her cheekbones are like bookshelves, above which sit eyes that speak volumes. "Just . . . okay?"

I look around the windowless room, with its gray

linoleum floor and acoustic tile ceiling, desperately hoping I might be inspired by the brilliant ghosts who once studied here: Kevin Kline, Robin Williams, William Hurt. In the hermetically sealed world of Juilliard you are literally breathing the same air as the stars.

I've got to say something, preferably true. But what? After having every move I make, every word I say vivisected, analyzed, and criticized in front of everyone, I don't know what to do anymore. Learning to act is like getting buried in the sand up to your neck, then having an Australian soccer team play footy with your head.

Marian Seldes sighs.

"Edward, when you first auditioned for us you laid yourself bare, exposing the fishy white underbelly of your soul."

Actually, I forgot my lines, had a total meltdown, and ended up incorporating the words *goddamned fucking asswipe shit-for-brains pussy-whipped toad* into Sophocles' *Antigone*. This somehow got mistaken for talent.

Marian Seldes continues. "But ever since then, you've been concealing something. Instead of truth, you're always giving us a *performance*." She splays her quill-like fingers in a Fosse-esque manner, but the effect's all wrong.

Lady Macbeth! The Musical.

She purses her mouth. "I'm afraid you're simply too . . . what's the expression . . . 'jazz hands' for Juilliard."

No. This can't be happening. I worked too hard to get here to be rejected. I sued my own father to make this dream come true, and that was after I tried to raise the money myself through embezzlement, blackmail, money laundering, identity theft, fraud, forgery, and (just a little) prostitution. "I'm sure I've got it in me," I say. "If I just tried harder . . ."

She places her hands to her breastbone, as if to quell the emotion burbling inside her. "Oh, my little bird, you're so young," she says, which is true. At least half of my classmates came to Juilliard after completing a bachelor's elsewhere. The drama division doesn't offer a master's, so we're all together, and the gulf between those in their mid-twenties and those of us who can't drink legally is vast. "What you need," she says, "is life experience. You need to get out into the world and discover Who. You. Are." She rises, gesturing to some unseen horizon. "Hop a freight train. Work on a fishing boat. Have a love affair and get your heart broken." She's all elbows and flying hands as she speaks, her fingers manipulating invisible marionettes.

"And then what?"

"Who knows?" Her eyes light with excitement, as if she and I were going off together. "That's the point."

"But I want to finish school."

"And you should. Listen, Edmund—"

"Edward."

"Of course. I'm so sorry. I keep thinking of Eugene O'Neill. He was expelled from college, too, you know."

The word *expelled* slams me in the chest.

"But then he went off and had *adventures*," she says, shaking a fist to screw my courage to the sticking place. "And that led him to become the first great American playwright."

"But," I hear a small voice say, "I want to be an actor."

It's all I've ever wanted.

Marian Seldes folds herself onto the chair again. "Here's what we'll do," she says in a soothing bedtime voice. "In a year's time, if you like, you can reaudition. Of course, there's no guarantee you'll get readmitted, but we'd certainly consider you again. How's that?"

I nod, unable to speak. Unable to feel.

"Now, *fly*, little bird," she says, tossing her arms like she's releasing a carrier pigeon. "Fly, and be *free*!"

It's an exit line. Except I'm the one who exits.

Two

Failure follows me wherever I go—a shadow, a stalker. It's infected every inch of me—a virus, a cancer. Each morning I wake up and it's written on the insides of my eyelids: EDWARD ZANNI GOT EXPELLED.

No wonder Eugene O'Neill's plays are so depressing.

It wouldn't be so bad if I'd been kicked out for doing something notorious. Years from now, when I'm famous, I could sit on the couch next to Johnny Carson and tell him about the time I took a bath in the Lincoln Center fountain or got drunk at a party and felt up Marian Seldes. And Johnny would laugh until he wiped a tear from his eye the way he does, and his sidekick Ed McMahon would laugh even harder because he'll laugh at anything, and everything would be okay because I would be famous and not washed-up at twenty, which is what I am.

"You have nothing to be ashamed of—*nothing*!" Paula insists, emphasizing her point with the wave of a fleshy arm. "Your process is different, that's all. You and the faculty have . . . creative differences."

Yeah, I thought I could act and they didn't. I stink, therefore I ham.

Paula does as she has since we were in high school, bullying me like an officious Victorian nanny, insisting I periodically bathe, take invigorating walks in the park, and limit my consumption of beer before breakfast. ("Baby steps," she says. "You take enough of them and pretty soon you've gotten somewhere.") She's hard to avoid, considering we share a one-bedroom basement apartment, along with her boyfriend, Marcus, and Willow. In order to maximize our limited space, Willow and I sleep in the living room—in hammocks. We thought it would feel like *Robinson Crusoe*, but it's more like awaiting burial at sea.

None of my roommates can possibly understand how I feel. They're all successes at Juilliard—relatively, at least. The faculty continually hassles Paula about her weight and Marcus about his attitude, but, like Willow, they deliver the theatrical goods and, therefore, remind me daily of my failure.

So there's nothing Paula can say to convince me to join her on Memorial Day weekend for Hands Across America. Yes, I know it's the first and perhaps only time that five million people will hold hands to form a line across the continent. And if I lived in the Arizona desert with my mother, where there are so few people they have to line up sailboats and catamarans, I would go. (If only to find out why anyone in the Arizona desert owns a sailboat or a catamaran.) But New York is a mob scene, and I fail to see what difference I'd make. Besides, I don't want to feel at one with humanity. I just want to stay home in my boxers and eat ice cream.

I find an unlikely ally in Marcus, who boycotts the event based on a host of grievances, which he gladly enumerates afterward as the four of us cram onto a train headed to Jersey (five if you count my dirty laundry, which is the size of a body bag).

"They charged you twenty-five dollars to hold hands?" Marcus says, the ropy veins in his neck popping. He scowls at the car packed with people in red-white-and-blue Hands Across America T-shirts. " 'Age, thou art shamed!' "

Paula lifts her dark thicket of curls to cool her lily-white neck, her off-the-shoulder peasant blouse descending as her enormous breasts smush against each other like bald men kissing. "It was a fund-raiser for the homeless," she says. "Don't be vituperative." She adjusts her thick studded belt, which she wears over a gauze skirt, the overall effect being of a very trendy grape stomper. Unlike me, Paula hasn't let Juilliard stomp out her desire to express herself through fashion. I look down at my wrinkled oxford and khakis and feel shabby.

Marcus gestures to the crowd with the same haughty disdain he exhibited as Hotspur in Juilliard's production of *Henry IV, Part One*. "Baby, look at those T-shirts," he says. "Every one of them an ad for Citibank and Coca-Cola." He throws back his head, unleashing four years' worth of voice and speech training. "Pawns! Corporate tools!"

Marcus inherited these convictions. The grandnephew of Nikolai Sokoloff, the Russian director of the Federal Music Project, he is also the son of Martha Hopkins, the distinguished African-American soprano and civil rights activist. As a result, he possesses the kind of pure, socialist contempt for capitalism that only a trust fund can buy. He wears his usual uniform—a white undershirt and jeans—to demonstrate his solidarity with the workingman.

"I don't understand you," Paula says, snapping open a lace fan and flapping it over the canyon of her cleavage. "How can you be opposed to corporations donating money?" She looks to me for confirmation, but I don't have the energy; it's partly depression but mostly the heat, which makes me feel sticky and fat. Nominally, I suppose I'm slender, having burned excess calories this semester through sheer panic, but my body is still soft, like an un-baked pie.

"I'm opposed to corporations, period," Marcus snaps. "We shouldn't have to throw a continental block party to help the homeless." Aggression radiates from his taut, coiled frame like a furnace, and the passengers next to us inch away. Marcus tends to have that effect on people. Both his personality and appearance remind me of sand-paper, the latter due to an unfortunate set of pockmark acne scars.

"Well, I found it *exhilarating*," Paula says. "Didn't you, Willow? Will?"

Willow turns and looks at us as if she's just realized there are other people on the train. She shrugs her freck-led shoulders, which look like they've been dusted with cinnamon, and starts to sing:

We are the world . . .

"Oh, no. Don't you start," Marcus says, but he's drowned out by Paula.

We are the children . . .

A pair of senior citizens in shiny tracksuits chimes in, and soon all the people advertising Citibank and Coca-Cola are swaying and singing. No one knows the rest of the words, so they just la-la-la all the way to Jersey. I look at Marcus, feeling as saggy as my bag of laundry.

" 'What fools these mortals be,' " he mutters.

The bar is packed when we arrive, and not just with people. Lucky McPuddles is the kind of claustrophobic restaurant-pub where they nail as much crap to the walls and ceiling as they can and call it atmosphere: street signs, bowling trophies, rocking chairs, carousel horses. It looks like the set of *Cats*. Add in all the high-haired Jersey girls dancing around piles of purses like witches at a coven and you can barely see the band.

And the band is the reason we're here. Otherwise I wouldn't set foot in Jersey. Not that I've got anything par-ticular against my home state; I oppose all smug, compla-cent suburbs. As a result, I am not in the habit of eating mozzarella sticks while listening to a Bruce Springsteen cover band called Almost Bruce. But tonight is different. Tonight is the first time any of us will witness a perfor-mance of Almost Bruce's new lead singer, Doug Grabowski.

Doug.

Doug, Doug, Doug, Doug, Doug.

I take some credit for the direction his life has taken. For it was I who first sensed that Doug yearned for a cre-ative outlet beyond the Paleolithic pleasures of football. And it was I who convinced him to audition for Danny Zuko in the Wallingford Summer Workshop production of *Grease*, opening up a whole new world to him. But it was Doug who went to see Springsteen's *Born in the USA* con-cert, which inspired him to follow in the rocker's footsteps by dropping out of community college, taking up the gui-tar, and wearing very tight Levi's.

There are worse things he could do.

Willow and I lose Paula and Marcus in the crowd as we

push our way in. I still can't see the stage, but I can hear a growly baritone that sounds just like the man Jerseyites simply refer to as Bruce.

This gun's for hire,
Even if we're just dancing in the dark.

I'm not a Springsteen fan. For all the hype about Bruce's lyrics being poetry, it bugs me when he mixes a metaphor ("This gun's for hire, even if we're just dancing in the dark"?); that is, when I can understand what he's saying at all. Bruce Springsteen's mush-mouthed diction makes Bob Dylan sound like Henry Higgins.

No, as far as Jersey boys go, Springsteen may be the Boss, but Sinatra is still the Chairman of the Board. When Frank dances in the dark, he waltzes in the wonder of why we're here, looking for the light of a new love.

Now, that's poetry.

But since my failure is imprinted so firmly on my psyche, even Sinatra's music is spoiled for me. Just thinking of those classic Capitol recordings (easy to do—I know them so well I don't actually need to listen anymore) reminds me of Juilliard. You see, in order to pay for school, I kind of stole Frank Sinatra's identity. Well, not stole. More like borrowed. On the dubious advice of my cheese-head friend Nathan Nudelman, I used Ol' Blue Eyes's name to create a scholarship as a vehicle for laundering money so I could embezzle funds from my father when he refused to pay for acting school, which resulted in my actually embezzling the money from my evil ex-stepmonster, because she was embezzling from my father in the first place. That scheme didn't work out so well, forcing us to move to plan B, which entailed drugging my stepmonster and taking blackmail pictures of her passed out beneath Doug's absurdly large penis.

Y'know, just good, clean teen fun.

Memories of Doug naked—and of the one time we were nearly together—loom large in my imagination, so much so that I often question my mental health. Surely it's not normal to obsess so much about a straight guy. Not to mention pointless. And self-defeating. And humiliating.

And there he is.

Three

Doug shouts "Hey, baby!" and several women rush the stage. Suddenly there's a clearing in the bracken of Big Jersey Hair, and my heart stops beating, presumably because all the blood has traveled to my groin. Doug's outfitted in Bruce's trademark checked shirt with the sleeves cut off, a bandanna wrapped around his head, and a pair of 501s caressing his thighs so tightly I momentarily forget my troubles, as well as my name and Social Security number. With his cowlicky hair dyed darker, he bears a surprising resemblance to Springsteen, all flashing teeth and sparkling eyes.

As a saxophone wails, Doug grooves to the music, his whole body swaying to the beat. The smile on his face is unmistakable—he's drunk with the pleasure of performing—and he beams at the audience, flinging pheromones with each sweaty strut.

It's not just the heat he generates that infatuates me; it's the light he shines. Most straight guys are too macho and mumbly ever to express this kind of six-hundred-watt joy, but Doug's not embarrassed to share the Pan-like pleasure he takes in performing. He seems so at home in his skin, so effortlessly comfortable in the world, so assuredly, maddeningly heterosexual. That's the thing about guys with big dicks: They can be stupid, homely, poor—it doesn't matter. They still have that confidence about them, that cockiness that says, *Guess what I have in my pants?*

To the shrieks of the hair down front, he extends a veiny arm into the crowd and pulls a slender woman in a pink ruffled miniskirt onto the stage. She spins around once, twice, three—*whoa*—four times, her square-cut cotton shirt rising to reveal her flat belly, her blond ponytail flying, her pale pony legs rippling. She looks like a cross between a gazelle and Giselle.

Willow leans in to me. "Isn't that your old girlfriend?"

I nod.

"What's her name?"

Kelly.

I'm not surprised to see her—we planned to meet here, after all—but watching her rock out onstage with Doug gives me a pang. Last summer, when Kelly and I both worked at Six Flags Great Adventure, I didn't mind that she got cast in the revue while I spent two months baking inside a character costume. After all, she's the Bennington dance major, not me, and I'd like to think I brought something new to the interpretation of Chuckles the Woodchuck. This past winter, however, we both auditioned for summer stock and, well, I was under a lot of stress at school and was fighting a cold, which means Kelly's got her Actor's Equity card and I've got plenty of nuthin'.

I'm happy for her. Really.

I mean it.

No, really.

Okay, here's the thing: Kelly and Doug were like my

protégés. I'm the one who lit that flame inside them. Now they're both three-alarm fires and I'm burned out.

Kelly bobs like a piston, each limb throwing off sparks of enthusiasm. She shimmies at Doug, like she did when she played Sandy to his Danny in *Grease*, and he laughs in recognition. They look so comfortable together onstage, so free, so uninhibited.

It makes me want to shoot them both, then myself.

The song finishes and, as the crowd cheers, I hear a man's voice behind me say, "They look good together, no?" The accent is indeterminately Continental, which either means Lucky McPuddles has been discovered by Euro-trash or I've been discovered by Ziba.

I turn around and there she is, literally the height of fashion. Her new hairdo extends upward like a skyscraper, adding another five inches to what she refers to as her five-foot-twelve frame, making her look like a very startled Cleopatra. I try to hug her, but am impaled on a pair of earrings shaped like Calder mobiles.

"Come," she says, tickling me under the chin. "I can't bear watching Kelly flirt with men." To Ziba's endless frustration, Kelly continues to experiment with heterosexuality.

I leave Willow, who's dancing alone with her eyes closed, and follow Ziba through the crowd, which is easy to do because she's five-foot-seventeen and wears a pleather tube dress and patterned stockings.

Once we're in the bar I'm pleased to see I'm not carded. There's nothing like bitter disappointment to lend you an air of gravitas. I order a pair of tequila shooters, both for myself. Ziba observes me, her face as unreadable as the *Wall Street Journal*.

"You look awful," she says.

"Thanks," I mutter as I knock back my first glass of liquid amnesia. "I feel awful."

She retrieves a cigarette from a sleek silver case, tapping it on the lid with the assurance of someone who's watched lots of black-and-white movies. "Well, at least you're consistent." She dangles the cig between two fingers, the Internationally Recognized Signal for "Light me, darling." Or, to be more precise, "I'm too pretentious to light it myself." Or maybe, "I refuse to let you wallow in self-pity. It's not good for you, and you know how excessive displays of emotion make me uncomfortable."

I pick up her lighter and increase her chances of lung cancer. "You should quit, you know."

"Don't be ridiculous," she says, exhaling a long stream of exhaust. "No one likes a quitter."

Ziba.

"Besides," she continues, "if I'm going to quit anything, it'll be the Fashion Institute. You don't know how lucky you are to be out of school, Edward." Her voice drops an octave as she adds, "I'm so bored."

I remind her that her rigorous schedule of partying with other expat Persians actually prevents her from attending classes.

"That's why I'm so bored," she says. "I need a project. I called Nathan to see if he has any ideas, but his roommate said he was at home and his parents said he was at school. Have you heard from him?"

Of all of our high school friendships, none is more unlikely than that of the five-foot-twelve Persian lesbian and her five-foot-four Jewish sidekick. It's the Ayatollah Khomeini's worst nightmare. "I haven't seen Natie since New Year's," I say, nor do I want to think about what kind of trouble he's gotten into. Nathan Nudelman is like a headline—all bad news. "Maybe he's been recruited by the CIA."

Ziba exhales a dragon's breath of smoke. "No, he'd tell me if he were."

Just then, Kelly appears, breaking through Ziba's cloud like the sun.

"There you are!" she says, giving me an I-haven't-seen-you-since-you-got-kicked-out-of-school-but-I-love-you-anyway-even-though-you're-a-loser hug. Or, at least, that's how I interpret it. She brushes my bangs out of my eyes, which is hard to do when they've been moussed into sub-mission, and gives me a moist, soulful gaze. Her eyes are made up to camouflage her heterochromia, a condition that causes them to be two different colors, one favoring blue, the other brown. Kelly read somewhere that Vivien Leigh didn't actually have green eyes and that the effect in *Gone With the Wind* was accomplished through skill-ful makeup and lighting, so now she's got this compli-cated Bloomingdale's-makeup-counter regimen. Even with Monet's *Water Lilies* on her eyelids, there's no mistaking her pity. And I won't be pitied by anyone. Except, of course, myself.

From the other room the band starts up again. "C'mon," I say, feigning enthusiasm. "I love this song!" I don't, but I've got to get out from under the weight of her kindness. Grasping Kelly's hand like a lifeline, I squeeze into the back of the room, where we watch Doug perform with acrobatic abandon—jumping up on the amp, sliding across the stage on his knees, leaping into the crowd—and my body begins to ache. Not just for Doug, although that's easy to do when so many of the songs are addressed to love objects with an-drogynous names like Frankie, Ricky, and Terry and have titles like "I'm Goin' Down" and "Ramrod," but also for myself, for the person I used to be. Back in high school I was the madcap *bon vivant* who cavorted onstage and off, a puckish Pied Piper who led the parade of the Play People. But two years of being told I perform too much—that I push, show, and indicate—have made me timid. I went to school to learn how to act and I've become inert.

After the show we snag ourselves a table, but, having drunk four (five? okay, six) tequila shooters, I find that the print on the menu keeps rearranging itself into kaleidoscopic patterns, like showgirls in a Busby Berkeley musical.

"Whah goes wid tequila?" I ask Ziba.

"Blackouts."

I look across the room, which tilts like the deck of the *Titanic*, and see Doug surrounded by Jersey girls seeking autographs. Autographs! Back in high school he didn't know a whole note from a fried egg, and now he's signing autographs. I resist the urge to march across the room and pull his fans off of him, screaming, "Back off, bitches, he's *mine!*" Instead I order another shooter, wishing I could arrange for an intravenous drip.

I turn back to the table, where Kelly's telling everyone what it's like to join Actor's Equity.

"They've even got a newsletter," she says, pulling it out of her bag.

Marcus sneers. "You carry it around with you?"

"I brought it for Edward," Kelly snips, then, turning to me, adds, "I figured you could use it, now that you're . . . Well, it's got a lot of great inside information."

I flip through pages of casting calls, obituaries, and apartment notices, all of them swirling in formation, then fold the newsletter in quarters so it'll fit in my back pocket.

"Fanks," I gurgle.

There's an awkward silence, as silences are wont to be. A quick inventory of the participants doesn't bode well for conversation: Marcus is in a mood, Ziba's aloof, I'm drunk, and Willow is, well, Willow. That leaves Paula and Kelly to do the heavy lifting.

"So where are you working this summer?" Paula asks in a cheery, talk-show tone.

"Akron Under the Stars."

We all nod like we're impressed. Kelly tries to downplay being cast as Dream Laurey in *Oklahoma!* by explaining that she looks like the woman playing the regular daytime Laurey. *Her success has nothing to do with me,* I say to myself.

Eventually Doug struts over to our table. As usual, Paula takes charge. "Can you sit with us? Come, sit. Edward, let him sit. Pleeeze, sit, sit, sit."

Fine, I think, *just stop saying "sit."* I start to get up, a little miffed that I'm the one being asked to give up my seat, but Doug just nudges me over, sharing it with me. On the sound track in my mind, a thousand violins begin to play.

Paula continues as hostess. "Doug, have you met My Boyfriend, Marcus?"

If this were acting class, Marian Seldes would tell Paula she's telegraphing the subtext: "My little bird, don't *show* us that you're uncomfortable introducing your current boyfriend to a well-endowed man you used to sleep with recreationally. *Be* uncomfortable."

Doug and Marcus each give that upward nod of the head that guy-guys do, two alpha dogs.

"Hey."

"Hey."

Paula gestures to Willow. "And this is our roommate Willow."

Willow just laughs, as if someone told a joke only flakes can hear. She hands Doug a bar napkin. "Can I have your autograph?"

Doug reaches into his back pocket, his hand brushing against my thigh, and a shiver crosses my face and down my neck, making the hair on my arms stand on end. But then he pulls a pen out of his pocket and I feel myself die a little. Having autograph seekers is one thing; being ready is another. As he signs, Willow says, "You're a sweater."

Doug looks confused, a near-universal response where Willow is concerned. "I'm a what?"

"A sweater."

"Ya' mean, like a cardigan?"

"No. Like a big, wet, sweaty mess."

Doug Grouchos his eyebrows at me, the Internationally Recognized Signal for "The redhead's a freak, but I'd still bone her." If he does, that'll leave Marcus as the only person at the table with whom Doug hasn't had a sexual encounter.

I look down at the napkin, which he's signed, *Doug Grab.*

"Where's the -owski?" I ask. "Ya' need anudder napkin?"

"Doug Grabowski sounds like a teamster," he says. "Doug Grab is a rock star." He looks around the table. "Whaddya guys think?"

"It's a bit aggressive," Ziba says, swirling the Courvoisier in her glass. "But so's rock 'n' roll."

"I like it," Kelly says.

"Why don't you just call yourself Almost Bruce?" Marcus says, biting into a chicken strip.

Doug narrows his eyes. " 'Cuz that's not my name."

You can almost hear the Western showdown music.

"I've got it!" Willow says. "Why don't you call yourself the Sweater?"

For a moment we're all united in our shared opinion of Willow. "He can't call himself the Sweater," Paula says.

"Why not?"

Paula begins to explain and I tune out. Willow and I have conversations like this nightly while we lie in our hammocks: "How come, when you pick up a rock and there are all those bugs and worms and stuff underneath, how come they're not smushed? And how come, in *Cinderella*, the coach and the footmen and the dress all turn back to what they were at midnight but the glass slippers stay the same? And how come . . ."

Doug turns to me. "So?"

"Sew buttons."

"Whadja think, man?" he says. "How was I?"

He cares what I think. Of course, he doesn't know yet that I've been kicked out of school. That my opinion is obviously worthless.

I look straight into his eyes—all six (seven?) of them.

"You. Were. Great." I concentrate on each word to make sure they come out in the right order. "Raw. An' electric. An' . . ."

"And what?"

"I forgot whut I wuz gonna say. Oh! An' you were totalilly in the moment. Totalilly. And I'm not jussayin' that 'cuz I'm a lipple titsy . . . a tittle lipsy . . . 'cuz I'm drunk."

"Thanks, man," he says. "That means a lot to me." He puts his hand on my shoulder, and it takes every bit of self-control I have left not to lean over and lick him.

I am twenty years old and, thanks to a not unreasonable fear that sex with the wrong person will kill me, I have only gotten laid once in the last two years. Once! And even that wasn't so great. After a summer sweating inside the woodchuck costume, I finally hooked up with one of the dancers in the Six Flags revue, which we called Six Fags because all of the guys were gay. But he wasn't really my type. None of them were. Those swishy dancer guys just make me cringe. I mean, if I wanted to date a woman, I would. After all, women are still my second-favorite people to have sex with, but they're a distant second. I guess you could say I was on the "bi now, gay later" plan.

I'm brought back into the conversation when I hear Kelly mention a wedding Ziba's going to. I'm always eager to hear about Ziba's Persian social life, her "Arabian nights" at trendy bars with private rooms and subtle lighting.

"Why do you have to be so mysterious?" Kelly says, then announces to the rest of the table, "She's going to the shah's wedding."

"The shah of Iran?" Marcus says. "I thought he was dead."

"It's his son," Kelly says, "the one who would've been shah if his father hadn't been deposed."

"What do you call the son of a shah?" Paula asks. "The prince?"

Ziba hesitates just long enough for the rest of us to volley the possibilities:

Shah Junior

Shah Lite

The Man Who Would Be Shah

I Can't Believe It's Not the Shah

Shah-Nah-Nah

Shahma-Lahma-Ding-Dong

George Bernard Shah

Almost Shah

When pressed for details, Ziba answers in vague gener-alities, leaving us all to wonder just how close she is to roy-alty. Marcus won't let it go, though, and bores into her with his coal black eyes. "So you're a monarchist?"

Ziba opens her mouth just enough to let the smoke out, like when there's a fire behind a closed door. "Politics bore me."

"But you're going to his wedding. That's a political act."

Paula rests a tiny hand on Marcus's arm. "Honey, calm down."

"Why should I?" he says, rising. "That's the problem with all of you. You're too complacent in your bourgeois bubble." He then embarks on a Marxist diatribe I won't re-peat, mostly because I can't follow it. Something about the exploitation of the common people by the evil-white-male-military-industrial-corporate complex, which, somehow, is personified by a five-foot-seventeen Persian lesbian. He finishes by marching out without paying.

Paula apologizes for him. "The graduating class just did their presentations for agents and casting directors. Mar-cus didn't go over as well as he would have liked."

Willow nods as she sticks the paper umbrella from her piña colada in her hair. "Some agent said he had a face like a sea sponge."

The party breaks up from there, and I immediately mourn the demise of the evening. I don't want to leave my friends—not yet, not so soon. My petty neuroses aside, I never feel more like myself than when I'm with them, and I feel desperate to hang on to that feeling. I wish we could go everywhere together, like wolves or Japanese tourists. Not only are my friends a safe harbor in which to dock, they're the lighthouse guiding me home across storm-tossed seas.

But I have to make a duty call—at a port I have no desire to visit.

Four

It's after two when I stagger down the hall to my old room, swaying back and forth with my bag of laundry as if I were dancing with it. I don't know how my dad can stand living in a four-bedroom split-level ranch all by himself. Actually, I don't know how anyone could stand living in a four-bedroom split-level ranch period, particularly if you could afford any of Wallingford's many charming Colonials or Tudors. As always, Al's got financial reasons for keeping it—something about capital gains and a onetime exertion. (Excursion? Excretion? Whatever.) But it's a sad place, the house my mother walked out of when I was twelve, and the house I walked out of shortly before my eighteenth birthday, slamming the door on the Teutonic nightmare that was my evil ex-stepmonster. Plus, it's a four-bedroom split-level ranch, which just sucks.

I slip in the door to my old room as quietly as is possible when your body is do-si-doing against its will, unzip my pants, shimmy across the room, and flop onto the bed face-first.

Onto a sleeping body.

I'm not sure who screams first, me or the woman. I

scramble to get off of her, a task made easier when she knees me in the groin. While I cringe on the floor, she yells, "*AYUDA! AYÚDAME!*"

The door flies open, and I see the silhouette of a caveman with a club.

"*POP! IT'S ME! IT'S ME! IT'S ME!*" I yell, suddenly sober. Life-threatening terror can do that to you.

"Eddie?" He flips on the light to find me sprawled on the floor, my pants around my ankles, while a plump young woman sobs in Spanish.

"What the fuck's goin' on?" Al says, putting down the baseball bat. His furry frame is covered only by a towel, giving him the unfortunate appearance of a skirted dancing bear.

"I don't know," I gasp. "All I tried to—"

"Milagros, you okay?"

"Spanish Spanish Spanish Spanish," Milagros says.

"THIS. IS. MY. SON," he shouts, like she's retarded instead of foreign.

The woman pulls the neck of her oversize T-shirt up over her face, hiding her head behind the word RELAX. She looks to be in her late twenties.

"*Esto es mío . . .* Shit. Eddie, how d'ya say *son* in goddamned Spanish?"

I have no idea, having studied French because it seemed more elegant.

"Spanish Spanish Spanish Spanish."

"Milagros, *esto es mío . . . sol. MÍO SOL.*"

I may not know Spanish, but I believe my father just informed a hysterical Latina that I am his sunshine.

Milagros seems to get the idea. "Your son?" she says.

"*SÍ. SÍ. SÍ,*" Al and I both shout.

When I woke up this morning it never occurred to me

that I would need to know the Spanish word for *rapist*, so it requires a dictionary to explain to Milagros that she sleeps in my old room and I am not *el violador.*

In fact, once she calms down, she's as warm and sweet as the delicious doughy cheesy thingy she heats up for me. I'm not hungry—well, that's not exactly true; I'm always hungry—but I shouldn't be, having just gorged on mozzarella sticks and chicken strips. Since I left school I can't seem to stop eating. It's like I've got a giant hole inside me I can't fill.

"Who is she?" I ask after Milagros has gone back to bed.

My father drips melted cheese onto his broad, hairy chest. He's wearing a robe now, but it's one of those short ones, which is just too embarrassing. "She's my new domestic."

Domestic? This is not a word we Zannis have ever used as a noun, being just a generation or two removed from immigrant pushcart vendors ourselves. Employing a live-in domestic seems entirely too you-ain't-Kunta-Kinte-yo'-name-is-Toby-now for us.

"She lives here?"

"I was gonna tell ya', but I thought you weren't comin' home till tomorrow."

"Where does she come from?"

"Nicaragua. Fran Nudelman found her for me in Miami. It's a sweetheart deal. She cleans a bunch of the houses in the neighborhood and lives here in exchange for doin' the cookin'. I hope you don't mind I gave her your old room."

"No, it's fine."

"I thought about givin' her the guest room, but your room has the best light."

"I understand."

"You sure? 'Cuz if it bothers you, we should talk about

it. It's not healthy to let feelings fester inside you, y'know."
After my evil ex-stepmonster returned to whatever hellhole
vomited her onto this earth, Al got just enough therapy to
be really annoying.

"It's *fine*," I say.

"Aha!" he says, shaking a sausage-sized finger. "I knew
it. You do mind."

"IDON'TCAREABOUTTHEGODDAMNEDROOM!"

Al furrows his eyebrows, two mustaches colliding.
"What's botherin' you, kid?"

*You mean, aside from the fact that my most cherished
life's dream has turned into a nightmare? And that I have
no money and no job and no idea what I'm going to do next?
And that you're going to say, "I told you acting school was
a lousy idea?" And then bitch about all the trouble I caused
making you pay for it and how you've wasted twenty grand
and isn't it time I grew up and got a real job? You mean, besides that?*

"Nothing," I say.

I rise the next afternoon so hungover even my sweat
smells like tequila. The Tennessee Williams Wake-Up Call.
What's more, my teeth seem to have grown fur. I shower
until I use up all the hot water, then throw on my smoky
clothes and duck out to avoid my father. I know I'll have to
tell him eventually, but tuition's not due until August, and
it's possible he could get hit by a bus or a falling piano by
then, in which case what's the point of spoiling his final
moments on earth? I escape the house, hoping to leave behind the looming dread that sticks to me like tar.

I head across the street to find out what's happened to
Natie, a process otherwise known as Looking for Trouble.

Just last year, while engaged in a light-saber battle with a visiting friend from college, Natie broke the back of his mother's couch, then invited me over and purposely stood in a way so I'd lean against it and take the blame. When I later found out what happened, he said, "What do you care? Al paid for it."

Natie.

I press the doorbell, which is followed by a voice that sounds like Ethel Merman slamming her fingers in a car door.

"NATHAAAAAAAN! ANSWER THE DOOOOOOOR."

It's the Call of the Nudelmans.

"NATHAAAAAAAN? DIDJA HEAR ME?"

How could he not? Fran Nudelman could broadcast to our troops overseas.

Someone else shouts, "NATHAN'S NOT HERE." Someone meaning Natie.

"WHADDYA MEAN, YOU'RE NOT HERE?" Fran screeches. "WHO AM I TALKING TO, A GHOST?"

From the other side of the house her husband, Stan, answers, "DON'T YA' REMEMBAH? WE'RE SUPPOSED TO SAY NATIE'S NOT HERE."

"OH, RIGHT, RIGHT, SO SUE ME."

I ring the bell again.

"STAAAAAAAN! ANSWER THE DOOOOOOR."

Rather than endure round two, I try the knob and let myself in, just in time to see an Ewok scurrying out of the entry. I lunge after it, grabbing the hood of its Georgetown sweatshirt, revealing the fuzzy, teddy-bear head of Nathan Nudelman.

"It's all a mistake. I didn't do it," he says, putting up his hands.

"Natie, it's me."

He turns. "Jeez, you scared the crap outta me. Since when do you just walk in my house?"

"Since the fourth grade. What the hell is going on?"

"NATHAN, WHO IS IT?" Fran shouts.

"DON'T WORRY, MA. IT'S ONLY EDWARD."

"HELLO, EDWARD!" Fran screams in a tone usually reserved for yelling "Fire!" in a crowded movie theater.

"HELLO, EDWARD!" Stan echoes.

"C'mon," Natie says, motioning to his room. "We can talk in here."

Natie's room is a time capsule of his precollege self: Debate Team trophies, a model of the starship *Enterprise*, posters of each of the actors who played Doctor Who, and the *Revenge of the Nerds* lobby display. On his desk sits a disassembled computer.

"Why aren't you answering anyone's calls?" I ask. "Ziba's worried about you."

He thumps down at his desk, swinging the arm of a lamp around so he can examine the dissected computer guts. "Oh, I had a little run-in with the College Democrats."

"Over what?"

"Anti-Semitism," he says, squinting through his glasses. "Just 'cuz I was one of the few Jews at a Catholic university, they automatically assumed I misappropriated some funds."

"Did you?"

He turns, his baby face the epitome of hurt indignation. With his button eyes and orange fro, he could be Little Orphan Annie. "How can you say such a thing?"

I sit down on the bed, pushing aside a copy of the *New York Times*. "Well, you did help me embezzle ten grand from Al."

"Which had nothing to do with Judaism. In fact, may I point out that, out of the six of us who did it, four of you are Catholic. I shoulda mentioned that in my hearing."

"You had a hearing?"

"Inquisition is more like it. There I was, trying to further the Democratic cause using Republican tactics, and suddenly I'm a thief. Liberals have no understanding of the free market." He moves a monitor out of the way, revealing the words *Property of Georgetown University Computer Lab.*

"So you took the money?"

"I *invested* it." He reaches for the . . . what do you call it? The CPR? The C-3PO? The IUD? The boring part of the computer, the thing that's not the printer or the keyboard or the monitor. Oh, yeah, the "computer." Anyway, he reaches for that and unscrews the casing.

"Invested?"

"I've got two words for you," he says. "Wall. Street. I tell you, even guys our age are makin' fortunes. You watch— we're gonna take a bite out of the Big Apple."

In Eugene O'Neill's groundbreaking play *Strange Interlude*, the characters speak directly to the audience to reveal their inner thoughts, usually in a lifeless monotone to let you know it's profound. If my life were an O'Neill play, I'd step downstage and say:

(bitterly) . . . We? There is no we . . . "We" is a boat that ventures recklessly into the storm of your ideas, crashes on the rocks of their consequences, and capsizes in a sea of metaphors . . .

"What do you mean, we?" I say.

"It's the first-person plural."

"I know that, I mean—"

"I'm transferring to Columbia."

(fearfully) . . . How my heart quakes . . . I'm forever banished from the Met because of your Pavarotti scalping scheme. . . .

"Can you do that?" I sputter. "Y'know, with . . ."

"Oh, yeah," he says, "I'm already accepted. I'm switching from poli-sci to economics. I figure it's better to own a politician than be one."

(adverbially) . . . Perhaps commence with something smaller . . . a fish or a fern . . .

"Anyway," Natie says, "I figured since you got kicked out of Juilliard . . ."

I reach for his chair, swiveling him around. "What? How'd you know that?"

"My mom told me."

"Your MOM? How the hell did she find out?"

"She ran into Kelly's mom at the Pathmark."

That's it. I'll never be able to show my face in Wallingford again. I'm a has-been. No, worse: a never-been. I can see the write-up in the "College News" section of the *Wallingford Towne Crier*: "Hometown star burns out."

"You're hurting me," Natie says.

"Oh, sorry." I let go of his arms. "You've got to make Fran promise not to say anything to Al."

"Don't worry," he says. "The only thing they talk about is Milagros, the Merry Maid of Managua."

"Yeah, what's that all about?"

He shrugs. "She cleaned my parents' hotel room in Miami and Fran liked the way she scrubbed the tub."

The phone rings, followed by Fran bellowing, "SOME-ONE ANSWER THE PHONE. I'M IN THE JOHN."

Natie shakes his Brillo head. "I gotta get outta here before I lose my hearing." He plops down next to me. "How about we get a place together? Just the two of us."

"Oh, Natie, I don't know."

"C'mon, it'll be fun. The change'll do you good."

Perhaps, if my brain weren't still marinating in tequila, I'd stop myself from hitching my wagon to Natie's Death Star. But I also know that if I stay with Paula and Marcus and Willow, I'm going to wake up every day to the sickening aroma of my failure.

"Okay," I say, "if you find something . . ."

Natie slaps me on the back, his doughy face spreading in his lippy, no-tooth smile. It feels good to be wanted, even if it's by someone whose moral compass regularly leads you into shark-infested waters.

He opens up the *Times*. "Let's see about apartments. . . ."

"In the obituaries?"

"You know a better way?"

I reach into my back pocket and hand him Kelly's Equity newsletter. "I think I saw some cheap sublets in this."

As he scans the paper, I feel a spark of hope ignite inside me. Say what you want about Nathan Nudelman; with his blatant disregard for ethics also comes the sense that anything can happen. And often does. I'm actually relieved I don't have to go back to school this fall, because I now feel certain I am going to have the most marvelous adventures. I may not hop a freight train or work on a fishing boat, but I'm going to get out in the world and do . . . something. A whole lot of something. I don't know what it is, but I'm certain it's going to make me a better actor. No, not just a better actor. A great actor. A brilliant actor. And in a year I'll reaudition for Juilliard, and they will be amazed. I'll show them. I'll be the best damn me they've ever seen.

But before I can find myself, I need to find a job.

Five

In the days that follow I traipse all over Manhattan, not in the transcendental, one-with-humanity mode of Walt Whitman, but because I can't afford mass transit.

For two years Juilliard has been my whole world, an oasis where I spent every waking hour. Now, as I pound the pavement on the Yupper West Side, luxury condos sprouting up every other block, I'm keenly aware how Manhattan is twenty-three square miles of Not For You: windows full of products You Can't Buy, posters for events You Can't Afford, restaurants full of food You Can't Eat. You can't walk fifty feet in Manhattan without passing food: bagels, deli, pizza, ice cream, hot dogs, Chinese. I want to run into every Korean grocery I see and buy a softball-sized corn muffin, devouring the crunchy mushroom top, then working my way down to the spongy but gritty interior.

As I stagger through a heat wave so torturous I keep my sheet and pillowcase in the fridge until bedtime, I grade myself against the thousands of people I pass: Better Looking than Me, Better Dressed than Me, Better Shape than Me. So many suave urbanites in pleated seersucker shorts with skinny belts and baggy cotton socks that sag around their ankles like deflated concertinas. God, I wish I could afford baggy socks. My socks seem so inconsequential.

Lorenz Hart was wrong: I don't like New York in June.

When I say I'm broke, I don't mean it the way most people do, which is to say, not actually broke. No, I'm really broke, like borrowing-money-from-my-friends kind of broke. You know, the guy whose name is always accompanied by the rolling of eyes. The one whom they invariably wonder about years later, saying, "I don't know. After he got kicked out of Juilliard, Edward's life just spun out of control." If I don't get my act together, I'm going to end up like one of New York's many mad vagrants, wandering the city wearing a shabby overcoat and a woolly hat even though it's ninety degrees.

But two years of acting school have provided me with only such useful life skills as how to sit in a seventeenth-century tailcoat or analyze Chekhov. Apparently, a semester of typing at Wallingford High School is not enough to qualify for temp work, unless it's for a company where quick brown foxes jump over lazy dogs. And, thanks to the second-worst Broadway season of the century (the worst being the season before), restaurants now have more waiters than the chorus of *Hello, Dolly.*

I try to get on the lists to be a cater waiter but discover those jobs are controlled by the Gay Mafia. Invade their turf and you'll wake up with a head of arugula in your bed. I'm seriously considering getting a squeegee and a bucket to intimidate commuters into paying me for cleaning their windshields when Willow lands me a gig in the cosmetics department at Bloomingdale's. She needs a sub while she tours the tristate area as Titania in one of those shoestring productions where the actors travel in a van with the scenery. Shakespeare in the Truck.

Bloomingdale's cosmetics department is like a bazaar out of *The Arabian Nights*, packed with aggressive merchants hawking their wares. Every three feet someone entices you with magical elixirs, potions that promise to transform you into an object of desire: "Would you like to sample Fascination? Rhapsody? Midnight Rendezvous? Have you tried our Rejuvifying Skin Tonerizer?"

Two kinds of people work in the Bloomingdale's cosmetics department: beautiful women and the gay men who love them. On closer inspection, not all of the women are beautiful; some are merely ordinary but determined. The men, however, definitely give off the fussy, epicene air of boys who sewed their prom dates' dresses, and I feel ashamed to be in their company. Surely I'm not that nellie.

I stand on the outskirts, a sentry armed with an atomizer of something called Indulgence, while Willow trains me in how to get perfume onto a customer's skin before anyone else does. Like animals in the wild, we want to mark them with our scent.

Willow's approach is more holistic than her competitors'. "I don't think of myself as a fragrance model," she says. "I'm more like an aromatherapist." As such, Willow focuses on the underlying needs that compel someone to use cosmetics in the first place.

"Would you like to be happier?" she asks, beaming in the manner of an airport Hare Krishna.

Only the most hard-hearted New Yorkers grumble, "No," as they pass. Some laugh. But some stop, more bewildered than intrigued.

"Close your eyes," Willow says, waving her hand in front of the shopper's face. I'm half expecting her to add, "And click your heels three times." Instead she squirts the fragrance in the air and, leading the customer forward with the lightest touch on the elbow, says, "Step into the world of *Indulgence*!"

Really.

After watching her a few times, it's my turn. To my surprise, the first person I speak to stops, a dowager with a face like a crumpled paper bag.

"Close your eyes," I say.

"Why?" She's that kind of dowager.

"So you can step into the fragrance."

"Oh. All right."

She closes her eyes. Holding the bottle aloft with one hand, I reach down with the other to guide her forward. But as I touch her elbow, she flinches, opening her eyes just as I squirt her with a faceful of Indulgence.

"OWWWW! MY EYES! MY EYES!"

Someone calls security. Someone calls 911. Someone comes running with water, eyecups, and wet towels.

Someone gets fired.

Once again Paula comes to my rescue, such a Paula thing to do, by convincing Marcus to get me a job at the moving company where he's working.

"This is what you need, Edward," Marcus says. "Honest labor by the sweat of your brow."

It's not the sweat of my brow that I'm worried about; it's my hands, particularly as I stagger backward down the stoop of a brownstone hauling the end of a fish tank. "Shouldn't we have emptied this first?" I ask.

Marcus snorts. "And done what with the fish?"

I don't have an answer. My only experience in transporting marine life is carrying home a minnow in a baggie from the Knights of Columbus Italian festival. Still, lugging a five-foot-long aquarium full of tropical fish seems, well, fishy. I raise the tank to eye level and find myself staring at a sea creature resembling Mick Jagger. The muscles in my arms start to quiver.

"I'mnotsureIcanholdthisup," I grunt.

" 'Once more unto the breach, dear friends, once more,' " he shouts. Marcus, that is, not the fish.

Since graduating, Marcus has become belligerently Shakespearean, because the only casting calls he's gotten have been for Puerto Rican hoods, Harlem pimps, and Colombian drug lords. Having been trained classically (and raised like nobility), Marcus regularly rails against this egregious racism.

"I should be playing kings, not criminals," he says.

But what he doesn't see is that the problem is not just the color of his skin; it's the texture. And there's just no nice way to tell someone his face looks like an overcooked omelet.

As I descend the steps, I raise the tank above my head, the sweat stinging my eyes as Marcus continues with *Henry V*:

In peace there's nothing so becomes a man
As modest stillness and humility:

Step.

But when the blast of war blows in our ears,
Then imitate the action of the tiger;

Step.

Stiffen the sinews, summon up the blood . . .

Stiffen your own sinews, I think. *I'm dying here.*

Step.

Disguise fair nature with hard-favour'd rage;

Step.

Then lend the eye a terrible aspect;

If he doesn't shut up, I'm going to land on my aspect.

"Whew," I say when we finally reach the sidewalk, "I didn't think we'd—"

"Watch out for the . . ."

I glance over my shoulder just in time to get goosed by a fire hydrant, which sends me toppling backward onto East Sixty-fifth Street. I look up, but am blinded by a rushing waterfall followed by a noise that sounds like, well, a five-foot-long aquarium crashing onto a sidewalk. I wipe the water from my eyes and gape in horror as dozens of fish flop in the gutter before disappearing down the sewer, along with both our jobs.

Naturally, Marcus is furious, and doesn't laugh at my jokes about the fish returning from whence they came or that perhaps we should call it East Sixty-fish Street. No, as far as he's concerned, I owe him big-time.

Which is how I find myself bound and gagged in Central Park.

"I still don't get it," I say as Marcus ties my wrists to a six-foot-tall crucifix with the word CAPITALISM written across it. "Shakespeare in the Park is free."

"On a first-come, first-served basis," Marcus says, gesturing with his head to the crowd waiting outside the Delacorte to see *Twelfth Night*. "But the first served are the corporate sponsors."

Since Paula is putting in extra hours waiting tables at the Murmuring Peach and Willow is busy getting smacked in the head by the scenery whenever the *Midsummer* Mobile turns a sharp corner, I'm the one who has to sweat inside a velvet doublet and wool hose with a mask over my eyes and a dollar bill taped over my mouth. Our performance consists of Marcus reciting Shakespearean soliloquies, a sign around his neck reading, NOT FOR PROPHET, while I try to pose in complementary attitudes without falling over. When I ask him what it all means he accuses me of being too linear.

The whole endeavor reminds me of mask class, something I should have been good at, but wasn't. I mean, here was an approach to acting from the outside in, instead of the navel-gazing of all those three-minutes-alone-in-your-room exercises. By wearing a mask, we were supposed to absorb the chemistry of acting, adapting our physical identities by simultaneously engaging and controlling our feelings.

Yeah, I didn't get it either.

The crowd's reaction to our piece ranges from smirking ridicule to open hostility, which only makes me feel more idiotic. I've just leaned over as Marcus begins Hamlet's "How all occasions do inform against me" speech when I notice a pair of snub-nosed black Oxford shoes with white socks.

Cop shoes.

"Okay, fellas," says one of New York's finest, "time to move along."

Marcus ignores him, a foolish move considering the cop has that broad, bullnecked look that seems to be a requirement for the NYPD. He looks like a mailbox with a hat. New York's widest.

"C'mon, Shakespeare," he says to me. "Get a move on."

Marcus interrupts his soliloquy. "This is a free country. We have a first amendment right to free speech and assembly."

"Well, this is New York, and you can't perform in the park without a permit." The cop rests his hands on his belt, uncomfortably close to his gun, handcuffs, and billy club.

"C'mon, Marcus, let's go," I say, but, since my mouth is taped shut, it comes out, "Mhmm, mhmm, mmh mmh."

"What are you gonna do?" Marcus says to the officer. "Arrest us?"

"Mmh mmh, mmh mmhmmh." ("Shut up, you asshole.")

The cop takes a step forward. "If you don't disperse right now, that's exactly what I'm gonna do."

"MMH MMH. MMH MMHMMH MMH MMH MMH MMH."

("I'LL LEAVE. JUST UNTIE ME AND I'LL GO.")

Marcus sticks out his chin like he's angling for a fight. "Then take us away."

"MMMMMMMMMMMMMMMH!"

("FUUUUUUUUUUUUUUCK!")

Six

Marcus fails to see why getting arrested, handcuffed, frisked, fingerprinted, photographed, then served a stale bologna sandwich and a summons to appear in court for disorderly conduct might not be something I'd care to repeat.

"Next time we'll lose the cross and bind you with golden handcuffs instead," he says on the subway back from jail. "The symbolism's better, and you can run from the cops."

"How do you expect me to do this again?" I say, waving my summons. "I can't even pay the fine."

Marcus frowns, his onyx eyes as dark as a starless night. "Then don't. I'm not."

"But they'll put us in jail."

" 'I will stay in jail to the end of my days before I make a butchery of my conscience,' " he says. "That's what Dr. King said to my mother."

I rest my head on my crucifix. "Marcus, has it occurred to you that the corporate sponsorship of Shakespeare in the Park might not be a cause worth getting jailed over?"

Marcus purses his lips, like he's chewing on the idea. "No."

Despite Paula's disapproval, Marcus continues to pester me to be his partner in mime, suggesting *The Merchant of Venice* at the New York Stock Exchange, *Richard III* at Trump Tower, and *Othello* in front of any Korean deli that discriminates against blacks. But Paula reminds me that this is my second brush with the law—such a Paula reminder to make—having been arrested in high school for stealing a ceramic Buddha. (Not to mention nearly getting caught for embezzlement, money laundering, identity theft, fraud, forgery, and just a little prostitution, all of which occurred against her better judgment.)

"*Honestly*, Edward," she declaims, "another arrest would suggest a disturbing pattern of lawlessness."

I agree, but the more I resist, the tetchier Marcus gets, particularly since he has so few auditions. It's like sharing a cage with a panther. An angry, socialist panther.

So, when Natie calls to say he's found us an apartment, I'm off quicker than a tube top at spring break.

The building is right in the middle of Hell's Kitchen, a scab-colored tenement across from what can only be described as the Devil's Playground. Garbage cans crowd the curb; broken glass, cigarette butts, and the occasional derelict lie in the gutters. Air conditioners hang precariously in the windows like open drawers.

"The neighborhood's in transition," Natie says.

"To what? Landfill?"

He opens the front door and out flows a stream of Spanish—the only bit of which I can understand is, "Fuck you." We walk up a steep and very narrow stairway to a voice like a methadone addict. In withdrawal.

"On the plus side," Natie says, "we can make as much noise as we want."

I am not unfamiliar with shabby living conditions. This

past year I've resided on a section of Amsterdam Avenue sketchy enough to think of as the Amsterdamned. But at least I had a safe route to the subway. Walk out the door of this building and you're in Beirut. Hell, walk *in* the door and you're in Beirut.

The hallway walls are the color of phlegm. Granted, it's healthy yellow phlegm, not the army-issue green you snort out when you have a sinus infection, but, between the gunky amber walls and the fetid humidity, it's a distinctly mucous environment. When we reach the fourth floor he opens one, two, three locks, pushes back the door, and I gasp. It's like the moment when Dorothy steps out of her sepia-toned house into Technicolor Oz. The walls are a soothing Wedgwood blue, the floor painted a gleaming dark green. Overhead, faux sunbeams radiate from behind whipped-cream clouds. What's more, the place is crammed full of theater memorabilia: posters for *42nd Street* and something called *How Now, Dow Jones*; a swastika arm-band mounted with a shot of Mary Martin and a handsome young Nazi in the original *The Sound of Music*.

I peer at the photo. "Is this the guy who lives here?"

"Yeah," Natie says. "That's him, too, after he became a stage manager." He points to a middle-aged man in a tuxedo with Liza Minnelli and Chita Rivera. He's still blond and handsome, but weathered like an aging surfer.

"Why's he moving?"

Natie takes a sudden interest in a poster for *Willy!*, the deservedly forgotten musical version of *Death of a Salesman*, and I instantly know all. Handsome, weathered men working in the theater only give up great apartments for one reason. I get a prickly feeling as I wonder whether I can really inhabit the space of someone who died of AIDS.

Then I see the couch.

It's a claw-foot tub sliced in half and fitted with cushions, just like in *Breakfast at Tiffany's*. If it's possible to have romantic feelings for a piece of furniture, then I'm in love.

"What are we supposed to do with all his stuff?"

"We keep it," Natie says. "It's part of the deal."

"The deal? How did you find this place?" I sit down, rubbing my hand along the velvet cushion. Is it possible this is from the ill-fated musical version of *Tiffany's* starring Mary Tyler Moore? And is that the barber's chair from *Sweeney Todd*?

Natie explains: "I saw this announcement in Kelly's Equity newsletter about a memorial service for a guy named Eddie Sanders—don't look at me like that; it was very touching. Bernadette Peters sang 'Unexpected Song' from *Song and Dance*. Afterward, we were having cocktails at this place called Joe Allen's—cute spot, very theatery—and I overheard someone ask the executor of the estate what he was gonna do about Eddie's apartment."

"Natie, you didn't."

"Listen, this guy is taking care of, like, twenty sick friends. He's totally overwhelmed. If you think about it, we're doing him a favor."

I don't want to think about it. I don't want to think about AIDS or sex or gay men, the latter leading inexorably back to the first. And I seriously wonder which ring of hell Natie's going to inhabit for crashing a memorial service.

"Anyway," Natie says, "long story short, it turns out this place is rent-controlled, and I figured, what with your name being so close to Eddie Sanders's . . ."

"What are you talking about?"

Natie plops down where the Demon Barber of Fleet

Street slashed his victims. "You know what rent control is, right?"

"Sure. The rent is low and it only goes up a little each year."

"Exactly. But only until the tenant moves out or dies. Then it reverts to market value."

"But the tenant *did* die."

"You know that. And I know that. But the landlord . . ."

"Natie, no."

He goes over to the desk and retrieves a stack of canceled checks. "Look," he says, showing me a check for $400. "Here's Eddie's last rent check. See, Edward Sanders. Now all we have to do is go to the same bank, open a new account for Edward Zanni with the same address on the same-style check, sign your name Edward Scribble-scribble, and the landlord will never notice."

"Won't they notice my name printed at the top?"

"Not if the check looks the same. And we can camouflage it with a coffee ring."

I regard Natie's munchkin face, behind which lurks a sinister criminal mind. Baby Face Nudelman. "Is this even legal?"

"What's illegal? You're paying from an account with *your name* on it. If the landlord's too stupid to notice, that's his problem." He wags the check in front of me. "Do you have any idea how hard it is to find a rent-controlled apartment in this city? This is a gift."

"But two hundred bucks a month is fifty more than I'm paying now."

"For a goddamn hammock," he says. "C'mon, lemme show you the bedroom. It's got a loft with room for a futon underneath. You don't mind climbing a ladder, do you?"

. . .

Natie and I aren't the only ones with new domestic arrangements. After returning from the Almost Shah's wedding, Ziba moves into her aunt and uncle's Upper East Side town house; being the kind of people who use the words *summer* and *winter* as verbs, they needed someone to look after the place when they're not around. All six floors.

The town house is the size of my new apartment building. In fact, it is essentially a cleaned-up version, *The Prince and the Pauper*, its facade curving toward East Seventy-seventh Street to capture the light, bulging like a well-fed belly.

It also has columns. I can't believe I know someone with columns. It's like something out of Edith Wharton. But instead of our being greeted by an ancient family retainer, Ziba opens the door wearing a bikini top and a sarong, her bottle-shaped body anointed with oil. She looks like a character from a South Seas epic who wandered onto the set of a drawing room comedy.

"Boyzzz," she says, tickling under our chins with her fingernails, which are entirely too long to actually sew anything at the Fashion Institute.

The front foyer looks like a hotel lobby—black-and-white marble floor, crystal chandelier, potted palms—plus a swirling staircase, the kind where aging divas make entrances in musicals. It takes every bit of testosterone I have to resist racing up a flight and belting out a show-stopper about living life to the fullest.

Ziba leads us to the elevator instead, a gilded birdcage equipped with a brass-filigreed porcelain telephone. "It's too bad your aunt and uncle have fallen on hard times," I say.

"Yeah," adds Natie, "I'd be embarrassed to stay in a dump like this."

Ziba picks up the receiver. "Jeeves, would you please throw these gentlemen out?"

"So how was the wedding?" I ask.

"Oh, y'know," she says, adjusting her cockscomb hair in the mirror.

No, I don't. But I'd love to find out.

The doors open. "Here we are," she says. "Fifth floor. Ladies' lingerie."

We round a corner and ascend a narrow flight of stairs, the top of which opens onto an Arcadian vision so lovely it makes you want to write a poem about it. It's easy to imagine oneself chim-chimereeing from roof to roof, sailing along the top of Manhattan without ever having to mingle with the huddled masses below.

And there, in the middle of it, leaning against a wisteria-laden arbor, stands a nearly nude forest nymph.

"Surprise!" Kelly crows, thrusting her arms in the air like the cheerleader she once was. She wears a bikini, her pink skin looking distinctly undercooked. On the wrought-iron table next to her, a bottle of champagne chills in an ice bucket.

"What are you doing here?" I say, inhaling vanilla as I hug her, as if she were a yummy baked good. "Why aren't you in Akron?"

"I had a meeting," she says. She hugs Natie, who holds on to her too long.

"What kind of meeting?" People our age don't have meetings. And we don't open bottles of champagne on the roof gardens of million-dollar town houses, either. What the hell is going on?

"I had an interview with an agent," Kelly says. "And he signed me!"

Ziba pops the cork, which goes off like a gunshot.

"What?"

"Congratulations!" Natie says, taking advantage of the moment to hug Kelly again. The little horn dog.

"H-h-how?" I say. But this is not what I mean. What I mean is, *Why?* Specifically, *Why you and not me?*

Kelly explains that the choreographer for *Oklahoma!* was so impressed with her work as Dream Laurey in the dream ballet—not only as a dancer but as an actress—that he recommended her to his agent, who, get this, represents GWEN VERDON. "Can you believe it?" she squeals. "She's, like, my idol!"

Please. Kelly didn't even know who Gwen Verdon was until I made her watch *Damn Yankees.*

She continues: "Irving thinks I should take time off from school."

Irving? Already he's Irving? I want an Irving. How come I don't have an Irving?

"He said I'm perfect for commercials and soaps."

This is too much. "Are you s-sure that's a good idea?" I sputter.

"But of course," Ziba says, resting her cocoa brown arm on Kelly's pink shoulders. "She can stay here with me."

Great. Kelly gets an Irving and an Edith Wharton building with columns. Plus someone to have sex with on a regular basis. "What about school?" I ask.

Kelly raises an eyebrow, a consequence of hanging around Ziba too much. "I'm a dance major," she says, dropping a sugar cube in her flute. "It's not like a real degree."

"Exactly," I say. "You don't have any acting training."

"Edward!" Ziba says, her cat eyes flashing. "You sound like you don't want Kelly to succeed."

I know I'm being petty. If I were a rock 'n' roller, I'd be Tom Petty. If I were in the navy I'd be chief petty officer. If I were underwear, I'd be a petticoat. "Of course I want her to succeed," I say. I just don't want her to succeed before me.

"Actually," Kelly says, "I told him all about you."

And just like that, flowers bloom in my soul as I immediately envision the *New York Times* Arts and Leisure piece about how Broadway's newest sensations dated in high school.

"What did you say?"

Seven

Pinnacle Management sits high above the theater district, but it might as well be a world away. The lobby of the glass tower thrums with office-type people—men in suits carrying briefcases, women in suits wearing sneakers—all of them rushing to get upstairs to do whatever it is office-type people do.

I am not one of you, I tell myself as I dig out from the elevator, *I am not one of you.* Granted, I'm not meeting with Irving Fish to discuss my bright future on the Great White Way. During Kelly's interview Irving mentioned that he'd just lost his assistant and, faithful friend that she is, Kelly recommended me. Having just paid a $100 fine for disorderly conduct, I'm in no position to turn it down. Besides, who knows where a talent agency job might lead?

"I know who'd be perfect for the part," I imagine Irving saying as I take dictation. (Not that I know how to take dictation. But, hey, it's a fantasy.)

"Who?" I ask. In my fantasy, Irving has slicked hair and a pencil-thin mustache, like Adolphe Menjou in all those 1930s backstage musicals.

"Who?" he says. "Why, you, of course." Then he calls Ziegfeld and puts me in the Follies.

In reality, Irving Fish is a gargoyle with a lint-colored toupee that sits on his head like a nest. He looks like someone you'd meet under a bridge asking you to solve three riddles.

He doesn't look up when I come in, but instead reaches into a drawer and flops a blood-pressure monitor onto his desk. Then, without so much as a glance at me, he removes his shirt, revealing the body of a god. Unfortunately for Irving, that god is Buddha. He has the lumpen blobbiness of a half-melted snowman. As he straps the monitor on his arm he says, "So?"

"I'm Edward Za—"

"We've already got an Edward," he says. "You'll need to be somebody else. How about Alan? I had an aunt once named Alan."

"I'm not sure I—"

"So what's your story, Alan?" he says, still not looking at me. "You banging my client?"

"You mean Kelly?"

"No, four-time Tony Award winner Gwen Verdon."

"Uh, no," I say, less heterosexually than I would have liked.

"Why? You a pansy?"

I don't dare reach into the grab bag that is my sexuality for fear of what I might pull out, so I simply say, "We used to date."

"Type?"

"Gosh, I don't know. I kind of like blue-eyed blondes."

"No, you germ," he says, pumping the monitor. "Do. You. Type?"

"Oh. A little."

"Shorthand?"

"No."

"Keypad?"

"Maybe."

"Maybe?"

"I don't know what that is."

He examines the gauge, scowling at the results. "I'll take that as a no."

"I'm a very good speller."

"Excellent. You can represent us in the bee."

"I meant for filing and—"

"Working pulse?"

"I beg your pardon?"

He gives me a look that's equally malevolent and condescending, Rasputin teaching day care. "Does oxygenated blood empty out of your heart, course through your veins, deposit carbon dioxide in your lungs, which you then expel into the air?"

"Uh . . . yeah."

"Good. You can start right now by perambulating your body downstairs to get me a Fresca."

I learn very quickly why Irving Fish can't keep an assistant. As valedictorian of the Roy Cohn School of Charm, he oozes into the office every morning with all the vigor of an oil slick, the plants in the reception area wilting and dying as he passes. It's obvious he hates his job, his life, and, most of all, me.

And rightly so. I am a clerical disaster. Monks calligraphing illuminated manuscripts worked quicker. A simple cover letter can take me the better part of the morning. Luckily, Irving's clients don't work too much. Famed for having told Meryl Streep she should get her nose fixed,

Irving specializes in those who are either on their way up or on their way down, the former dumping him as soon as they hit it big, the latter clinging to him as their careers circle the drain. He's created an entire cottage industry representing stars who are forgotten but not gone, ex–movie queens who play Mame and Dolly in melody tents all over the country.

What's worse, I have to fill in for the receptionist, a high-haired girl from Staten Island who dials the phone with a pencil so she doesn't break a nail. She takes so many breaks I begin to wonder whether she suffers from a chronic bladder infection.

I dread these moments most of all, gaping at the phone like I'm a transplanted aborigine: *Ooh, the blinking lights of your magical talking machine frighten and confuse me. Please give me an errand so I may go on walkabout.* One day I accidentally disconnect the artistic director of Play-wrights Horizons and Irving throws a paperweight at me, narrowly missing my head and shattering a framed photo of Martha Raye on the wall.

"My *goddess*," my mother says when I call to complain. (I figure, with all the long-distance calls the agency makes, no one will notice a few to Sedona, the latest stop on her Magical Mystery Tour. Suffice it to say her spiritual quest has greatly enhanced Natie's stamp collection, such a Nudelman thing to collect.) "Why would you manifest that?"

"What are you talking about? I didn't want him to—"

"Edward, he aimed for your head. Don't you see what that means?"

"He's a homicidal maniac?"

"No. You're so desperate to open your mind, you willed this Irving person to do it for you."

"Oh, Mother . . ."

"I'm serious. If you don't find a spiritual outlet you could end up manifesting an aneurysm or a brain tumor. I know you think I'm crazy, but I'm not the one getting paperweights thrown at me, am I?"

"No, you're the one in the desert trying to contact aliens."

"Zoozook isn't an alien; he's a Pleiadian star being."

She says it like everyone lives in a teepee on an abandoned ranch in Sedona so they can listen to the hallucinations of a Utah housewife who hears the voice of a five-thousand-year-old Pleiadian star being whenever she turns on her microwave.

"You're just like your father," my mother says. "So earthbound. You really should come to Sedona and experience the healing energies of the vortexes."

She means vortices.

"New York is sucking your soul dry," she adds.

She's got a point. There's a big, Juilliard-sized vacuum in my life, and working as an assistant to the Prince of Darkness certainly isn't going to fill it. But how am I ever going to achieve a success large enough to redeem such an enormous failure?

Naturally, Natie sees my employment as an opportunity for ill-gotten gains. "For Chrissake, you're his assistant," he says. "You pick up the phone, you say you're calling for Irv, and you can go to any audition you want."

But the mere thought of auditioning gives me gastric reflux. I compare my résumé, which sucks even when it's padded, with the hundreds that come across my desk, and I can't conceive of competing against actors who have more to show for their careers than a summer spent as Chuckles the Woodchuck.

Still, I can't help thinking I sound pretty good singing

along with the London cast album of *Les Misérables*, which is coming to Broadway next season. I mean, it's not like I'd expect to get a part, but surely I'm good enough for the chorus, right? Or maybe an understudy. One vocal coach in particular crops up on the better musical theater résumés, so, armed with a spiffy new Walkman-sized tape recorder, I spend fifty bucks for a lesson with Morgan Firestone, who's responsible for Mandy Patinkin's voice, though not the part that sounds like musical sinusitis. I choose the song I think of as my personal anthem: "Corner of the Sky" from *Pippin*.

I've got to be where my spirit can run free,
Got to find my corner of the sky.

After my particularly heartfelt rendition, Firestone looks up from the piano and says, "That wasn't bad, but you smile too much for *Les Miz*."

It's not my fault. Two and a half years of orthodontics couldn't eradicate an overbite, which, to be fair, was so severe to start with I could've eaten apples through a picket fence. The photographer who took my head shots said I have a mouth "built for smiling." I originally took it as a compliment, like I have a congenital capacity for happiness, but, after being called too jazz hands for Juilliard, I worry it means I'm just a lightweight. Of course, this is the same photographer who rendered me virtually unrecognizable by slathering too much foundation on my face. When Irving noticed the shot on my desk one day, he said I looked like I should be down on one knee singing "Mammy."

No, I can't audition for *Les Miz* or anything else. Everything about me is wrong, wrong, wrong. My spirit doesn't run free; it runs into brick walls. I have the emotional depth of a Very Special Episode of *Growing Pains*. If I were a river, I'd be shallow enough to cross without rolling up your pants.

I need help.

That's why I accept Willow's invitation to join her at a free, introductory consciousness-raising session with EGG, the Enlightened Growth Group. Following the lone algebraic equation I remember—if $a = b$ and $b = c$, then $a = c$—I figure that since Willow is both a gifted actor and an EGG practitioner, maybe it'll help my acting, too.

The session takes place in a meeting room at the Sheraton, a rather bland environment for a psychological breakthrough, but I'm determined to keep an open mind. After all, I don't want to manifest an aneurysm or a brain tumor.

There are hundreds of us assembled on those chairs that connect so you're sitting closer to a stranger than you'd like. A lot of the people seem to know one another, judging from the overlong hugs and soulful stares. As a group of Growth Facilitators motions us to our seats, Willow turns to me with the panicked look of someone who just remembered she left the water running. With a child in the tub.

"Did you pee?" she says.

"You mean just now? No, I'm continent, thank you."

"I mean—"

She's interrupted by an explosion of applause as a team of radiantly happy people takes the stage, led by a middle-aged man with a gleaming cue-ball head and a glassy-eyed expression. He wears a collarless Indian shirt, which marks him as a Spiritual Person. He joins in the applause and soon we're all clapping rhythmically. For five minutes.

It's a funny thing about five minutes. If you're running five minutes late, it speeds right by; but try clapping rhythmically for longer than thirty seconds and the novelty wears off fast.

The leader motions us to sit down, then stares at us so long I find myself nostalgic for the clapping. Finally he says, "I see you."

"I see you," responds the crowd, or at least those who know what the hell's going on.

This exchange warrants more applause. "Happy birthday!" the leader shouts.

"Happy birthday!" shouts the crowd, followed by an even bigger ovation. I swear, I haven't seen this much unwarranted appreciation since the high school musical.

The leader quiets us again.

"Today is your birthday, the day you begin a new life. The day you become who you are truly meant to be." He closes his eyes. "Let us begin."

He leads us through a guided meditation in which we are to envision laying an egg. That's right, an egg. Large enough to accommodate a human baby. He's a little hazy on the anatomical details, telling us only that "it emanates from your kundalini," wherever that is. All around me people grunt and puff, Lamaze-style, but I can't get past the idea that I'm supposed to be shitting an oversize egg. I can see why Willow asked me if I needed to go to the bathroom. With all the pushing, now I really need to pee.

Still, I manage to pass my egg, which apparently contains my inner child, who must peck, peck, peck his way out until he finally gets fed up and punches a hole in his shell with a tiny, inner-child-sized fist.

"That is why you're here," the leader says, "to break out of your shells. Most of us go through life protected, held captive in prisons of our own making. Not us. Not here. Not now." He pauses, as if he's about to say something profound, or perhaps shit another egg. "Not. Ever."

More rhythmic applause. My palms look like smoked salmon.

We're then instructed to wander the room, letting everyone else see us for who we truly are, our "unshelled selves." (Try saying that ten times fast.) "And when you see someone, truly see them," the leader says. "Stop and tell them." He demonstrates with an assistant, bearing down on her with a spotlight stare until he finally says, "I see you."

Seems simple enough.

I stroll around the room, making eye contact with people, but they just glaze past as if I weren't there. Finally a man stops in front of me, a cadaverous executive with gray hair and a gray face to match.

"I see you," I say.

He stares into my eyes, like he's looking for something he lost in there, then just shakes his head and skulks off.

I turn and there's a leathery woman with skin like a topography map. Even her tan has a tan.

"I see you," I say.

She breezes right past me. "Sorry."

I begin to sweat. I'm trying too hard. I'm not capable of revealing myself, of making myself vulnerable. Once again I'm Morales in *A Chorus Line*, feeling nothing. Except the feeling that this bullshit is absurd.

I approach a tiny woman, no more than five feet tall, slender, but with hips like parentheses. Before I can say anything, she grabs me by the elbows.

"Can you see me?" she asks.

"Yes."

"You sure?"

I take a moment to look at her. She wears the short, layered haircut of someone with neither the time nor the inclination to bother, a pair of round tortoiseshell glasses, and the kind of worried expression you see on child actors when they say, "Please, mister, don't hurt my dog." Her eyes have gray circles under them, like she's been up since 1972, and her mouth is surrounded with those hairline fractures that smokers get.

"I see you," I say.

"Oh, thank Gawd," she squawks with the distinctive nasal whine of the outer boroughs. "I was beginning to lose it."

"Can you see me?"

"Of course," she says. "You're right in fronta me." She puts out her hand. "I'm Sandra Pecorino," she says. "Like the nutty, flavorful cheese."

"Edward Zanni."

"No talking!" says one of the Growth Facilitators.

Sandra grabs me by the hands. "Don't leave me," she whispers. "I can't take any more rejection."

We stand there awkwardly, a pair of thirteen-year-olds at their first slow dance. Finally Sandra whispers, "I came here to work on my relationship issues. And because I thought there might be men who are triple-S."

"Triple-S?"

"Sensitive, single, and straight." She rolls her owl eyes at me. "Two outta three ain't bad."

Yikes. Does it show? I feel like gay bits of me are just slipping out every which way. I'm about to tell her that women are my second-favorite people to have sex with, that I'm not so much gay as gayish—Almost Gay—when she says:

"I don't know what it is, Edwid. I'm a magnet for the gays. Like Barbra Streisand or Bette Midlah. Lemme guess. You're an actor, too."

"How'd you know?"

"Also a magnet. Hence my relationship issues."

A gong sounds and once again we clap rhythmically. Then we're informed that we're to separate into two groups—those who have already done EGG's three-day introductory course and those of us who have not. Willow takes her place with the Haves, while Sandra and I remain with the Have-nots, which are then split into smaller "Hatcheries." As I follow Sandra into a meeting room, I ask one of the Growth Facilitators where the bathroom is.

"After," he says.

"Excuse me?"

"You can go after."

"But—"

"Don't say 'but.' "

"Why?"

"It's like your body. The only thing that comes from a but is shit."

And an egg, I suppose, but I don't want to argue. Instead I sit down, crossing my legs to keep from wetting myself. The chairs are arranged in pairs so that each one of us gets our own personal Growth Facilitator; mine is a guy with the wide-eyed look of someone who uses coffee-bean suppositories. His name tag reads Bruce. Or Bryce. I can't tell.

"Why are you here?" he asks, his eyes like headlights.

"I don't know."

"Don't say, 'I don't know.' You do know. That's an excuse you use to avoid taking responsibility for your shit."

I'm a little miffed at his presumption. This guy doesn't

know me. Still, he's got a point. So I tell him what's been going on, how I need to figure out who I am, how I'm afraid to feel. And he listens, which I enjoy, even though it freaks me out a little that he doesn't blink.

"You have to do this course, Edward," he says.

"I'd like to, but—"

"Don't say 'but. . . .'"

". . . I don't have the money."

"Bullshit! You don't have *any* money?"

"I mean, I don't have enough money."

"You don't even know how much it costs."

"How much does it cost?"

"Three hundred dollars."

"I don't have that kind of money."

"You know what your problem is, Edward? You're limited by your scarcity consciousness."

At this moment a woman in the corner bursts into tears, thrusting her arms around her Growth Facilitator.

"Yes! Yes! Yes!" she cries.

"See?" Bruce/Bryce says. "If she can do it, why can't you?"

"I don't even know who she is."

"No, you don't know who *you* are. Aren't you tired of being unhappy?"

"I'm not unhappy."

"Liar! You just told me you're a miserable, unfeeling loser. Why do you lie so much?"

"I don't—"

"Why are you a big fucking liar?"

From the ballroom next door I hear a chorus of people sing "Happy Birthday."

"I just want to—"

"Don't say 'just.'"

"I'm trying to—"

"Don't say 'try.' "

"I need to go to the bathroom."

"NO!" he shouts.

"But—"

"Don't say—"

He's interrupted by a voice that sounds like a duck getting a root canal. "STOP!"

I turn around as Sandra stalks across the room. "I swear to Gawd," she says, pointing a chipped fingernail in my facilitator's face, "if you say 'don't say but' to this poor kid one more time, I will reach down your throat and rip out your lungs."

Bruce/Bryce finally blinks.

Sandra and I sit on stools at someplace called Frozert, eating fat-free, sugar-free, taste-free frozen yogurts. Chemicals in a cup. She laughs, a sound like an upper respiratory infection. "They really said you were too 'jazz hands' for Juilliard?"

"Yeah. I guess deep down I'm very superficial." Over the sound system, Cyndi Lauper sees my true colors shining through.

"Nah, you're just like me," Sandra says, gesturing with a plastic spoon. "You're too nice." (This from the woman who threatened to remove a vital organ.) "You're a people pleazah, that's what you are, a people pleazah. Am I right or am I right?"

I scrape the remaining frozen caulk out of my cup. "I guess so. I can't really relax until everyone else is happy."

"See, I knew it!" she says. "Edwid, today is your lucky day!"

Eight

The following weekend I venture out to Sandra's studio on "Lawn Guyland" to begin my training as a party motivator.

According to Sandra, having a guy in a shiny shirt and tight pants encourage a roomful of thirteen-year-olds to dance is the latest thing at bar and bat mitzvahs so lavish she calls them "bash mitzvahs." *La Vie de la Fête* Productions currently employs four male motivators: two older guys around twenty-five who also emcee and two younger ones who just dance. Sandra used to have one other, but he did a sweet sixteen where he did the sweet-sixteen-year-old, and now he's doing sixteen months on Rikers Island.

Luckily, you don't have to be a dancer-dancer. "Your job is to boogie with regulah people," Sandra says. "Ya' need to be a little sloppy." In which case I'm eminently qualified.

Still, I learn how to do the Robot and the Moonwalk from Rex, her star motivator, a fledgling entertainment journalist who combines an effortless cool with the kind of canine conviviality that makes you want to be his best friend. Sandra says Rex strikes the perfect "bash mitzvah balance": He's hip enough that the boys want to be him, sexy enough that the girls want to do him, and professional enough that the parents want to pay him. At a hundred bucks a party, I definitely want to be him.

The rest of August passes with Xerox monotony, each day a photocopy of the one before as I wait until my first gig. The only thing I'm learning working for the Agent of Evil is that bitterness is a contagious disease, a virus spread by aural contact. I try to remain immune by embracing my alter ago, telling myself that it's not Edward Zanni who has to deliver a cup of Irving's pee to his urologist on a sweltering subway; it's Alan, Lucifer's piss boy.

It doesn't work.

Even more dispiriting are the entreaties I get from former Juilliard students. Now that they're enrolled in the School of Hard Knocks, they've apparently confused me with someone with clout. Graduates I've never met contact me like we're long-lost friends, which is just embarrassing. The only one I don't hear from is Marcus, because it turns out Irving was the ray of happy sunshine who made the crack about him looking like a sea sponge.

Meanwhile, Kelly breezes in and out on her days off after auditions. I can see why—you could easily picture her as a girl with slow-motion hair in a shampoo commercial, or as a doomed prom queen in a slasher flick. She even got an audition for *Starlight Express*, the latest assault on theater from Andrew Lloyd Webber, in which actors on roller skates portray trains. It's a big hit in London, which Natie says just proves how the birthplace of Shakespeare has deteriorated since Margaret Thatcher took over.

The nadir, however, comes on one of those brutally hot New York days, the kind that cause neighbors to kill each other in Bensonhurst. The intercom on my phone beeps, and the receptionist tells me there's a Ted Lucas out in the waiting room to see me.

Ted Lucas? I think as I step out of my office. *Surely it can't be . . .*

Mr. Lucas.

My high school drama teacher releases one hand from the crutches that circle his wrists, deftly sliding it up his forearm so he can shake my hand. "Edwaaaard," he says in a voice too theatrically sonorous for the space.

"It's great to see you," I say in a tone that unfortunately conveys the subtext of *What the hell are you doing here?* Hoping to make up for it, I add a chipper, "Come in my office."

"Your office?" he says, raising his eyebrows. "My, my, my." Mr. Lucas gives a Victorian tilt of his head to our receptionist. "Nice to meet you, Valli."

I offer him some water, which he declines, though he looks like he could use it, his pale linen suit wilting around him as he sits. He unstraps the leather carrying bag we gave to him on the opening night of *Godspell.*

"You have a view," he says. "Very impressive." He strokes his beard, a gesture that used to intimidate me, but now seems like a nervous tic.

"I have to be next to Irving's office," I explain. "It makes me look more important than I really am."

Through the wall I can hear my boss screaming at the Bucks County Playhouse about the color of Ann Miller's dressing room.

"I hope you don't mind me barging in like this," Mr. Lucas says. "I chanced upon Fran Nudelman recently and she told me what you were up to, so I thought I'd stop in and see for myself."

"I'm just taking a year off," I say. "I'm definitely going back."

Subtext: *Please don't think I'm a loser.*

"*Eggz*elent," he says. "A *Wanderjahr* will do you good. Give you a little seasoning."

"Exactly." It's possible he's just being kind, but I'll take it.

"I'm making some changes myself," he says.

"Really?"

"As you know, I haven't acted in some time"—he makes a vague gesture at his legs—"but I've been encouraged by some colleagues to pursue voice-over work."

He pronounces the last words slowly, as if they were foreign.

"Great," I say. "You'd be terrific at that."

"I'm glad you think so, Edward. Perhaps you won't think it too presumptuous, then, if I ask you to pass along my demo tape to Mr. Fish."

I get an itchy feeling across my back, like I've just gotten my hair cut. I mean, I'm a nobody. A failure. A dud. Anyone coming to me for help has got to be, well, less than that. And I don't want Mr. Lucas to be less than anything.

"Happy to," I say.

He reaches in his bag and hands me a cassette, as well as a head shot and a résumé.

"I know it isn't necessary," he says. "But you never know."

I look at the picture. Judging from the mustache and the open shirt, it's at least ten years old.

The intercom blares. "Alan," Irving bleats. "My office."

Mr. Lucas raises an eyebrow. "Alan?"

"Long story. Listen, I've got to go."

"Of course," Mr. Lucas says. "Well, it's been—"

The intercom blares again. *"Today."*

"Sorry," I say, rushing out as he struggles to his feet. "Sorry."

I round the corner into Irving's office.

"What are you doing in there?" Irving snaps. "Carving the Rosetta stone?"

"Sorry, I—"

"What's that in your hand?"

I glance down and see that I'm holding Mr. Lucas's résumé and tape.

"Oh, this is, uh, a voice-over actor I thought you might be interested in," I say, handing him the résumé. "As you can see, he trained at the Royal Academy of Dramatic Art in London, and worked in a number of regional houses . . ."

Irving scans Mr. Lucas's credits, then flips over the page to look at the head shot.

". . . then he had a spinal cord injury and now he's kind of, y'know, disabled . . ."

Irving picks up a Sharpie marker.

". . . but he's got this terrific voice. Really, uh, stentorian . . ."

My own voice trails off as Irving doodles a goatee and devil horns on Mr. Lucas's face. Taking a moment to admire his handiwork, he crumples it up and tosses it in the trash can, along with any illusions I had about show business.

"Anything else?" he says.

Two words: I. Quit.

C'mon, Edward, say it.

Say it.

"No," I say, "nothing else."

• • •

The morning of my first *La Vie de la Fête* gig, I'm awoken by the phone. I squint at the digital clock, which appears to say LOSE, but, upon closer inspection, actually reads 10:58, Edward Standard Time, which means it's . . . Oh, fuck, who can do math this early? I fumble for the phone while Natie makes sleepy piggy sounds in the futon below.

"Hlllluh?" I mutter.

"WHAT THE HELL'S GOING ON?"

Since moving in with Natie, I'm used to people shouting on the phone. Just hearing Fran Nudelman say, "Hello," is like removing ear wax with an electric drill. But this shouter is different. This shouter is pissed.

This shouter is my father.

"Uh, so solly," I say. "This Kolean deli. You have long number."

"Cut the crap, kid, I know it's you. Why haven't you answered my calls? I've left you a bunch of messages."

"Really?" I can just picture Al, pacing the floor with gorilla menace while he jingles his pocket change. "Uh . . . Natie must've forgotten to give them to me."

From below Natie mutters, "Sure, blame it on the Jew."

"So," Al says, "the reason I'm callin' . . ."

"That's how it started in Germany, y'know."

"Shut up!"

"Whah?"

"Not you, Pop. What did you say?"

"I sent your tuition check to Juilliard . . ."

Uh-oh.

". . . and I got a letter sayin' you're not enrolled."

Silence. Deadly, cavernous silence.

"You wanna explain?" he says.

No, I'd rather have a Strange Interlude:

(fearfully) . . . Explain? How can I explain? . . . All sum-
mer long I've hoped that you might suffer a freak head
injury while golfing, rendering you temporarily feeble-
minded so that I need not explain. . . .

"Well," I say, "my professors think, and I agree, that my acting would benefit from taking a year off. Y'know, to get a little seasoning."

"Seasoning? What are you, a steak?"

I sit up, bumping my head on the ceiling. "You see, this is why I didn't tell you. I knew you wouldn't understand."

"Don't start with me," he says. "I know you got kicked out."

And, just like that, my failure rushes into the room, throws on the lights, and shoves its nasty, dirty ass in my face. "Who told you that?"

"One of your teachers. Marian something."

The thought of the grande dame of the finest drama school in the country talking with the chief financial officer of the nation's foremost toxic-waste facility makes me cringe. "Did she also tell you I could reaudition next year?"

"Oh, for Chrissakes . . .".

"But—"

"Eddie, face facts. It's over. You tried and you fai . . . It didn't work out. Cut your losses and move on."

"But next year—"

"There ain't gonna be a next year. That's just throwin' good money after bad."

Suddenly my whole body is on fire. "But you . . . you have to. It says so in the divorce agreement." I throw off the covers.

"Fuck the divorce agreement. You wanna sue me again,

go right ahead. *You will lose.* I gave in last time becuz I knew how much it meant to you, but there ain't a judge around who'll say I gotta continue payin' for this nonsense. I'm done. It's over. Finished."

I pull my knees up to my chest, feeling defeated and exhausted before I've even gotten out of bed. He's probably right. Besides, there's no guarantee Juilliard will take me back, anyway.

Frailty, thy name is Edward.

"Listen, son," he says, downshifting into a less hostile gear. "I know you're disappointed, but, c'mon, dreams only come true in dreams."

Al always says that.

"You're a smart kid," he says. "Why don't you come home? You can live here rent-free, work at the plant, take some business classes at night."

Sure, then bury me in the backyard, because I'll already be dead. "I don't think so, Pop."

"Eddie, you're twenty years old. It's time to grow up."

And at that moment, somewhere deep inside me, beneath the nasty-ass failure and the humiliation and the shame, a small, still voice whispers, *No.* Just like that. *No.* Not if growing up means becoming like my father, some miserable guy with a tie like a noose around his neck, sitting at a desk in an office, counting the minutes until he retires.

The thought stops me cold, like someone in a horror movie who realizes he's already ingested the alien antibody or has turned into a zombie. I *am* a miserable guy with a tie like a noose around my neck, sitting at a desk in an office. How did this happen? In the space of a couple of months I've gone from being an actor to being someone who makes a living off of people who are doing what I should be doing myself.

"Don't you want me to be happy?" I say.

Al groans.

"Listen, if you wanna think I'm a monster 'cuz I won't let you throw your life away at some la-di-da acting school, fine. I'm just tryin' to save you a lot of heartache and pain. You have no idea what it's like to be poor. You never hadda stuff cardboard in your shoes when they wore out."

Yeah, yeah, and walk ten miles to school in the snow. Uphill. Both ways.

"You think the world owes you something," he says, "but I've got news for you—the world doesn't give a shit about you or me or anyone else. The sooner you learn that the better.

"Happy?" He snorts. "Kid, you can't afford it."

I place the phone in its cradle and shut my eyes. Fuck him. He doesn't understand me. Never has. Never will.

But I'll show him. I'll show everybody. And I'll do it my way. I'll get more gigs and save up my money and pay for college myself. I'll be the most motivated party motivator there ever was.

I refuse, *refuse*, to turn out the lights on my life. Ever.

Nine

My first party motivator gig of the season is the Schlon-sky bash mitzvah, or, as Sandra calls it, the Schlonsky BM. Sandra refers to all of the bash mitzvahs as BMs, list-ing them on the calendar behind her cluttered desk (Yohalem BM, Schwartz BM, Krumholz BM) as if she were charting bowel movements at a Florida retirement home. But the Schlonsky BM will be the biggest of them all. In-spired by his son's Torah portion about Noah's ark, Joel Schlonsky, aka "the Wizard of Wall Street," has invited seven hundred of his closest friends for an overnight cruise on the SS *Europa*, an ocean liner so luxurious it makes the *QE II* look like a pontoon boat.

The Midtown pier terminals are as confusing as they are unfamiliar, and I just manage to get on board before the ship departs for its fifty-mile cruise to nowhere. From there I'm directed below to a windowless cell on something like Z deck, where my bathroom is so small I can shit, shower, and shave all at the same time. Then I report to re-hearsal on the ship's basketball court. That's right, bas-ketball court. The *Europa* also boasts a tennis court, two swimming pools, a theater, casino, disco, spa, and planetarium, all available this evening for the Schlonskys' guests.

I arrive at the gym to find Sandra quivering on the sidelines like a hummingbird. With Parkinson's. In the center court hover two of the male motivators—a pair of haircuts with hips named Hector and Javier—and a trio of busty comic-book superheroines named Courtenay, Kate, and Robyn. Sandra sees me and rushes over with the speed of someone walking on hot coals. "Edwid! HaveyouseenRex?"

"No."

She raises her arms, addressing the heavens. "Why? Why? Whyyyy?"

I cross to the group. "What's going on?"

"Rex missed the boat," Hector says.

"What am I gonna do?" Sandra says, munching on a cuticle. "The *New York Times* is here. The *New York Post. Women's Wear Daily*. I'm fucked. I'm totally fucked."

She's right. Zach, the only other motivator who emcees, is currently in Great Neck doing a BM.

"I swear to Gawd," she says, "Rex had better be lying in a ditch somewhere or I will kick him until he's dead."

Hector steps forward. "I can do it."

"You?" says Javier. "You can't find your ass with two hands."

"I never heard your mama complain."

"Oh, yeah . . . ?"

"Shaddap," Sandra says. "Neither of you can do it."

"Why not?"

"Because Deborah Schlonsky watched our video like *this*." She demonstrates by putting her palm up to her face. "If either of you emcees, she's gonna know I filled in with a backup. No, the only way this is gonna work is if she thinks I got somebody bettah."

"But you don't have anybody better," says Courtenay.

"I've got Edwid."

I gulp. "Me?"

Courtenay looks at me like I'm smelly cheese. "He's not better."

"She's right," I say. "I'm not better."

"What about one of us?" Robyn says.

Sandra shakes her head. "Trust me, these people don't want women or minorities telling 'em what to do. I know, I know, I don't agree with it—I went to Sarah Lawrence, for Chrissakes—but that's how it is. It's gotta be Edwid. Now lemme think." She points a finger at me like a prosecuting attorney. "Can you do an English accent?"

"Well, sure . . ."

"Great. You're a veejay for British MTV. You're in town filming promos and, because this is such a spectacular occasion, I managed to convince you to emcee this party. Got it?"

"Uh . . . okay."

"That doesn't sound British to me."

"Uh . . . awlraight."

"See, you're a cinch. Now you just need a new name, something not so ethnic."

The words tumble out of my mouth like change from a slot machine. "How about Eddie Sanders?"

"PerfectIloveitnowcomewithme."

In less than an hour I'm outfitted in the most MTV-looking duds we can find at the men's store—a silver double-breasted sharkskin suit over a turquoise T-shirt with a pair of bright white bucks. It's more *Miami Vice* than MTV, but it does make me feel snazzy. Not that I have much time to feel anything. Once I'm dressed, we rush up to the deck where the guests are gathered for the cocktail hour.

The crowd is a society page come to life: men in tuxedos ornamented by women in gowns that shine like jewels, a whole ship's worth of Freds and Gingers. In keeping with the nautical theme, models dressed as mermaids float in the pool, while handsome waiters in sailor suits pass seafood appetizers to guests like Mayor Ed Koch, all to the accompaniment of a string quartet dressed as pirates. The perfectly temperate September night only contributes to the self-congratulatory sense that this is the place to be, that the gods of the air and sea bestow their blessings on this gathering.

Then there are the kids.

It seems irredeemably cruel that Jewish tradition requires thirteen-year-olds to make a public show of themselves, for it's an age when few of us will ever be more homely: boys with just enough facial hair to look dirty; girls with torsos as thick as Russian wrestlers. Then there are the extremes: the awkward, female pituitary case slouching to appear shorter; the elfin midget boy who compensates for his height with sheer obnoxiousness. Taken individually, each one could break your heart with their gawky vulnerability. Together, they're a band of marauding pygmies. Due to a lethal combination of limited supervision and unlimited funds, they swarm through the party as if the ship were their personal playground, brazenly unintimidated by the swank surroundings. They make me feel like I'm back in the seventh grade myself, which, as an athletically inept, show-tune-loving reader of movie star biographies, was about as successful as you'd imagine.

My panic attack is interrupted as a helicopter approaches the ship, landing on the deck above with great gusts of wind and generating a chorus of chatter about the identity of the late arrival. I kind of hope it's a celebrity, preferably someone who'll recognize my rare genius and jump-start my career.

Instead, a man who looks like Santa Claus in a tuxedo steps out of the helicopter, and the crowd erupts in delight. "It's Rich Whiteman! It's Rich Whiteman!"

"Who's Rich Whiteman?" I ask Sandra.

"I think he owns banks in Texas."

I didn't realize you could own a bank.

"He also wrote that book," she says, "y'know, *A Heapin' Bowl of Values*? He gives millions to the Republicans."

Ho-ho-hum.

Dinner is announced, and suddenly my lungs feel like they're in a trash compactor. How am I going to do this? I'm not effortlessly sexy and cool, like Rex. Or Doug. Oh, why can't I be like Doug? (Well, for starters, I don't have a dick so big it requires its own zip code.) I'm going to fail. Again. What was I thinking? Swallowing my panic, I wobble into the ballroom with all the resolve of lime Jell-O.

Then it hits me: Why *can't* I be like Doug? What's stopping me? These people don't know who I am. When they look at me, they won't see twenty years' worth of accumulated neuroses. Or that I'm an actor, which is kind of the same thing. All they'll see is Eddie Sanders, British MTV veejay.

I hope.

The Europa's ballroom rises three decks to a curved stained-glass ceiling. At one end of the dance floor stands the stage where the Miami Sound Machine will perform; at the other, a replica of Noah's Ark with waving automaton animals on its deck. I quiver at the top of a sweeping two-story staircase while Sandra signals a deep-voiced actor dressed as a crustacean to do the offstage introduction:

"And now, your surprise emcee for the evening, straight from London, British MTV's hottest veejay, Eddieeeeeee Sanders!"

There's an audible "ooh" in the room, followed by an indecipherable applause. Will they love me or hate me? Am I to be the lion or the gladiator?

Then the spotlight hits me.

I'm temporarily blinded, and I grasp the brass handrail for support. Seven hundred people wait for me to say something, to do something, anything. What would Doug do? For that matter, what would I do—not me today, broken and battered on the rocks of Juilliard, but the high school me, the puckish Pied Piper who led the Play People Parade?

I would slide down the banister.

Taking a deep breath, I hop up on the rail for a two-story ride.

I hit the ground running, slipping across the dance floor and finally landing on my ass, which the drummer punctuates with a rim shot. The crowd laughs, but I can't tell if it's an oh-what-fun or an oh-what-an-asshole laugh. I hop up, brush off my shiny suit with what I hope is a swagger that says, *Guess what I have in my pants?*, and holler, " 'Ello, America!"

Apparently Eddie Sanders is Cockney.

I hadn't planned on it, but I suppose it makes sense. British MTV certainly wouldn't hire John bloody Gielgud, now, would they? Luckily, I have an extensive working knowledge of *My Fair Lady*, *Oliver!*, and *Sweeney Todd*. I just hope I don't sound like Dick Van Dyke in *Mary Poppins*.

"Blimey," I say, surveying the surroundings. "Wot a pity the Schlonskys 'ave fallen on such 'ard times, eh?"

The crowd laughs and I instantly know that they're mine. Oscar Hammerstein called the audience the "big black giant," a living, breathing creature that every performer has to go out and slay. And that's what you say when you succeed: I slayed 'em, I killed 'em, I knocked 'em dead. And when you fail, it's the opposite: I died out there. But, after two years being trapped behind the invisible fourth wall, I realize that this giant doesn't care whether I'm publicly private or emotionally transparent; it just wants to drink as much free booze as possible without throwing up.

That's showbiz, baby.

I station myself at the base of the stairway like a tenor in the Ziegfeld Follies singing about the most beautiful girl in the world, then introduce the members of the family, who are escorted by the other motivators to a throbbing Latin beat. Depending on the guests' abilities, my coworkers either dance with or around them; indeed, nine-year-old Shoshana struts like Tina Turner, which suggests someone actually gave her a cocktail during the cocktail hour. After the entrance of Joel and Deborah Schlonsky, who have the slick good looks of a game-show host and the model who gestures to the prizes, we turn our attention to a large screen above the ark, which shows a video parody of *Gilligan's Island*:

> *Just sit right back and you'll hear a tale,*
> *A tale of a boy named Dan,*
> *And how he read his Torah portion,*
> *Then became a man.*

At the end of the video, the door to the ark opens and out pops Daniel, a miniature version of his father, as if he'd been shrunk in the laundry. It's a great piece of theater, but having Mayor Koch hand him the key to the city is a bit much.

During the six-course dinner I hang out with the marauding pygmies, building a bond so that they'll want to dance later, even though they are so uniformly awful it's like they came off a production line in hell. I swear, if one more kid sucks the helium out of a balloon and tells me to follow the Yellow Brick Road I'm going to rip out his larynx. Once the music starts, however, my primary function is to shout, "Lemme hear you say, 'Yeah!'" and get people to clap above their heads. I lead every conga line, judge every dance contest, and draggle across the floor with every elderly aunt from Boca. I bound, I cavort, I joke, I flirt, I wiggle, I strut. I do the Robot and the Moonwalk. I'm hip enough that the boys want to be me, sexy enough that the girls want to do me, and professional enough that the parents want to pay me.

And, for the first time since I did *Godspell* in high school, I feel totally, exhilaratingly alive.

After it's over, I stand alone at the ship's stern, staring out at an inky black sea. I've always wanted to stand alone at a ship's stern staring out at an inky black sea. We're about as far from the coastline as Wallingford is from Manhattan, but we might as well be in the middle of the ocean. A *Yentl* "Papa, Can You Hear Me?" moment.

My reverie is interrupted by the arrival of a seventh-grade girl.

"Okay, here's what I wanna know," she says. No "hi,"

no "hello," no "Do you mind me interrupting you while you stare out at an inky black sea?"

She's a spindly puppet of a girl, but fashionable, with a permed, asymmetrical bob that drifts to one side like she's standing downwind, and a vaguely galactic silver dress with sleeves like atomic-bomb clouds. She has unusually bushy eyebrows, which she wears parted in the middle.

"Were you really the emcee for Prince Andrew's wedding to Fergie?"

I laugh. "No."

She turns and shouts to her friends gathered on the deck overlooking ours, "I TOLDJA, MARCY. YOU OWE ME FIFTY BUCKS." The girls giggle and scatter. My companion rolls her eyes. "They're *so* immature. My friend Marcy? She still wets the bed." She taps her hands on the railing, unsure of what to say next.

"So wot's your name?" I ask.

"Lizzie Sniderman. You've probably heard of my dad, Shel Sniderman?" She pauses. "The producer?"

"Cahn't say I 'ave."

"Oh. Well, everyone thinks Aaron Spelling invented Jiggle TV, but it was really my dad. He did this show called *Hollywood Vice Girls*, about female cops who go undercover as prostitutes . . . ?"

"Never seen it."

"It was ahead of its time."

"So you live in Los Angeles, do you?"

"I wish!" She collapses against the railing for emphasis. "I live *here*. With my *mom*. She's a lawyer for a big accounting firm." She mimes sticking her finger down her throat. "She's all pissed becuz she wasn't invited. But I'm the one who goes to Daniel's school, not her. She doesn't even know Daniel's parents." She pops up again. "But my dad? He says when I'm sixteen he'll throw me as big a party as I want, which is way better than having a bat mitzvah, 'cuz you get just as many gifts and you don't have to go to Hebrew school. You'll emcee it, right?"

We're interrupted by a sound that's either my boss calling or a seagull flying into the side of the ship.

"THERE YOU ARE!"

Sandra charges over. "Who do I love? Who! Do! I! Love!?"

"Uh . . . Barry Manilow?"

"Eddie Sanders, that's who!" She leans into me. "We need to tawk."

I start to say, "Will you excu . . ." to Lizzie, but Sandra grabs me by the arm and heaves me starboard.

"What's going on?" I ask.

She's about to answer when we find ourselves in a gaggle of giggling girls.

"Eddie!" / "Hi!" / "Can I have a picture?" / "Hi!" / "Will you sign my shoulder?"

"Later girls, later," Sandra says, steering me inside and shutting the door on them. "Listen," she whispers, "we've gotta—"

Just then, a band of boys appears at the end of the hallway. "Hey, Eddaaaaay!"

I wave and am abruptly yanked around a corner. Sandra opens the door to the ship's library and pushes me in, motioning for me to duck behind one of those immense freestanding globes. Outside, the boys clomp past the door.

The library is the kind where Hercule Poirot would gather suspects to reveal the murderer: rosewood paneling, Chippendale wingback chairs, and shelves so high they require a library ladder. As you'd expect on a night when guests have such late-night choices as laser tag or the vocal stylings of Miss Lainie Kazan, the room is empty.

"Listen up," Sandra says. "We've got some guests from London and, get this, there's no such thing as British MTV. I know, who knew? Anyway, I told 'em that it's coming, and you're gonna be the star, but we've gotta get you belowdecks before they find you and start asking questions."

"Got it." I rise.

"But first," she says, grasping my hand, "I wanna say thank you. You really saved my ass out there. From now on you are my number one motivator." She pokes me in the chest. "BMs, corporate events, weddings, funerals, circumcisions: Edward Zanni is my go-to guy."

"You mean Eddie Sanders."

She gives an adenoidal laugh. "Trust me, that name'll come in handy. Otherwise, you'll have thirteen-year-old girls crank-calling you in the middle of the night." She looks at her watch. "Speaking of, I've gotta round up the fire dancers. Can you make it downstairs on your own?"

"Yeah. But as long as I'm here I think I'll find a book to read before I go to bed." My head's too light to try to set it down.

"You rest up. There are a lot more gigs where this one came from." She speeds out, practically leaving skid marks.

A lot more gigs! If my life were a musical, this would be the moment when the spotlight would hit me and I'd do a celebratory uptempo showstopper called "A Lot More Gigs!"

In fact, the minute Sandra leaves, I leap onto the library ladder and slide along the shelves. Maybe I even go, "Wheeeeee!" And why shouldn't I? I'm a hit! I'm a star! I'm—

I hear a long, loud sniff.

I'm not alone.

Ten

I turn around and there, in one of the wingback chairs, sits a man in his thirties so improbably handsome he must have been created in a petri dish mixing DNA from Paul Newman and Robert Redford. He has blond hair you imagine some gnome has spun into gold, eyes as green as spring, and a chin like a fist. The only flaw in his otherwise perfect visage is a crooked nose, proof that he, indeed, is real.

"Sorry to eavesdrop," he murmurs in a voice that can only be described as postcoital. "I didn't want anyone to know I was here." On the coffee table in front of him lies a neat row of white powder. "You want to do a line?"

"No, thanks." The few times I've done cocaine, it just made me want to stay up all night cleaning my bathroom.

The improbably handsome man takes a snort with a rolled-up dollar bill.

"Listen," I say, "you won't tell anyone, will you? Y'know, about my not being English?"

He runs his index finger along the table, then rubs the remaining dust on his gums. "I'm good at keeping secrets," he says, sniffing. He rises and offers his hand, not the one that was just in his mouth.

"Chad Severson."

Even his name is gorgeous.

I try to give him an assertive, masculine handshake, like I'm priming a water pump, when all I really want to do is cue the violins and sing "He Touched Me."

"Edward. Zanni."

He holds on to my hand just a moment longer than he should. "I watched you tonight," he murmurs. "And you know what? You have a great ass."

Did I just hear him right? Did this perfect specimen of manhood just tell me I have a great ass?

"And do you know what that asset is?"

Never mind.

"You're a people person." He slides a business card out of his breast pocket. "I could use a guy like you."

A week later I'm back in the snazzy sharkskin suit, but this time I'm the one who's being entertained.

The Café Carlyle is a low-ceilinged room, smaller than I expected, but every bit as swank as its reputation. The walls are covered with murals done in a loose, brushy style that seems typically French in a way I can't define, and surreal in a way I can't understand: a shirtless youth embracing a horse, a spaniel dancing in a dress, a nude woman painting. The waiter leads us to a spot in the corner, where he pulls out the table so I can scooch into the velvet banquette. I've had waiters pull out chairs for me before but never a whole table.

This is glamour.

I gaze at Chad basking in the glow of the little lamp between us on the table and hear myself nattering on about how "I've always wanted to see Bobby Short perform at the

Carlyle, I mean, who wouldn't, the man's an institution, right, the epitome of Upper East Side elegance, of course, I'm no expert, but I do have a friend who lives just around the corner in an enormous town house, she's Persian and she went to the shah of Iran's wedding, well, not the shah-shah, his son, the Almost Shah . . ."

Meanwhile, another Edward, a sensible, more mature Edward, sits next to me groaning, *For God's sake. Shut. Up.*

Luckily, the waiter appears with our drinks, allowing me to gather my wits and remind myself to take a "sincere interest" in Chad. (On Sandra's recommendation, I've been reading Dale Carnegie's *How to Win Friends and Influence People.*) Of course, the only sincere interest I have in Chad is what he looks like naked.

"So what does a broker do, actually?" I refrain from adding, ". . . in bed?"

Chad gives a spreadsheet of a speech that I'm sure would fascinate my father, and I nod like I understand when he talks about call options, put options, and Morgan Stanley, whoever she is. We pause only to order from a menu where everything sounds like haiku:

> *New Zealand spring lamb*
> *Leeks and baby artichokes*
> *Dandelion greens*

Then Chad leans across the table, his jade eyes lasering into me, and says, "How would you like to be a spy?"

A spy? He might as well ask me to be an astronaut. Or a cowboy. "You mean, like, in a trench coat, passing secrets to the Soviets?"

Chad smiles, flashing a row of tall, straight teeth, like

the picket fence that will someday surround our cozy cottage for two. "No," he says. "A spy for me."

I take a sip of my Scotch, which I only ordered because he did and now regret because it smells like makeup remover. "Brokers use spies?"

He sits back, his jacket falling open to reveal a shirt as crisp as paper. He's probably fifteen years older than me and is in much better shape. I resolve to start dieting. Tomorrow. Because they have crème brûlée on the menu. " 'Information is the currency of democracy,' " he says. "You know who said that? Thomas fucking Jefferson."

In that case, I guess spying's all right. Though, to be honest, I'm so smitten with Chad, I'd poison pigeons in the park if he asked me.

"What would I have to do?"

"That's the best part," he says, his green eyes shining like the Emerald City. "You're already going to corporate events, right? All you have to do is talk to people about their businesses and report back to me what they said. I'll give you a hundred bucks each time. Plus bonuses, if the information pays off."

A hundred bucks! That's already what Sandra pays. In other words, I'd get double the amount for the same work. Even without bonuses, I could quit working for Irving. And save up for college. And maybe buy some of those baggy socks.

"What kind of information are you looking for?"

He glances over his shoulder to make sure no one's listening. "Let's say a company has a new product they're going to launch, or they've got some new spank-ass technology, or they're expanding into a new market. Or maybe there's going to be a change in leadership, or in federal regulations, or, best of all, they're part of a merger or an acquisition."

I'm watching his mouth, but all I'm hearing is, "Blah, blah, blah."

"So I just tell you this stuff . . ."

"And we get filthy fucking rich. I tell you, Edward, you'll be rolling in so much dough we could put you in an oven and bake you."

I like the way he says *we*.

"But," he adds, "it's got to be our secret. You can't tell anyone."

"Why? It's not illegal, is it?"

He gives a wry smile as crooked as his nose. "Does that really matter, Buddha boy?"

I freeze. How'd he know I was arrested in high school for kidnapping a three-foot-tall ceramic lawn ornament?

Chad seems to read my mind. "'Information is the oxygen of the modern age.' You know who said that? Ronald fucking Reagan. Now, is that the only suit you've got?"

"What's wrong with my suit?"

"Nothing, if you're headlining in Vegas."

Maybe I shouldn't have rolled up the sleeves.

"Tomorrow morning take yourself to Brooks Brothers," he says. "I'll arrange for you to put it on my account."

The conversation proceeds amiably from there, particularly since this is the second time in less than a week someone has bought me a new suit. Our food arrives and, with it, a bottle of wine, and soon I've banished whatever worries I have that Chad knows anything about my past dealings with embezzlement, money laundering, identity theft, fraud, forgery, and (just a little) prostitution. He tells me about his old Kentucky home, where his family raises racehorses, and about going to business school at Stanford, but I just luxuriate in his low bedroom voice, not to mention the ambrosial wine and the sophisticated surroundings. The men's room even has those thick, napkin-like towels embossed with the Hotel Carlyle's crest.

What a week it's been. First, to be the Life of the Party at a party written up in the *New York Times*, *Women's Wear Daily*, and the *New York Post*. None of them mentioned me but I'm thrilled just to have been at an event that made Page Six, right next to a photo of Andy Warhol at a gallery opening with James Freeman Foster, the Brown University junior who's the talk of the town with his debut novel, *Coke Is It*. And now, at last, an adventure! It may not be hopping a freight train or working on a fishing boat, but, still, it's an adventure. Corporate espionage. Clandestine meetings. Maybe even a secret romance. Of course, I don't know whether Chad is gay or not, but he did suggest we see Bobby Short. And is very well groomed.

Just when I think the night can't get any better, the lights dim and a cherubic man with a cannonball head and skin the color of cognac bounces into the room and springs onto the platform where a grand piano sits gleaming in the spotlights. Bobby Short smiles, his grin as white and wide as the piano keys, and he flings out his arms as if he were trying to give every one of us a hug. He is tastefully turned out in a tuxedo, yet has an eager, boyish quality to him, like the child performer he was in the 1930s. He hops onto the piano bench, plays a flourishing arpeggio, and begins to sing:

The man who only lives for making money
Lives a life that isn't necessarily sunny . . .

I don't recognize the song, but am immediately struck by his husky voice, which has a tremulous, fluttering vibrato, the way you'd imagine a bird's wings would sound if you could hear them. It's a voice that invites you to inhabit the song with him, and his nimble, rolling style on the piano doesn't so much accompany the lyrics as converse with them.

When he reaches the chorus, I finally recognize the tune. It's the Gershwins' "Nice Work If You Can Get It."

I take it as a sign.

Eleven

I'm roused, as usual, by the sound of construction, my alarm clock a wrecking ball. This after repeated wake-up calls from New York's dedicated Department of Things that Go Bump in the Night, which apparently uses my street to crash-test crosstown buses. Even at the building's quietest, I can still hear the scuttle of roaches and mice in my apartment walls, fighting for turf like the Jets and the Sharks. No wonder New York's the City that Never Sleeps. Still, I feel invigorated because I'm off to Brooks Brothers. That is, after playing the following Neil Simon scene with Natie:

NATIE: So how'd it go?

EDWARD: How'd what go?

NATIE: Your meeting. I thought you said this guy had a job for you.

EDWARD: Oh, yeah. He wanted to talk to me about the internship program at Thorpe, Sharpton, and Riley.

NATIE: You mean Sharp, Thornton, and Wiley.

EDWARD: Right.

NATIE: The internship program? To be a stockbroker?

EDWARD: Yup.

Natie goes to the window and looks outside.

EDWARD: What are you doing?

NATIE: Just checkin' to see if black is white and up is down. Oh, look, there's four men on horseback.

Edward gets dressed.

EDWARD: You're not the only one around here who knows something about business.

NATIE: Yes I am. Where ya' goin'?

EDWARD: For a walk in the park.

NATIE: Good idea. I'll come, too.

EDWARD: You can't!

NATIE: Why not?

EDWARD: I'm going to Brooks Brothers.

NATIE: Brooks Brothers is in the park?

EDWARD: No, it's on Forty-fourth and Madison. I'm going after.

NATIE: Great. I need a new dress shirt. Mine's got pit stains.

EDWARD: No!

NATIE: It's just pit stains.

EDWARD: I mean . . . I need to shop alone.

NATIE: Why?

EDWARD: I've developed a phobia.

NATIE: To shopping?

EDWARD: I can't do it in front of other people. It's like being pee shy.

NATIE: Fine. We'll walk in the park; then you can shop alone. Hopefully, you won't have to pee.

EDWARD: Actually, I'm going to Brooks Brothers first, then to the park.

NATIE: I thought you said you were going after.

EDWARD: I changed my mind.

NATIE: If you don't want me to come . . .

EDWARD: No, I just find that a walk in the park helps relieve the stress brought on by shopping.

NATIE: And peeing.

EDWARD: Exactly.

If I'm going to lead a double life, I'm going to have to become a better liar. No wonder I got kicked out of acting school. The moment I step outside, however, I get another chance.

"Eddieeeee! Hi! Remember me?"

"Oh, hallo!" I say, instantly becoming British. "Of course. From the boat. Uh, Lizzie, rawght?"

She smiles, revealing braces like the grillwork of a '57 Chevy. "My friend Marcy and I looked you up in the phone book."

Damn. Of all the pseudonyms to use, I'm stuck with one belonging to a man who worked on Broadway for twenty-five years as a chorus boy and a stage manager. If Eddie Sanders's name gets in the paper, the entire cast of *42nd Street* will see that I stole his identity.

Lizzie bends one leg against the other, like a flamingo. "Marcy would've come with me, but she had to go to therapy."

"Sorry to 'ear that."

"She just does it for attention. Do you like my shirt?" She spins around to model an oversize Union Jack T-shirt, which she wears belted over a pair of leggings tucked into baggy socks.

I wonder if Brooks Brothers sells baggy socks.

"I'm, like, totally into everything British now," she says. "America sucks. Do you know Morrissey? He's so profound. Nobody at my school gets him." She fidgets with the multiple jelly bracelets on her wrist. Across the street a drug deal takes place on the Devil's Playground.

"This neighborhood isn't really safe," I say.

"It's okay," she says, reaching into her shirt. "I've got a whistle."

It's pink.

"Still," I say, "why don't I walk you over to Broadway?"

"Okay. Where ya' goin'?"

"Just out to do a spot of shopping."

Her eyes widen. "I *love* shopping," she gasps, as if this were evidence of our deep, spiritual bond. She thrusts a skinny arm through mine. "I know all the best places."

As we walk, Lizzie fills me in on All Things Sniderman: how her father's girlfriend takes laxatives to stay thin, and that her brother knows the Preppy Killer, and her mother makes her carry condoms in her purse. ("In case I get raped.") She also grills me on All Things British, so I teach her some Cockney slang, all of which I make up.

"So," she says, "if you're confused, you say you're wonkysocks?"

" 'At's rawght," I say. "You also use it when somefin's rubbish. Y'know, when someone acts like they're all hump, but they're really a Wimbledon."

Lying is much easier when you're using a phony accent.

Meanwhile, I try to figure out how to ditch her, but I can't very well prevent her from entering Brooks Brothers. And I can't very well tell her that British MTV's hottest vee-jay has a shopping phobia.

Once we arrive at the store, Lizzie charges in ahead of me, as if she were my publicist, announcing, "This is Eddie Sanders from British MTV. He needs a suit. Now." The saleswoman directs us upstairs, giving me and my barely pubescent companion a look like she's going to call Child Services. As Lizzie and I ride the escalator, she asks, "So, what kinda suit are you looking for?"

"Somefin' conservative," I mumble. "I thought maybe black."

She rolls her eyes. "Black is for limo drivers and dead people."

The third floor of Brooks Brothers has the Old World look of a private gentlemen's club: cherry paneling, egg and dart molding, and a wooden chandelier with carved deer heads holding crystal lamps in their mouths. The saleswomen look like the Daughters of the American Revolution. The actual daughters.

So, as we ascend the winding, Colonial-style staircase to the fourth floor, I can't help but notice the shapely pair of showgirl legs heading my way. As they approach I take in the snug fit of the skirt on the hips, the high-necked blouse accentuating rather than concealing the breasts, her frosted hair swirling like a meringue, obscuring her face.

"Excuse me," I say, letting her pass.

The showgirl raises her head to acknowledge me, and my blood turns to ice.

It's Dagmar. My ex-stepmonster.

"You!" the Terminator cries, her blood-red lipstick like a gash across her face. "Vaht are you doink here?"

I opt for outright denial, answering in Eddie's jaunty cockney, "Beg your pardon?"

"You stole from me, you son uffa bitch," she says, wagging a crooked finger in my face. Despite her Bond-Girl beauty, her hands are as gnarled as tree roots. "You ruined evertsing. It is because of *you* I hef to verk here."

Please. It's not my fault if no one wants to buy her creepy photographs of decapitated dolls and rotting meat.

"I don't know whut you're tawkin' about." I try to pass her but, like a bird of prey, she grabs my wrist, her talons digging into me. *"Liar!"*

Being a Manhattan kid, Lizzie doesn't seem remotely fazed by the confrontation. And, being Lizzie, she's not afraid to step in. "Eddie, who the hell is this?"

"I dunno," I say, shaking free. "I've nevuh seen 'er before."

"Dat is not true!" Dagmar shrieks. "You are a liar! And a tsief! And an azz*huuuuuuuuuull!*"

She accompanies this last little endearment with a decisive shove to my chest, sending me hurtling down the steps.

Twelve

Actually, I send myself hurtling down the steps. In my second display of stairway spontaneity in just over a week, I realize that the best way out of this situation is to incriminate Dagmar, so I put two years' worth of stage combat to use and take a very convincing fall. Naturally, the manager comes running to my aid. When he learns that I am not only British MTV's hottest new veejay but also a referral from a valued customer, he fires Dagmar on the spot. What follows is something akin to a Godzilla movie, with Brooks Brothers standing in for Tokyo. After a flurry of accusations, as well as the destruction of a rack holding camel-hair jackets and tartan vests, the scene ends with an unhinged Austrian being escorted from the building, frothing at the mouth and vowing revenge.

Okay, maybe she doesn't froth, but that's how I reenact it when I get together with my friends to go bowling, the sound of falling pins punctuating the action. I'm thrilled I have stories to tell them, for there is no audience I want to please more. Laughing with your best friends is like eating cake—you do it till your sides hurt. I just wish I could tell them everything. It doesn't feel natural to keep secrets from them.

Bowling was Paula's idea. "Never disdain mindless activities," she says. "They are the only refuge for the brilliant and the only option for the ordinary." If the sentiment sounds out of character, it's because she's been cast as Lady Bracknell in *The Importance of Being Earnest* and insists on living the role. "Artifice requires rigorous preparation," she explains. "That is why politicians are so rarely young."

She's got a point. The preparation for my first gig as a stealth guest certainly has been rigorous—and terrifying. Chad messengers me packets of indecipherable annual reports and business prospectuses, then takes off for the Cayman Islands before I can get him to explain what the hell I'm looking at. And I can't ask Natie for help because I don't dare tell him how I got this stuff. As it is, he's been looking at me funny ever since the shopping-phobia debacle. So it's up to me to figure out how to be the Life of the Party for events thrown by Boring, Monotonous, and Drab, Inc.

In the absence of information, I choose to get hammered with my friends.

Ziba and I have just gone to the bar (she's paying; I'm carrying) when a snack-sized Asian guy with spiky platinum hair flounces in. He's cute—with a flat, friendly face like the "Have a Nice Day" smiley and a compact body like a Chinese acrobat—but he's so gay, just looking at him makes my ass hurt.

Kelly spies him—which is easy to do because he's wearing a buttercup yellow bowling shirt and purple velvet pants tucked into ankle boots—and the two of them spring into each other's arms, shrieking like junior high girls. Kelly brings him over.

"You remember Ziba," she says.

"Of course," the strange little stranger says. "Akron will never be the same."

He must be someone Kelly worked with this summer. Judging from the outfit, I'd guess it was in the costume department. He has a tiny wind chime hanging from his right ear.

"And this," Kelly says, gesturing to me like I'm a museum display, "is Edward."

"Well, hello*oh*," he says, licking me with his eyes. Then, leaning into me, he murmurs, "I'm hung."

I flinch. "Excuse me?"

He places a hand on his hip. "Don't get your hopes up. It's a name, not an adjective. Capital H."

He winks.

I hate people who wink.

"I know," he says, "it's not enough to get airlifted out of Saigon, survive a refugee camp, and grow up gay in Texas. But then to find out you've got a name that sounds like a personal ad . . . It's even worse with my last name."

"What's that?"

"Promise not to laugh," he says, tilting his head coquettishly.

"I promise."

"It's Manh."

"Your name is Hung Manh?"

"You promised not to laugh." He covers his mouth as he giggles like a geisha, and I feel myself cringe. Swishy guys make me intensely uncomfortable, with their hinge-like wrists and hips, and their liberal use of double entendres and sexual innuendo. This is not who I want to be.

But the fact that he's wearing a vintage bowling shirt

with the name Mitch stitched on the breast pocket does inspire us to create appropriately trashy *noms de boules* to appear on the screens above the lanes. Paula, Willow, Ziba, and Kelly sign in as Hildy, Toots, Gladys, and Trixie; while Marcus, Natie, Doug, and I bowl as Tito, Zog, Porch, and Brawth.

The game grows more esoteric from there. When Lady Bracknell breaks a nail, she opts to sit out the game, stating, "Simple pleasures are often neither." This decision prompts Willow to bowl as if she were Paula, all sashaying hips and twiddling fingers, like a hen trying to fly. From there, we each bowl as the person who preceded us: Marcus capturing Willow's dazed, somnolent shuffle; Ziba performing a surprisingly accurate imitation of Marcus's lupine tread; Natie doing an hysterical rendition of Ziba's runway strut; and Kelly transforming herself into the homunculus that is Natie. Unfortunately, I land on my ass when I attempt to do a high kick as Kelly, jettisoning the ball into the neighboring lane. And I feel a little cheated when Hung imitates me; if his splashy portrayal is to be believed, I fall somewhere on the masculinity meter between Elton John and Bea Arthur.

The only person who doesn't seem to get it is Doug. I'm sure he doesn't welcome the prospect of bowling as Hung, a guy so nelly you can tell he's gay from outer space. But Doug is also the only one of us who doesn't view the game ironically. Through some kind of mystical groupthink, the rest of us arrived here tonight knowing it was a goof. But for Doug, bowling is a legitimate pastime, something he actually does with his other friends. When Willow compliments him on his bowling ability, Doug gives a hangdog Elvis thankyavurrymuch look, mumbling, "I've always been good at sports."

"Any activity that can be performed while imbibing spirits is not a sport," says Lady Bracknell. "Bowling is just alcoholism with unfortunate footwear."

Doug escapes to the bar to watch the Mets.

From there our game morphs into a version of charades as we bowl in the manner of state capitals, historical figures, movies, and plays, the latter causing a debate when Kelly chooses *The Music Man*.

"That's not a play," Marcus says.

"It is so," replies Kelly. "It's a musical."

"Musicals are bourgeois entertainment for tourists," Marcus says. "That's not theater; that's commerce."

This probably isn't the right thing to say to someone on her third callback for *Starlight Express*.

"Millions of people go to musicals," Hung says. "They can't all be wrong."

"Yes, they can," Marcus replies. "That's how Reagan got elected."

"What's Reagan got to do with *Starlight Express*?"

Marcus flies at him with his crow black eyes, saying:

Why, man, he doth bestride the narrow world
Like a Colossus, and we petty men
Walk under his huge legs, and peep about
To find ourselves dishonourable graves.

I recognize the speech. It's Cassius from *Julius Caesar*, which would be a good role for Marcus. He, too, has a lean and hungry look. Every frustration Marcus has, all of his righteous indignation, flows into Shakespeare's words like molten lava.

"My dear boy," Paula says, "please refrain from this disputatious display."

Marcus wheels around, eyeing her murderously. "Don't call me boy."

"Oh, you know what I mean," she says, dropping character. She gestures to the rest of us, suddenly Victorian again. "Why don't we pause for libations and light refreshment?"

Marcus skulks off to the bar while Paula and Hung visit what Hung refers to—excruciatingly—as "the sandbox." When they're gone, Kelly bounces over to me as if she were about to lead a Fourth of July parade.

"So?" she says. "What do you think of Hung?"

What do I think of Hung? He's gayer than a purse full of rainbows. He's gayer than a Liza Minnelli concert on Fire Island. He's gayer than figure skaters eating corn dogs.

"He's okay," I say, avoiding eye contact. Behind her I notice Willow lining up the bowling balls so that they look like a row of faces.

Kelly gives a conspiratorial glance at Ziba. "He likes you, y'know."

"Ooooooh," Willow says. "Eddie's got a boyfriend."

"What is this, seventh grade?" I pick up a ball to give a practice throw, but it just rolls into the gutter. "Shall I meet him at the bike racks after school?"

I don't want to have this conversation. It's not like I've got a problem with my sexuality; I just don't want to be defined by a bunch of leather-clad loonies, drag queens, and the Gay Men's Health Crisis. Gore Vidal famously said that *homosexual* is an adjective, not a noun, but I think of it more as a verb, something you do, not something you are. Unless, of course, you're living during a plague, in which case I'm not homosexualing anything.

Even worse, I hear from Natie (aka the *Daily Nudelman*)

that the Supreme Court ruled in a case called *Bowers v. Hardwick* that it's okay for a cop to just barge in and arrest a man in his bedroom for having sex with another man, which is fascistic and medieval and terrifying, not to mention embarrassing that a gay defendant is named Hardwick.

I pick up another ball. "I'm just really busy," I say. "Sandra's got all these corporate events planned for me. Pretty soon I'll have enough gigs that I can quit working for Irving."

Kelly's water-lily eyes grow murky. "Why would you do that?"

"Uh . . . because he's a raging sociopath?"

"Of course he is," Ziba says. "That's what you want in an agent."

I throw another gutter ball. This game sucks.

"You can't quit," Kelly says. "How's that going to look for me?"

I look at her, her seashell skin hiding the roar of the ocean inside. "Kells, he made me scrape dog shit off his shoes."

Willow drifts into the conversation. "Why don't you just screw up so much he has to fire you? That's what I do."

"Good thinking," says Natie. "That way you're eligible for unemployment."

"Really?" Willow asks. "I didn't know that."

While Natie outlines the finer points of defrauding the government, Ziba explains why feigning ineptitude won't work: "No offense, darling, but I can't imagine you could be any more incompetent than you already are. And we have to consider Kelly's career."

No, we don't. Kelly's career is doing great. Just last week she flew to Palm Beach to do an industrial show for

Kraft Foods, playing a dancing wedge of cheese in an *Evita* medley entitled "*Velveeta.*"

"Promise me you won't quit," Kelly says. She bats her eyes, everyone's idea of the girl you bring home to meet your mother.

I sigh. "I've got to get out of there."

"Why don't you say you're sick?" she says. "I can tell Irving how worried I am about you, y'know, maybe cry in his office?"

"That would be a good way of showing your range," Ziba says. "Maybe he'll start sending you out for soap operas."

"Do you think?"

No, no, no. For a sexually ambiguous young man to suddenly develop mysterious health problems leads naturally to one fatal assumption. And that makes you a pariah. Not to mention dead within a year, which would be really hard to fake.

There's got to be another way.

In the Irving-infested days that follow, I resist the urge to leave at lunchtime and never come back, reminding myself that a promise is a promise, even though I've never really understood what the phrase means. What else would a promise be? A jelly doughnut? A wingback chair? *A promise is a three-legged dog.* Still, when Irving rips the phone out of the wall and aims for my head, I find myself wondering whether my mother was right. If I work for the Dark Overlord much longer, maybe I will end up with an aneurysm or a brain tumor. Or at least a concussion.

And that's what gives me the idea.

A brain tumor—who could argue with that? Sure, when our receptionist had to take time off for her grandmother's funeral, Irving made her bring a copy of the death certificate, but surely he's not going to put up with an assistant who suddenly goes numb on one side.

I start off with small, telltale signs, wearing sunglasses inside because the light hurts my eyes, walking into walls, and giving him phone messages from people who didn't call. ("Oh, I'm sorry. Did I say Patti LuPone? I meant James Lapine.") Then, claiming I hear bells, I start picking up phones when they don't ring and (best of all) dropping coffee on Irving's desk. It's so much fun, I wish I'd gotten a brain tumor weeks ago.

Finally I shuffle into his office one day after lunch in what I hope is the manner of someone with a terminal illness.

Scene:

"Irving?" I say, my voice quavering. "I need to talk to you about something."

Irving looks up, his eyes launching scud missiles.

"God, this is harder than I thought it would be," I say, giving a nervous laugh.

I mean this, but not in the way it sounds. In my mind I hear Marian Seldes say, *Stay in the moment. Use the discomfort.*

"I've, uh, been to the doctor," I say, swallowing. Swallowing's good; it shows the character is uncomfortable, dry-mouthed. "I have a growth on my brain." I heave a deep breath, hopefully approximating someone struggling to put on a brave face. That's what good actors do—instead of playing the emotion, they struggle against it, the way you would in real life.

Edward, you're not in the scene, Marian Seldes says. *I see you watching yourself.*

Damnit. I can't help it. Every time I act I want to yank

my eyes out like Oedipus and put them on the other side of the room to see how I'm doing.

I had the same problem with my Chekhov scene, although it wasn't entirely my fault, because I got assigned the opening of *The Three Sisters*, which is full of that clunky Chekhovian exposition ("As you know, you are my sister . . ."). What's more, I couldn't relate to any of those world-weary Russians in mourning for their lives. I mean, if you long to go to Moscow, then fucking go already.

I look at Irving, who doesn't say anything, the maggot. "They think it may be from too much aspartame."

He puts down his Fresca.

"I need to have . . . an operation."

I feel myself pushing for an emotion. Why can't I feel it? What's wrong with me? I'm an uptight, airtight box, an empty space. I quiver my chin and hope for the best.

"So I'm sorry to say that I'm going to have to quit."

Irving sinks back in his chair, momentarily at a loss for words. Then he bangs a fist on his desk, looks up at the ceiling, and addresses an unseen and fickle deity, crying, "Why, God?"

I'm shocked. And thrilled. This is more than I hoped for. Maybe I'm a better actor than I thought.

Irving continues to address the heavens, his palms outstretched, his voice rumbling like thunder. "Why does everything happen to ME?"

The rest of the office buys me a get-well card.

Once I am freed of Irving, Manhattan instantly becomes a happier place for me, the autumn in New York that Sinatra sings about, the one that transforms the slums to Mayfair. Dappled light dances among the trees, shimmering in the cranberry-, saffron-, and pumpkin-colored leaves, and I feel more motivated than ever to motivate these party-goers to my advantage, to live a life of mystery and intrigue. I turn my full attention to my first corporate event, a party for Beautonics®, Inc., a Midwest-based beauty-product company and the makers of the mousse that keeps my hair from looking like a tumbleweed.

"You're really gonna need that acting training," Sandra explains. "These executive types don't wanna socialize with perky chorus boys, even if you're dancing with their wives. There's no shiny shirt or tight pants. You've gotta fit in."

Apparently, some of us are too jazz hands for the corporate world.

Eager to get my beloved Chad the information he needs, I ask Sandra if she has any suggestions for talking to businesspeople.

"Just remembah," she says, "they're there to have fun. Tell 'em jokes. Talk about real estate or electronics. Oh! And sports. These guys love to talk about sports."

Great. I'm as fond of sports as truck drivers are of knitting. If I'm going to converse about it, I'll need help from the only jock I know.

Thirteen

The members of Almost Bruce live in Jersey City in two skinny houses crammed against each other, as if the buildings were afraid of the neighborhood and decided it's best to stick together. The walk from the PATH station could charitably be described as "life-threatening."

Doug waves to me from the shared front porch, where he's sprawled on a weathered couch strumming a guitar. He wears baggy army fatigues and a thermal shirt so tight it looks like he's been vacuum-packed. "Hey, man," he says, "just in time. I wantcha t'hear somethin' I'm workin' on."

I welcome any opportunity to stare at him directly.

He sings:

*Car lights, bar fights, a parasite suburbanite with
    gerbils in a Habitrail,
Got a rocket in my pocket and little Davy Crockett reads
    the telephone book in Braille.
A nighttime enzyme climbed into a pantomime and
    asked for a louvered grenade,*

Then took a Persian excursion with an adolescent
  version of a terry-cloth masquerade.

"Whaddya think?" he says.

I hate it.

"Catchy," I say. "What's it mean?"

"It's poetry," he says. "It doesn't have to mean anything."

"Well, then, you succeeded."

"Cool."

Not content with just being Almost Bruce, Doug then subjects me to a medley of songs that are Almost Original: rock anthems about cars, New Jersey, driving cars in New Jersey, and the plant closing in our hometown. When I point out that the only plants in Colonial Wallingford are ornamental, Doug says he's "expressing the collective pain of the displaced American worker."

What about the pain of those of us who have to listen? I think.

Luckily, we're interrupted when one of the doors on the porch creaks open and out tumble three musicians wiping their noses. Doug introduces them in quick succession, so I only catch the drummer's name, which is Napalm. Apropos of nothing he sets the conversational tone by asking, "Have you ever taken a dump so big your pants felt looser?"

"No," I say, far snippier than I intended, like I'm the prim schoolmarm newly arrived in Prairie Gulch; but he's too high to notice. Doug and I follow them in the other door, where we're going to watch game one of the National League Championship Series, which, apparently, is something that needs to happen before the World Series.

Inside I meet two more guys: Brian, the guitarist, and Vernon, the saxophonist, who are a study in contrasts. Whereas Brian is cadaverously pale and thin, as if he's kept in some dark cupboard between shows, Vernon bursts with life, his brown, bull-sized body bulging against his muscle T-shirt and zebra-striped weight-lifting pants. I swear, the man has forearms the size of my calves. He offers me a beer and I settle on the floor to watch the game, although I'm more intrigued by the fish tank, which isn't decorated with the usual fake plants and castles but with little green army guys, McDonald's Happy Meal toys, and a veiny black dildo the size of a peppermill.

I turn back to the Mets game, afraid someone will see me staring at it.

Nominally, I'm a Yankees fan. I say *nominally* because at some point in elementary school every boy must name his team whether he cares or not. I chose the Yankees because they're the only baseball team to inspire a Broadway musical. As a New Yorker, naturally I'd prefer the Mets beat the Houston Astros, but, frankly, I'm not rooting for either to win. When I look at the screen all I see are the kind of guys who beat me up in elementary school. And junior high. And high school. If there were a sport in which both teams lose, I could root for that. Or maybe a game in which they threw stones at each other. Massive Head Trauma Ball. Whoever gets the most concussions wins.

I'm not that much more impressed with the company in the room. These guys may not be jocks, but they're still guy-guys, and, consequently, they yell a lot, either at the TV or each other.

NAPALM: "A strike? That ain't no fuckin' strike. Is that a fuckin' strike?"

GUY WHOSE NAME I DON'T KNOW: "That ain't no fuckin'
   strike."
NAPALM: "That's what I'm fuckin' sayin'. I mean, that
   first one . . ."
GWNIDK: "Sure."
NAPALM: "But that one . . ."
GWNIDK: "No fuckin' way."
NAPALM: "That's what I'm fuckin' sayin'."

It's like a David Mamet play. But, unlike Mamet, where
the inane vulgarities are weighted with subtext, these guys
are just idiots. And I'm disappointed that this is what
Doug aspires to. Frankly, I don't know how he can stand
these cheeseheads.

The answer to my question comes rushing into the
room.

She's the kind of woman you might describe later in life
as handsome. Slender, leggy, with flinty cheekbones and a
tomahawk nose, a young Marian Seldes, though I can't
picture the grande dame of the Juilliard drama division in
a denim vest with a Mets cap and ponytail.

She tousles Doug's hair, which always looks like he just
had sex, even if he hasn't. "Outta my chair, junior."

Doug is at least four years younger than the others and
is the second Bruce they've had, having lost the first to a
competing tribute band from Princeton called Tramps Not
Unlike Ourselves. He grins at her, smitten, and I wonder if
his attraction to slender, boyish women signals repressed
homosexual desires.

The woman plops herself in the chair with the confi-
dent air of someone who's one of the guys. She places a
Styrofoam wig head between her thighs and starts brushing out a lustrous red mane. "Who are *you?*" she asks,

the Jersey equivalent of "Charmed to make your acquaintance."

"I'm Edward."

"Oh, yeah, I heard of you."

She has? That means Doug's talked about me. I refrain from doing a little happy dance.

"This is Theresa," Doug says. "She sings backup."

"And duets."

He smiles. "And duets."

I point to the wig. "I didn't recognize you, y'know, without the . . ."

"Yeah, when I get famous I want it to be as myself, not Patti Scialfa."

"You will, baby," Vernon says. "You will."

A commercial comes on, demonstrating how drinking beer will make you desirable to bikini-clad women.

"Doug says you're some kinda dancer," Theresa says.

"Sort of. I get thirteen-year-olds to boogie at bar mitzvahs."

"He's being modest," Doug says. "He's totally the life of the party. Those kids love him."

I swat the compliment away. "They love Eddie Sanders."

The name catches Vernon's attention. "The football player?"

"No, that's Eddie Zander," Brian says.

"Who's Eddie Zander?" I say.

The superlatives come tumbling out faster than I can make sense of them: College Football Hall of All-American Most Valuable Heisman blah blah blah. As I understand it, in the mid-1950s Eddie Zander led the University of Oklahoma to the longest winning streak in Division I history. What's more, he somehow managed to be more offensive and more defensive for more minutes than anyone else, which apparently is a good thing. There wasn't anything this guy couldn't do with a football, short of frying it up in a pan and eating it. Unfortunately, his football career came to an abrupt end when he suffered a tragic buttock injury.

"Y'know, my old man met him once," Napalm says, reaching for what appears to be a clarinet but turns out to be a bong.

"Get out," Vernon says. "What's he doing now?"

"He's home watchin' the game with my mom."

"No, you tool, Eddie Zander."

"Oh, he sells fake limbs."

"Fuck you, he does not."

Napalm pulls a bag of weed out of his pocket.

"He does so. I read it in *Sports Illustrated*. He's got a big warehouse in one of those O-wa states."

"O-wa states?"

"Y'know, in the Midwest: Iowa, Ohio, Oklahoma, Omaha."

"Omaha ain't a state, you dipshit."

"I meant Idaho."

We stay ahead beers and bong hits to innings until the Mets finally lose. Everyone seems to drift away after that, but it could just be the beer and the bong hits. The room keeps going all cubist on me, and I inform Doug that I'm going to have to crash on the couch. He responds by turning off the lights so we can mellow out in front of the fish tank, because that's the kind of thing you do when you're stoned.

We sit on the couch in the dark, mesmerized by the phosphorescent glow of the tank, the fish proving to be surprisingly good entertainment. Some are Vegas show-girls, with sparkling iridescent gowns and fins like feather boas; others are flamenco dancers, with slender bodies and wide, fanlike tails. The rest come straight out of Central Casting circa 1940: a google-eyed Peter Lorre, a fat-lipped Edward G. Robinson, and a spotted catfish with a Fu Manchu mustache.

"Explain this to me," I say. "Eddie Zander wuz a hunch-back. . . ."

"Halfback."

"And tha' means . . . What does tha' mean?"

"Here, I'll show ya'." Doug arranges some Cheetos in a line on the coffee table. "Here'za line of scrimmage, right?"

"Whassa scrimmage?"

"It's . . . Don't ask me that."

"Okay. Where am I?"

"You're right here," he says, patting my knee. "Next to me."

"Yeah, me, too."

He moves a Cheeto, then another. "So the fullback is here, behind the quarterback. And the halfback is behind him."

I stare at the Cheetos. Such a strange word, Cheeto. Cheeeeee-tooooooh.

"That doesn't make sense," I say. "It should be quarter-back, halfback, fullback. Y'know, like two quarterbacks make a halfback and two halfbacks make a fullback."

"And four fullbacks make a gallon," Doug says.

"Yeah. But only God can make a tree."

We laugh for a long time. Or maybe a short time. I'm not sure. Then we sit back and watch the tank. A reptilian, eel-like thing scales the bottom. I think it's an eel.

"What were we just talking about?" I say. .

Doug squints to remember. "Something."

"Yeah," I say, shaking a Cheeto. "It was definitely something. What was it?"

"What was what?"

"The something we were talking about."

"I dunno," he says. "I don't even know what I'm talking about right now."

I stare at the tank. The dildo is like a baseball bat. "Sports. We were talking about sports."

He nods like I've said something profound, his head bobbing on an unseen ocean. "Riiiiight." Nod, nod.

"I mean, whas the point?" I say. "In the end, somebody loses, somebody wins. It doesn't teach you anything about life."

Doug scooches around to look at me. "No, no, no, man, you're missin' the point. When you play a game, it's like you're a part of somethin', somethin' bigger than you."

Looking into his blue eyes is like finding two tiny robin's eggs.

"It's like when I'm singin'," he says. "And the band is wailin' and the crowd is jumpin' up and down. There's like this . . . wave. Y'know? Sometimes Theresa comes up to sing a duet and we lean in real close . . ."

He leans in real close.

". . . and it's like we're fucking. Except we're not, 'cuz she's fucking Vernon. Fuckin' Vernon. But when we're *singing*, it's just the two of us in this other world together. Like I'm Bruce and she's Patti. And nobody can touch us. Ya' know what I mean?"

My mind is Teflon. I watch his mouth move but all I see are lips, tongue, teeth.

He leans back and gazes at the tank again. "Do you think they mind?"

"Who?"

"The fish. They just swim back and forth in there. It's like a fuckin' fish prison." He rises. "C'mon. Let's give 'em some exercise."

What follows is the kind of thing that only makes sense when you're using recreational drugs. Doug fills a bucket with tap water, into which we transfer the squirming fish with one of those little nets. Then we slosh down the hall to the bathroom, fill the tub, and pour the fish in. We both kneel next to the tub and watch them. The fish don't seem to know the difference, still swimming the length of the tank, rather than the tub.

"They don't look happier," I say.

"They need waves," Doug says, then swooshes the water around, sending the fish twirling, an aquatic kaleidoscope.

"Cooooool."

He does it again, this time splashing me.

I splash him back. And he me. Then him again. Back and forth until we're both soaked to the skin. Doug leans against the wall, his shirt clinging to the contours of his chest, his nipples nippling through the fabric. He reaches up and pulls down the towel hanging over his head, pats himself, then peels off his shirt.

He's grown hairier, but you can still see the striations in his muscles, as if he'd been woven together in a very sexy arts-and-crafts class. My whole body aches with *I want you.* Doug is like an addiction: The more I get of him, the more I need.

He hands me the towel. I take off my shirt and rub myself dry, sucking in my stomach, ashamed of my softness. I pull my knees up to my chest, wishing I had a body like his. It's like they say about sculptors: Michelangelo looks at a block of marble and carves away everything that isn't David. If I were a statue, I'd be unfinished.

We sit in silence, the only sound coming from our breathing.

Doug leans his head against the tub. "I gotta go to bed."

I look at the fish. "What about them?"

Doug lifts himself up, the muscles in his chest flexing. "Tomorrow," he mutters. He shuffles to the door, then turns to look at me. "You got everything you need?"

No, I don't have what I need at all.

"Yeah."

Wuss.

I stagger back into the living room and reach for the nubby blanket that looks like someone's grandmother crocheted it when I'm suddenly aware of the disembodied redhead sitting on an amp that doubles as an end table.

"Hello," I say. "You've got no body." A wave of sadness pours over me. "Me, neither." I take the wig head in hand, fascinated by it. I am Salome with the head of John the Baptist. I pull the wig off. I am Hamlet with the skull of Yorick. I sing to him.

"It's up to you, New Yorick, New Yorick . . ."

I look down at Theresa's Patti Scialfa wig in my hand, and wonder, *Why am I holding this? What am I supposed to do with . . . Oh, I know; I'm trying it on.* I place the red hair on my head and stumble over to the dark windowpane to examine my reflection. With my long, dark eyelashes and the softness at my belly, I look, well, Almost Pretty. At least in dim light. I take the blanket and drape it on my shoulders. Suddenly I am Vanessa Redgrave in the opening scene of the movie version of *Camelot*, wrapped in fur as

Guinevere is led to meet King Arthur for the first time. A lousy movie, but a luminous performance and . . . someone's talking to me.

I turn around and there's Doug with a pillow in his hand.

"Patti," he says.

"Bruce."

Fourteen

I'm awoken by the sound of a woman screaming. I try to brush the hair out of my eyes, but there's so much of it, all of it red. Am I bleeding? I reach up and feel my scalp move. Oh, God, my head is cracked open. I'm lying in a pool of my own blood. I'm . . .

Wearing a wig. I look over at Doug, who lies asleep next to me on the couch with his boxers around his knees, his morning erection bursting from his crotch like an angry child raising a fist.

I nudge his leg. "Waig up. Waig up."

Now I hear a man yelling in the other room, too.

"WAKE UP."

Doug stirs, moaning, "Whutthefug . . ." He looks at me. "Patti?"

Doors slam. Footsteps pound down the hallway.

And now Doug is wide-awake.

"SHIT!" With astonishing speed he leaps up, his cock bobbing like an eager puppy. He pulls up his boxers, yanks off my wig, and wraps the blanket around himself as Theresa comes storming into the room, screaming:

"WHAT THE FUCK HAPPENED TO MY FISH?"

We fumble into the bathroom, I-don't-knowing and What-are-you-talking-abouting, only to encounter an empty tub. Well, empty except for about a dozen dead fish.

Doug glances at the drain. "I guess we need a new stopper."

Theresa kicks him in the shin.

Doug limps with me to the station, mostly to escape the drama. We try to laugh off the mishap but, after this past summer's accident on East Sixty-fish Street, I can't deny that I'm now a serial fish killer. We lapse into silence, the air between us heavy with the unspoken. Finally I say, "About last night—"

He puts up his hand to stop me. "That can never happen again."

No. Don't say that. Rewind. Do-over. No backsies.

"I understand," I mumble.

Wuss.

More silence. Thick, muggy, humid silence.

"It's just that . . ."

"What?"

I scuff my foot along the pavement, which I shouldn't do because I hate it when white sneakers get dingy. "What *did* happen?"

He stops. "You don't remember?"

This is almost physically painful for me to admit. Three years I've been waiting for this moment, imagining it and reimagining it in my mind—the feel of his lips parting and yielding to mine, his skin against my skin, his heavy manhood in my hand. Or possibly hands. And now I can't remember anything beyond, "Oh, Bruce." It makes me want to run around in circles screaming like the crazy homeless guy who hangs out across the street from my apartment wearing a colander on his head.

I swallow, trying to moisten my mouth. "Do you?"

He stares at the crooked sidewalk. "No." He looks up, his sky blue eyes cloudy. "But whatever it was, it can't happen again."

Yes, it can. It will. It must. Inside me, Jennifer Holliday wails:

You're gonna luuuuh-uhuh-uuuuuh-huh-huh-
   uhuhuhuuuuuve . . .
(gasp)
   . . . meeeeeeeeeeeeeeeeeeeeeeeeeeeeeeeeeh.

Unlike *Dreamgirls*, no intermission follows, forcing me to cope with my roiling emotions in the time-honored method of Miss Effie White and thousands of other spurned lovers: I go home and eat a half gallon of ice cream in one sitting.

Luckily, I don't have much time to sit around feeling maudlin and showstopping. The following night is my Beautonics® gig, so I suit up in my new Brooks Brothers uniform, a gray-blue single-breasted two-button suit that makes me look like an insurance salesman, and show up at the Waldorf=Astoria, an atmosphere so swank that even the pissy punctuation of the hotel's name intimidates me. Much as Einstein probably had a blackboard's worth of notation to prove $e=mc^2$, the answer to what makes Waldorf equal Astoria is not for mere commoners to comprehend.

I tread down the hallway of the fourth floor, past photos of former guests like Charles de Gaulle, Winston Churchill, and the Duke and Duchess of Windsor, wondering how I'm going to pull this off. *Jokes, real estate, electronics, and sports,* I tell myself. *Jokes, real estate, electronics, and sports.* I touch my hair to make sure it's still in place and am relieved that I slicked it back with so much mousse it feels shellacked. Adjusting the nonprescription reading glasses I'm wearing to look older, I round the corner into the Louis XVI suite.

The room is what you'd expect—a blue-and-gold baroque fantasy of padded silk walls and heavy velour drapes—but what surprises me are the guests. It's not like I imagined a beauty-product company would only employ people in black turtlenecks with severe wedge haircuts, but now I understand why Chad had me buy the gray-blue single-breasted two-button suit. I'm looking at a roomful of my fathers. From the Midwest.

This is never going to work, I think. I don't know how to talk to my own father, let alone a roomful of them.

I glance past murals of French châteaus and immediately pick out the stealth guests: There's Zach, circulating with apparent ease, all backslappy and how-ya-doin', while Courtenay, Kate, and Robyn effortlessly command the attention of several middle-aged middle managers. The female motivators have it easy, because these guys neither expect nor want them to act like businesspeople; it's enough to look pretty and feign interest in what they have to say, which is a skill in and of itself. The only reason to keep up any pretense at all is so the out-of-towners don't think they're hookers.

Nearby, a cluster of my fathers listen to another tell a joke.

"So there's this new colonel at the Foreign Legion," the guys says. "And, after a coupla weeks in the desert, he asks his sergeant, 'What do our soldiers do to satisfy their physical urges?'

"And the sergeant says, 'Well, sir, we've got a camel in the stable.'

" 'A camel?'

" 'Yes, sir.'

"This sounds pretty strange to the colonel, but it's been a while, so he figures, Why not? The sergeant brings him to the stable, and the colonel steps up on a stool, drops his pants, and fucks the shit out of this camel. And when he's done, he pulls up his pants and says to the sergeant, 'So, is that how the enlisted men do it?'

"And the sergeant says, 'Actually, sir, usually they just ride the camel into town.' "

When the laughter subsides, I say, "I've got one," and the men turn around and see me for the first time. I smile, trying to be the Life of the Party, albeit in a backslappy, how-ya-doin', insurance-salesman way. "This wino is pan-hassling on the subway, right, and he comes up to this businessman and says, 'Loan me a dollar?' And the businessman says, ' "Neither a borrower nor a lender be"— William Shakespeare.' And the wino says, ' "Eat shit and die, motherfucker"—David Mamet.' "

They stare at me like I suggested boiling babies.

"So," I say, "how about that real estate, huh?"

Nothing. My forehead starts to rain.

"Yeah," I continue, "it sure is, uh, real."

I try switching topics, but apparently my little anecdote about how I can never tell which side my cassette player is playing isn't the kind of electronics discussion these guys have either. I escape to the bar.

I'm fortifying myself with beer when a hedgehog of a man sidles up to me. "Hi, there," the hedgehog says, used-car-salesman friendly. "Gus Gunderson."

"Eddie Sanders," I mumble. I suppose I should come up

with a different name when I'm not being MTV's hottest new veejay, but Sandra says it's important to keep your party aliases close to your own name, so you remember to answer to them. Plus, I forgot.

He cocks his head to hear me better. "Eddie Zander? Like the football player?"

And, just like in a comic strip, a lightbulb switches on in my brain. "Shore as yer born," I drawl. "He's mah daddy."

"No!"

"If I'm lyin', I'm dyin'."

"Well, how do you like that."

"I like it vurry much, thank yew."

He slaps his knee and laughs. I'm not sure I've ever seen someone actually slap his knee.

"Y'know, I saw your dad play . . ."

And he's off, relating some incomprehensible tale of running, passing, blocking, and tackling, which gives me time to hastily cobble together a plausible autobiography for Eddie Zander, Jr. That way, I'm ready when he asks the inevitable:

"Did you play ball like your dad?"

There's no way I can fake my way through that conversation. "No, sir," I say. "I wish I could've. I was born without kneecaps."

It's the best I could do on short notice.

"I thought all babies were born without kneecaps."

Shit. Who knew? No wonder babies' legs look like sausages. "That's true," I say, "but mine never grew in." I put my foot up on the rung of the bar stool, leaning my forearm on my thigh in a folksy, Western fashion. All I need is a lasso and some chewin' tabacky. "One hundred percent plastic," I say, tapping my knee. "Mah daddy said

I wuz the bionic boy. That's why he got into the artificial limb business. Once he said ta me, 'Sprout . . .'—that's whut he calls me, Sprout—'dreams only come true in dreams. The sooner you learn that the better.' "

Gus Gunderson gives a sage nod. "So what brings you here?"

"I'm fixin' to take over Daddy's business when he re-tires, but he wants me to get out in the world first. Y'know, get some seasoning. So I became a sales rep for this here company."

I'm about to extol the virtues of the Beautonics® prod-uct line, most especially their Ready-Set-Go Spray Mousse, when Gus Gunderson puts a paternal arm around my shoulder and says, "Let me introduce you around." He waves to a man across the room. "Hey, Ted, you'll never guess who this is."

Before the evening is over, I've met an alphabet soup of executives—PR, VP, GM, IT—all of whom get the same gleam in their eye when they hear Eddie Zander's name. In an instant they're twelve-year-old boys, and soon I've got a group of them around me as if I were at a bash mitzvah. Mostly the guys just want to talk, to share with me the seemingly magic qualities Eddie Zander had on the field. And how their innocence ended when Zander suffered his tragic buttock injury. A couple of them even get dewy-eyed about it. I assure them that my father went on to live a ful-filling life, even with only one ass cheek.

Finally, after several drinks (and several hints that I need guidance in my fledgling sales career), Gus motions me aside with a boozy wave and mutters, "Now, son, don't tell anyone I told you this. . . ."

Fifteen

I ride down in the elevator with my new friends, whom I'm eager to dump so I can call Chad. But they cling to me like socks from a dryer, unaware that they're talking and laughing too loud. I glance around at the ballrooms flanking each side of the lobby, concerned we might be making a spectacle of ourselves, when a voice calls out:

"Eddie! Eddie, it's me!"

I wheel around and there's Lizzie Sniderman, rising from an overstuffed chair by some potted palms, wearing a leather bomber jacket with a plaid miniskirt and combat boots.

I keep walking.

"EDDIE!"

Shit. Doesn't this kid have parents?

Gus Gunderson turns around. "Is that little girl calling your name?"

"What little girl?"

"That one."

"Oh, *her*. That's, uh, my sister."

I wave, giving Lizzie the Internationally Recognized Signal for "Don't come over here, you crazed harpy, or you'll fuck up everything."

She gets the message. Unfortunately, Gus Gunderson doesn't. "A sister!" he shouts. "Do ya' hear that, boys! That's Eddie Zander's little girl."

They advance on her like they're a pack of dogs and she's a hamburger that just dropped on the floor. *Okay,* I think, *I can do this.* I actually have a sister. She's a drug-addled craps dealer in Reno, Nevada, but acting's all about making substitutions. Faced with the collision of my British and Oklahoman alter egos, I simply put my arm around Lizzie and keep my mouth shut.

"Well, hello, there, little lady," Gus says. "What's your name?"

Lizzie seems distracted by my hand on her shoulder, probably because I'm cutting off her circulation. "Lizzie?" she says, like she's not sure.

"Lizzie! Why, you're the spitting image of your dad."

She gives a metallic grin. "You know my dad?"

"Of course. We all do. We're big fans."

"Really? You've seen his movies?"

"Movies?"

"*Debs Behind Bars* and *Debs Behind Bars Two: Muffy's Revenge.* They're mostly on cable, but they're real popular in Germany."

Gus turns to me. "I thought you said he sold prosthetic limbs."

"What's a prosthetic limb?" says Lizzie.

Suddenly they all go silent, undoubtedly wondering why Eddie Zander's daughter doesn't know what he does for a living.

"Would you excuse us?" I say in what I hope is an Anglohoman hybrid. I pull Lizzie a few steps away, saying, "Listen, poppet, be a dearie and wait for me over there. I just need to talk with these gentl'mun about a wee bit a' business."

"Why'd you say my dad sold—"

"I didn't. They're just pissed."

"At what?"

"No, pet, pissed means drunk."

"Oh. Ya' mean, like, in English?"

"Yes. Like in English. And some of those blokes fancy young girls. So just wait for me by the door."

Lizzie scuffs down the steps to the front door, giving the alleged child molesters murderous looks. I saunter back, maybe just a little bowlegged for effect.

I'm sure this situation will help me in my acting, that it will someday make a great anecdote for a profile in the *New York Times* Sunday Arts and Leisure section about how this year's Tony Award winner first got his start, but right now it's got me more nervous than a maid at the Helmsley Palace.

"I'm shore sorry you had to see that," I drawl. "Poor thang got dropped on her head when she was little and she ain't been right since."

They all shake their heads, tsk-tsking. "That's awful," says Gus Gunderson.

"Yeah, bless her heart. I need to get her outside. Otherwise she's liable to start barkin' like a dog."

I say good night, then dash down the steps, shoving Lizzie through the revolving door.

"What are you doing here?" I say, the night air slapping me in the face.

"I came to see you."

"How'd you know where I was?"

"I called your apartment. I mean, your flat. Some bloke told me." She pulls a pack of cigarettes out of her purse. "You want one?" she says. "They're Silk Cut. I had me dad get 'em from the duty-free shop."

I find it really irritating that she's affecting an English accent. I mean, it's one thing for work, but this is just pretentious. "I don't smoke."

"Me, neither," she says. "But these are British."

"Do your parents know where you are?"

"I don't even know where *they* are. Me dad lives in Beverly Hills, y'know."

"You said."

"And me mum is always at work or at parties for work. I just take the phone off the hook so she thinks I'm talking to Marcy all night, which is what I usually do anyway, because Marcy's so fucked-up."

As she trails me heading west, Lizzie shares some of the more sordid details from Marcy's life—how her dad had an affair with the nanny, how her mom threw all his suits off the terrace onto East Seventy-fourth Street, and how Marcy goes to therapy three times a week to deal with her habitual bed-wetting. All of this is interspersed with a running commentary on the sights we pass and how they figure into the rich, eventful life of Lizzie Sniderman: Saks ("It's okay, but I do all my shopping downtown"), St. Patrick's ("Marcy and I went once and I dared her to drink the holy water"), Rockefeller Center and Radio City ("I used to go a long time ago, but it's strictly Bridge and Tunnel").

I stop on the corner of Broadway, where *Cats* is playing Now and Forever, which sounds more like a threat than a promise.

"You should catch a cab here," I say. There's no way I want to be responsible for a thirteen-year-old in Hell's

Kitchen. My neighborhood's so tough even the rats are armed.

"Why don't you come over?" she says. "I've got some really trippy Kate Bush records. Have you heard her? There's, like, whales on 'em and stuff. We could turn down the lights, have a glass of wine. . . ."

As if I didn't have enough problems, now I'm being propositioned by the Lenox Hill Lolita. I shove her in a cab and hurry home. According to the genuine fake Movado I bought on the street, it's 11:05 Edward Standard Time, which means it's actually 10:54 and not too late to call Chad to tell him my inside information: Beautonics® newest blow-dryer, the Beau-Sonic 2000, is being recalled because it overheats and sets consumers' hair on fire. It's less of a blow-dryer than a blowtorch. I dash up the four flights to what I've come to think of as Sanderland, only to find a note on the door:

Be quiet. I'm baking.

I'm not sure what the latter has to do with the former. Natie might as well have written, *Be quiet. I'm knitting.* Or *Be quiet. I'm sandblasting.* And since when does he bake? I unlock the door and am immediately intoxicated by the aroma of vanilla, accompanied by the sight of Natie tiptoeing toward me, raising a finger to his lips like he's Elmer Fudd hunting wabbits. "Don't let the door ba—"

Behind me, the door bangs shut.

"Never mind," he says. He shuffles back to the kitchen, his slippers scuffing against the floor. Natie's the only person my age I know who wears slippers. "I have very soft feet," he says.

I follow him into the kitchen, where he opens the oven door. "Good," he says, "it didn't fall."

"That only happens on TV."

"That's what you think. You didn't grow up with Fran Nudelman cooking."

Actually, I did. When my mom left town I pretty much lived at the Nudelmans'. Fran followed the sacred Jewish tradition of taking perfectly edible meat and vegetables and torturing them until they gave up every last nutrient.

"What are you making?"

"Banana-nut upside-down cake. Eddie's mother sent the recipe."

"She did? When?"

"In 1965. I found it in his journal." He hands me a sallowed newspaper clipping from the *Des Moines Register*.

"Natie."

"What? Don't look at me like that. As coexecutor of the estate, it's practically my responsibility."

"You're not the coexecutor."

"De facto coexecutor. And who else is gonna read it? His little old white-haired mother in Ohio?"

"Maybe."

"Yeah, well, I've got two words for her: Butt. Love." He fans himself with the book.

"Then why are you reading it?" I ask. "Is there something I should know?"

He gives me a look like just-'cuz-I-like-musicals-and-can't-get-laid-doesn't-mean-I'm-gay. "There's a lot of fascinating theater stuff in here."

"Like . . . ?"

"Like after Eddie left *The Sound of Music*, he did this show about homeless people called *Subways Are for Sleep-*

ing. I know. *Poverty! The Musical.* Anyway, the show was a dog, but it almost broke even because the producer, David Merrick, was a fucking mastermind. He found seven guys with the same names as the theater critics of the seven daily newspapers, gave 'em free seats, then took out a full-page ad in the *Herald-Tribune* with quotes like, "Best Musical of the Century!" Natie smiles, his squishy face like a baby's butt. "Genius!"

I sit down at the table, pushing aside Natie's textbooks (something called *Quantum Microeconomics: Structural Theory of Discrete Data and Econometric Applications*, as well as a phone-book-sized tome simply titled *Psychology*) and study Eddie's personal effects, including a stack of souvenir record albums from industrial shows like General Motors' *Diesel Dazzle* and American Standard's *The Bathrooms Are Coming*, as well as a collection of 1960s soft-porn physique magazines like *The Grecian Guild Pictorial* and *Manorama*.

I pick up Eddie's diary and flip through it, wondering whether I should come up with some excuse to go out so I can call Chad from a pay phone. "Anything else going on in 1965?" I ask.

"Yeah, Eddie got chlamydia from a guy who blew him in Central Park."

"What's chlamydia?"

"I dunno. But it makes it hurt when you pee."

I put down the diary.

Without a trace of irony, Natie unpeels a banana. "Gay guys don't still have sex in the Ramble, do they?"

"How should I know?"

"I just figured, y'know, since you wanted to be alone in the park the other day."

"Don't be a cheesehead."

He plops down next to me. "So what happened with your gig tonight?" he asks. "Didja go to the wrong place?"

I explain to him how he was duped by the delinquent detective.

He frowns, his forehead wrinkling like a pierogi. "So you were *supposed* to be at the Waldorf?"

"Of course."

"Okay, don't bite my head off."

I glance at something called *Muscles A-Go-Go*. "Anyone else call?"

He hands me a pile of pink While You Were Out slips that I swiped from Irving's office before I quit: *7:45—Hung called to say hi. 8:50—Hung called to see if you were back. 9:30—Kelly called to find out why you're not calling Hung.*

I cringe. Not only am I not interested in Wei Tu Gay, but Kelly's still pissed at me for quitting the way I did. Apparently another assistant already had a brain tumor.

As usual, I'm awoken by the Garbage Truck Derby. Normally I'd try to eke out whatever sleep I could, but this morning I'm instantly alert with Chad on my brain. I realize it's just as well that I didn't call him, because I would have squandered an opportunity to see him in person.

The only problem is how I can reasonably show up at his office. Our arrangement is supposed to be secret. I lie in my loft bed, Natie snoring below, while I ponder who might visit a brokerage firm. Probably the same people who visit Pinnacle Management: clients, UPS and FedEx guys, delivery boys, and bicycle messengers. Of the list, the last feels like the easiest to pull off; plus it allows Chad to see how good my butt looks in spandex. I climb out of bed as quietly as possible for someone sleeping on the top bunk, gather up the appropriate clothes, and creep into the living room, where I slip on tights with a T-shirt and windbreaker. I don't have one of those little cycling caps, so I tie a bandanna around my head to look more Latino.

Natie appears in the doorway, wiping sleep from his eyes like he's an enormous toddler.

"Why are you dressed like a *Solid Gold* dancer?"

"I'm, uh, going to an audition."

I grab a clipboard, a pen, an envelope, and a pad.

"I thought you said auditioning gave you gastric reflux."

"I . . . got over it."

"Is that so?"

"Hypnosis. Amazing stuff."

I toss everything in my messenger bag.

"You didn't tell me you were seeing a hypnotist."

"I'm not. It's self-hypnosis. I'm actually in a trance right now."

I grab my Walkman, because messengers always seem to have them, though how they can listen to music without getting hit by a bus is one of life's great mysteries.

"Affirmation tape. Ooh, look at the time," I say, glancing at my wrist despite the fact that I'm not wearing my watch. "Gotta go."

I fumble for my keys and tumble out the door. As I descend the stairs, greeting my downstairs neighbors, Mr. and Mrs. Crackhead, I ponder why I have no trouble claiming to be a British TV star or an Oklahoman without kneecaps, but I find it so hard to lie when I'm being myself.

Lower Manhattan feels as if it were an entirely different city, a quainter, more colonial one, like Boston or

Philadelphia, with narrow streets and winding alleys and Greek Revival buildings like Federal Hall, where Washington was inaugurated. I get turned around twice trying to find Chad's office because there's water to the east, west, and south. But I finally find the building, a glass-and-metal skyscraper that looks like an immense honeycomb attracting very busy bees. Making note of the coffee shop adjacent to the lobby, I go upstairs.

The reception area of Sharp, Thornton, and Wiley resembles the drawing room of an English manor, all mahogany paneling and brass fixtures. There's even a mantelpiece, above which hangs a portrait of a heavily whiskered man with the fierce, frowning countenance of someone passing a kidney stone.

The receptionist looks up. Unlike the high-haired gum chewer at Pinnacle, she has the pretty, self-possessed air of a Miss Porter's School for Girls grad, her blond—but not too blond—hair pulled back in a severe ballerina bun, as if she were punishing it. Her nameplate reads, SHANNON RIEKE, the friendliness of the Irish first name punctuated by the Teutonic officiousness of the last. Trying to remember Milagros's accent as best I can, I inform the receptionist I have a "letter for Shat Severson."

"Who?"

"Shat Severson." I show her the name on the envelope and give her a look like, *Don't you speak English?*

"You can leave that with me," she says, more Rieke than Shannon.

"I need his signature."

"Can't I sign for it?"

"No. I need Shat Severson."

The fraulein frowns, picks up the phone, and relays the message to Chad, who, judging from her response, isn't happy about it. I'm forced to wait just long enough to feel I've made a horrible, horrible mistake when the object of my affection comes banging through the doors. He has his jacket off, revealing a blue pin-striped shirt with a white collar, his yellow tie knotted tight around his neck. He frowns, his chest heaving against his suspenders. He glances at me, then does a double take.

"Shat Severson?" I say.

He nods, cartoon-eyed.

I hand him the clipboard. As he signs, I flick my eyes at the envelope, which contains a note saying, *I have news. Meet me downstairs in the coffee shop.*

I get into the elevator, my shirt clinging to the small of my back. In less than twelve hours I've been three differ-ent people—four, including myself. Shakespeare was right: All the world *is* a stage.

Once in the lobby, I head into the coffee shop and take a seat at the counter, setting my bag on the stool next to me. I examine the menu, willing myself not to stare at the door like a faithful dog, when a voice behind me says, "What the hell are you up to?"

It's not Chad.

Sixteen

I whirl around on the stool and find myself face-to-muffin-face with Natie. He folds up the brim of his fishing hat, making him look like a burlesque comic.

"What are you doing here?" I hiss.

"Me? What about you?"

"I can't explain. Just go."

Through the window looking out on the lobby, I see Chad stop to buy a paper. I turn my back on Natie, who decides to make my life a living hell by plopping down on the next stool over. He's wearing the sweatpants he slept in. "You don't know me," I mutter.

I reach for a napkin to wipe the sweat off my forehead. I am the worst spy ever. The waitress approaches and, just as I'm about to order, I hear Chad behind me, demanding a coffee. I move my bag, as if I'm making room for a stranger.

"Thanks," he says, then whispers, "pretend you're listening to your Walkman."

It's all very cloak-and-dagger. I put my headphones on and bop my head to unheard music. Chad unfolds a copy of the *Times* and starts filling out the crossword puzzle.

"W-H-Y-R-U-H-E-R-E," he writes in 37 across.

I softly sing my answer, as if I were singing along to a tape. "I want-ed to call youuuu, but it was too laaaa-hay-hay-hay-hayaaate." Natie peers over Chad's right shoulder, an even more inept spy than I am.

Chad doesn't notice him, as he's sort of hunched my way so I can read what he's writing. "W-H-A-T-H-A-V-E-U-G-O-T."

I like this game. This time I answer with a real melody, to the tune of Springsteen's "Dancing in the Dark."

You can start a fire;
Your hair can go right up in flames,
If you buy a blow-dryer,
Beau-Sonic 2000 is its name.

It's not a perfect fit, but it's pretty good on short notice. Chad writes, "B-O-S-O-N-I-C-2-0-0-0," in the puzzle, adding, "N-O-T-B-A-D." Meanwhile, Natie holds up a spoon as if he's examining it for spots, when it's perfectly obvious he's trying to see what Chad's writing. Chad scrawls a note in the margin:

Next time call me at home,
no matter how late.

I feel a twitch in my groin.

Use a pay phone.

I nod in a bopping manner. Seeing him in his natural habitat makes me want to please him even more. He seems so grown-up, so put-together, with his slick hair, tight pores, and tailored suit, like he's been assembled in a factory. I don't think I'll ever feel the way he looks.

Chad snaps his fingers for the waitress and tells her he wants his coffee to go. He opens his wallet, pulls out two bills, and places them on the counter. One is a dollar he leaves for the waitress. The other is a hundred for me. As he rises, he flicks his eyes downward at my crotch. "Cute tights," he mutters.

Then he winks. I love people who wink.

Natie and I walk to the East River, which I'm seriously considering tossing him into. "Why did you follow me?" I cry.

"I had to. You've been acting so strange. First you tell me you're being recruited for the internship program at Sharp, Thornton, and Wiley, which is just a Dumbo ride short of Fantasyland. Then, all of sudden you've got shopping phobias and this thirteen-year-old stalker. . . ."

"No, she's for real."

He shrugs, the Internationally Recognized Signal for "I don't believe you, but I'm willing to concede the point." He continues: "I just figured, since we're at the age when people can turn schizophrenic . . ."

"Oh, I see. One psych class and suddenly you're Carl Jung."

"Of course not. Jung collaborated with the Nazis."

"That's not what—"

"You can't blame me for being suspicious," he says. "After all, your mom is kind of a dipsy doodle."

He's got a point. This is the woman who moved to Sedona to contact extraterrestrials. Any similarity between her reality and ours is completely coincidental.

We lean on a fence and take in the view of the Brooklyn Bridge, the autumn wind whipping off the water. There's so much sky down here, as if the world suddenly opened up. I tell Natie everything about my burgeoning career in corporate espionage.

It's such a relief. What's more, Natie offers to help. "My friend, with your acting skills and my business know-how, we are gonna get rich."

"How?"

"Whaddya think Chad's gonna do with the information you gave him today?"

I have to confess I don't exactly know.

"He's gonna trade on it."

"But the Beau-Sonic 2000 is being recalled. That'll send the stock price down, won't it?"

"Yeah, but he can buy options."

"Options?"

"Meaning he'll short the stock. It's kind of like betting it'll go down."

"Sounds like gambling."

Natie claps me on the back. "Welcome to Wall Street."

"So, what's that got to do with us?"

"Chad's not the only one who can trade on that information."

It never occurred to me that I could buy and sell stocks. That's for men in suits who work in offices, not for guys in spandex. But if I invest the money I'm earning from Sandra and Chad in the stock market, I won't have to work in an office. I can make my own way on my own terms. I'd be totally self-sufficient. Then I could show Al once and for all that I don't need his goddamn money. And maybe once he saw what I'd accomplished, he'd be so proud that he'd offer to pay for Juilliard anyway, so I could use my money for myself. And finally buy some baggy socks. Those suckers are expensive.

When we get back to the apartment, Natie examines the Beautonics® annual reports and business prospectuses that Chad sent me and informs me that the Beau-Sonic 2000 accounts for too little of Beautonics® business to make a huge difference in the stock, and that "we" should keep looking for other information. "We" meaning Eddie Zander.

Being the son of a legend opens doors (an invite to a lake house, several promises to fix me up with single daughters, and, once, an offer of some choice Colombian cocaine), but it doesn't guarantee information. Reasoning that businessmen have kids, I expand my search to the bash mitzvahs.

Unfortunately, no one wants to talk business with British MTV's hottest veejay.

Luckily, my commitment to winning friends and influencing people doesn't escape Sandra's notice. Overwhelmed by the administrivia of running her burgeoning business, she hires me to do some of the grunt work, providing me a view of the underbelly of the overprivileged. For weeks Sandra's been fretting about a sweet sixteen thrown by oil and commodities trader Will Owens for his daughter from his first marriage, Windy, so Sandra has spent the better part of her time running interference between the first and second Mrs. Owenses, the former being much embittered because the latter isn't much older than sweet sixteen herself. Since Owens's company, Petrolox, is a big woofy deal, the party is only slightly less elaborate than the Radio City Christmas spectacular.

Still, no amount of gossip prepares me for the surrealism of the event, which is held in the backyard of Owens's estate on Long Island's oh-so-exclusive North Shore. And by backyard I don't mean a place where you set up a grill and a few lounge chairs. I mean a state park. The house itself, a stone manor with ten chimneys, is so grand it must require serfs. Even though it could easily accommodate hundreds of tenants, let alone guests, Owens throws the party under a circus-sized tent erected over the tennis courts, which are repainted "Windy Pink."

This kind of arrangement typifies the decadent logic of party planning. Sandra has produced events where she's assembled an arbor of wisteria in a hotel ballroom to create the feeling of being outdoors. (Here's an idea—throw the party outdoors.) Conversely, she's also used slide projections to replicate the ceiling of the Sistine Chapel inside a tent, an odd choice for a bash mitzvah.

The inside of the Owenses' tent glows with projections of pink clouds, as if a storm system of cotton candy just blew in. Since the birthday girl is a passionate equestrian, life-size horses made of rose petals flank the entrance. Windy herself makes an entrance on a white stallion dyed her signature color for the occasion. With a haughty lift of the tail, the steed expresses our shared opinion that this is horseshit.

Still, the evening is a sparkling success, with the most popular attraction being a booth marked DADDY'S MONEY, where guests try to catch dollar bills that are blown around by a fan. I do my usual shtick while trying to avoid the guest entertainment, British singer Robert Palmer, who corners me before he goes on and asks about the plans to launch MTV in Europe. I mumble something about Margaret Thatcher not wanting her MTV before dissolving into a coughing fit, possibly the most convincing part of my performance.

After introducing him, I retreat to the back of the tent, where Sandra is having an Alka-Seltzer-and-vodka. She points at Windy. "You see that tiara on her head? That cost more than I made last year."

"What does an oil and commodities trader do?"

"You're asking me?" Sandra says. "I don't even know what a commodity is."

I look around at the splendor surrounding us. "How do people afford to live like this?"

Sandra glances around to make sure she's not overheard. "I might as well tell you. It's gonna be in Monday's paper."

I head into the house to find a phone, which I discover in a bathroom the size of my apartment, all dusty rose and sea-foam green, like a spa. I've never seen a bathroom with a phone, let alone a television, which is mounted from the ceiling, like in hotels or hospitals. I lock the door and call Chad.

He picks up on the third ring, not that I'm counting. I just happen to notice.

"Hello."

It's a statement, not a question, which strikes me as ineffably sexy.

"Hi!" I squeal. "It's Edward!" My voice sounds uncannily like Lizzie Sniderman.

"Hey, I was going to call you."

"Really?"

"Yeah. I got a call from someone named Dagmar."

Seventeen

This is my worst nightmare. Well, not exactly. My worst nightmare is being chased by an angry mob, falling off a cliff, and hanging on by the tips of my fingers; but being hounded by my stepmother the succubus ranks right up there. Inside my chest, someone starts playing basketball with my heart.

"How did she find you?"

"I don't know. Someone at Brooks Brothers must have told her you charged the suit to me."

"What did she say?"

"That you're a liar and a thief. And an asshole."

"She's crazy, you know." My heart is beating so loudly I can hear it, like the pounding of the drum on a Viking ship to keep the crew rowing.

"She's just bitter because I told my father she was stealing from him," I say. "You shouldn't believe anything she says."

"I didn't."

Actually, that's not my heart at all. It's Robert Palmer's drummer. I pull some toilet paper off the roll to wipe my forehead.

"Are you calling on a pay phone?" Chad asks.

"Uh . . . yeah," I say. Imitating Sandra's adenoidal whine, I add, "Please deposit twenty-five cents," then tap on the receiver a couple of times.

"Sorry about that," I say. "So, what did you tell Dagmar?"

"The truth. That you work for *La Vie de la Fête* Productions and I bought you a suit."

"How'd you explain that?"

"I didn't. My personal life is my business."

Let's pause for a moment to consider this last statement. Buying me a suit was a business decision. A Business Decision. To help him gain information. But that's not what Chad said. He said, "My *personal life* is my business." Buying me a suit was part of his personal life. I am a part of his personal life. What's more, straight people don't say things like, "My personal life is my business." That is, unless they have something to hide. Which he does. Me.

In the tent outside, Robert Palmer sings "Addicted to Love."

Of course, while I'm thinking all this, I'm still talking as fast as I can. Because he asks me, "And who was this girl you brought with you?" and I hear myself saying, "My friend Ziba. You know, the one I told you about, the one who went to the shah of Iran's wedding. She goes to the Fashion Institute."

I don't know why I do this. My brain is like a gumball machine. You put in your nickel and, whoosh, out comes the thought. Too bad if it's a color you don't like. But saying Ziba was with me somehow sounds better than, "I'm being stalked by the Bad Seed."

Chad reminds me to be discreet, and I say, "Of course, of course, of course," and then hope to redeem myself by telling him what Sandra told me—that Will Owens's ex-wife said that Owens is about to be indicted for tax evasion and illegally trading with Iran during the hostage crisis. "If he doesn't flee the country, he'll probably go to jail," I say. "Either way, that'd affect the price of the stock, wouldn't it?"

"Sure," he says, "if his company was publicly traded."

"What do you mean?"

"Petrolux is privately held."

What? Can he do that? Corporate espionage is so frigging complicated.

"But I like how you're thinking," he says. "I'll mail your hundred bucks tomorrow."

I'm glad to get the money, but I really wanted him to say, *Oh, Edward, you're a mastermind. Come right over and we'll celebrate by wrestling naked.*

"Don't be such a baby," Natie says the next night. "Dagmar's not gonna do anything."

"But what if she told Chad we stole ten grand from her?"

"She won't."

"How do you know that?"

" 'Cuz she stole that ten grand from your da—"

He's cut off as a Persian on roller skates crashes into him.

It was Ziba's idea to throw a skating party to celebrate Kelly being cast as a swing in *Starlight Express*, which is not, as the name suggests, another anthropomorphized inanimate object but an understudy who covers multiple roles, and a job Kelly didn't even know existed until she was hired.

"What better way to celebrate?" Ziba asked, a question

I hadn't thought to answer at the time. While I'm not bad on skates, I'd prefer an activity that doesn't require strapping wheels on Nathan Nudelman. I offer him my hand, but that only lands me on my ass, an apt metaphor for our friendship.

"What if Dagmar contacts Sandra?" I ask as we struggle to our feet. "I could lose my job."

"Jeez, such a worrier," Natie says. "We'll burn that bridge when we get to it."

We trundle out of the rink, the other skaters swirling around us as Madonna tells her papa not to preach. Ziba circles languorously with her Persian girlfriends, their arms and hands coiling to the music like serpents, as if they were harem girls dancing for the Persian guys, who huddle on the sidelines, smoking and looking hip with their artfully wrinkled linen jackets and carefully cultivated two-day razor stubble. Meanwhile, Kelly and the musical theater people zip around with exuberant abandon, attempting stunts, throwing their heads back with laughter when they fall, and singing along to all the songs. I fall somewhere between the two, while Natie just falls, period. Both groups intimidate me—the former with their effortless cool, the latter with their uninhibited enthusiasm. I tell myself I'm being stupid; when I'm at a bash mitzvah or a corporate party I'm the hippest, happiest guy in the room. I regularly mingle with the city's elite, for Chrissake, the Life of the Party at parties that make Page Six. (Once again, without mention of me. The Owens sweet sixteen got a lot of ink, right next to a photograph of the ubiquitous Andy Warhol at a fund-raiser for Save the Squirrels. I swear, that man would go to the opening of a tuna can.) But at those parties I'm Eddie Sanders or Eddie Zander. When I have to be Edward Zanni, I feel like a total cheesehead.

I feel even worse when Kelly zips up in front of us and says, "Isn't it great about Doug?"

"What about Doug?" I haven't talked to him since the no-pants/fish-killing incident.

"Didn't he tell you? Almost Bruce got a cruise ship job. They're going to be in the Bahamas from Thanksgiving until spring break."

I can't believe he didn't call to tell me. I've ruined our friendship with my unwanted sexual advances. I repulse him. My only hope is that he can't face me because he's tortured and confused by his own repressed homosexual desires. Oh, dear God, please make him tortured and confused by his own repressed homosexual desires, though not so much that he throws himself overboard in a fit of self-loathing.

She dashes off just as Paula arrives, marching in like she's Mama Rose in *Gypsy*, wagging a pinkie-sized pointer finger in my face. "Where *were* you?" she cries. "You didn't come see *Earnest*."

How do I explain? I wanted to go but just the thought of stepping through Juilliard's glass doors gave me an asthma attack. And I don't have asthma. Everyone would ask me what I'm doing, and I'd have to explain that I go to work in a shiny shirt and tight pants, a job only slightly more dignified than playing Chuckles the Woodchuck. And then I'd have to watch them onstage, doing what I should be doing myself.

"I had gigs," I say.

"During *every performance*? I thought bar mitzvahs were only on Saturdays."

"Yeah, but there's a lot of . . ." I make vague motions in the air, as if that explained it.

Paula takes off her coat and thrusts it in my hands. "I thought so."

She wears her usual outfit for physical activities—an oversize black cotton T-shirt (with shoulder pads, of course) and a pair of black stirrup pants. She's dressed up the ensemble with a metal Slinky around her waist and a pair of bent forks around her wrists.

She eyes Natie. "What's your excuse?"

"I had my wisdom teeth out."

"That was last year."

"Yeah, but it haunts me still."

Now, I may have been kicked out of Juilliard, but one thing I learned is that the best way to distract actors is to get them talking about themselves. "So how'd it go?"

"I made a real breakthrough," Paula says. "You know, Marian thought I was *insane* for speaking like Lady Bracknell offstage, but it really worked, it *really, really* did. It's so difficult to make Wilde organic. He's like Restoration comedy—you can easily end up playing the style, not the substance. All frosting and no cake. But being epigrammatic is positively *exhausting.* No wonder Wilde died so young."

She glances down at my skates. "Oh, dear, is brown the only color those come in?"

As we move to the counter, I see Hung round the rink dressed in full 1970s roller-disco duds: tube socks, tight satin shorts, and terry-cloth shirt, with a long silk scarf around his neck. He blows a whistle and shakes his groove thing.

Mama said there'd be gays like this.

Paula gets her skates and plops down on a bench. "I still haven't forgiven you two," she says, "but I have a way you can redeem yourselves."

Eighteen

Paula slips off her shiny silver flats. "It all started that night we went bowling."

This is how Paula tells a story. Ask her what she did last weekend and she'll say, "Well, first dinosaurs ruled the earth. . . ."

She pulls a pair of socks out of the Prada knockoff she bought on the street. "You remember how upset Marcus got when Kelly insisted *The Music Man* was a play? Well, he positively *fulminated* on it for days; he truly can be impossible. As it was, we'd been fighting over what to call his company. He wanted to name it the Death to the Patriarchy Players, then got absolutely *incensed* when I said that might make it hard to get funding. Then we came up with the Public Play Project. But if you say that too fast it sounds like Probably Profit, which sort of defeats the purpose. We finally settled on the Coup d'État Group, which at least has a Continental flair, and started planning to perform *Waiting for Godot* in an elevator in Penn Station. But then we went bowling and Marcus decided he had to do *The Music Man*?"

"*The Music Man*?" I say.

"That's right," Paula says, "with the question mark. He's deconstructing the text based on the principles of Brecht's alienation effect and Artaud's Theatre of Cruelty."

"With *The Music Man*," I say.

"No, *The Music Man?* It's ironic." She throws her feet onto Natie's lap, wiggling her fingers to indicate he should lace her up. "Natie, I need you to talk some financial sense to him. Marcus refuses—simply *refuses*—to accept any money from his mother, because she's an opera singer, and opera is part of the elitist power structure."

"Then how's he gonna pay for the rights?" Natie asks.

"He's not. He says that's contributing to the commodification of the arts."

Natie whistles through his teeth. "The publisher ain't gonna like that."

"I *know*," Paula says. "I'm positively bereft."

"What about me?" I ask.

"Well . . ." ("In the beginning, God created the heavens and the Earth . . .") ". . . Marcus has cast a blind woman as Marian the Librarian and a deaf man as Harold Hill. Don't roll your eyes; it's a *brilliant* concept, underscoring the way we're blind and deaf to the corruption of the Reagan administration." She glances at the Persians huddling nearby, then whispers, "You know he sold weapons to Iran?"

"It's okay," Natie says. "These are the people who escaped."

"Oh, it's so confusing. As far as I can make out, our government sold weapons to Iran, our enemy, to make money for the Nicaraguan contras so they could fight the Sandinistas because the Sandinistas are sympathetic to the Soviet Union, which is also our enemy. Honestly, what's the point?"

I could ask the same thing about Marcus's concept.

"Anyway," Paula continues, "we need you to coach the Harold Hill."

I see the glitter of crashing cymbals. And hear the thunder of rolling drums. The summer I was fourteen I played Harold in the Wallingford Summer Workshop production of *The Music Man* and my performance was compared to Kevin Kline. Granted, it was by Paula's Aunt Glo, but I've seen the video, and I must say I was damn good. After all, I was the youngest one in a cast that included graduating seniors. Still, coach a deaf actor?

"I don't speak sign language," I say.

"Gavin reads lips," Paula says. "And speaks *perfectly*. He just needs to learn how to sing."

"Sure," I say. "And when I'm done, I'll teach the blind how to paint. Then heal the sick and raise the dead."

"Don't be negative," she sniffs. "It doesn't suit you."

As always, she's right. And, in the following weeks, I try to keep a positive attitude, even though I continually come up with nothing that fulfills Chad's vision of us getting filthy fucking rich. The fact is, after two months, I've already had it up to my kishkes with bash mitzvahs. There's something inherently creepy about flirting with prepubescent girls, not to mention middle-aged women starving themselves to look prepubescent. Likewise, I'm growing tired of watching thirteen-year-old boys take off their ties and wrap them around their heads.

I'm no longer impressed with the sumptuous surroundings, either. I've come to expect round banquet tables with gold bamboo chairs, gold charger plates, and centerpieces that look like the female guests, with enormous heads propped precariously on stalky bodies.

Natie and I hold out hopes for my gig with Pharmicare,

the Jersey-based pharmaceuticals giant, which is holding its corporate retreat the weekend before Thanksgiving in Atlantic City. Natie drills me like he's Henry Higgins readying Eliza Doolittle for the embassy ball. Except we don't have a chorus of servants in their bathrobes coming in to tell us to quit. He quizzes me on the names of the people in R & D (which, I learn, stands for research and development, not rhythm and dance); he reads me passages from *The Art of War* ("All warfare is based on deception"); and teaches me trivia about Eddie Zander's native Oklahoma (soon to be celebrating the fiftieth anniversary of the shopping cart, invented in an Oklahoma City Piggly Wiggly in 1937).

Even though I'm Eddie Zander for this party, my tasks are closer to those of Eddie Sanders, requiring that I flirt and dance with neglected wives, which kind of bums me out. There's already something inherently depressing about Atlantic City, with its tattered remains of broken dreams being bulldozed over for the glitzy promise of quick cash. And I can't help feel for these women whose husbands won't dance with them. I don't get it. The middle-aged women I meet at these parties are almost uniformly vivacious and attractive, yet most of them are married to paunchy, dull men. What is it about being heterosexual that makes so many men boring? Monotony is so prevalent among straight men it's practically an epidemic.

They remind me of my mother, these women, and, as I hold a particularly lonely wife of an R & D executive in my arms, I feel the weight of her life against me. She tells me that her husband is a stranger, that he's been working eighty hours a week for months, and I wonder if that's why there are so many boring straight men—they've had all the magic whacked out of them. I lean in, holding her closer, vowing never to become that man.

"I'm sorry," I say. "What could he possibly be working on that's so important?"

She glances around us then says, "I really shouldn't tell you this. . . ."

Thanksgiving morning Natie and I take the train out to Wallingford, still giddy from my Pharmicare coup.

Natie pulls out a spreadsheet he's written on graph paper—such a Nudelman thing to have. "Okay," he says, clicking a ballpoint, "how much have you managed to save these past two months?"

"Four hundred bucks."

"Not bad. Plus the hundred we just got from Chad. So that's five hundred."

"Yeah," I mumble.

I don't want to sound ungrateful, but I'm bummed that Chad didn't make a bigger deal about my news. I mean, Pharmicare is developing a new diet pill that allows you to eat what you want without absorbing the fat. That's *huge*, pardon the pun. Who wouldn't want to take that pill? The woman in Atlantic City told me that it's scheduled to be approved by the FDA in just a few months. You'd think information like that would warrant a celebratory dinner. Or some mutual masturbation. Instead Chad sends cash without even including a note. It makes me feel like a hooker. Without the benefit of getting laid.

Natie hands me an open envelope. "Plus you got this credit card application."

"You opened my mail?"

"How else was I gonna read it?"

"That's a federal offense."

"Blah, blah, blah." He pulls the application out of the

envelope. "Look, you qualify for $1,000 worth of credit. Once you receive your card, you can take out a cash advance and invest $1,500."

"But won't I owe the credit card company the money?"

"At a minimum monthly payment of twenty bucks."

"But that'll take me . . . let me see . . . twenty bucks a month is $240 a year . . . *four years* to pay back a thousand bucks."

"Actually, it's longer, because you're charged interest."

"And this is a good idea because . . . ?"

"Because you're borrowing the money at sixteen percent interest, but you're investing it for much more."

"How much more?"

He hands me his spreadsheet and pulls out the *New York Times*. "Let's see. Pharmicare stock is currently selling at $30 a share. So, with $1,500 you can buy fifty shares. If the stock goes up to $60 a share—"

"Can that happen?"

He looks at me over his glasses. "Eddie, they've got a pill that prevents your body from absorbing fat. Sixty bucks a share is conservative."

"So, if the stock doubles, does that mean we double our money?"

He takes back the spreadsheet.

"Sure, but you can do way better if you buy options. With options, you don't buy the stock at $30; you buy *the right* to buy it at some later date, in this case at $35."

"Why would I want to pay more?"

"You don't. Because the option only costs *$2* per share. So you take your $1,500 and buy seven hundred and fifty shares instead of fifty. Then, when the stock doubles to $60, you've contracted to buy it at $35, so you immediately sell it for $60 and pocket the difference."

"How much is that?"

He scrawls in the margin. "Well, $25 profit per share times seven hundred and fifty shares equals $18,750."

I stare at him, stunned.

"Profit," he says. "Plus, you get back your initial $1,500."

My heart flaps its wings.

"That's . . . $20,250. That'll pay for two years of college."

Natie's glasses fog. "I think I'm gonna cry," he says.

Al pulls up to the station in a boxy burgundy Volvo the size of a Brinks truck. Citing carsickness, Natie claims shotgun, an irrelevant argument when you consider we live two miles from the station. The ensuing conversation is like a Pinter play—minimal dialogue with lots of silence filled with incomprehensible subtext.

ME: What happened to the Corvette?
AL: I traded it in.
ME: How come?
AL: Ah, y'know.

(Incomprehensible subtext-filled silence.)

AL: So, Nathan, your mom says you switched majors to business.
NATIE: Econ.

(More incomprehensible subtext-filled silence.)

AL: Good.

(Still more silence.)

Finally, I can't stand it and start to fill up the Pinteresque void with rapid-fire screwball comedy dialogue. How I'm a big, big hit with *La Vie de la Fête* Productions, the toast of the town with the crème de la crème. If Marian Seldes were listening, she'd say, *My little bird, you're pushing too hard. You're avoiding your feelings by barreling over them with an avalanche of words.*

Of course I'm avoiding my feelings, I'd say to her. *Who wants to experience bad feelings?*

Actors, she'd say.

She's right, even though she's just a figment of my imagination. I can hear in my voice how much I want my father's approval. I don't understand why. The man is everything I don't want to be, with his *dese*, *dem*, *dose* and his "dreams only come true in dreams." If I met him at a party, he'd be the last person I'd want to talk to.

Yet I still want him to be proud of me.

Damn him.

We don't say anything for the rest of the ride, the silence filling the empty space like rising water. We drop off Natie, I hop in the front, and we head to my aunt Lydia's.

But at the first red light, Al turns to me and says, "We need to talk."

Nineteen

Why do people start conversations with the phrase
We need to talk? It only makes you assume the worst, like
they have cancer. Better to start off casual and ease into
it, like, "Hey, a funny thing happened on the way to work
today—I got cancer."

Al shifts so he can look at me, the seat belt cutting into
his belly like the string around a pot roast. "Milagros is
pregnant."

It takes me a moment to figure out who he's talking
about. "The domestic?"

"Yeah."

I'm not sure why the personal life of the woman who
cleans my father's house is any of my con . . .

"No," I say. "How?"

Al winces, like I'm a splinter. "How do ya' think?"

In the time-honored way, I suppose. The lord of the
manor creeps up behind the saucy scullery maid as she, I
don't know, sculleries?

"Is she going to keep it?"

His nostrils flare. "Of course she is."

"Okay," I say. "Don't get all Vatican on me."

Al grips the steering wheel, his simian brow drooping over his eyes. When did he get so old? He could use a pair of shoes to go with those bags.

"What are you going to do?" I ask.

"Whaddya think I'm gonna do?" he says. "I'm gonna marry her."

Ay, caramba.

The next day, while Natie and I take the train into Hoboken for the Coup d'État Group's first rehearsal, he offers a financial analysis of the coup occurring in *mi casa*:

"You're fucked."

"Really?"

"Think about it," he says. "How old is this Menudos?"

"Milagros. I don't know. Twenty-seven. Twenty-eight."

"Right. So when Al dies, all his money goes to her. And since women live longer than men, you can kiss your inheritance good-bye."

"Shit."

"Yeah, my mom's real upset."

"About my inheritance?"

"No. She just lost the best housekeeper she ever had."

The rehearsal is held at the Church of the Holy Redeemer in Hoboken, one of those parishes you hear about from time to time, the kind where a much-beloved priest suddenly disappears because he's been trying to anoint the altar boys with massage oil. Things have improved greatly, however, since the arrival of Paula's cousin, Father Angelo, a scholar so stuffy he wishes everyone would take the holy host by hand. "All those tongues," he says, shuddering, "like frogs eating flies." According to Paula, whatever sexual urges her cousin has he sublimates into a passion for opera.

Since Father Angelo's idea of a good Mass is the first act finale of *Tosca*, I'm not surprised to find the actors rehearsing in the sanctuary. Marcus has assembled a cast of ten: the blind Marian, the deaf Harold, and eight others whose only handicap is their misguided faith that this idea can work. They sit in the front pews, all wearing black. It's like a funeral for a very unpopular person.

"I've chosen to rehearse in a church," Marcus says, "because an actor is a kind of priest."

Actually, Marcus chose to rehearse in a church because it was free. But he makes a good point.

"Since the Greeks, whose plays were a part of religious festivals, the theater has been a sacred space. And the church," he says, gesturing to the stone arches and stained glass windows, "is a kind of theater." He holds up a worn copy of Jerzy Grotowski's *Towards a Poor Theatre*. "The Coup d'État Group rejects the spectacle of bourgeois entertainment. Theater cannot, should not, *will not* compete with film and television. We need to strip away anything that isn't necessary and focus on what's essential—the relationship between the actor and the audience."

I read somewhere that jaguars kill their prey by biting through their skulls, slaying them instantly by ripping into their brains. That's how it is with Marcus. Sure, he's combative and humorless. But there are times when he grabs hold of my mind and just shakes me until I'm helpless to the ferocity of his beliefs.

"Okay," he says, "let's warm up. Ten laps around the church." The cast leaps to its feet and jogs around the perimeter of the sanctuary, as if the stations of the cross were an Olympic event (*Jesus falls, Jesus rises, Jesus falls . . .*). Bringing up the rear are Paula and Willow, both of whom give wan waves at me and Natie, like they're Abbott and Costello drafted into the army.

A tickly, carbonated happiness bubbles up inside me. I'm so excited to be at a rehearsal again. When you're rehearsing, everything is possible. There is still a chance to get it right. The Germans call it *die Probe*, the French *la répétition*. And therein lies the pleasure: to probe repeatedly. To hearse again and again, from the Old French *hercier*, to rake or harrow.

And this rehearsal certainly is harrowing.

After a series of truly gruesome facial exercises, it becomes abundantly clear that Marcus's concept is also Brechtian, which is another way of saying it's dark and pretentious. Brecht believed that an audience should not get emotionally involved in a play, that a cathartic experience clouds the audience's reason and leaves it complacent. I guess if I were writing as Hitler came to power on a wave of emotionally manipulative propaganda, I'd be cranky, too. Still, it's unnerving to watch Marcus stage "Pick-a-Little, Talk-a-Little" by having the four women beat the blind singer while the men read copies of the *New York Post*. I don't care if the song is about character assassination. If the purpose of Brecht's "alienation effect" is to alienate the audience, then we've got a hit.

The scene gets even more surreal when, from a side door, Father Angelo enters the church with his mother, otherwise known to the world as Aunt Glo.

Aunt Glo.

Her apple-pie face warms with recognition as she spots me and Natie, crying "The LBs!" (As a MOP—Mother of

Priest—she refrains from saying Little Bastards in church.)`
Paula, who's busy assaulting a blind woman, responds
with an aggressive *shh*, which only causes Aunt Glo to call
more attention to herself as she does a silent-movie tiptoe
up the aisle, genuflecting before she enters the pew, then
thrusting her plump arms around me. Her hug feels like
home, as if she's trying to make up for all the mother love
I may have missed. She beams at me, her globular eyes
overflowing with tears, like two cups filled above the brim.
To Aunt Glo I'll always be a star.

Her son slips in behind us, giving me a pious nod.

Father Angelo makes me uncomfortable. For starters,
he's way too good-looking for a priest, his dark bedroom
eyes and athletic build arousing exactly the kind of impure
thoughts you're supposed to go to church to get rid of.
What's more, two years ago Aunt Glo got me a job here as
a soloist and I kind of flaked out. In my defense, it's hard
for anyone to hold down a job while attending Juilliard. It's
like boot camp for actors. I try to concentrate on the cast
rehearsing "Wells Fargo Wagon," which, for reasons having
to do with Reagan cutting taxes for the rich and driving the
national debt sky-high, requires that the citizens of River
City writhe with orgasmic pleasure as they list the items
they've ordered, doing Fosse-esque pelvic thrusts every
time they say the wagon is "a-*comin'*."

It's not the kind of scene you want to watch with an old
lady and a priest.

When the cast takes a break, Aunt Glo says, "Y'know,
my Angelo here wanted to be an actor, just like you." She
turns to her son. "What was that show you did in high
school? The one with the carousel?"

"Carousel."

"That's it. So beauteeful, his voice."

"Oh, Ma."

Willow comes over to say hello to Aunt Glo, who gives her a hug and calls her Wilma.

"What do you think of the concept?" Willow asks.

Before I can answer, Aunt Glo says, "Y'know, I saw Ken Berry do *The Music Man* at the Paper Mill Playhouse."

Willow nods like this makes sense, which, being Willow, it very well might. "I think Marcus is really onto—the problem with most experimental theater is that it doesn't reach—but here, my God, they're going to be like, 'Oh, look, it's *The Music Man*' . . . then WHAM, right between the eyes. Like Lillian Hellman. Are you familiar with her work?"

Aunt Glo shakes her head. "No. But I love her mayonnaise."

Paula brings the deaf Harold Hill over to meet me. Gavin is a slender reed around thirty, with shoulders like a coat hanger and the drooping posture of a gooseneck lamp, as if someone had punched him in the chest. He wears a T-shirt reading GAY MEN'S HEALTH CRISIS, and shakes my hand with both of his. "Thanks for helping me."

I'm shocked at how well he speaks. You'd never know he was deaf.

He's also exceedingly appealing, with tendril curls that flop over soft, doleful eyes set just a little too far apart. With his plump, fleshy mouth, he reminds me of the koi I exterminated in my fish-killing sprees.

"Angelo helped me with the rhythm," he says, "but he insists I need a real singer for the notes." A bemused, secret smile spreads across his face, like he's in on a joke I don't get.

Father Angelo clears his throat. "Gavin's deaf dance troupe rehearses here." Even though he's speaking to me, he faces Gavin, presumably so he can read his lips.

Gavin and I retreat to the back of the church, Gavin moving with the wan, spectral tread of someone who slept in an airport. Not exactly what you'd expect for a thundering, outsize role like Harold Hill, but a production paying the actors with Aunt Glo's homemade cannoli can't be too picky.

"SO," I say, trying to look at him and walk at the same time. "YOU. READ. LIPS."

"You don't have to work so hard," he says. "I'm deaf, not blind."

"Sorry."

"Here," he says, stopping. "Let me show you."

He turns and faces the front of the church, where Paula and Natie are engaged in a conversation I can't hear.

"Paula's telling that little red-haired guy that now's not a good time to talk to Marcus," Gavin says. "She says he gets *frightfully* irritable when he's rehearsing."

"Wow," I say. "You should work for the CIA."

"I can't. The other ushers at the Eugene O'Neill depend on me."

"You're an usher?" I say, far more music-theatery than I intend. He's an usher; I'm a gusher.

"The theater is my life," he says, with a grand Master Thespian gesture.

Marcus gives an irritated *shh* from the altar that Gavin can't hear.

I like him.

The plan is for Gavin to talk his way through all of Harold's songs, which will probably work better on some than others. Not that Marcus cares. "Enjoyment is a bourgeois indulgence," he says. But Gavin is determined to sing the last few lines of "Till There Was You."

"Come over here where there's some light," he says, leading me to an altar to Saint Jude. From the plaque, I learn that Saint Jude is a) a man; and b) the patron saint of lost causes, not a good omen. Gavin positions me facing him, close enough that I can feel his breath on my cheek.

Then he reaches into his pocket, his jeans slipping down his narrow hips, and pulls out . . . a condom.

Mama said there'd be gays like this.

Giving me that same enigmatic smile, he tears the package open with his teeth, hands me the wrapper, and proceeds to blow the condom up like a balloon, tying it off with a knot.

"Balloons are a natural amplifier," he explains. "I forgot to bring one, but I never go anywhere without a rubber."

He takes the balloon, which is ribbed for our pleasure, and tucks it under his chin. Then, placing his hands on my shoulders, he guides me closer until the condom is against my throat. Our faces are now inches away from each other.

Gavin reaches up and places his long, sinewy fingers on my neck. "Okay," he says. "Go slowly." I can feel the vibration of his words through the rubber. I check the first note on a pitch pipe—not an easy thing to do when you have a condom balloon under your chin—and start to sing:

> There was love all around,
> But I never heard it singing . . .

Gavin laughs. "Well, *duh*."

He asks me to sing the first note again, then attempts the seemingly impossible task of matching a pitch he can't hear. It's painstaking, frustrating work. Words like *higher* and *lower* don't mean anything to him so it's totally trial-and-error, with me saying *no* over and over while his reedy fingers grope my face and neck to memorize the position of my larynx, my jaw, my mouth. All the while I'm singing "Till There Was You" into his wistful hazel eyes, watching his fleshy lips wrap around the words. Now I understand why Father Angelo didn't want to do this task.

Still, Gavin is a tireless pupil, having had rigorous speech training. While we break for Aunt Glo's homemade lasagna, he tells me that he lost his hearing from measles at the age of three and that the teachers at the school for the deaf taught him to speak by flicking him on the tongue with their fingers every time he got something wrong. He also tells me how he didn't find out until he went to college that farts made noise.

We work the rest of the evening this way, note by note, each a hard-won victory. But since the first three notes repeat three times, at the end of rehearsal Gavin is actually able to stand before the cast and sing:

There . . . was . . . loooooove . . .
All . . . a . . . rouuuuuund . . .
But . . . I . . . neeeeee-ver . . .

It's like watching a baby take his first steps. For all its hesitancy, his voice already has a croony, caramel quality, like a 1940s band singer, perhaps a young Sinatra. He even uses a vibrato. If I hadn't heard it with my own ears, I wouldn't have thought such a thing possible.

Paula turns to me, tears streaming down her dove white cheeks. "He sounds just like you."

I swell like a condom balloon and leave the church feeling a kind of good I've not felt before. For the first time in I don't know how long I've thought about someone else, done something worthwhile. Rather than obsessing about what's going to happen to me, me, me, I think about what's going to happen to him, him, him.

I bask in that good feeling all the way home, exhausted yet exhilarated as Natie and I climb the four sticky flights to our apartment. I slide my key in the lock, eager for a good pee and a satisfying sleep, when panic goes off inside me like a car alarm.

The door is unlocked.

Twenty

I turn to Natie.

"Did you forget to lock the door?"

He shakes his head. Of course he didn't. There are three locks.

Faced with the probability of an intruder in his apartment, any moron would head down the stairs and call the cops. But I am not any moron. I am an über-moron, the moron to end all morons. If stupidity were a sport I would letter in it. So, despite Natie urging me downstairs by pulling on my sleeve and whimpering, I push open the door, calling, "Hello?" because I am, as I've already established, a total cheesehead. I'm sure if you put your head up against my ear, you could hear the ocean.

To my surprise, someone within responds.

"Eddieeeee? Is that you?"

"Who the hell is that?" Natie asks, flinching like the Cowardly Lion.

I'm not sure. The voice is female, and childlike, and the only female child I know is . . .

"Lizzie!"

She looks up from the couch, where she's reading Eddie Sanders's diary. "Is this yours?" she sneers. "It's gross."

I advance on her. "How did you . . . I mean, 'ow did you get in 'ere?"

She grins a barbed-wire smile. "I picked the locks."

"Wot? 'Ow?"

She holds up a small kit. "Marcy and I bought 'em at Spy City on Fourteenth Street." She raises her chin with smug, know-it-all satisfaction. "You must be Nathan Nudelman. I saw your textbooks."

"She's good," Natie says.

"Listen, Nancy Drew," I say, "you cahn't break into people's apartments. I mean, flats. It's illegal. And immoral. And scary."

Natie looks at the lock-picking kit. "How much did this thing cost?"

"Twenty bucks."

"That all?"

"Natie!"

Lizzie stretches out on the couch, putting her feet up on the coffee table. "So, who's Edward Zanni?"

"Wot?"

"There's a credit card application for someone named Edward Zanni. Who is he?"

I feel a Strange Interlude coming on:

(anxiously) . . . Who is Edward Zanni? Who knows? . . . That is a question for the dark night of the soul. . . .

"Awlright," I say, "that's enough. You. Out."

"But—"

"I mean it. Stop followin' me around or I'll call the cops. Or your mother."

"That's not fair. I just—"

I grab one of her twiggy arms and yank Lizzie off the couch. "Now!"

Note to self—there are some dangerous things you should not touch: hot stoves, live wires, and thirteen-year-old lunatics. Remember Linda Blair in *The Exorcist*? Compared to Lizzie, she's Rebecca of Sunnybrook Farm.

"Fuck you, you fuckety fuckwad!" she screams, then smacks me in the shoulder with Eddie's diary. She stomps to the door, undoubtedly disturbing my downstairs neighbors, the comparatively calm Crackheads. Pointing an accusatory finger at me, she says, "You're gonna be sorry."

Luckily, bash mitzvah work tapers off with the holidays, so I don't risk running into her until January. In the meantime I'm still booked for corporate holiday parties, which provide multiple opportunities to seek inside information from imprudent drunks. Not for myself, of course. Once my credit card arrives, Natie invests my $1,500 in Pharmicare stock options, informing me that our investment won't pay off until February, when our option comes due. But I still hold out hope for a lead so spectacular that Chad takes me out and gets just drunk enough to act on his heretofore unexpressed homosexual desires. I'm so horny it hurts.

My final chance of the year comes at a holiday party for the accounting firm of Hibbert & Howard. As the second-largest firm in the country (after I. J. Sloan, according to Natie), neither Hibbert nor Howard has spared any expense, renting out the Temple of Dendur at the Metropolitan Museum of Art. When I tell Ziba what I'm doing, she insists on joining me.

"I need to scout locations," she explains on the phone.

"I'm in charge of my cousin's twenty-first birthday party in April."

"But you can see it anytime."

"Not decorated. Oh, please, darling. With Kelly in rehearsals, I'm living like a nun."

"What about your Arabian nights?"

"Oh, I'm so bored with being hip. I'd much rather do something with you."

We arrive early because I need time to change into an Egyptian pharaoh's costume. We walk down a long corridor past mummies, scrolls of papyrus, and charcoal gray sentinels, then turn a corner into the room containing the temple.

No, *room* is the wrong word. It's like stepping into another world.

Naturally, the sandstone temple stands untouched, but uplighting casts it into high relief. I wish the whole world were uplit—it's so much more dramatic. Hundreds of votive candles float in the surrounding moat, as if reflecting the starry night sky, which is projected two stories high on the museum's stone walls. With black cloths masking the buffet tables, all you see is shimmering light, towering palm trees, and the temple. After all the garish displays I've witnessed this fall, I'm dumbstruck by the sheer eloquence.

I'm snapped out of my reverie by a voice that sounds like someone stepping on a cat.

"Edwid!"

Sandra dashes over, her brow fraught with worry, as if she doesn't expect me to live to the end of the conversation.

"Thank Gawd you're here," she says. "It's a disaster.

First, I hadda deal with the coked-up photographer, and now . . ." She stops and stares at Ziba. "Who are you?"

"This is my friend Ziba," I say. "She's—"

"Perfect! That's what she is. Oh, Edward, what would I do without you?"

"Excuse me?"

"Courtenay quit on me, the skinny bitch. She met a millionaire at the party we did at the Founders Club and now she's engaged. Engaged! Twelve years I've been in this business and you know how many millionaires I've dated? Zero. My therapist says I'm not aggressive enough." She peers over my shoulder. "Hey! You, next to the statue. You break it, you buy it." She turns to Ziba. "The costumes are over there."

"Oh," Ziba says, "I don't think—"

"No, please, it's me who should be thanking you."

"That's not what I—"

"You'll do fine, honey. Just slouch a little—men don't like women who are too tall."

The guests pour in like water from a burst pipe, and I'm immediately swept into the conversational current. I'm doing my usual hello-how-are-you-tell-me-corporate-secrets when I spy Ziba across the room, which is easy to do considering she's five-foot-seventeen and dressed as Nefertiti. I walk over to her and, just as I arrive, she's approached by a stocky, square-headed guy with a Guido pompadour that looks like it was blown dry in a wind tunnel.

"Nice costume," he says to her.

Ziba emits a "thanks" like a puff of smoke.

"You know where it would look even better?" he says, leaning into her. "Piled in a heap on my bedroom floor."

She gives him a Diana "That's-Miss-Ross to you" look. "Do you know what I'd like to see?"

"What?"

"You piled in a heap under the Queensborough Bridge."

The man slams his empty glass down on the bar. "Bitch."

Ziba turns to me. "This is a terrible job. Why do you do it?"

"For money."

"Oh, that." She looks around the room, her fingers twitching for the cigarette she can't have. "Honestly, I don't know why Kelly would want to date a man. They're so tiresome. No offense."

"None taken. Does she still want to date men?"

Ziba rolls her Cleopatra eyes. "She doesn't know what she wants. She says she loves me, but she's not sure if she's gay."

"She's like Doug is for me."

"*Exactement.* Except she doesn't have a comically large penis."

I hitch up my cotton kilt so that it sits above my pudge. "I guess it's confusing for her. I mean, she's so girlie."

"What are you saying? That I'm not?"

"No, no. You're just very . . . tall."

"It's the haircut, isn't it?" she says, touching the cockscomb atop her head. "It makes me look too butch."

"Not too butch."

"I see. Just butch enough. Midbutch. Demibutch."

"I didn't say that." I'm such a lousy liar. I'll never get back into Juilliard if I don't learn to lie better.

Ziba straightens her dress. "Excuse me," she says, pushing me aside. "I'm being paid to flirt with the *heterosexual* guests."

She slinks into the crowd, Delilah in search of a Samson. I go the opposite way, hoping to do some heterosexual flirting myself. Natie read in *Fortune* magazine that corporate raiders are rushing to buy out companies before new tax laws take effect January 1, so I pump the drunk secretaries for as much information as I can. But it's hard to have a serious conversation when you're enlisted to Walk Like an Egyptian while a band called the Bangles does a song by the same name. I tell myself that my willingness to do anything for a laugh (or a buck) is evidence of my outsize, wacky personality, but as I look around at all these well-dressed people with their suits and cocktail dresses and six-figure jobs, I feel less like the wily court jester than the clueless village idiot. After making a spectacle of myself, I go to the bar to get something to take the edge off my humiliation. Ziba joins me, this time on the arm of a guy who looks like he was the homecoming king in high school before his life went downhill and he took to drink; although perhaps I'm overanalyzing.

"Edward, thisss is Greg." Her voice is thick and slurry, like she's been gargling with cottage cheese. "He's a paramedic."

"Paralegal," Greg burps. "And iss Craig."

"In't that whut I said?"

"No, you said paratrooper."

They're both shit-faced. Ziba smoothes her hair with immense self-satisfaction, a Siamese cat grooming itself.

"So, what does a paralegal do?" I ask.

"He works for me," a voice says behind me.

I turn, and there's a skinny, middle-aged woman who puts the *pow* in power dressing: Nancy Reagan red with NFL shoulder pads. Her thick eyebrows are brushed fashionably against the grain, contributing to a sense of menace.

"Judith," Craig says, "meet Ramses and Nefertiti. Ramses and Nefertiti, this is my boss, Judith Utzinger."

I smile at her, trying to win her over with my Southern charm. "Eddie Zander," I say. "Right pleased to meet ya', ma'am." If I had a hat I'd tip it.

She reluctantly shakes my hand, then stares down her employee. "Ease up on the booze," she says. "We still have work to do tonight."

Craig gives a military salute. "Yes, sir. I mean, ma'am."

She frowns, her eyebrows caterpillaring toward each other, then turns, cutting a swath through the crowd like a Western movie villain sauntering down Main Street.

"Wow," I say. "She's certainly a ray of sunshine."

"She's psycho. Lass week she hit me in the head with a yogurt."

Naturally, this comment invites me to share Boss from Hell stories, of which I have many, courtesy of Irving Fish. As Craig leers at Ziba, I ply him with alcohol and various *Tales from the Crypt*, including the time Irving cut off my tie, all of which primes him for the crucial moment when I ask, oh-so-casually, "So what is it you're working on?"

Given that the avenues in Manhattan are numerical, one could reasonably assume that they begin with First. But beyond First, tucked along the river between Fifty-third and Fifty-ninth, lies Sutton Place, a neighborhood so exclusive I hadn't even heard of it.

Chad lives in a postwar building, the kind with a glass-fronted lobby, which I now enter carrying a pizza. The doorman looks up, one of the uniformed members of Sgt. Pepper's Lonely Hearts Club Band.

"Hey, how you doin'?" I say, imitating any number of Zanni relatives. "This is for"—I consult a name I've scrawled on the outside of the box—"Severson."

The doorman picks up a phone. This is an idiotic idea. I mean, Chad's probably not even home. But I'm determined not to lose my last chance this year for a one-on-one encounter.

"Good evening, Mr. Severson," the doorman says into the phone. "Your pizza is here."

He looks up at me. "He says he didn't order a pizza."

"Damn. Musta been some kinda mix-up."

He talks into the phone. "Sorry to bother you, Mr—"

"Hang on, hang on," I say. "Ask him if he wants it anyway. Tell him it's from Zanni Pizzeria. It's a merger of pepperoni and sausage."

He relays the message like it's a colossal bother. After a few *mm-hmm*s and *uh-huhh*s, he puts down the phone.

"You can go up."

Twenty-one

Thank God there's a mirror in the elevator. Without it I wouldn't have noticed the Egyptian eyeliner still on my eyes. Please note: If you ever have occasion to line your eyes in the ancient Egyptian fashion, nineteen floors is just enough time to smear it all over your face. I look like a mime who just got dumped.

I walk down the hallway, which is carpeted like a hotel, and ring Chad's bell. He opens the door, wearing nothing but a towel and a smile. "You caught me coming out of the shower."

Volumes of poetry have been written to describe the kind of exquisite beauty now on display before me. Chad's body is muscular, but not intimidatingly so, and is coated lightly with peach fuzz, as if he'd been doused with gold dust. The remaining moisture from his shower coats his tawny skin like he's been decoupaged for an extremely gay crafts project.

"Come on in," he purrs, his voice like a Burt Bacharach song.

The apartment is smaller than I expected, and barely furnished, with parquet floors and a sliding glass door onto a narrow terrace. Chad leads me past one of those flying-saucer lamps hanging in an empty dining room and to a black leather couch, which faces a television the size of a bank safe, flanked by a pair of stereo speakers like sentries.

"Just move in?" I ask.

He shoves some papers off the glass coffee table and I put down the pizza. "Nah, I've been here seven years."

There's nowhere else to sit, so we place ourselves on opposite ends of the couch. Chad opens the pizza box and, after taking a moment to blot it with a napkin, grabs a slice. All I can think about is how he's naked under that towel.

"You're tan," I say, displaying the rapid-fire wit for which I'm renowned.

"I was in the Cayman Islands."

"You were just there in September."

He pulls on the end of the slice with his teeth, like a dog playing tug-of-war. "It's the only place I can really relax." Oil dribbles into the ledge between his lower lip and his chin. "So whaddya got for me?"

Two words: Hard. On.

I start my story with a Paula-style, "Once upon a time, in a galaxy far, far away," preamble, partly because I want Chad to know how tirelessly I work for him, but also to prolong the conversation so I can track the progress of a drop of water as it journeys down his breastbone, through the ridge of his abdominals, and finally wells in his navel. Even if he is gay, he probably wouldn't be interested in me. While some people might consider me short, dark, and handsome, Chad's out of my league. If it weren't for his crooked nose, he has soap-opera looks.

But that doesn't stop me from mooning about him like a junior high girl lingering by the lifeguard station. I hear myself blather on about Ziba's cousin's birthday party and the Temple of Dendur until I finally tell him what I learned:

"Hibbert and Howard is being acquired by I. J. Sloan."

Chad's green eyes flash like traffic signals. "Are you sure?"

"The deal's going through in the next couple of weeks. They're working on it right now."

Chad leaps off the couch. "Yeah!" he shouts. "That's what I'm talkin' about. That's what I'm fuckin' talkin' about." He leans down and grabs me by the shoulders. "Oh, Edward, baby, I could kiss you."

I stop breathing.

Instead he shakes me, grunting with pleasure, his perfect teeth as white as the towel I wish would fall from his waist. His eyes crinkle when he smiles, the wrinkles suddenly appearing like starbursts. He releases me. "Okay, you'd better go," he says, pacing the floor. "The doorman's gonna notice how long you've been up here."

"Oh, right." Those of us without doormen don't think of these things. The only people who'd notice anything in my building are the Crackheads downstairs or the guy across the street with a colander on his head.

"Sorry," he says. "I'd love to hang out, but in my business I can't risk anyone gossiping about my personal life."

There's that phrase again. As much as I relish the role of the private paramour, I'm getting fed up with the whole love-that-dare-not-speak-its-name thing. If I'm going to put up with the constraints of being the secret love, then I'd actually like to have some secret lovin'. Instead, I wait while he goes into the bedroom without me to get my hundred bucks.

"When this deal comes through, we'll celebrate," he says, patting me on the shoulder as he hands it to me.

The hair on my neck stands on end. "Okay," I say.

Wuss.

I go back to Wallingford for Christmas and discover that my childhood home has been transformed into Little Managua: Multicolored blankets drape over couches; folk-art masks of parrots and toucans hang on the wall; you can't even pee without being watched by a statue of the Blessed Virgin. You'd think I'd mind feeling like a tourist in my own house, but I've seen this play before—with the original cast. When Dagmar moved in she transformed the place into a SoHo gallery, with hardwood floors, track lighting, and her scary black-and-white photographs.

No, it hasn't been my house for a long time.

Milagros's family has joined us for the wedding: her cheerful parents, Ignacio and Perpetua, with whom I communicate solely through frequent nods, smiles, and an English-Spanish dictionary, making me feel even more like a tourist; and her younger brother, Fernando, who was a university student until the war with the U.S.-backed contra rebels forced him to quit school. As if the Che Guevara T-shirt weren't enough of a hint, he quickly informs me that Ronald Reagan is a war criminal.

He and I get along just fine.

Al and Milagros honeymoon in Miami, and I return to the city, where I find a postcard from Doug. It's a picture of the ship, the *Caribbean Destiny*. On the back he's written:

Hey, buddy,

The ship is AWESOME. You should work here.
They've got party motivators. See you in April.

Doug

P.S. Have you read ▬▬▬▬▬▬*? Made me think*
of you.

I dissect each word with the care of a Talmudic scholar.
"Hey, buddy," for instance, firmly establishes the I-like-
you-but-not-that-way boundary, as does the friendly
promise to see me in April. Clearly, all is forgiven, and that
is the best Christmas/birthday present I could get. Reading between the lines, I decide that meeting party motivators on board helped him realize that he can fraternize
with homosexuals without fear of molestation.

What's maddening is the postscript. No matter what I
do—hold the card up to the light, examine it with a mag-
nifying glass—I can't figure out the smudged title. It appears to be about eight or nine letters, but it depends
whether it's one long word or a few short ones. What could
it be? *The Iliad*? *Ragtime*? *Catch-22*? None of those would
make Doug think of me. Neither would *Emma*, *Jane Eyre*,
Saint Joan, or *Lolita*, although they'd certainly make an interesting poker game. I briefly consider *Pygmalion*—Doug
and I have something of a Henry Higgins/Eliza Doolittle relationship, but it doesn't seem like something you'd find on
a ship. I just hope it's not *The Plague* or *The Dead*.

I obsess about the smudge the entire week between
Christmas and New Year's, ruling out the Greeks (*Lysis-
trata*, *Antigone*, *Electra*, *Medea*) and Shakespeare (*Hamlet*,
Macbeth, *King Lear*, *Othello*) on the principle that Doug

would assume I had already read them and therefore wouldn't need to ask if I had. And why would he be reading the Greeks or Shakespeare anyway?

This is what happens when you have too much time and too little company. Natie's off skiing with Ziba and her Persian posse, or, to be more accurate, keeping her company in the lodge. (When asked what kind of skiing she prefers, Ziba replied, "*Après.*") Willow's visiting her family in California, and Kelly's so beaten up from *Starlight* rehearsals she has to nightly soak her bloody, swollen feet in a bucket of rubbing alcohol.

"You have no idea how hard this show is," she says on the phone. "Every day grown men cry. One of the guys is a vet, and he says it's harder than Vietnam."

That should be on the poster: *Tougher than 'Nam!*

My only outlet is helping with the Coup d'État Group's *The Music Man?*, which has run into trouble. Not only has the cast not been available for rehearsals, but Marcus had to fire the Marian. It turns out she wasn't blind, just nearsighted and desperate for the role.

I enter the Church of the Holy Redeemer through the side door next to the lady chapel, stomping the snow off my feet. Paula and Marcus stretch on the floor.

"Well, look at chew," Paula cries, suddenly Southern. "You're just covered with God's dandruff."

"Let me guess. Juilliard's doing *Summer and Smoke.*"

"Oh, you are a caution," she drawls. "Marcus, isn't he a caution?"

Marcus gives me a look like, *He's something, all right.*

"As a mattuh of fact," Paula says, "we're performing anothuh play by Mistuh Tennessee Williams, *Cat on a Hot Tin Roof.*"

"Congratulations," I say. "Who are you playing?"

She clears her throat. "Big Mama. I know, I know, heyuh I am—poised to graduate from the finest institution for the dramatic arts in the nation—and I have never once played someone mah own age. It's a *disgrace*." She fans herself like she has the vapors.

"You got robbed," Marcus says, doing a stretch that makes him look like a swastika. "You've got more talent than the others."

"Well, apparently, there's some rule in Mistuh Aristotle's *Poetics* that the fat girl has to play the mothuh."

"You're not fat. You're juicy."

"You lie so prettily. If I get any larger, you could take your exercise by sprinting around my perimeter."

He rises. "Baby, I'm not going to let you starve yourself to fit into some narrow, commercial concept of beauty. You're gorgeous the way you are." He kisses her and starts jogging around the church.

Marcus.

Paula sighs. "Ah wish ah could believe him, but how can you trust the opinion of someone who casts a musical with a deaf man?" She flops onto a kneeler, leaning her head on the pew in front of her, her ringlets hanging like vines. "Do you know how Mistuh Tennessee Williams describes the charactuh of Big Mama? Like a Japanese wrestluh. One of those sumo people decorously draped with a napkin. I tell you, it's positively *galling*."

I put my arm around her and rub her shoulder. She places a tiny finger under each eye to stop the tears. "I just wish the good people at the FDA would hurry themselves up and approve that new diet pill."

"What new diet pill?"

"The one that company is developing. Pharmisomething. Didn't Nathan tell you about it?"

"Uh . . . no."

"Ow," she says, breaking character, "you're pinching me."

"Sorry."

She resumes her mint julep drawl. "I'm surprised he didn't inform you. Mistuh Nathan's positively absorbed with matters of commerce. These Pharmipeople are developing a revolutionary new diet pill that allows you to eat whatever you want without absorbing the fat content. Isn't science *miraculous*? Naturally, the innovation has financial implications, and Nathan has been kind enough to invest mah little nest egg. Why, Edward, don't gawk at me like that. If our little theatrical endeavor is going to survive, it requires seed money. We have to rent space, run advertisements. . . ."

"How much did you give him?"

She glances over her shoulder. "Five hundred dollahs," she whispers. "Don't tell Marcus—he doesn't even like taking the number four or the number five train because they stop at Wall Street."

"Mendacity, mendacity, mendacity," I say.

"Oh, shut up."

Gavin arrives and we commence another grope session in the back of the church, a privilege usually reserved for altar boys. As he caresses my neck and jaw, I sort out how I feel about Natie investing Paula's money. I suppose there's no harm. Clearly he didn't mention me or Chad, so why not spread the wealth?

Let's see. With $500 she can buy options for two hundred and fifty shares at $2 apiece. With $25 profit per share that's . . . two hundred and fifty times twenty-five, carry the two, then twelve-fifty, carry the one . . . that's $6,250. All for a good cause.

Doing math helps keep my mind off the fact that I'm in a man's arms singing "Till There Was You," this time without a condom between us. As I stare into his wide, wistful eyes we work on the last note over and over, our mouths *you*-ing and *you*-ing just inches away from each other, his breath caressing my cheeks until there is no *you* and *you* any longer, just we, inhaling and exhaling as if we were one.

It's so fucking sexy I could break boards with my cock.

Finally Gavin lays his long, slender fingers on my chest, and I can't stand it any longer. Like someone slipping a spoon into a lush and creamy dessert, I kiss him.

His soft, plump lips cushion mine, as if to break a fall, but he pulls away.

"I'm sorry," I say.

"No, it's—"

"I shouldn't have—"

"It's okay. I just can't . . . I've got . . ." He hesitates.

No, it can't be. He has AIDS. I just got the kiss of death. How could I be so reckless, so stupid? I have to get tested and . . . Wait a sec, can you get AIDS from kissing? They say you can't, but are they sure?

". . . a boyfriend."

Respiration resumes. "Oh."

His head droops like a sunflower, his floppy curls casting a shadow across his face. "I would if I could. But I can't."

Why am I only attracted to guys who are unavailable to me? First Doug, then Chad, now Gavin. Does my subconscious actively seek them out because of some kind of internalized homophobia? Or self-loathing? Am I not worthy of love?

Or is it self-preservation? After all, in the age of AIDS, rejection keeps you alive.

I console myself with that thought as I spend New Year's Eve alone reading about Eddie Sanders's libidinous, preplague sexcapades. It was just ten years ago, but gay Manhattan in the 1970s seems like a land before time, a paradise lost, a coke-infused fantasy with a cast of thousands fucking to a disco beat. And I'm mad as hell that I missed the party, that by the time I arrived love was wrapped in plastic like leftovers. I'm young. I'm alive. I want to dive into another man's body and never come up for air.

Instead, I'm going to spend my twenty-first birthday with my friends, channeling my sexual frustrations into full-throated renditions of show tunes at our favorite piano bar, Something for the Boys. After so many years of drinking there illegally, I guess it's appropriate, but, for a gay bar, Something for the Boys feels awfully . . . I don't know . . . dickless.

The night of the party, I'm just stepping out of the shower when the phone rings. I hop across the apartment the way you do when you don't want to drip on the floor. Not that it works.

The phone slips out of my hand and lands with a clunk.

"Hold on! Hold on! I'm here!" I shout. My towel falls off as I reach for the phone, which shouldn't matter because Natie's still skiing with Ziba, and why should I care if I'm naked in front of him, anyway? I guess I have body issues.

I place the phone against my ear and begin the conversation. "Sorry."

"Edward? Chad."

Funny, the last time we talked *he* was wearing a towel. It's kismet.

"Have you heard the news?" he says.

"What news?"

"The Hibbert and Howard merger went through and the stock closed today at fifty-eight."

"Is that good?"

"Considering I bought it at twenty-two this morning, fuck, yeah. How about that dinner I promised?"

"Sure! When?"

"I'll see you at eight o'clock. Do you know Caprice?"

"No, but if you hum a few bars I can fake it."

I love making him laugh.

"It's on Seventieth and Lexington. I know the chef."

It amazes me how he automatically assumes I'm not doing anything, like I'd just drop everything for the mere privilege of sharing molecules with him. But I can't just blow off my friends for the possibility of a cash bonus and an after-dinner tryst.

"Eight it is," I say.

Twenty-two

Okay, one drink. Maybe an appetizer. Then I'll leave around nine, which'll get me downtown for a fashionably late entrance by 9:30—9:45 max. I mean, it's not like any of my friends will be on time anyway. I call Paula to let her know I'll be late, but I get the answering machine.

I'm uncharacteristically early for my sort-of-maybe-not-sure-if-it's-a-date with Chad, so I wait in the bar and watch the dining room, which is full of blond wood and blond women, both polished to a shine. You'd think that after all the society parties I've worked I'd feel comfortable in these surroundings. But repeated exposure to the lifestyles of the rich and fatuous has made me keenly aware of my lowly station in the world: my cheap haircut, my scabby cuticles, my genuine fake Rolex I bought on the street. In my neighborhood, the locals look at your shoes and want to kill you for them. Here they look at your shoes and you want to kill yourself.

Chad enters, Achilles freshly returned from battle and a celebratory fuck with his boyfriend Patroclus. The hostess greets him like he's a movie star and leads us to his "usual table" in the corner.

Caprice is one of those places where the waiter gives a litany of incomprehensible ingredients so exhaustive it sounds like he's under federal mandate to disclose them: *"Tonight we have a vodka-infused portobello cake in a peanut–pine nut sauce, with charred chard and a persimmon risotto made by monks who've taken a vow of silence."* What arrives is a miniature tower of food so painstakingly constructed it's obvious that someone's hands have been all over it. The tower stands alone on the hubcap-sized plate, like a grain silo on a lonely prairie.

Chad orders a bottle of champagne. Champagne! I mean, to not finish the bottle would be rude. I wonder if I should just slip away for a moment and call Something for the Boys, but I'm afraid to leave this table. First off, I can't imagine that anyone answering the phone at a gay piano bar would be able to hear over a chorus of men belting out, "I Enjoy Being a Girl." More important, I don't want to do anything that will break the spell.

For Chad is charm personified: attentive, relaxed, and real. He wants to know all about me, laughing at my exploits as Eddie Sanders and Eddie Zander, asking question after question about my past and planning our bright future together—professionally, of course, but who knows where that might lead? Like a detective searching for clues, I parse fragments of what he says to make my deduction:

"I feel like we understand each other" + "It's hard to find someone you trust" + "That suit looks good on you" = "I want you. Let's have sex in the bathroom."

We don't get nearly that intimate, but I do get drunk enough to ask about his crooked nose. Did he break it in a fight? An accident?

Chad replies by sticking the tip of his thumb in his mouth and hooking his finger over the bridge.

"Thumb sucker," he says. "Until I was seven. Don't tell anyone."

It makes me adore him all the more.

It's after eleven when we finally stumble out of the restaurant, laughing at nothing as we share a cab downtown, which gives me less than twenty blocks to figure out how to make him love me.

As we turn onto Sutton Place, Chad arches to reach his back pocket, his knee grazing mine, sending a little shudder up my spine. He pulls out his wallet and hands me a wad of cash.

"For a job well done," he says. The bill on top is a hundred and there appear to be four more underneath.

"Wow. Thanks."

The cab stops.

"I'd invite you up, but the doorman . . ."

That's it. I've had it with him and his nosy doorman. What is the point of living in an expensive apartment if you can't invite a horny twenty-one-year-old upstairs to have sex?

"I understand," I say.

Wuss.

"I'm sorry," he says. "It's just that, in my business, I can't afford to be . . . well, you know."

But that's exactly why we should be together. In a world of AIDS and *Bowers v. Hardwick*, Chad's repressed sexuality and my celibacy are a perfect match. It's safe, contained. And all I'd ever need.

But am I all he'd ever need? Maybe he's not inviting me up because he'd rather date someone whose abs aren't insulated by a protective layer of fat, nature's bubble wrap. I disgust him. That's it, starting tomorrow I'm going macrobiotic.

Chad smiles, and I feel the earth turn toward the sun. "Listen," he coos, "you keep finding winners like this and I'll take you to the Caymans with me. You got anything coming up?"

Yes, in my lap.

"The bash mitzvahs start again next weekend," I say. "And we're doing your firm's Super Bowl party, but I'm just working the door. You guys only wanted female motivators."

"I'll see you there, then," he says. "In the meantime, keep your ears open. Even if it turns out to be a dog like Pharmicare."

My vision goes into freeze-frame. "Pharmicare? What about Pharmicare?"

"Didn't you hear? It was in the paper. The FDA didn't approve that diet drug."

"What? Why?"

He laughs.

"What is it? Tell me."

"It caused 'excessive anal leakage.' "

"What the hell is excessive anal leakage?"

"Gas followed by mass."

I'm going to lose it. Right here in the taxi. The driver will have to drive straight to Bellevue.

Chad continues: "After that, the stock went into a fuckin' free fall. It's gonna be years before it recovers."

That makes two of us.

After he leaves I lie down on the seat, curling into a fetal position while I try to absorb the realization that I invested $1,500 in volcanic diarrhea, my Juilliard dream literally disappearing down the toilet.

Plus I have to pay for the fucking cab.

. . .

With its brick facade and arched doorway, Something for the Boys might have once possessed charm, but now it looks tired and battle scarred, the architectural equivalent of the frail, hollow-cheeked men who haunt these twisting streets of Greenwich Village. From the street I can hear the voices of men singing "I Am What I Am."

The door opens and out springs Hung, arm in arm with a guy who looks a lot like me, except cuter. The upgrade has the unmistakably muscular frame of a gymnast or a dancer, his shoulders and thighs stretching the fabric of his leather jacket and tight jeans. If Michael Bennett were directing a musical about me, this is who'd he'd cast.

"Edward!"

"I know," I say, "I'm so late."

"What happened?"

"I had a . . . work thing."

"*Whell*, Miss Paula's *furious*. Kelly came all the way down here with bloody feet, y'know."

"Shit. Are they inside?"

"No, everyone's gone. You missed it. Some deaf guy sang 'Till There Was You.'"

"That was so moving," says And-Starring-as-Edward. "Even with a condom next to his neck."

"Oh! Where are my manners?" Hung says. "Edward, this is Tom."

"Todd."

"Same alphabet." Hung tosses his scarf over his shoulder. "Now, if you'll excuse us, we're going to find out whether it's better to be ribbed or tickled." He kisses the air in front of my face. "Happy birthday, sweetie."

I stand alone on the street, wondering whether I should still go in. The windows of the bar glow invitingly, but without my friends, I'd only be going in for one reason. And I just can't imagine doing that. I mean, some of these guys are walking time bombs. How does Hung do it? Does he ask if they have HIV? Or does he just assume they do? And what's really safe, anyway?

I turn around and go home.

The days slush by. Everyone's mad at me and I don't blame them. Why do I do such stupid things? I knew there was no way I could meet Chad and get down to the Village in time but I still went. I couldn't help myself. I'm like a big walking id. My brain ought to sue me for neglect.

What's worse, Natie won't be home until Sunday, and I have no idea how to contact him. Still, I've got plenty of party-motivator gigs coming up. Surely there'll be more insider information to trade on, right?

Right?

My first chance comes that Saturday at the bash mitzvah of Tamara Katz. Given their surname, Tamara's parents have decided on a *Cats* theme. A Katz mitzvah. They've even re-created the junkyard set in a SoHo warehouse. A very hard to find SoHo warehouse.

I come dashing in, panicked and panting.

"Where the hell have you been?" Sandra screeches.

"I—"

"Never mind, we don't have time. Like I don't have enough to deal with, with this new photographer. Here. Hurry up." She tosses me a costume.

I'm not sure which feline I'm supposed to be—Pointlesstheater or Bourgeoispleaser—and I don't care. The only thing worse than sitting through *Cats* is having to pretend you're in it. There's only enough time to draw on some whiskers, then take my place "backstage," a curtained-off area next to an oversize prop stove.

"Nice of you to show up," Javier hisses.

I pull my tail between my legs and wank it, just in time to notice the shocked faces of Leon and Nancy Katz.

Over the PA comes the announcement to which I've grown accustomed, as if it really were for me: "And now, *La Vie de la Fête* Productions is proud to present everyone's favorite emcee, British MTV's hottest new veejay, Eddieeeeee Sanders!"

I enter, swinging my tail in a jaunty manner that hopefully communicates I'm aware how stupid I look, then leap onto the trunk of a prop car that sits beneath a marquee featuring the yellow-eyed logo with the word *Katz*. I notice immediately that the applause is less enthusiastic than usual, and, just as I'm about to crow Eddie's trademark, " 'Ello, America!" it starts:

Boos.

My heart lurches in my chest like I've popped the clutch. Instantly I'm covered in sweat. I've performed for audiences that were indifferent (in high school I sang at a nursing home while a man had a stroke), but boos? I don't know what to do. For some reason the kids have turned on me. The parents murmur to one another, as confused as I am.

Sandra sticks her head out through the curtain.

"Edwid!" she hisses. "Get off!"

I jump off the trunk and hurry offstage to jeers that give new meaning to the term *catcalls*. Sandra grabs my mike and hands it to Javier, who hastily introduces Mr. and Mrs. Katz. The crowd applauds, and the evening continues as planned. Without me.

"What's going on?" Sandra says. "Why did they react like that?"

As if on cue, the reason steps through the curtain.

Twenty-three

"**Lizzie!**" **I shout.** "What the hell's going on?"

She crosses her arms and gives a smug smile. "I just thought my friends would want to know that you're a pervert."

"What are you talkin' about?" Sandra says.

"I saw his diary in his apartment," Lizzie sneers. "It's disgusting."

Sandra turns to me. "What was she doing in your apartment?"

"She broke in. With these little tools," I say. "And that's not my diary, you little crook."

Lizzie narrows her eyes. "Liar. It has your name on it. You're not even English. You're from Ohio. That's why you were talking so strange that night at the Waldorf."

Sandra shrieks like a pterodactyl. "YOU TOOK HER TO THE WALDORF?"

"I-I did not take her to the Waldorf," I stammer. "She met me there."

Sandra grips her forehead. "Oh, Gawd . . ."

I grab Lizzie by the shoulders. "Tell her what happened."

"Let go of me!"

"Tell her!"

Lizzie knees me in the nuts, then reaches into her bodice and blows a whistle. "RAAAAPE!" she screams. "RAAAAPE!"

People spill backstage, led by an hysterical woman screaming, "LIZZIE, MY BABY, LIZZIE!"

I look up from my crumpled vantage point on the floor and see Lizzie's mother for the first time. Make that the second time, because I've met her before. At the party for Hibbert & Howard. In the Temple of Dendur.

It's Judith Utzinger, the psycho boss.

"Are you all right?" she cries. "What happened?"

Lizzie points at me. "He touched me!"

"Where? Show Mommy where."

Lizzie reaches up and touches her shoulders.

"Your breasts?" Judith says. "Did he touch your breasts? C'mon, baby, use your words."

Lizzie responds by sobbing. Judith turns to me.

"YOU MONSTER!"

She advances toward me, smacking my head with her beaded clutch bag, which, from the feel of it, contains a lead weight. Within moments I'm seeing stars. No, not stars, flashbulbs. The fucking photographer is document-ing my assault. Good. I'll have a record.

"I want those pictures," I shout. "I want those pictures!"

The photographer lowers her camera. "Tsey are all yours."

No, it can't be. I must be hallucinating. It's my ex-stepmonster, the villainous Valkyrie.

This is my worst nightmare. Well, actually, my worst nightmare is still being chased by an angry mob, falling off a cliff, and hanging on by the tips of my fingers, but something tells me I'm just a few steps away from that.

"Get the cops," Judith screams. "This man molested my little girl."

"Wait a sec," Sandra says. "He didn't—"

"It's true," Dagmar says. "I saw tsem shopping at Brooks Brothers. He's a tsief. And a liar. And an *azzhuuu-uull.*"

"MONSTER!" Judith screams, kicking me in the ribs.

"I didn't touch her," I shout. "I'm gay! I'm gay! I'm gay!"

It's the first time I've been glad to say it.

I'm waiting for Natie when he comes through the door Monday afternoon. He has that strange tan you get from ski goggles, making him look like a marmoset.

"Where have you been?" I cry.

He struggles with the zipper on his jacket, which still has his lift pass attached.

"Our flight got in late," he says, "so I stayed at Fran and— Jesus, what the hell happened to you?"

He's referring to my black eye.

"You can read all about it," I say, holding up a copy of today's *Post.* There, on the front page, is a picture of me dressed as a cat while fending off an attack by an unseen assailant. The headline reads: PARTY MONSTER.

"Holy shit." He pulls off his jacket. "Read it to me. I've had to pee since Newark."

"The city's elite got a big surprise—"

"Louder."

"The city's elite got a big surprise at the Saturday-night party celebrating the bat mitzvah of thirteen-year-old Tamara Katz when they discovered that their star 'party motivator' is a fraud. Passing himself off as Eddie Sanders, a supposed veejay for British MTV, twenty-one-year-old Edward Zanni has charmed enthusiastic teens and their parents at such glittering events as financier Joel Schlonsky's legendary party aboard the Europa *for his son's bar mitzvah, and disgraced oil and commodities trader William Owens's blowout for his daughter's sweet sixteen just before he fled the country."*

"Makes you sound pretty important," Natie shouts from the bathroom.

"Just wait."

" 'I'm as surprised as anyone else,' said Sandra Pecorino, owner of La Vie de la Fête Productions, the event planning company that employed Zanni. 'Anyone who's met him can tell you he's a very convincing con artist. I feel so betrayed.' "

Natie flushes. "That's bullshit."

"I told the cops she knew who I was. My name is on the friggin' W-9."

"The cops?"

"Hang on; there's more.

"Zanni, a Juilliard drama school dropout, was identified by one of the young partygoers with whom he's allegedly formed a friendship. Witnesses say the girl's mother confronted Zanni at the Katz event, but no charges have been filed against him as yet.

"'He's a pervert,' said thirteen-year-old Marcy Glickman. 'I can't believe we ever liked him.'"

"Jeez," Natie says, emerging from the bathroom. "You okay?"

"Sure. If throwing up six times a day is okay." I flop into Sweeney Todd's Chair of Death and put my head between my knees.

"How about some tea? I'll mix Mint Magic with Tension Tamer. You'll be magically relaxed." While he clanks around the kitchen, I tell him the rest of the story, from the assault with a deadly purse to the police interrogation.

"Hang on," Natie says, handing me a cup of warm brew. "Tell me exactly what you said. Did you have a lawyer?"

"No."

"Jeez. I go away for two weeks . . ." He sits across from me on the coffee table. "What did you say?"

"I told them that Lizzie was stalking me."

"Did you tell 'em she broke into our apartment? I can testify to that."

I nod, blowing on my cup. "I also told them to check with Spy City."

"Good thinking. So they let you go?"

I sip at the tea, but it's too hot. "Yeah, but the cop made a report."

"What's that mean?"

"It means the complaint won't appear on my record because no charge was made."

"That's good."

"But there's a seven-year statute of limitations. If Lizzie changes her story, I could go to jail for child molestation."

"That's not so good."

I hand Natie the newspaper. "It gets worse. Look at the photo credit."

There, in tiny print, it says, *D. Teufel.*

He drops it like it's contaminated. "How'd she find you?"

"I've been going over and over it in my mind. All I can think is that when Chad told her I worked for *La Vie de la Fête* Productions she must have sought out a job there."

"Just to sabotage you?"

"I did cost her a job at Brooks Brothers."

"And ten grand."

"And her marriage."

"It's too coincidental to be random." Natie puts his cup down, spilling some, then claps his hands together, all business. "Okay, let's review. You've been fired, accused of child abuse, beaten with a handbag, pursued by a mad Austrian, and humiliated in the press. Anything else?"

"Yeah. Pharmicare."

"Oh, that."

I follow him as he carries his suitcase into the bedroom.

" 'Oh, that'?" I yell. "You told me I'd earn twenty grand and now I'm out fifteen hundred. I'm no math whiz, but I would say that's significantly less."

He tosses his suitcase on the futon underneath my loft bed. "Eddie, money's like the tide: It flows in; it flows out. Trust me: It'll flow in again."

"How? I just lost my job, you cheesehead."

He ducks to avoid the book I throw at him.

"Violence doesn't solve anything."

"That's easy for you to say. You're not the one who lost $1,500."

"That's not true," he says, opening his suitcase. "I invested just as much as you did."

"Plus Paula's money."

He takes out a full set of embroidered towels reading TELLURIDE INN. "She told you, huh?"

"Natie, that five hundred bucks is probably all she has."

"You mean had."

It's a good thing I believe in gun control.

"You're paying her back," I say.

"Sure, as soon as I pay off my credit card from this trip."

"Natie."

"Hey, you try keeping up with a bunch of rich Persians. Those guys order $200 bottles of wine. I could get a hundred bottles for that much."

Silence. Itchy, scabby silence.

"Has Paula said anything about it?" Natie asks.

I shake my head. "She's too busy being Miss Corn Bread of 1987."

"Good. That gives us five or six weeks to figure out what to do."

I suppose a more dispassionate person might ask, *Us? Who's us? This is your problem.* But I am not a dispassionate person. I am a desperate, unemployed pariah who is breaking out in hives. Natie's all I've got. That is, assuming I let him live.

Messages on my answering machine pile up, particularly after the article in the *Daily News* ("Bizarre Mitzvah") and a reference in the *New York Times* about Manhattan's elite not realizing there isn't any British MTV. My first appearance in the Arts section and it's as a duplicitous drama school dud.

(Beep) "Eddie, it's your father. What the hell is goin' on? Call me."

(Beep) "Edward, Ziba. How dare you do something illicit without telling me? Let's have lunch."

(Beep) "Hello, gorgeous. It's your future ex-lover. I hear those bitches at Cats are furious. Call me and I'll give you all the dish."

(Beep) "Hiyeee, it's Kells. Oh, my God, I can't believe it. I'm so sorry. I'd say call me but I'm being held hostage at rehearsals. So, um, I'll try you again. Or stop by! The theater's, like, practically around the corner. I love yooooou."

(Beep) "Oh, honey chile, what on God's green earth is going on? Marcus, Willow, and I are just sick with vexation about chew. What? I'm not going to say that. Give me back that phone."

"Edward? Marcus. Great job of stickin' it to the ruling class. Oh, Willow says hi."

(Beep) "Am I taping? I hate these machines. Baby doll, it's Aunt Glo. I had no idea you were in Cats. I'm gonna get tickets even though I already saw it."

The one person who doesn't call is the one I want to hear from most. I leave Chad a couple of messages—okay, six—but he doesn't respond, which sends a message all by itself. I am on my own. There will be no more clandestine meetings, no envelopes with cash. There will be no *frottage* in the Cayman Islands.

I'm such a cheesehead.

Mercifully, the gods arrange for everyone's answering

machines to be on when I return calls, partly because I call at times I'm pretty certain they'll be out. I can't bear being an object of pity yet again. So I leave chipper messages, giving the performance of my life as I say everything's fine and it was all a misunderstanding and don't believe everything you read in the papers, ha-ha-ha. By the fourth or fifth call I sense the beginnings of a party piece, an amusing anecdote we can laugh about for years to come. (*Remember when you almost got arrested for child molestation? That was hilarious!*) In fact, I feel so much better I'm tempted to open the phone book and start calling strangers. (*Hello, is this Adam Aalberg? This is Edward Zanni. Just wanted to let you know I'm not a crook or a pedophile.*) After a few days the hives fade and I start to feel like I can move on with my life.

Then I get a letter from something called the Securities and Exchange Commission.

Twenty-four

I've never visited Columbia University, and I gasp when I see its sprawling, snow-covered lawns and columned Neoclassical buildings. It's like someone plunked down the Washington Mall in the middle of Harlem.

I bolt into the Parthenon-like library and up to the second floor, where Natie regularly meets with his study group. The room is a temple to learning, with soaring ceilings and a stained-glass window depicting New York's Dutch settlers. Natie sits at a table in the corner with the Indian and Asian versions of himself. If they were puppies, they'd be the runts their mothers threw away.

I toss the letter down on the table. "We need to talk."

The Indian runt reaches for it. "Is that from the SEC?"

Natie snatches the letter. "It's not the SEC you're thinking of," he says, folding the paper.

"There's another?"

"Of course. The, uh, Saudi . . . Electric Company."

The Asian guy looks at me, pushing his glasses up his nose. "Why did you get a letter from the Saudi Electric Company?"

"Don't you guys read the news?" Natie says. "The Arabs

are taking over everything." He turns to me and, enunciating very clearly, asks, "Abdul, Do You Need Help Understanding Your Bill?"

"Yes, thank you," I say. "Uh, praise Allah."

"Sorry, guys," Natie says, gathering his books. "But if he doesn't pay, they'll cut off more than his electricity."

My panic is too enormous to be contained indoors. I need air, I need space, I need a place to throw up. As Natie reads the summons, we walk over to Morningside Park, where I feel reasonably sure I won't get mugged because I'm ranting like a lunatic.

"WHY DIDN'T YOU TELL ME INSIDER TRADING WAS ILLEGAL?"

"Calm down," Natie says. "It's only illegal if you get caught."

I seriously consider adding homicide to my expanding dossier of crimes.

"Everyone does it," Natie explains. "It's practically an industry standard."

I see. Almost Legal.

I start to hyperventilate, my breath making clouds. "Then why did I get a letter requesting . . . What is it again?"

Natie looks at the page. " 'A *voluntary production of information*.' "

"Yeah, that."

"Well, the government believes—and I disagree—that trading on information the public doesn't know about destroys a level playing field."

"Then why'd you let me do it? Never mind, I know the answer to that question."

"C'mon, Eddie. Where in life is there a level playing

field? Most people get ahead because of who they know or what they know."

"And hard work."

He looks at me over his glasses. "Don't be naive."

I gaze at the park. The low afternoon sun casts long shadows, while the dome of an immense Gothic cathedral rises above the bare trees. I've never seen a church that big.

"What's the punishment for insider trading?" I say.

"Usually a couple of years in jail."

An industrious Boy Scout ties a knot in my colon. "WHAT? It's not like we robbed a convenience store."

"Calm down. The SEC's not interested in locking up a little pisher like you. They want you to finger Mr. Big in bed."

"What?" I thought the Supreme Court outlawed that kind of thing.

"They want to know who you're working for," he says. "I bet if you tell 'em about Chad trading on the Hibbert and Howard merger they'll grant you immunity and overlook our little Pharmicare trade."

"Which. We. Lost. Money. On," I say, punctuating each word by hitting him with my hat. I flop down on a bench. "Why are they coming after me? Why don't they just go after Chad?"

"I dunno," Natie says, pacing. "Someone probably got suspicious and reported you. I'm guessing it's the psycho lawyer who thinks you're molesting her kid. Hey, don't lie down on that bench; it's filthy."

I pinch my eyes shut, hoping the nightmare will end. "So now what?"

"We've gotta act fast. First one to squeal gets the best deal."

"Is that what you and the Geek Patrol are studying?"

"Hey, those guys are sharp. I'm gonna have a helluva time explaining the Saudi Electric Company, Abdul."

I sit up again, resting my head in my hands. "I don't know, Natie. I mean, ratting Chad out to protect myself. It's so slimy."

"Don't get sentimental," he says, wiping his nose with the back of his ski glove. "You think he wouldn't do the same? Why do you think he didn't want you to call at his office? And always sent you cash in an envelope with no return address? He wanted to make sure there was nothing linking you to him, in case you got caught." He sits down next to me. "Jeez, how can you sit here? This thing's an iceberg."

"He promised to take me to the Cayman Islands."

Natie's button eyes go wide. "The Cayman Islands?"

"Yeah, he says it's the only place he can relax."

"Sure, 'cuz he can visit his money."

It's then that I learn about offshore accounts.

"Obviously we're up against a pro," Natie says, rising. "We're gonna need some hard evidence to prove he made that trade."

"Oh, God . . ."

"Stop scratching your face. You'll leave marks." He takes me by the hands and pulls me off the bench. "All you have to do is tape-record a conversation with him. We've got until, what?" He consults the letter. "Friday, February thirteenth. Ooh, that can't be good."

I lean against him while we walk, as limp and wilted as if it were a hundred degrees. "How am I supposed to tape him if he won't even answer my calls?"

"Tell him you've got a new piece of information."

"From where? Everyone in the tri-state area knows I lost my job."

"Y'know, you really are a naysayer."

I grab him by the collar. "Well, it's hard to be optimistic when you're GOING TO JAIL."

"Calm down, calm down. Rome wasn't burned in a day."

"How can you stay calm? You traded on that information, too."

"Sure, but I did it all under your name."

"WHAT?"

"I didn't think there was any point in both of us—"

I can't make out the rest of what he's saying with my hands around his neck.

"Uhddi, yr chkng muh."

I let go.

"Y'know, you're stronger than you look," he says, rubbing his neck.

"I'm going to have to be, to fend off attacks in the prison yard." I pace. "Okay, you're saying all the trading was done under my name. So at least Paula's safe, right?"

Natie fiddles with the ski pass hanging from his jacket zipper.

"Natie . . ."

"Her trade came after ours. So, naturally, it's under her name."

"Great!" I shout. "It's not enough I'm going to jail; I'm taking down innocent people."

"Stop being so dramatic. I told you, all we need is some evidence proving you worked for Chad. Didn't he say he would be at his firm's Super Bowl party?"

"I can't go there," I moan. "It's a private party for their top clients."

Natie scrunches up his face, which is pink and mottled from the cold, like a carnation. "Details."

Rather than go home, I suggest we stop by Ziba's because a) she has a supple, if slightly criminal mind; and b) it's dinnertime and she always pays.

Natie's a little reluctant. Things have been tense between them since they got back from their trip to Telluride.

"I don't get it," I say as we walk up the front steps of her town house—with the columns. "What happened?"

"You know how every clique has the tagalong friend, the one who doesn't fit?" he says. "Y'know, kind of like you are for us?"

"I'm not the tagalong friend. You are."

"What are you talking about? I'm the nexus of our group. Without me, nothing would get done."

If I suffer from a lack of confidence, Natie suffers from an overabundance.

"I don't wanna fight about it," Natie says, ringing the bell. "My point is: Ziba is the tagalong of the Persians. I'm tellin' ya, she gets so worked up around them. It made her very snippy."

"Ziba? Snippy?" I can't imagine. It takes energy to be snippy.

"Sure," Natie says. "Why else would she seem so embarrassed to be around me?"

The door opens.

"Boyzzz," Ziba says, tickling under our chins with her fingernails. She wears her hair slicked back, bringing her back down to her five-foot-twelve height. With her bolero jacket over a velvet unitard, she looks like a matador. "Your timing is purrfect. Hung's teaching me how to cook Vietnamese."

She does a runway pivot and leads the way into the kitchen. I gesture to Natie by putting a finger to my lips, the Internationally Recognized Signal for "Don't say anything about the Feds." Hung's got a mouth bigger than the Lincoln Tunnel.

We go into the apartment-sized kitchen, which is large enough to have one of those hanging pot racks with shiny copper cookware. The Blabbermouth of Broadway stands at the island, chopping herbs, a bib apron clinging to his compact frame. I take off my sunglasses and he nearly slices off his thumb. "Good God, what happened to your eye?"

"I got in a fight with a clutch purse," I say as I head to the fridge.

Ziba blows a smoke ring, as calm as the caterpillar in *Alice in Wonderland*. "Accessories are so difficult."

My soul smiles. Count on Ziba not to make a big deal.

Natie peers into a kettle. "Does this have MSG? 'Cuz MSG makes my ears itch."

"It's homemade," Hung says. "Or perhaps I should say homo-made."

"What is it?" Natie lifts a spoonful to his mouth.

"Dog-meat stew."

Natie does a burlesque spit take.

"I'm kidding," Hung says. "It's beef noodle soup."

Natie grabs my Saigon Beer and takes a swig. "No wonder we lost the war," he grumbles.

"Hung is a great talent," Ziba says, eyeing me as she leans decoratively against the counter. "He can cook, sew, cut hair, arrange flowers. You should see his costume designs."

I wish Ziba and Kelly would stop trying to foist him on me.

Hung gives a little curtsy like he's auditioning for *The*

Mikado. "When you're Asian and gay there's twice as much pressure to overachieve."

"What's all this?" I say, referring to a pile of brochures on the counter.

"My rent," Ziba says. "In lieu of it, I'm in charge of my cousin's twenty-first birthday party. It's a bore, but at least it's something to do."

"When is it?"

"April eleventh. Everyone wanted Au Bar or Xenon or the Palladium, but those places are so done."

I nod, even though I've never been.

"I chose the Starlight Roof at the Waldorf." Ziba picks up a sprig of mint and smells it. "It's very 1930s Café Society. Marlene Dietrich and Mae West ate dinner there every night."

"And each other," says Hung, turning up the heat. "Of course, we'll have to get rid of those murky drapes and lay a black-and-white tile floor over that truly unfortunate carpeting. But if we light it right, it'll look like the big white set of an Astaire and Rogers movie. Oh, and palms, lots of palms."

Natie frowns, like he's not happy Ziba may have found another five-foot-four sidekick. "Are you sure that's what your cousin wants?"

"All that matters to her is the music," Ziba says. "She wants my uncle to pay for someone like Bon Jovi or Bruce Springsteen."

"Oh, is that all?"

She exhales a serpent of smoke. "I suggested he hire Almost Bruce and hope no one notices the difference."

"You couldn't get away with that," Natie says.

"Why not? Douglas is very convincing. And half the

guests are from Europe. I thought we'd bring him on late when everyone's drunk, have him do a couple of songs, then whisk him out."

"It's too risky," I say.

"Is that your opinion, or British MTV's hottest vee-jay's?"

"My point exactly. Look what happened to me."

"That's because you were working alone," Hung says, untangling a pile of noodles. "Deception requires a team effort."

"You two seem to have it all worked out," Natie says.

Ziba gives her enigmatic Mona Lisa smile. "Hung's been a great help."

Natie looks back and forth between the two of them, a leprechaun who just lost his pot of gold, then says the only thing he can that will top his rival:

"Edward's wanted by the feds."

Wildfire burns across my cheeks. "Natie!"

"It's serious," he says. "He could go to jail."

My head ping-pongs between Ziba and Hung. "It's probably nothing. Really."

Of course, they want to know every sordid detail, starting with the Schlonsky BM and ending with the Saudi Electric Company. Telling them actually helps alleviate my sense of gloom. In their eyes I am both a lovable rogue on a quest for adventure, as well as an unfortunate naïf, trapped in hell by the three-headed Cerberus of Chad, Dagmar, and Lizzie.

When I finish my tawdry tale (and a couple of Saigon Beers), Ziba says, "What are you so worried about? You'll just go to Chad's party in disguise."

Having impersonated a priest in order to launder money, I am not unfamiliar with this approach. "But I'd have to be totally unrecognizable."

"Hung can do it," she says. "He works at the most prestigious costume shop in the city." She turns to him. "You don't mind, do you, darling?"

Hung looks at me like he's a hound dog and I'm a veal chop. "I'd love to dress Edward."

Twenty-five

Over the course of dinner (delicious, although I learn the hard way not to bite into a hot chili), we bat around various ideas, with an emphasis on the heavily bearded. But neither Santa Claus nor a lumberjack seems a likely guest at a financial services party, and a Saudi prince feels beyond my capacities as an actor. We eventually decide to follow the Andy Warhol–will-go-to-an-opening-of-an-envelope model and have me crash the party as the famous French mixed-media artist you've never heard of, Etienne Zazou. We choose to make him French so I'll have an accent to hide behind, as well as a cultural identity known for rudeness.

Meanwhile, Paula gets me a job. "Ah am still not on speaking terms with yew after the disgraceful way you treated us on the occasion of your birthday," she says. "But ah feel it is my duty as a Christian woman to make you aware of a substantial moneymaking opportunity. All it requires is a willingness to use Mistuh Alexander Graham Bell's fine invention, with which I trust you are familiar, despite the fact that you seldom use it to contact those who love yew best."

I apologize again, thank her for the lead, and promise, promise, promise I won't miss *Cat on a Hot Tin Roof*. And a promise is a wingback chair.

The following night I show up at a dubiously downscale building in the mid-Thirties and report to a dingy room furnished only with banks of phones on tables. It's the kind of operation you could easily envision disappearing in the night, like in a psychological thriller where everyone thinks the heroine is insane: *But I swear there was a whole roomful of phones here last night.*

My task is to sell diet supplements.

"It's so easy!" gushes the supervisor. Everyone gushes here. The room is full of would-be and wannabe actors whose enthusiasm derives not from a belief in the efficacy of the herbal product we are hawking, but from the gullibility of the stooges who've already bought it from an infomercial and to whom we're trying to sell more. Starving artists preying on the overfed masses.

I'm led to a folding chair at a table, where I review my script, which has a flowchart of answers to "overcome objections." Apparently, the key to sales is overcoming objections, although these objections seem entirely reasonable to me—specifically, why would someone buy additional quantities of a product that hasn't even arrived yet? I'm told that we put the customer in a "yes" frame of mind by asking lots of questions to which the answer is yes:

"Aren't you tired of carrying around that extra fat?"
"Yes."
"Don't you want to look good for bathing suit season?"
"Yes."
"Aren't you worth at least a dollar a day?"
"Yes."

"Will you go to the bank, withdraw all your money, and send a cashier's check payable to Edward Zanni?"

"Yes! Yes! Yes!"

It's so easy!

While we telemarketers go with the flowcharts, our supervisors hover behind us, crouching and pumping their fists, saying, "Go! Go! Go! Go!" which is supposed to motivate us, but just makes me nervous. Every time one of us makes a sale (and by *us* I mean *them*), a supervisor dashes to the front of the room, rings a bell, and makes a check mark on a blackboard next to the salesperson's name.

For three nights bells ring, fists pump, and fortunes are made, while I come up zero. I am the worst telemarketer in the room. People who've just started that night are already ahead of me.

You'd think that someone who could convince hundreds of truculent thirteen-year-olds to dance could convince a handful of gullible consumers to part with their money, but I can't motivate that party motivator energy. It all feels so hollow and fake, so game-show-hosty. So jazz hands.

And I desperately need the money. Not only am I broke once I pay February's rent, but I got a letter from the landlord saying that New York City rent-control laws clearly state that the only person authorized to write rent checks is the one whose name is on the lease. Namely, Eddie Sanders.

"C'mon," Natie says. "This is New York. There's gotta be squatters' rights." He says he'll look into it.

It takes me three nights to finally make a sale. "Way to go, Edward!" my supervisor says, giving me an "attaboy" shoulder rub and holding up my arm in a victory gesture.

The other telemarketers cheer supportively, as if I were the short bus kid who finally hit the ball in gym.

Thus encouraged, I return to my task with renewed vigor, picking up the phone and calling a buyer in Arkansas.

"Hulloh-oh?" a woman's voice drawls. She sounds like the offspring of first cousins.

"Hi!" I say. "Is this (insert name here)?"

I introduce myself, ascertain that her shipment hasn't arrived yet, and ask if she'd be interested in taking advantage of our special supplemental seven-week package for just $49.95.

"Ah don't know," she says.

"Aren't you tired of carrying around that extra fat?"

"Well . . . yeah. I still ain't lost the weight from mah baby."

I instantly picture her at the stove in her double-wide, stirring a pot of Kraft Macaroni and Cheese while an infant mewls in her arms.

"Don't you want to look good for bathing suit season?"

"Ah don't know. Mah huhzband? He don't laahk it when I get skinny. He gets jealous."

I imagine her husband—an unshaven do-nothing in a KEEP ON TRUCKIN' tank top tossing empty Coors cans at the TV, which he pronounces by putting the emphasis on the first syllable. The fact that he gets jealous of his wife whenever she loses weight leads me to conclude that he has control and possible anger-management issues, the kind of guy who doesn't let her have friends and has alienated her from her family. Probably a wife beater. I know about these things. I saw Farrah Fawcett in *The Burning Bed*.

"Aren't you worth at least a dollar a day?" I say.

"Ah guess so. But I don't got a job, see, on account of the baby. And, well, I'm still in high school."

"Wait. You're still in high school?"

"Uh-huh."

"And you ordered fifty bucks' worth of diet products?"

"Well, it said on the TV it works real good." She pronounces TV with the emphasis on the first syllable. Behind me, the supervisor chants, "Go, go, go!"

No, no, no.

This is not who I want to be. Sure, when I was in high school I engaged in embezzlement, blackmail, money laundering, identity theft, fraud, forgery, and (just a little) prostitution. And, okay, since then I've taken part in corporate espionage, insider trading, more identity theft, and rent-control fraud. But that doesn't mean I have no morals.

"Listen to me," I say into the phone. "When that package arrives, you send it right back, you understand?"

In each ear I hear my customer and supervisor say, "What?"

"Save your money," I say, my voice rising. "You need to finish school. And take care of your baby. And—"

I'm about to tell a stranger she needs to get out of her abusive marriage when my supervisor reaches down and hangs up the phone. "What the hell do you think you're doing?"

I stand up. "I'm quitting."

There are some things even I'm not willing to do.

Plus, I would've gotten fired anyway.

That said, I have no ethical dilemmas regarding entrapment. Come Super Bowl Sunday, my only concern is the feasibility of a scheme devised over too many Saigon Beers. I mean, Eddie Sanders and Zander are one thing, but Etienne Zazou, the famous French mixed-media artist?

"What are you so worried about?" Natie says while I shave. "You're an actor."

"Not according to Juilliard."

"What do they know? Did De Niro go to Juilliard? Did Nicholson?" He leans on the door frame like a koala clinging to a tree. "It couldn't be simpler: You crash the party . . ."

"That's the first thing I'm worried about."

". . . then find Chad and start talking about stocks, casually mentioning you heard that Fuji is taking over Eastman Kodak."

"How did I hear that?" I'll never remember any of this.

"I dunno. Your Japanese dealer told you."

"Got it." This is a terrible idea.

"Now, listen closely; this is the important part: The only way to nail Chad is if he actually trades on that information, which he won't, because the tip's no good. So you have to lead the conversation around to how mad you are at your broker for missing out on the I. J. Sloan takeover of Hibbert and Howard and see if you can get him to brag about it."

"Who's—ow—my current broker?" I nick my Adam's apple, which is why you should never shave and plan espionage at the same time.

"It doesn't matter. Be evasive. You're a famous artist. Act temperamental."

"Shit, I'm bleeding."

Natie hands me a piece of toilet paper. "Then, while he's talking, you reach into your jacket pocket to pull out a cigarette, and simply press down on the tape recorder. Got it?"

"Yes, yes, yes." I dab the toilet paper to my throat.

"Okay," Natie says, "you bought a new tape?"

"I've got an old one I can tape over." Damn, it's not stopping.

"Did you change the batteries?"

"I just put them in." I'm going to look like I've had a tracheotomy.

"Did you check to make sure the recorder's working? 'Cuz sometimes you can put the batteries in upside down and—"

"For God's sake, leave me alone. I'm bleeding to death."

Natie hovers restlessly, tapping Morse code on the doorjamb.

"I'll just check," he says.

Hung lives in Chelsea, a neighborhood where the men make eye contact even after they've passed each other. I'm surprised more of them don't get run over or fall down manholes. Hung's building is a tatty walk-up like mine, with the word *fuck* graffitied on the front door, as if it were a business name.

I climb the stairs to the fifth floor, ring the bell, and a small Asian woman answers the door. She has lustrous shoulder-length hair and wears a navy blue Chanel-type suit with red piping and white buttons. The kind of outfit you'd expect Anita Bryant to wear to a DAR luncheon.

"Hell*oh*," she says.

It's Hung.

I'm not sure how to respond, so I say hi and try to be culturally sensitive by asking if I should take off my shoes.

"By all means," he says, "and everything else."

I give a curt, no-teeth smile. Teeth only encourage people.

"Seriously," he says, "how else do you expect me to dress you?"

I look around the apartment, which is possible to do from the doorway, as it's only one room, as tall as it is wide, painted traffic-cone orange and decorated like it was ransacked by Cossacks. Everywhere you look there's fabric, feathers, beads, hats, and shoes. The stifling atmosphere is exacerbated by the steam heat, which is so tropical the window is wide-open.

"Don't be shy," he says. "At the *Les Miz* fittings they have to get naked because everyone wears this baggy nineteenth-century underwear. You should see those guys flopping around onstage. They should call it *Les Missiles*."

I take off my coat, draping it on the shoulders of a dresser's dummy, and remove my sweater.

"So?" Hung says, twirling. "Whaddya think of my outfit?"

"You look very . . . pretty."

"And witty and gay. I know. Don't you recognize the dress?"

I smooth my hair, which is all staticky from the sweater. "Should I?"

"Honestly, what kind of gay man are you?" He plops a wide-brimmed white hat on the back of his head. "Here's a hint." He sings:

"Diamonds, daisies, snowflakes . . ."

He pauses.

"*That Girl*?" I say.

"Yes!" he says, jumping up and down. "It's an exact

copy of the outfit Marlo Thomas wore in the opening credits. I made it myself." He puts his arm around me and gestures with the other toward some unseen horizon, the way people do in musicals before a number about how we're gonna do it, just you and me.

"Scene: a lonely Gaysian boy arrives in Houston in the summer of 1975, knowing no English. He's a resourceful lad, as clever as he is attractive. While his parents are at work, he engages in an English tutorial by watching syndicated reruns: *Green Acres*, *I Love Lucy*, *The Flying Nun*, *I Dream of Jeannie*, *Bewitched*. All burgeoning feminist mythologies about independent, misunderstood women thwarted by the confines of their surroundings. Women with dreams and ambition and false eyelashes. But of all the rerun heroines, only one manages to escape the stifling expectations of her bourgeois upbringing." He pauses again.

"*That Girl?*"

Hung hugs himself. "From that summer on I wanted to move to New York, get completely overdressed, and fly a kite in Central Park."

I take off my jeans first, because my legs look better than my chest. "Is that what you're doing today?"

"Of course not, silly. I'm going with you."

"I beg your pardon?"

"Don't pop the head, Cassie. You said you needed an assistant."

"No, I didn't."

"Yes, you did. At Ziba's. You asked for my help."

"With a *disguise*."

He grabs my pants.

"Fine. Go in your underwear."

"B-b-but . . ."

He dashes across the room and dangles my jeans out the window.

"No!" I cry.

"Can I go?" he asks.

"Hung, that's not fair."

He drops them onto Eighth Avenue.

Twenty-six

The party is being held at the Limelight, a deconse-
crated church turned disco, and one of the city's hottest
spots. I suppose it's an odd choice for a brokerage house,
but Sandra suggested it because of the video screens.

The line goes down the block, every man uniformed in
a wool coat with his neck exposed. What is it about
straight guys and scarves? It can be so cold your snot
freezes, yet businessmen, politicians, and newscasters
wear those useless felt handkerchiefs, if they wear scarves
at all. Don't they get cold? If so, it seems a silly thing to get
macho about.

Of course, I'm hardly in a position to criticize clothing
choices, dressed as I am in a big, swoopy stole, a vast
kimono-like jacket with bat-wing sleeves, and the kind of
wide, stiff collar you put on dogs to keep them from biting
themselves. My face is obscured by an enormous white
fright wig, a huge pair of Elton John sunglasses, and a
scrubby Vandyke, also white. I look like a character out of
Dr. Seuss. The Zazou. ("Can you Zazou? Me, too!")

"Remember," I say to Hung as we pull up in the taxi.

"You're my Japanese art dealer." Who, for mysterious Asian reasons, feels compelled to dress as That Girl.

"Sorry again about your jeans," he says. "I forgot about that tree."

I open the door to the taxi, saying a silent prayer to Saint Jude. We step out into the frigid air and head straight to the door, if Hung can ever be said to head straight to anything. Ignoring the jeers of the waiting crowd, I walk right up to Hector and Javier, guarding the entrance.

"I hev arrived," I say, pronouncing the last word like I'm spitting up a hairball.

Hector consults his list. "And you are . . . ?"

"I am Zazou!" I huff. "Ze *artiste*."

"You got a Zazou?" he says to Javier. "I don't got a Zazou."

"Zees eez absurd," I say, like I'm going to slap him across the face with a glove. "Do you not know 'oo I em?"

He doesn't have time to answer because there's a whoosh of sound behind me. I turn and a man with a snowy white beard emerges from a limousine like Santa stepping out of his sleigh. The crowd erupts in delight.

It's Rich Whiteman.

Whiteman smiles and waves just like he did when he landed on the deck of the *Europa*. Businessmen with exposed necks swarm toward him to bask in his reflected glory.

Which gives me an idea.

As Whiteman and his entourage approach I throw out my arms in welcome, crying, "Ree-shaaaaaahrt." Whiteman flinches, not an unreasonable reaction when encountering a dandelion with attitude, then grasps my hand with the automatic friendliness of someone who meets too many people to remember them.

"Nice to see you," he says. (Translation: "Who the hell are you?")

"And you, as well," I say, air-kissing each cheek.

My credibility established, we sweep in the door as if on a wave.

I can hardly see the interior of the club through my sunglasses, but it feels like a looted church filled with marauding pirates. Except these pirates are former frat boys in khakis and Gucci loafers.

While we check our coats, Hung mutters, "Do you know who we just walked in with?"

"Sure. Rich Whiteman."

"Don't you realize who he is?"

"Some banker from Texas." Behind him, a large screen displaying a car commercial obscures a stained-glass window.

"Rich Whiteman is one of the biggest backers of the Moral Majority," Hung says, unpinning his hat. "He went on *The 700 Club* and said if God hadn't invented AIDS, he would've."

"That's awful," I say.

"Yeah," Hung says. "I'm thinking trunk of the car, duct tape, cement shoes. You're from Jersey. Surely it can be arranged." He removes his white gloves and puts them in his purse.

I peer around the room and reconsider whether my disguise was a good idea. With free booze, big-screen football, and Sandra's best-looking female motivators, why would Chad be interested in the freak with the hay bale on his head?

I peek over my glasses and see Chad working the room,

gliding through the crowd like the best skater at Rocke-feller Center. Even on a Sunday he's starched and creased, as if his oxford and khakis had been constructed around him.

He stops to say hello to Rich Whiteman, who may or may not know him, and I wish I'd brought Gavin along to read their lips. As Hung and I make my way across the floor, snippets of conversation waft past:

"Nine and a half? That's fuckin' givin' it away."

"You're gonna pay a premium."

"Fuck video. The future is in laser discs."

"So I told that bagel over at Goldman to stick a dreidel up his ass."

"He's very senior."

"You call that piece of shit a vacation home?"

"That's a statistical aberration."

"Me likey that Asian chick."

"I'm tellin' ya, that bitch's lawyer has got my dick in a vise."

"And the sergeant says, 'Actually, sir, they usually just ride the camel into town.'"

I lose sight of Chad in the throng. I lower my glasses to get a better look when I hear a voice behind me that sounds like a chimp stapling its hand to the floor.

"Hey! Hey!"

I keep walking.

"Hello-oh?"

I feel a tap at my sleeve. I turn and there's Sandra, looking at me as if I had a bomb strapped to my chest.

"Who the fuck are you and why are you here?" she says. Actually, that's what her expression says. Her mouth says, "Hi." But it says it in a way that sounds like she's go-ing to ask us to leave or else she's calling security.

"I'm Sandra Pecorino, the party planner."

And I'm screwed.

"I em Zazou. Ze *artiste*. But, of course, you know zat."

I glance around, looking for exit signs.

"Oh! Of course," she says, "I'm a huge fan."

She doesn't recognize me.

I gesture to Hung. "Zees eez my dealer from Japan." Hung gives that intake of breath that precedes an ebullient homo hello. "Unfortunately, she speaks no English."

Hung's mouth purses like he's got something stuck in his teeth.

"So," Sandra says, "what brings you here today?"

"Ze Concorde."

She laughs. I laugh. Hung continues to sulk, his face like a cat's ass.

"I em, how do you say in English, an investor. And I adore ze footbull *américain*."

Sandra laughs again. "Who doesn't?"

I know that sound. That's the sound of sucking up. The laugh of flattery. I am two feet away from her and she believes I am who I say I am. What's more, I believe it. It's as if Etienne Zazou's wig, sunglasses, and beard transfuse his essence into my system. I don't need to push or show that I'm a famous mixed-media artist. I just am—or, in this case, em. Is this what was supposed to happen in mask class?

We exchange pleasantries about Paris, which I've never visited, and I'm so in character that Sandra doesn't seem to notice I don't know what an *arrondissement* is. Finally she asks if she might take a picture.

"*Bien sûr*," I say, finally putting my high school French to good use.

She lifts a walkie-talkie to her mouth. "Where's the

damn photographer? I've got a photo op here." She turns back to us, giving a nervous laugh. "I'll be right back."

The moment she's gone Hung says, "You could've let me have a line, you know."

"Come on," I mutter. "Let's find Chad before she gets back."

"Don't you want your picture in the paper?"

"I've had enough publicity."

I can't see shit with these sunglasses, so I suggest we head upstairs to the choir loft to do reconnaissance. As we emerge from the narrow stairs into the balcony, I see that someone else is already doing the same—with a camera.

It's Dagmar.

Twenty-seven

Naturally, my instinct upon seeing my ex-stepmonster is to run screaming in the opposite direction. Instead I plunge into the empty deejay booth, pulling Hung in with me.

"Hallo?" Dagmar calls.

We hold our breath. I can tell because Hung's lying on top of me.

Another voice answers, "I hope I'm not intruding."

It's Chad. He must have come up the other side.

"Not tat tall," Dagmar says.

Silence. I imagine them each giving smoldering film noir looks.

"A beautiful woman like you ought to be in front of the camera, not behind it," Chad says.

"I vas, in tse past. But now I am too olt."

Hung sticks out his tongue like he's gagging.

"I prefer a woman with experience."

As the crowd below cheers the Giants, I imagine myself a sports announcer: *There's the pass. . . .*

"Vat kind of experience do you like?"

"What kind are you offering?"

He's running with it. . . .

"I didn't say I vas."

"You didn't say you weren't."

Look at him go!

"Chad Severson."

"Chat Severson? I am Dagmar Teufel. I used to verk at Brooks Brothers."

The TV in my mind suddenly goes black.

"Oh, yeah," he says. "We talked on the phone, right? About, uh"—he snaps his fingers—"what's his name . . . ?"

"Edvard Tsanni."

"Right. I saw something about him in the paper, didn't I?"

Liar. Phony. Jerk.

"I thought he verked for you," Dagmar says.

It suddenly occurs to me that he might say something worth taping. I try to reach my recorder, but I'm trapped underneath That Girl.

The tape, I mouth to Hung.

What? he mouths back.

I flick my eyes at my chest. *The. Tape.*

Meanwhile Chad says, "I tried to help him out. He's a troubled kid."

Prick. Slimeball. Sleaze.

"Tsat boy belongs in *chail*. Ach, tse tings I could tell you about him."

Hung slips his hand inside my jacket . . .

"Really?" Chad says. "Why don't you—over dinner?"

. . . he grasps the tape player . . .

"There's this sweet place on Seventieth and Lexington. I know the chef. How about this Saturday?"

. . . he presses the button . . .

"I vould like tsat."

. . . and my chest suddenly screeches . . .

I'VE GOT TO BE WHERE MY SPIRIT CAN RUN FREE,
GOT TO FIND MY CORNER . . . OF THE SKY.

Hung and I both make a mad scramble to turn it off. Outside the booth I hear Chad say, "What the hell is that?"

With lightning speed, Hung hikes up his skirt and starts bucking his hips like he's riding me, shouting:

"FREE ME, ETIENNE, FREE ME!"

Chad and Dagmar appear and I freeze, a deer in the headlights. A strange, French deer with troll-doll hair. Hung, on the other hand, doesn't waste a second. Leaning over, he thrusts his face in mine and gives me a thorough dental exam with his tongue.

"Oh! Zo zorry," Dagmar says.

Hung whirls around. "Well, you ought to be," he says, or something approximating that, because he has a mouthful of white facial hair in his teeth.

Chad scowls. "What the fuck?"

I push Hung off of me and struggle to my feet, my sunglasses falling to the floor. "*Excusez-moi*," I say. Then, grabbing Hung by the hand, I dash for the stairs.

The last thing I hear is Dagmar saying, "Who vuz Tsat Girl?"

I lie awake that night, obsessing about Chad and Dagmar and what she could tell him about me. What if Natie's wrong? What if she finds a way to nail me for embezzling that ten grand I stole from her in high school? Or, worse, goes to Lizzie and Judith and starts stirring up trouble? It doesn't matter whether it's true or not. She's capable of anything, particularly when she's hopped up on steroids for her allergies. By morning I've convinced myself that she's doing everything in her malevolent power to ensure that I spend my life picking up trash on the side of the highway. I won't rest until I know what they talk about on their date. Actually, I won't rest until I can produce some evidence for the SEC by Friday the thirteenth. No, I won't really rest until I'm completely in the clear, have found a way to pay for Juilliard, and convinced the faculty to let me come back.

Then I'll relax.

In the meantime, I turn to the only person who can help me. Tuesday night I go to the box office of the Eugene O'Neill Theatre and ask to speak to Gavin O'Casey.

The box office woman sighs, clearly annoyed. Broadway box office people never seem happy about anything. They're like the tollbooth attendants of the theater world. Without leaving her perch, she leans over and opens a little Hobbit door, muttering instructions.

While I wait, I scan the cast list of *Big River* to see if there's anyone I know, a little game I play to torture myself. Either I feel shitty because I don't know anyone in the cast, which means I'm obviously a nobody; or I feel shitty because I do know someone, which means I'm obviously a nobody. I have enough self-awareness to know how destructive I'm being, but I can't help myself. I'm a hostage to my feelings.

Eventually Gavin pops his head through the gold metal doors, his tangled seaweed curls flopping over his wide, amphibious eyes. "Ouch," he says, referring to my black eye.

"You should see the other guy," I say. "Not a scratch."

Not to get metaphysical about it, but there's a particular energy to an empty theater. How could there not be? Audiences at the Eugene O'Neill have laughed at eight Neil Simon comedies, wept at the original production of Arthur Miller's *All My Sons*, and jeered at one of the most notorious flops in recent memory, *Moose Murders*, a play so bad Frank Rich said its dialogue was only improved by its inaudibility. All of those experiences get trapped in the dusty theater air, which I inhale as if my life depended on it, breathing in as many magic moments as human biology will allow, then exhaling, leaving an invisible part of myself for future audiences.

This is where I want to be.

Gavin and I sit on the steps to the mezzanine stuffing inserts into *Playbills*, Gavin making bridges with his long, skinny legs, like he's doing yoga. I explain to him that this guy I've been seeing is cheating on me, and would he be willing to use his lipreading skills to help me spy? I feel bad lying to him, but I can't risk him telling Paula about my insider trading. "We'll get to wear disguises," I say, hoping it all sounds like a madcap lark.

"When?"

"Saturday night."

He frowns.

"What?" I say. "Will your boyfriend mind?"

"No, he works weekends, too. That's the problem. I'm supposed to work." He tosses his hair, the way pretty girls do. "I'll try to get a sub. Hey, that reminds me, do you want to get on the list?" He looks down. "I, uh, saw in the paper that you lost your job."

I lean over so I can see him. "That'd be great."

He smiles. What a nice face he has, so sweet, yet melancholy. "Most of the ushers are old ladies," he says, "but, for some reason the subs are gay guys. And, well, lately we've been short."

The reason hovers in the air between us.

He writes a number on the back of an insert. "Call the union and ask for Hela. Tell her I recommended you."

Sensing an opportunity for Natie to earn back Paula's money, I ask Gavin if my roommate could do it, too.

"You mean the little guy helping Paula make money?"

Lose money, but why argue semantics?

"Sure," he says. "He's gay, right?"

"Yes," I say.

Serves him right.

I come home to find Willow curled up on my couch, all snuggly in an oversize mohair sweater and paisley leggings as she talks on the phone. She waves like there's nothing unusual about her being here. "Oh, he just walked in," she says. "Well, it was great talking to you, Joy. Yeah, *namaste* to you, too." She hands me the phone. "It's your mother."

My mother's name is Barbara.

"Mom?"

"Hello, dear one."

"Who's Joy?"

"I am," she says.

"You changed your name?"

"I have your father to thank for it, which isn't something you hear me say every day. When you told me he was getting married again, I thought, 'Why am I still carrying this identity around with me? Who's Barbara Zanni? She's one of those legless suburban mothers you only see waving from the window of a station wagon as she ferries her children around.' "

"You never ferried us anywhere," I say. "You sat in the house with the shades drawn, smoking."

"That's because I was miscast in my life as a suburban mother. And I did so ferry you. You just remember the bad parts."

Actually, I remember a childhood spent in front of the TV imagining myself trading quips with Merv Griffin.

She continues: "So I thought to myself, 'Who am I? What am I? I'm Joy! I'm *Joy*!' "

"Joy Zanni?" I say.

"No, your father's name no longer serves. But neither does *my* father's name. I was just telling Willow, women are property in this culture. That's why they call them *sur*-names."

One advantage of living far away from your mother is that you can roll your eyes at her as much as you want.

"Okay," I say, "so what's your new last name?"

"Shapeshifter."

"That's not a name."

"It is for the native people."

"But you're Polish."

"This lifetime," she says. "In the past I was a shaman."

No one ever does anything ordinary in a past life. In past lives, believers always kneel and weep at the feet of the crucified Jesus or have their hearts yanked out by Aztec priests in a ritual sacrifice. You never hear about someone being a medieval serf sleeping in a mud hut with goats and pigs, then dying of cholera.

"That's what your driver's license says—Joy Shapeshifter?"

"Yes. I was gifted it by Zoozook."

"Can you give it back?"

"Don't be fresh. People come from all over to hear Zoozook's teachings. Why, just the other day . . ."

And she's off, sharing the mystical insights of a five-thousand-year-old Pleiadian star being as channeled by Odeen Huckins, the former Utah housewife who is now so disconnected from the earth plane her acolytes push her around the desert compound in a wheelbarrow. I *mm-hmm* and *uh-huh* her, but my mind drifts—not to the cosmos, but to my own surreal life. It's official, I think. I'm an orphan.

"Edward, are you listening?" she says. "What Zoozook is trying to tell us is that we're all star beings. When the universe first began it exploded into an infinite number of atoms. And that's all we are—people, plants, furniture, cars—everything is starlight. There is no you. No me. No son. No mother."

Barbara.

I mean Joy.

Whatever.

I hang up, deflated. Every good-bye with my mother is the first good-bye, a searing reminder of the day she walked out of our house in Wallingford and left on her magical mystery tour. I try to shake off the feeling by turning my attention to Willow, who seems positively logical by comparison.

"I hope you don't mind me picking up your phone," she says, "but I was sitting here—actually, I was sitting there—and it feels weird when someone talks on your answering machine like you're not there but you really are—well, you weren't, but I was. So I picked up and this woman says, 'Who's this?' and I'm like, 'Willow, who's this?' and she says, 'Edward's mom,' and I'm like, 'Oh, my God, I love Edward's mom,' so, naturally we got to talking about your spiritual health."

Naturally.

"She said it was no accident that I'm moving in."

"Whoa, wait, what?"

"Didn't I tell you? I had to get away from Paula and Marcus. It's like *Who's Afraid of Virginia Woolf* over there."

"What happened?"

Willow rises and scoops up a set of darts from a cup. To his immense pride, Natie recently designed a dartboard made up entirely of prime numbers, creating a complicated scoring system that always seems to favor him. Willow throws a dart, missing the board by at least a foot. "Paula started taking these herbal diet pills that this friend of hers sells over the phone—which is really sad, because—well, I don't know what's in them, but they make her like *wooh*—and, c'mon, I left the apartment unlocked, what, two or three times, and she went—well, you understand, right?"

Actually, no. Willow always sounds like she's translating into Chinese and back again.

She throws another dart at the wall. "And Marcus! Well, all I've got to say is . . . really, it's kind of sad, if you think about it. He should be playing kings, not trying to . . . and I don't care if Stanislavski did rehearse *The Cherry Orchard* for seven months; I still see no reason why we should jog around the reservoir at eleven o'clock at night in February."

A third dart lands in the wall.

"Y'know, the object of the game is to hit the board," I say.

"Anyone can do that," she says, tossing a fourth. "Look, I've almost got the Big Dipper."

I give up. "Where's Natie?"

"He's out buying bolts to install my hammock. Isn't that thoughtful? He's just about the most considerate, selfless person I've met in my whole life."

"You sure we're talking about the same guy? Red hair? A little cross-eyed?"

"When I told him I needed a place to stay, he didn't hesitate. Of course, I'll pay a third of the rent. Let's see, $600 split three ways . . ."

"It's $400."

"What? How do you get $400 when you divide $600 three ways?"

"No, the rent is $400."

"Each? You're paying $1,200 to live *here*?"

I swear, talking to Willow is like knitting a sweater out of mashed potatoes.

"The. Rent. Is. Four. Hundred. Total."

"Oh," she says. "I could have sworn Nathan said it was $600."

I clear a spot on Sweeney Todd's chair. "Welcome to my life."

"Oh, there was another call, too," she says. "Some girl screamed, 'Fuckwad,' and hung up."

One of the things I learned in high school is that when you impersonate a priest you are rendered both conspicuous and invisible; whether I was buying beer or laundering money, all anyone ever saw was the collar. Following this crooked line of reasoning, a Hasidic rabbi in a hat with a beard and curls looks pretty much like any other.

So Saturday night, two Hasidic rabbis walk into a bar, which sounds like the setup for a joke. (*Two Hasidic rab-*

bis walk into a bar. And the bartender says, "Why is this night different from all other nights?")

The Orthodox disguise was my idea. Not only does it provide a way for me and Gavin to watch Chad and Dagmar without being recognized; it also ensures that we can do it without That Girl tagging along. With our black fedoras pulled down low, we look like kosher gangsters.

Unfortunately, my only contact with Hasidic Jews comes from the time Paula and I went to 47th Street Photo to buy a camera and discovered it's run entirely by men with curls like telephone cords. When an announcement came over the PA with a call for Shlomo, three guys reached for the phone. With only the vaguest idea of how Hasidic Jews talk, I go for a generalized shtetl-speak, which I learned when I played the tailor Motel Kamzoil in *Fiddler on the Roof* in the eighth grade.

"Ve had a bris around the corner," I tell the hostess at Caprice. "Now ve're feeling a little peckish."

"I'm sorry," she says in a tone that indicates she isn't. "We don't have any tables until ten o'clock."

"Oy," I say. "Then ve'll just sit at the bar and have a little glass tea."

This is all part of my plan. Assuming Chad and Dagmar are seated in Chad's regular spot, we can easily watch them from the bar without having to buy a meal I can't afford. We go to the bar, which is full of malnourished women and the men who love them, and order wine served in glasses the size of fishbowls. I'm glad they're so large, because we're going to need to make them last. The only reason I can afford them is because my rent went down.

I look around the room, gauging the other patrons' reactions to us. Some cast curious glances our way, but none of them has the smirk of someone suspecting a practical joke. They all seem to think we are who we appear to be, and I once again relish the power that comes from acting behind a mask, of truly convincing someone you are another person. It makes me feel ready to live in the scene. One of the biggest problems I had at Juilliard was "playing the outcome," somehow telegraphing to the audience with body language that I knew how the scene was going to turn out, as opposed to seeming like a real person who has no idea what will happen. "Acting is like tennis," Marian Seldes would say. "You show up with your technique, but you don't know what the other actor is going to do."

Here at Caprice, I truly have no idea what will happen, and, my apprehension aside, I feel giddy at the sensation. This is what acting is supposed to feel like. Maybe Juilliard should hold classes in public places instead of those gray, windowless rooms. I imagine a whole new curriculum in which actors are taught to act out in the world before bringing those skills into the classroom. They could call it the Zanni Method.

Suddenly the hostess is in our faces.

"Excuse me, Rabbis," she says. "We can seat you now."

"Vot?"

"We've had a cancellation."

I suddenly wish I knew how the scene will end.

Twenty-eight

"Great," Gavin says. "I'm hungry."

I can't very well tell him I have no money in front of the hostess, so I find myself skulking through the dining room while I sift through the muck in my brain for a nugget of an idea.

We're seated at an undesirable table in the middle of the room, the other diners wedging us in on all sides, as if we were performing Yiddish theater-in-the-round. As God's chosen people, however, we're blessed with an unobstructed view of Chad's regular table, which sits empty, awaiting his arrival.

I hope.

While I undo my napkin origami, Gavin scans the menu, his bulbous eyes widening to make him look even more like a koi.

"They must charge by the ingredient," he says.

I open my menu and see that the entrées cost more than a pair of Reeboks.

I've got to tell him, but I'm worried the other diners might overhear me. Then I realize that I don't need to make any sound for Gavin to understand me.

This is so embarrassing, I mouth, *but I only had enough money to pay for drinks.*

Gavin smiles. "That's okay. We can put it on my credit card."

Are you sure? I'll totally pay you back.

"Don't worry about it."

Why don't we just do appetizers? Otherwise I'll have to donate plasma.

"You can't," he says. "You're gay."

The weedy woman at the next table flinches, toppling her artfully constructed wigwam of food.

"You're uh, talking a little loud," I say.

While homosexuals and Hasidim are not uncommon on the island of Manhattan, you'd be hard-pressed to find them at the same table. Forget the commandments; the haircut alone is a deal breaker.

I'm about to ask why gay people can't give blood when I realize the answer, which makes me feel like a leper. It's only a matter of time before we have to wear bells around our necks.

"So," I say, "how's the show coming?"

He sighs. "Have you ever eaten one of those hot dogs they sell on the street?"

"Yeah."

"It's worse. Marcus is impossible. Now he's in a big feud with Angelo."

"Who?"

"Angelo. You know."

"Oh, of course. It just sounds funny not calling him Father."

"It would sound funny if I did."

"Why?"

"It's one thing to call your boyfriend daddy. . . ."

"WHAT?"

"Didn't you know?"

"No. You're dating *a priest*?"

The man at the next table chokes on his bowl of wine.

"I don't get it," I say, lowering my voice. "Isn't that breaking a commandment or something?"

"Why? He's not coveting his neighbor's wife."

"But priests are supposed to be celibate."

"Technically he is. Celibacy is the renunciation of marriage."

"I thought it meant you couldn't have sex."

"Only by extension. Catholics aren't supposed to have sex outside of marriage."

I shouldn't be surprised. Catholicism is the ultimate loophole religion (sin, confess, repeat), so it makes sense that a priest would know better than anyone how to work the angles. Still, when you go to confession and say, "Forgive me, Father, for I have sinned," you don't expect him to say, "So, who hasn't?"

Gavin goes on to explain, without a whiff of irony, that Angelo considers Marcus's refusal to pay for the rights to *The Music Man* a violation of "Thou shalt not steal." He's interrupted, however, by the arrival of Dagmar and Chad.

"That's him," I say, pointing with my bearded chin.

Gavin cranes his slender neck to see. "He's cheating on you with a woman?"

I must confess that I hadn't thought how I was going to explain all this to Gavin, particularly if Dagmar starts ranting about my past misdeeds and Chad admits my current ones. Naturally Gavin will tell Angelo, who'll tell Paula, who'll be furious with me for breaking the law. Not to mention implicating her.

My vision of disaster is interrupted by the waiter, an

animated actor type currently starring in a one-man ex-
travaganza called *Our Specials Tonight.*

Polenta! The Musical.

"I'll have the wood-fired shrimp in crab sauce," Gavin
says.

"Oh . . . kay," Our Specials Tonight says. "And you,
sir?"

"I'll hev the Black Forest ham vit goat cheese."

His eyebrows descend under the weight of heavy skep-
ticism. "Really?"

"Yeah," I say, giving him the evil eye. "You gotta problem vit that?"

"No, no," he says. He backs away as if I might explode.

"Why do you think he looked at us like that?" Gavin
asks.

I shrug Hebraically, like a Catskills comic.

I glance over my shoulder at Dagmar and Chad, who
are scanning their menus. "So what are they saying?"

Gavin peers across the room. "He's telling her the veal
is excellent. She says she's a vegetarian."

"So was Hitler."

He then relates a banal litany of Dagmar's various food
allergies and her boneheaded theories on food combining.
Gavin narrates as they swap autobiographies, the way
people do when they're getting to know each other, the sun
shining bright on Chad's old Kentucky home, Dagmar
blessing her Austrian homeland forever. Eventually, while
we're dismantling the sculpture of our appetizers, Gavin
says, "Oh, wait. Chad's saying how disappointed he was
when you got in trouble, that he didn't know you that well,
but he thought of you as someone he could mentor. Just
like a rich, wide man mentored him."

"Rich Whiteman?"

"Yeah, he's saying something about a role model, an inspiration. I don't know; I can't tell—he's got bread in his mouth. Hang on. He's swallowing; he's leaning in to talk to her; he's putting his hand on hers; he's saying: 'How would you like to be a spy?' "

The rest comes in a blur: " 'Call me at home, no matter how late . . . information is the currency of democracy . . . Thomas fucking Jefferson . . . filthy fucking rich . . . Ronald fucking Reagan.' "

There it all is, everything I need to turn Chad in to the feds, and I have no way to tape it. I'm a failure as a spy. I'm a failure as an actor. And, what's worse—what's far, far worse—I'm a failure as a human being. Because of my stupidity and greed, I helped Chad get information that made money for Rich Whiteman, the religious wing nut who would rather see people like me dead.

Suddenly I feel like I'm going to be sick, like there's something gnawing at my gut, trying to devour me from the inside out. Gavin signals for the check, then just makes it worse by assuming the best, telling me it's a good thing I got away from this creep before he tried to turn me into a spy.

Our Specials Tonight returns, handing Gavin his credit card. "I'm sorry, Rabbi O'Casey," he says, "but your card has been rejected."

Gavin's face goes slack, like a marionette whose puppeteer suddenly had a stroke.

"That's all right, vaiter," I say. "Ve can use mine." I pull my credit card out of my wallet and hand it to him.

"Thank you, Rabbi . . . Zanni."

As soon as he's left, Gavin says, "I thought you said you didn't have any money."

"I don't. Let's go."

We rise and make our way to the door.

"Excuse me," Our Specials Tonight calls across the room. "Excuse me!"

"Faster," I say, but, being deaf, Gavin doesn't hear me. "Stop them!"

I push on Gavin's back and two renegade rabbis tumble onto the sidewalk. We both seem to understand that this is the kind of neighborhood where the cops come right away, so we dash across Lexington Avenue, a taxi screeching to a halt and blaring its horn.

As we round the corner I start shedding clothes, pulling off my hat, coat, and prayer shawl, then yanking at the curls bobby-pinned to my head, pulling fistfuls of fake hair off my face. Seeing me, Gavin does the same. By the time we reach the subway, shivering in our shirtsleeves, we look like two sweaty waiters on their way home from work. Tomorrow morning, the residents of East Sixty-ninth Street are going to find a trail of Hasidic couture and wonder why two of God's chosen people suddenly evaporated. A Rabbi Rapture.

The following day I call the credit card company and tell them I left my card at 47th Street Photo and, when I went back to get it, it wasn't there.

"Sure," Natie says, "blame the Jews. Everyone else does."

In the weeks that follow, I stake out Chad so I can "accidentally" run into him and record an incriminating conversation about his trading of Hibbert & Howard.

It's not as easy as it sounds.

Every afternoon I go to the coffee shop in the lobby of his office building, getting jacked on refills while masses of humanity pour out, cascading down the steps and into the ground like a waterfall. I keep thinking of Sondheim's "Another Hundred People":

It's a city of strangers. . . .

And every one of them has a life, just like me. They leave and go home to friends or families or roommates. Even the most misanthropic must know at least ten people, and each of those ten knows ten more and ten more after that, multiplying onward and upward until thousands become millions and millions become billions. Coming and going every minute of every day. The enormity of it makes my head spin, although that could just be the coffee.

I thought when I got into Juilliard that I would become something special, that I would live a life set apart from and above the maddening throng. But as I sit here watching that throng I realize that I'm just one of billions of people, most of them with dreams that will never come true. One tiny ant in a colossal colony, an extra in a big cosmic picture show.

It sucks.

As the crowds go and come, my mind wanders and I keep forgetting to look for Chad. It takes over a week before I finally spot him striding out of the building like a lifeguard rushing into the water. I follow him, but he flies down the steps and into a waiting Town Car.

He's virtually untouchable. Every day he leaves his apartment in a taxi, gets driven to Wall Street, then reverses the process. There's no bumping into him as he walks to the subway, while I pretend I'm on the Upper East

Side visiting Ziba, or on Wall Street, where I have no business being.

I have even less luck on the weekends. Sutton Place is not like my neighborhood, where Lizzie could wait on my stoop for hours. Sutton Place has doormen who brush you away like dirty snow and threaten to call the cops. I manage to get in some surveillance from a pay phone on the corner of First Avenue, but can't linger there long enough to be effective.

The Friday-the-thirteenth deadline from the SEC is less than a week away, and I've got nothing. Literally. I have $139 in my bank account, $133 for my share of rent, which is due on the fifteenth, and $6 for the rest of my living expenses. I trudge home in the cold, my head congested with impending doom and a burning sinus infection.

I'm just passing the Nowhere subway station when I notice one of the many mad vagrants who wander New York's streets every day. Grizzled and prematurely old, he wears a baggy overcoat and a woolly hat.

"Will you help me?" he cries. "Won't someone help me?"

Pedestrians circle around him, immune to beggars, lost in their Walkman worlds. Unlike everyone else, I make eye contact with him. There's something different about this guy.

He holds up a bank deposit envelope, the kind you use at ATMs. "Can you help me? I-I-I found this and I don't know what to do." His face is tanned with a layer of city grime.

I look inside the envelope and see half a dozen antique coins. While the only thing I know about numismatics is the definition of the word (courtesy of Natie's coin collection, such a Nudelman thing to collect), the largest coin does say 1864 and has a portrait of someone with the regal profile of Marian Seldes. I close the envelope, noticing that there's a phone number on the outside.

"Someone probably dropped these on the way to the bank," I say. "You should call this—"

The guy presses his hands to his head, like he's trying to silence the people who live there. "No! No! No! No! No!"

"Okay," I say in the most therapeutic tone I can muster on short notice. "It's okay. How about if I call for you?" He gives a hesitant nod and follows me to a nearby pay phone. I dial.

"Sterling residence. This is Clark speaking."

"Uh, hi, my name is Edward Zanni and this . . . um . . . gentleman on the street handed me a bank envelope—"

"You found our coins!"

Clark Sterling immediately launches into a monologue about how relieved he is, that his wife will be so pleased, and if the person who found them would just come right over to the East Side, there's a $100 reward.

I relay the good news to the guy, who responds in the same disoriented fashion as before:

"I'm not goin' . . . I just wanna . . ." He covers his eyes and, for reasons known only to him, starts singing "Camptown Races":

Camptown ladies sing this song,
Doo-dah, doo-dah.

I speak into the phone. "He's kind of freaking out."

"Listen," Clark Sterling says, "I hate to ask you this, but I have to get those coins back. Is it possible for you to get to an ATM and give him the $100 yourself? I'll pay you back, of course. And just to make it worth your time, I'll pay you an extra $100, as well."

A hundred bucks for doing a good deed? It's a sign from the gods. I must be owed from some self-sacrificing past life as a goat-snuggling serf.

I explain the situation to the crazy guy between doo-dahs, then get the Upper East Side address from Clark, who tells me he'll reimburse me for a taxi, as well.

I go to the ATM, sneering at the lady who sneers at me for bringing a smelly street person into the bank lobby. I give him the money, tell him not to buy booze, then hail a cab. I love hailing cabs. It matches my vision of the life I'm supposed to lead. As we sail through the park, New York suddenly feels sunnier and prettier to me, the Manhattan of Gershwin songs or Woody Allen movies.

I arrive at the Park Avenue address and tip the driver generously—I'm being reimbursed, after all—then hop out of the cab with the exuberance of a movie star exiting a limo at a premiere. I approach a mustached doorman clapping his hands together to stay warm.

"Hi! I'm here to see Clark Sterling."

He laughs, revealing a gold tooth. "Yeah, you and about ten others."

I must appear as confused as I feel, because he says, "There's nobody here by that name."

"But . . ."

"Look in the envelope."

Twenty-nine

Thoughts rattle around my brain like sneakers in a dryer: *How did he know about the envelope? What's going on? Oh, my God, I just emptied my bank account to a total stranger.* My hands trembling, I pull open the envelope and find a half dozen quarters. The crazy guy must have switched them on me. Except he wasn't crazy. He's a con artist. An actor. If I weren't so hosed, I'd appreciate the verisimilitude of his performance.

I stagger down the street, my brain in a fog. A hundred bucks, gone. Plus cab fare, which is just cruel. I mean, he'd already gotten my money. Why did he and his cronies have to stick me with cab fare, too? How could someone be so vicious? At least my own brand of swindling is a victimless crime. (Okay, I did dine and dash. But that was an honest dishonest mistake.) I mean, when Natie and I bought Pharmicare options, no one got hurt, right?

Right?

As I once again trudge across town, cursing the malevolent syndicate that preys upon trusting innocents like myself, nagging doubts about my own innocence start to nip at my heels. Is it possible that whomever we bought the options from had to hold on to the shares until the options expired? In which case, they couldn't dump the stock when it plummeted. If someone owned Pharmicare at $30 a share and committed to selling it to me at $35 a share, but it went down to $10, that meant they lost, let me see, 750 shares times twenty equals, . . . $15,000? Did I do that?

I don't want to know.

The pressure—both in my sinuses and my life—finally gets to me and I sink into a Nyquil-induced coma for a few days. Natie periodically hydrates me with herbal teas, mixing Sweet Apple Chamomile with Sleepytime for sweet dreams. He and Willow offer to make up the difference on the rent while stalling on the utilities by sending the phone company the check for the electric bill and vice versa. I do my best to ignore the February thirteenth deadline from the SEC, praying that Reagan's pledge to reduce the size of government means the office is understaffed.

This cold must be going around, as I start getting calls to substitute usher. Of course I take them, infecting the old ladies and guaranteeing job security for me and Natie, who takes the gigs so he can pay back Paula. Maybe it's the head cold, but what I see onstage depresses the hell out of me. There are only fourteen shows playing, most of them ranging from at-least-it-didn't-suck disappointing to what's-that-smell awful. The lone bright spot is John Guare's *House of Blue Leaves*, which has a monologue that would be perfect for my reaudition to Juilliard. That is, assuming I don't go to jail. For several nights in a row I fidget in the back of the theater, restraining myself from leaping onto the stage because the actor playing the role is totally underplaying it, which is wrong, wrong, wrong. I mean, the character is plotting to blow up the pope because his father doesn't pay attention to him. He's so crazy he gets mistaken for retarded. I would make a meal out of that role. I'm sure the only reason this Ben Stiller got the part is because he's Jerry Stiller and Anne Meara's son. It's obvious he'll never amount to anything.

Even more dispiriting are the audiences. Up until now, I never really noticed who goes to Broadway shows. I guess I was too wrapped up in my excitement at what was happening onstage to look. But as I meet the Bridge and Tunnel crowd face-to-face, I discover that a disturbing number of them are the kind of people who, when asked about the show, will tell you about their seats. The middle-class New Jerseyites I was rebelling against when I decided to become an actor are the very ones I'm going to have to entertain. Suddenly my dream of glittering Broadway stardom doesn't shine quite as much.

Disillusionment! The Musical.

The dream dims even more when an usher at the Gershwin gets pneumonia, resulting in my first long-term temp assignment. When I tell Kelly I'm going to be ushering *Starlight Express*, which goes into previews next week, she says, "That's great! It'll be like we're working together."

Sure. *At this performance, the role of the bitter spectator will be played by Edward Zanni.*

As a swing, Kelly doesn't perform at the first preview, so she's waiting for me in the lobby after the show. As I descend the escalator (the Gershwin being one of those newer theaters that feels like a hotel) she smiles and gives a Miss America wave, not in a too-many-teeth Miss Texas way, but as if she were from some low-key, likable state, like Kansas or Vermont. She wears her new *Starlight Express* satin show jacket, which is the Broadway equivalent of the varsity letterman jacket, announcing to the world that she's one of the cool kids.

A more evolved person than I would marvel at it, asking her to model it, then jumping up and down, screaming, "Look! You made it!"

So that's what I do, summoning every acting skill I have to simulate euphoric delight. By way of contrast, I'm clad all in black, so I can blend in. That's my job. To be blendinable. Blendinadvertent. Blendinadequate.

"So?" she says, as blithe and untroubled as spring. "Whadja think?"

What did I think?

To call *Starlight Express* garbage is an insult to sanitation workers. A noisy, epilepsy-inducing assault on the senses, it is the Chuck E. Cheese of musicals, a show so astonishingly vapid it makes *Cats* look like *A Lion in Winter*.

I know it shouldn't bother me so much. I mean, it's only a musical, right? But the show inflames me with rage. I feel soiled by it. Abused. Cheated. I want to hand out flyers that say, *Warning: This performance contains material that may insult your intelligence.*

Don't get me wrong. I'm not opposed to light entertainment: *Guys and Dolls; Little Shop of Horrors; You're a Good Man, Charlie Brown*—these are frothy diversions that at least have a satiric edge to them, shows that entertain without condescending. But the Greeks did not invent theater so we could spend sixty bucks to watch *The Little Engine That Could*. They invented it so we could have an emotional catharsis. And the only emotion I feel at *Starlight Express* is the desire to flip the circuit breakers and send everyone home.

What did I *think*?

"It's astonishing," I say.

"Really?" Kelly says. "You're not just saying that?"

Of course I'm just saying that. Don't push your luck.

"No, no, no," I say, gauging her reaction for signs of irony. "I just can't wait to see you do it."

"Wow," she says. "I really thought you'd hate it. C'mon, I'll show you the set."

She links her arm through mine and I see she has a wrist brace, on which is scrawled, *Kell on Wheels*, *Kellraiser*, and Cats *is for pussies.*

"What happened?"

"You should see the girl I ran into," she says. "She got ten stitches. Now we have our own unit at St. Clare's on standby."

This isn't theater, I think; *it's vehicular homicide.*

Kelly leads me through a door to backstage, which, I have to admit, makes me feel pretty cool.

Of course, it's not like I haven't been backstage at a Broadway show before. I know this makes me sound like a colossal dork, but back in high school we used to wait at the stage door for autographs. Sometimes, if there were just a few of us, we'd get invited backstage. But that was as a fan, an outsider. This time it's as a friend.

Being a newer building, the Gershwin has none of the dusty romance that its name implies. It's just concrete hallways with fluorescent lights. Still, there's an electric vibe in the air, and the cast is pumped with the excitement of the first preview. Seeing them up close—makeup streaked, costumes half-off to reveal sweaty T-shirts, heads encased in wig caps—gives me an ineffable thrill.

As much fun as backstage is, with its giddy dancer banter, I feel the stage itself calling to me like sonar. I'm relieved and excited when Kelly finally leads me into the wings.

Wings are appropriately named because they're the part of the theater that allows the play to take flight. Dizzyingly tall as a Gothic cathedral, they have a hushed mystery to them, and I feel compelled to lower my voice even though the show is over. The wings are my favorite place to watch from, because you can see what's happening on- and offstage at the same time. It's like being able to watch the whole world at once, one part brightly lit, the other in shadow. I imagine this is how astronauts feel. Or people who die and come back.

As we hover in the wings, Kelly points out the components of the three-story set, which looks like a discotheque for androids. With a budget of $8 milion, *Starlight* is the most expensive musical ever mounted on Broadway, and it looks it. Three steel bridges connect stage right and stage left: "Kong," which hangs overhead like a chandelier and can tilt, fly, rotate, and do everything but wash the costumes; the "Teeter-Totter," which allows the cast to skate uphill from the stage to either side of the second level (and down again), depending on whether it's teetering or tottering; and the unimaginatively named "Front-of-House Bridge," which looms thirty feet up, parallel to the proscenium. Each bridge comes equipped with hydraulic gates that lower like guillotines to prevent the actors from flying off into space, which has already happened once. "This shit's dangerous," Kelly says. "It's like skating on a building while it's being built."

As much as I hate the show and everything it represents, I can't help but admire the actors. The sheer athletic achievement of racing up and down ramps and movable bridges thirty feet in the air at thirty miles an hour—plus doing flips on roller skates—is nothing short of remarkable. It gives new meaning to the word *training*.

As Kelly plays tour guide—over a hundred thousand pounds of steel, fifty miles of cable, blah, blah, blah—I can't resist the magnetic pull of the stage. Without asking, I step out of the wings, inching down a sloping bowl that leads to the stage floor.

Behind me, Kelly says, "Edward, I don't think you should . . ."

I don't care about *should*. Not anymore.

The auditorium looks cavernous, nearly two thousand empty seats. I walk downstage, where ramps circle the first ten rows, and stare out at the house. From where I stand, my post in the rear mezzanine looks microscopic, a light-year away, and I ache at the thought of my irrelevance. This is where I belong, down here. Center stage.

It feels like home.

But each night I return to a balcony so high up you could probably see Jersey on a clear day. That first week Kelly goes on for two previews, each time as an electrical component, whatever that is. I'm excited for her, but, to be honest, I can't tell which one she is. Between the cartoon costumes and amplification so artificial they might as well be lip-synching, they could switch actors two or three times a night and no one would know the difference.

After seething in the dark for a week, I finally figure out why the show makes me so angry. When I go to a musical I am looking to be more than entertained. I am seeking a transformative experience, a transcendental one. There's something about that Broadway sound—the swell of the orchestra as the King thrusts his arm around Mrs. Anna, the entire chorus telling Mame she's just sensational—that sends a shiver across my cheeks and down my neck, making the hair on my arms stand on end. The most stirring moments in symphonies or operas and the pulsing beat of rock and gospel may thrill me, but only musicals chill me. *Starlight Express*, on the other hand, leaves me cold. The only moment that comes close is when Rusty gets religion and sings, "I am the starlight," but even that feels like the musical equivalent of a Hallmark card.

Audiences eat it up with a spoon.

Unless Kelly's on, I hang out in the mezzanine lobby with my ushering partner, Mrs. Fiamma, a gray, wheezing smokestack of a woman who reminds me of Dustin, the roly-poly hopper car in the show, particularly because she has her Ash Wednesday ashes on her forehead when we meet. She doesn't do anything during the performance— neither reads nor does crossword puzzles nor knits—she just sits there like a barnacle.

"Whatcha readin'?" she croaks. She's got a voice like a shovel being dragged across a driveway.

"*Act One*, by Moss Hart." I found it on Eddie's bookshelf. It's a memoir by the playwright of *You Can't Take It with You* and *The Man Who Came to Dinner*. I dove into it to escape from my worries and haven't come up for air since. Like a toddler who covers his eyes so no one will see him, I'm hoping if I forget about the SEC, they'll forget about me and the fact that I ignored their deadline. "Have you read it?"

She shrugs. "He directed *My Fair Lady*, right?"

"I think so."

"I met him."

I blink. "You did?" This feels inconceivable to me, as if Broadway's Golden Age were the Bronze Age. Moss Hart isn't someone you meet.

She fans herself with a *Playbill*. "Back in the fifties I worked the Mark Hellinger. I musta seen *My Fair Lady* a thousand times."

I put the book down, ravenous to devour the real thing. "What was it like?"

"Well, the Hellinger was a nothin' house," she says, warming to the tale. "One flop after another. *Ankles Aweigh*, *The Girl in Pink Tights*. Real dogs. There was that musical about the Amish, what was it called? It had what's-her-name, Barbara Cook, but she wasn't really Barbara Cook yet. Anyway, there I am, with the flops, while my girlfriend Maxine is at the St. James workin' *The King and I* and *Pajama Game* back-to-back. In those days, when you had a hit, everybody came to see it and the show was all over *Life* magazine and Rosemary Clooney's singin' 'Hey There' on the radio. It was so different back then. And they dressed up, too. Furs and diamonds. Not like today, with these tourists and their hairy legs. Now they show up lookin' like they're gonna wash a car. Anyways, I'd been an usher since the war. Ya' think I woulda gotten a decent house by then, but I always hadda mouth on me. So there I am at the Hellinger, thinkin', 'A musical based on Shaw? It'll last a month, but feel like a year.' Which goes to show ya' how much I know. Opening night, there's the director, Mr. Hart, wearin' out the carpet in the back of the theater, pacin' back and forth, and I'm at my station, watchin' the show, and thinkin', 'This is pretty good.' But the audience is kinda polite, and Mr. Hart is so nervous he actually walks out of the theater with Mr. Lerner and Mr. Loewe. Just walks out."

I hear these names and they scarcely seem real to me.

"A half hour later they come back, smellin' of booze, just in time for 'The Rain in Spain.' And I am tellin' ya', the audience blows the roof off. It's like nothing I have ever seen. And then, two minutes later, Julie Andrews steps downstage and sings, 'I Coulda Danced All Night.'"

Mrs. Fiamma lays her hand on her breast, almost in supplication.

"It was like goin' to heaven. And Mr. Hart turns to me, so handsome he was, with those dark eyes, and he says, 'We're a hit.' Just like that, like I wuz somebody." She smiles, her eyes misting. " 'Cuz that's when he knew. He was a very nervous type, y'know, did a lotta psychoanalysis—I'm not gossiping; he talked about it in the papers. But that's when he knew the show was gonna be okay. And I was Right There. Oh, you shoulda seen it. When it was over the audience came runnin' down the aisles to the stage, standin' on their seats, clappin' with their hands over their heads. From then on it was the hottest ticket in town, sold out for two years, the number one record album in America. People camped out in sleeping bags to get standing-room tickets. Everybody came to see it. You name 'em, and I showed 'em to their seats. Cary Grant, Lucille Ball, Eleanor Roosevelt. During the show you'd look out at the audience and they wuz all smilin'. Like they wuz in love." She pauses, lost in the memory.

"What other shows did you work?" I ask, a child stalling at bedtime. *One more story, please, please, please.*

"Well, it musta been, I dunno, 1958, they opened the Lunt-Fontanne over on Forty-sixth Street and I got assigned over there. Boy, was I mad. For me, *My Fair Lady* was better than church. But I hadda go, and it opened with this thing starring the Lunts, *The Visit?* You ever heard of it? I still don't know what the hell it's about, and I thought, 'Uh-oh, here we go again.' And then we got *The Sound of Music.*"

"With Mary Martin."

"No, Dean Martin. Of course Mary Martin. The critics hated it, called it *The Sound of Mucous*; oh, they were so mean, but I loved it. So beauteeful, it was. I watched it every single time. The curtain went up, and there was Mary Martin in a tree. In a tree! She hadda be forty-five years old, but she seemed half that. She really was Peter Pan. And people would come back five, six times.

"One night, just before we open the house, there's a blackout. Poof. The whole city goes dark. So the house manager goes out on the street and tells everybody waitin' that it's so dark backstage nobody can put on their costumes or their makeup; they can't even move the set. But the audience won't budge. So Mary Martin's husband, who was also the producer, sends the crew out to get as many flashlights as they can. Naturally, they ask all us ushers if they can use ours, too. Then they do the show in the dark holding flashlights under their chins. Like they're tellin' ghost stories at camp. Oh, it was so much fun. No costumes, no sets. Just . . . *The Sound of Music*. About a half hour inta the show the lights came on, and there they all were, in their bathrobes and street clothes, like a spell had been broken. So they took a little break and the crew moved the set and the actors put on their costumes, but we wuz almost disappointed. It was so . . . magic."

From inside the theater we hear the siren announcing another train race onstage, and my rage returns. If New York was plunged into a blackout, you couldn't do *Starlight Express* by flashlight. The orchestra isn't even in the goddamn theater; they're piped in from a studio on the fourth floor by the men's john. It's so dishonest, asking us to root for a plucky little steam engine while garishly reveling in electronic overkill. They ought to call the show *Starlight Excess*.

I got to the theater too late. Broadway is dying, just like Eddie Sanders and his friends.

Thirty

After the show, I walk Mrs. Fiamma to the subway, pressing her for details, hoping for more stories of Broadway's Golden Age, maybe a tale of New York during the war—a night entertaining soldiers at the Stage Door Canteen, a quickie marriage with a sailor before he ships overseas? Or perhaps a melancholy tale of dreams deferred—the failed chorine who resigned herself to a life taking tickets. I want to—need to—go back to a time when the theater still seemed to matter. When the only steel onstage was Ethel Merman's vocal cords. When doing a hit song in a hit show could land you on the cover of *Life* magazine. When Moss and Kitty Carlisle Hart lived a Cole Porter–infused fantasy.

But Mrs. Fiamma is tired. She tells me she grew up in Brooklyn, where she still lives, got a job ushering through a family friend, and has been doing it ever since. It's rough on her knees, the audience has no manners, and she hates the commute. Her son keeps tellin' her to retire.

"Why do you still do it?" I ask as she waddles down the street, purse in one hand, tote bag in the other, like a pack mule.

"You know that joke about the guy who shovels after the elephants in the circus?" she says.

"No."

"There's this guy. He works at the whaddya call it, the Barnum and Bailey's Irish Circus, and it's his job to shovel after the elephants, y'know, shovel their, uh, bowel movements, right? So he's shovelin', and some guy who's just seen the circus comes out all excited—he's eatin' Cracker Jacks and swingin' one of them little flashlights. He says to the guy shovelin', he says, 'Buddy, you're one lucky fella. It must be real exciting workin' here.' And the guy shovelin' says, 'Excitin'? Look what I'm doin'. Every day I stand around these smelly elephants and shovel their bowel movements. Then I come home and my wife makes me sleep on the fire escape 'cuz I stink. Believe me, brother,' he says, 'This is the lousiest job in the circus. No, no,' he says, 'this is the lousiest job in the world.' So the other guy says, 'If you hate it so much, why don'tcha quit?' And the guy shovelin' says, 'What? And leave show business?'"

She laughs, like a car needing a new muffler. We stop in front of the Fiftieth Street station, the Nowhere station.

"You need help down the steps?" I ask.

"Nah, I can manage." She heaves her purse onto her shoulder.

"Well, good night, Mrs. Fiamma."

She pats my hand. "Call me Lily."

Lily.

As I pace down Broadway, a veil of sadness descends over me and I speed up, trying to shake it off. Maybe it's enough for her, but, when I'm Mrs. Fiamma's age, I don't want my theater stories to be about a three-word conversation with a director in the back of a theater, or having my flashlight shine on the face of someone else, even if it is a Broadway legend like Moss Hart or Mary Martin. I don't know what I'm going to do with myself, but I know I don't want to spend thousands of nights in the dark in the rear mezzanine while someone else stands in the spotlight center stage. I will not play a minor role in my own life.

As I pass Colony Music I scan the covers of the vocal selections in the window—Huck and Jim in *Big River*, the dancers in *A Chorus Line*, the urchin from *Les Miz*—my face reflected in the glass. How did I end up on the outside looking in? When I was in high school I thought for sure I'd be the next Kevin Kline, a serious Shakespearean actor who also does Broadway musicals and movies. When I saw him romping around as the Pirate King in *The Pirates of Penzance*—at the Gershwin, as a matter of fact—I knew that's who I wanted to be, albeit a shorter, stockier version. It was the same feeling I had after I saw *Annie* when I was eleven and spent months bumping and grinding while belting out "Easy Street." I'm sure my parents took one look at me and thought, *My son'll come out—tomorrow.*

Then, as if I were actually peering into my past, I spy Paula wearing a tartan tam-o'-shanter with a matching scarf, a large rhinestone pin attached to her herringbone overcoat.

She glances up and immediately starts talking, as if I can hear her, her fingers knitting sweaters in the air. She heads toward the entrance, bumping into another shopper as she goes. I enter the store, relieved to get warm.

"I shouldn't be happy to see you," she says. "I should be bitter and resentful that you missed *Cat on a Hot Tin Roof*. I should walk right past you like I don't see you."

"I'm so sorry—"

"What has gotten into you?" she says, swatting me with a glove. "You abandon us on your birthday. You don't answer my calls. It's so *rude*."

She punctuates the statement with an exceedingly noisy fart.

"You'll have to excuse me," she says, embarrassment rouging her cheeks. "It's this wretched diet. You're supposed to stay full by eating as much cabbage soup as you want." She pulls a bottle of perfume out of her purse and spritzes the air. "And do you know how much cabbage soup I want? NONE! But otherwise I'd be reduced to eating paint chips."

She continues talking as she leads me outside.

"It's positively *mortifying*," she says. "The other day I was rehearsing my scene for the presentation to agents, and, at the climactic moment when Mrs. Kendal touches the Elephant Man's hand . . . fffftttttttpppppp. Don't laugh; it was like a truck backfiring. I tell you, I'm at my wit's end. And don't even ask how things are going with Marcus. . . ."

"Why? What's going on with—"

"I can't even talk about it. He's completely unreasonable. If I didn't love him so much I would hate him, loathe him with every fiber of my being." She thrusts her arm through mine and starts walking in the exact direction from which I came. "He simply isn't qualified to run a theater company. There's no schedule, no organization. We keep losing actors. I'm like, 'Who's going to rehearse on their off hours in Hoboken for no money for *three months*? I don't care if it is deconstructed and ironic, it's still just the fucking *Music Man*.' "

"You said that to him?"

"No. But I thought it really hard." She pulls her scarf around her neck as a bitter wind whips down Broadway. "I tell you, I can't *sleep*, I'm so worried. I'm just hoping that, once I get a little seed money for the company, we can start paying . . . What? Why are you looking like that? What happened?"

I stop, the cold stinging my cheeks. "It's about your money."

"Oh, my God. Natie lost it."

"Sort of, but—"

"I'm having palpitations. Look at my hands."

"Let me explain."

She grabs my arms and shakes me. "DON'T YOU UN-DERSTAND? MY RENT IS DUE!"

"We have it; we have it!"

She clutches her hand to her chest. "Don't do that to me. I'm very vulnerable these days."

I explain to her what happened, and how Natie's earning back her $500 by ushering.

"That's very decent of him," she sniffs. "Y'know, it says a lot for Natie that he would return my money."

I don't tell her the part about the trade being Almost Legal.

There's the usual pile of take-out menus on the floor of the vestibule, branded with the footprints of neighbors who couldn't be bothered to throw them away. I swear, this building is like Gorky's *The Lower Depths*. I scoop them up without looking, trying to convince myself how delicious my cup of Top Ramen is going to be.

But my appetite disappears the moment I open my mail:

UNITED STATES SECURITIES AND
EXCHANGE COMMISSION
Washington, D.C. 24601

SUBPOENA

Pursuant to Section 10b-5 of
The Securities Exchange Act of 1934

EDWARD ZANNI

Is ordered to appear at
3 World Financial Center, Suite 400
No later than 10:00 a.m., Friday, March 20, 1987

**Failure to appear will result in a charge of
contempt, with a possible fine or incarceration.**

Thirty-one

I'm covered in sweat by the time I reach my apartment. Four floors, steam heat, and possible incarceration will do that to you.

I need evidence. I need a lawyer. I need a Valium.

I need my father.

Damn.

Damn. Damn. Damn.

Get a root canal. Work in a bank. Watch Sally Struthers in the female version of *The Odd Couple*. These are trials I would rather endure than admit to my father that I need his help. He's going to go ape shit.

I look at the genuine fake Cartier I bought on the street, which reads 11:15 Edward Standard Time, which means it's 11:04. Clenching everything clenchable, I succumb to the last refuge of the truly desperate, I call home.

A woman answers, her accented "Hello" indicating it's *mi madre nueva.*

"*Hola, Milagros,*" I say, trying to sound chipper and bilingual. "Uh, *esto es Edward. Como estás?*"

I figure I should make an effort now that we're family.

"Spanish Spanish Spanish Spanish," she says. "Spanish Spanish Spanish."

Unfortunately, my facility with pronunciation far exceeds my comprehension. "*Despacio, por favor,*" I say, "*despacio.*"

"Slower Spanish. Slower Spanish. Slower Spanish."

"*No comprendo, no comprendo,*" I say. "Uh, *dónde está mi papá?*"

"Slower Spanish . . ."

"*Mi papá! Mi papá!*"

"*Alberto,*" she calls, "*tu hijo loco.*"

I hear the *thunk, thunk, thunk* of the three locks to my apartment opening, followed by the thud of the door dislodging. I put my finger in my other ear and hear my father say, "*Gracias, mamacita,*" before taking the phone. "Eddie?"

"*Mamacita?*" I say, trying to sound casual. "That's cute."

"Well, she's moved in for a while."

"I should hope so, being your wife and all."

"Huh? No, that was Milagros's mother. She's come to help out now that she's on bed rest."

Natie shuts the door, another *thunk*.

"What? How can she help if she's on bed rest?"

"No, Milagros is on bed rest. On account of the twins."

"Jeez," Natie says, "it's like an oven in here."

I snap my fingers to get him quiet. "Milagros is having twins?"

"Didn't I tell you? Sorry, it's been crazy here, what with . . . *Hey, Fernando, turn up the news, will ya'? There's gonna be una cosa sobre Ollie North.* I tell ya', Eddie, it's criminal what those fuckers in Washington did. Since the

Nicaraguans went to war with the contras, wages have gone down ninety percent."

"What's Fernando doing there?"

Al pops his gum. "I got him a job at the plant. The kid was an engineering student in Nicaragua and he was mopping floors in Miami. But that Fernando, he ain't afraid of hard work."

I flap the letter in the air for Natie, who grabs it while trying to unzip his parka.

"So," Al says. "You got a job yet?"

I'm no Gavin, but I can read Natie's lips when he mouths, *Shit.*

"Eddie? You there?"

"I'm sorry, what, Pop?"

"Everything work out with that stuff in the papers?"

"Sure, sure. I told you, it was all a misunderstanding." Where do I even begin? Why can't I tell him?

"You got a new job yet?"

At least I've got good news there. "Yeah, I'm ushering."

My father backfires a laugh. "Finally made it to Broadway, huh, kid?"

I cringe. "Yeah. Something like that."

Why do I talk to this man? Why do I keep setting myself up? I don't care how much therapy he gets, how many Nicaraguan refugees he takes in; he will never understand me. He doesn't know who I am. My whole life I've tap-danced as fast as I can to win his approval, and all he's ever said is, "Cut out that racket, will ya'?"

Al.

"Oh, hey, my thing's on," he says. "Can we talk later?"

"Sure."

"All right. Stay outta trouble."

I hang up the phone, swallowing the teeth he kicked in.

"Son of a bitch," Natie says.

"I know, can you believe it?"

"No, my jacket. The zipper's stuck."

"Natie, I'm going to jail."

"One thing at a time. Right now I'm dyin' of heatstroke." He pulls out of his sleeves and tries to shimmy out of his parka, but it gets caught on his hips. "Dammit."

"Here, let me help you." I kneel down in front of him and try to pull the waistband away from his crotch so I can jimmy the zipper. Because it's twisted, I have to reach around inside, my knuckles pressing against him.

"What is this thing?" I ask.

"I hope you're talking about my ski pass."

"Why are you still wearing it?"

"I thought it made me look cool."

I pull the pass around and grab it in my teeth to keep it out of the way. Outside, I hear the clanking of keys and the *thunk* of the door.

"Come on, come on, come on!" Natie says, beads of sweat dripping off his face.

Out of the corner of my eye I see Willow.

"Oh, I'm sorry," she says. "I'll come back later."

No amount of explaining seems to help when she returns. ("It's okay, guys," she says. "I'm from Berkeley.") By then, at least, Natie has come up with another plan to finger Chad before my SEC appearance.

"All you need to do is get a job for the janitorial company that cleans Chad's building, then go through his desk," he says. "Ya' see it in the movies all the time."

I didn't say it was a good plan. Because not only would

I have to get assigned to the exact building and exact floor, I would also have to get hired. Which I don't.

You know you've come down in the world when you can't even get a job as a janitor.

Natie promises to come up with plan D. Or are we up to E? Whichever it is, we have to work fast, because the March twentieth deadline is just a few weeks away. Meanwhile, I continue ushering at the Gershwin. Since Kelly covers six roles, I end up watching *Starlight Express* more times than any person should ever have to. But even I'm not petty or bitter enough not to enjoy her performance as Dinah, the dining car, an Ado Annie/Miss Adelaide hybrid who performs one of the only decent numbers, a country-western takeoff on Tammy Wynette's "D-I-V-O-R-C-E" called "U.N.C.O.U.P.L.E.D." Kelly's adorable and funny and sounds great, and I'm so proud of her I could cry, if I were capable of such a thing. Watching her take bows to the cheers of the crowd, I remind myself that her success has nothing to do with me. She's worked hard for this and deserves it.

She deserves better, in fact.

Meanwhile, Natie gets to usher *Les Misérables*, the one show worth seeing this season, although he denies it to make me feel better. ("Two words," he says. "Dow. Ner.") But watching the chorus of desperate homeless people gives him the idea of how to infiltrate Chad's apartment, which, at this point, seems to be our only chance of finding evidence to take him down. Natie gathers our growing crime syndicate—Ziba, Hung, and now Willow—to plan a little guerrilla theater of our own.

It's a collaborative effort. Willow and I coach Ziba and Hung in their roles (apparently I can explain to someone else how to act; I just can't do it myself); Hung teaches us how to distress costumes ("You're ugly," Natie says to a pile of clothes. "I hate you. Your aunt Gladys is dead."), while Natie shows Hung how to use the lock-picking set we bought from Spy City on Fourteenth Street. It's fun, in a Mickey Rooney/Judy Garland backyard-musical kind of way—that is, if Mickey and Judy embarked on a life of disorganized crime:

"Hey, kids, let's commit a felony!"

Actually, if our latest scheme were a musical, it would begin with one of those ensemble numbers that establish the community, like "Tradition" in *Fiddler on the Roof* or "Iowa Stubborn" from *The Music Man.*

The curtain rises on the entrance to a luxury building on Sutton Place, with an awning extending over the sidewalk. A uniformed DOORMAN enters, sweeping the sidewalk. He addresses the audience.

DOORMAN: Oh, good mornin'! You're up early. Usually I'm the only one out here at this time of day. But you're just in time to see the mornin' rush. (He sings.)

Oh, there's nuttin'
Like Sutton . . . Place.

From there, various tenants of the building appear: men in suits, their shiny shoes gleaming like sports cars, skinny women in workout clothes walking children to school.

The music switches to a calypso beat for "The March of the Caribbean Nannies," followed by a contrapuntal duet for "The Ladies Who Lunch and the Ladies Who Clean Their Apartments." Delivery guys and dog walkers come and go, taxis and Town Cars pull up, and soon the entire cast is singing:

> *There's nuttin',*
> *Like Suh! Ton! Plaaaaaaaaaaaace!*

The stage clears and a spotlight picks up a homeless man, one of the many mad vagrants who wander New York's streets every day. Grizzled and prematurely old, he wears a baggy overcoat and a colander on his head. He sings one of those plaintive, "somebody, somewhere" songs.

> *Somebody please help me,*
> *Even though I smell like pee . . .*

In real life that vagrant is me, weaving along the sidewalk in the late morning, moaning, "Will you help me? Won't someone help me?" I approach the doorman, who doesn't respond in the cheery manner of someone who just performed the opening number of a Broadway musical.

"Okay, buddy, keep it movin'," he says.

I'm amazed at how comfortable I feel playing this role. Even though we're plotting to illegally enter Chad's apartment, I can't help but luxuriate in the pleasure of losing myself in a character. I know this guy. I see him every day.

I hold up a bank deposit envelope. "But I-I-I found this, and I don't know what to do."

"Neither do I. Now get the hell outta here."

An Asian woman of indeterminate age approaches. She's in china-doll slippers with white socks, and wears leggings with a worn-out down coat, a plastic rain bonnet on her head. She could be any of the number of house-keepers who come and go: conspicuously Not White, yet, paradoxically, almost invisible because she isn't. I slump down on the sidewalk, pressing my hands to my head like I'm trying to silence the people who live there. "No! No! No! No! No!"

"That's it," the doorman says, "I'm callin' the cops." He makes a move to turn, but I reach up and grab his fore-arms because I don't want him to see the Asian woman. I start singing "Camptown Races."

Camptown ladies sing this song,
Doo-dah, doo-dah.

"Let go of me," he shouts. "Let go of me."

Behind him the Asian woman slips in the front door, and I wrestle with the doorman until I feel certain she's gotten in the elevator. Then I let go, dashing down the street yelling, "Wait for me, Jesus! Wait for me!"

If this were a musical, the Asian lady would remove her disguise and Hung would perform a comic showstopper called "All in a Gay's Work."

While Hung breaks into Chad's apartment, I ditch my homeless duds, wipe off the residual dust I have on my suit underneath, and head to the pay phone on the corner of First Avenue, standing behind a fashionable woman with one of those fur wraps around her head.

"Any word?" I ask.

"Nothing yet," Ziba says.

I look across First Avenue, where Natie is stationed at another pay phone. He, too, appears to be talking, al-though that could just be for show. Or perhaps he's already talking to Hung, coaching him as he goes through Chad's apartment, explaining to him what he's looking at. That is, if there's anything to look at. If he's even gotten in. So many ifs. Once they're done, Hung will call this phone, and Ziba will cross the street to distract the doorman in the way that only an exotic five-foot-twelve beauty in a slit skirt can.

If this were a musical, she'd do a big femme fatale number called "I Love a Man in Uniform," dancing on the doorman's desk in the lobby, stealing his hat and wearing it at a rakish angle.

But this isn't a musical. This is real life. Where a real taxi pulls up in front of the building. And out steps Chad.

Thirty-two

I look across First Avenue, where Natie's still on the phone, or appears to be. Traffic zooms past. I wave my arms at him, pointing to the building, and making a series of gestures I hope communicates that Chad has come home and Hung needs to get out now. Natie waves back in a way I cannot interpret.

The light changes and I dash across the street in time to see Natie hang up the phone.

"Were you talking to Hung?" I ask.

"Yeah, he—"

"Did you tell him to get out?"

"No, why?"

"Chad's back."

"What?" Natie says. "Why'd you tell me to hang up?"

"I wasn't— Never mind."

I grab the phone and dial Chad's apartment, praying that the volume on his answering machine is turned up.

"Hung's not going to answer," Natie says. "I told him to call back in five minutes."

"Shut up. I've got to think." Chad's answering machine message finishes and I say, "Chad, uh, hey, it's Edward. I just called your office and they said YOU WEREN'T THERE so I figured I'D CATCH YOU AT HOME. So give me a call when you get there WHICH SHOULD BE ANY SECOND NOW."

I dash across First Avenue again to rejoin Ziba at her phone booth. She sucks on a cigarette with unaccustomed energy.

"Any sign of him?" I ask.

"No."

Five impossibly long minutes drip by. Any second I expect a squad car to pull up and Hung to be led away in handcuffs, which will lead inexorably to my being arrested and sent to jail, where I'll be gang-raped in the group shower until my asshole becomes Moon River, which is to say, wider than a mile.

Ten minutes. What will I do if I go to jail? I can't even pee in front of other people. I'll die of a burst bladder. Or some awful urinary tract disease that comes from not peeing. Or else suffer the pain and indignity of forced catheterization.

Both Ziba and I are staring so intently at the building we don't notice someone coming up behind us. That is, until we hear a voice say, "You're under arrest."

I take back what I said about peeing. I nearly wet my pants. Gritting my teeth, I turn around and there they are: Natie and Hung.

We all start talking at once:

"Jesus, you scared me."

"You shoulda seen your face."

"You boyzzz."

"What happened? Did you hear my message?"

"You were like, 'Waaaaah.' "

"Let's get out of here before someone sees us."

We flee the scene in a cab as Hung explains what happened.

"*Whell,*" he says, "it appears Miss Chad is packing up."

"No," I say. "That's just the way he lives."

"With moving boxes?"

"Moving boxes?"

"With a Swiss address."

"A Swiss address?"

"Is there an echo in here?" Hung says.

"I don't unders—"

"Ssh," he says, placing a finger to my lips. "All will be revealed." He goes on to explain that he did a quick scout around—Chad leaves whiskers in the sink and doesn't lift the toilet seat when he pees—then started sifting through papers on the coffee table.

"What were they?" I ask.

"I don't know," he says. Motioning to Natie, he adds, "I was just asking him when you told him to get off the phone."

"I didn't tell him to—"

"You went like this," Natie says, making a cutting gesture across his throat. "That's the Internationally Recognized Signal for 'Cut it short.'"

"Yes, but then I pointed to the building and mimed Hung walking out."

"Oh, I thought you were being a drum majorette."

"Why would I be a drum majorette?"

"I wondered the same thing."

"Hello?" Hung says, pointing to himself. "Attention must be paid."

"Sorry."

He continues. "Imagine the scene: I'm standing in the middle of the apartment when I hear a key in the lock. . . ."

"Didn't you hear my message?" I say.

"Shaddap. I work alone."

"Sorry."

"There I am, trapped like a . . . well, like something small and defenseless that gets trapped. . . ."

"Mice?"

"Rats?"

"Bugs?"

"Forget it," Hung says. "I'm not telling the story."

We cajole him with repentant entreaties until he finally relents, like an opera diva who has to be talked into singing a little something at a party, then performs "The Ride of the Valkyries."

"So there I am," he says, "helpless, mere seconds to spare, and nowhere to hide but the closet, which, as you undoubtedly realize, I haven't been in since I got caught blowing Conrad Birdie backstage at my high school production of *Bye, Bye, Birdie*. Anyway, I hop in, wrap myself in a yummy cashmere coat while you squawk on the answering machine. Then Chad picks up the phone and calls his travel agent to book a red-eye to Geneva on April eleventh."

"That's the night of my cousin's party," Ziba says.

Hung explains how he sneaked out when Chad went to the bathroom, taking the stairs to the basement, where a door led him out the back of the building, but I'm already playing chess in my mind. I've got no evidence to implicate Chad, and he's preparing to flee the country.

Checkmate.

Luckily, Natie was the president of our high school chess club, such a Nudelman thing to do. By the time we've arrived at Sanderland and ordered pizza, he's already devised a characteristically risky solution.

Based on the fact that I can't get near Chad, Natie decides we need to lure him to us. And he wants to use Bruce Springsteen as bait. Not the real Bruce, of course—Almost Bruce. Since Ziba's uncle has already hired Doug to convince a roomful of unsuspecting Persians he's the real thing, Natie suggests we invite Chad to the party, telling him that Bruce needs a new broker. Then, while Doug is interviewing Chad (in a suitably dim room), he'll get Chad to admit on tape that he's used insider trading to get ahead. Hopefully without playing "Corner of the Sky."

Hung and Ziba think it's a terrific idea, despite its depending on Chad both accepting the invitation and admitting to a rock 'n' roll legend that he broke the law. What's more, we're not even sure Doug is willing or able. I mean, Lucky McPuddles and the *Caribbean Destiny* are one thing, but this stunt requires some real acting. Still, it's the only plan we've got.

Since Doug only receives his mail once a week when the ship returns to port, we agree not to call Chad until we confirm that Doug's on board, so to speak. Plus, we don't want to give Chad too much time to think about it. Unfortunately, that leaves me plenty of time.

Worse still, I get another letter from the SEC saying that they're subpoenaing my bank account. My bank account! I don't even know how to balance my checkbook, depending as I do on the bank machine to tell me what I've got. Anytime I'm overdrawn, I just close the account and start over again.

If the SEC knows where I bank, they must know where I work. So, once the March twentieth deadline passes, I simply stop ushering, choosing instead to sit at home with the shades drawn, leaping out of my skin every time I hear a rat in the wall. Which, in my apartment, is often. Willow tries to engage me in her usual late-night musings from her hammock in the living room ("What do the Chinese call Chinese food?" "Do you think Daffy Duck and Donald Duck are related?" "Why do we say 'tuna fish'? We don't say 'chicken bird' "), but she might as well be a thousand miles away.

Meanwhile, to add insult to insanity, my father sends me an article about the returns on the investment in education. Apparently, by middle age physicians earn a sixteen percent return on the money they spent on school, surgeons eighteen, lawyers twenty-three percent, and businessmen twenty-six percent.

He underlines that last one.

Days become nights and nights days. I spend all my time in the private tree house of my loft bed, subsisting on cereal and Agatha Christie mysteries. I have agitated, looping dreams where I wake up sweaty and panicked: I'm in high school and have forgotten to go to biology for a semester, and now I'll never graduate; my teeth disintegrate into powder and fall out of my mouth; I'm chased by an angry mob until I fall off a cliff and hang on by the tips of my fingers.

I'm in Sedona. Everywhere I turn I see jagged mountains so red they look like they've been left outside to rust, a Martian landscape filled with hundreds of teepees. I approach one of them looking for my mother, but I can't find the way in. I circle it, rubbing my hands along the leather, searching for the opening, but none of the flaps gives way.

"Mom?" I cry. "Where are you?"

I can hear her voice calling me—"Edward?"—but I can't find her. Is she in this teepee? Or the next one? Or the next?

"Mom?"

"Edward?"

"Mom?"

"Edward?"

"Edward!"

I open my eyes, squinting to adjust to the light, and there she is, her mane of hair backlit like a halo.

Paula.

She clacks across the hardwood floor and throws open the shade, a shaft of white-hot daylight piercing the gloom. I recoil like a vampire.

"Rise and shine, rise and shine!" she singsongs, suddenly Southern.

I roll over.

"Oh, come on," she says. "You know the line."

I do. It's from *The Glass Menagerie*. Paula and I played mother and son my sophomore year of high school.

"I'll rise but I won't shine," I mutter.

"*Splendid*," Paula says. "Now suit the action to the word."

I prop myself up on my elbows to get a better look. Her fleshy body is poured into a yellow sundress the color of an Easter peep.

"Yikes," I say, shielding my eyes. "Turn off your dress."

She smiles. "Fuck you very much."

I flop back on my pillow. "How'd you get in?"

"Willow loaned me her keys. We had lunch and she said you hadn't left the house."

"Did she say why?"

"If she did, I couldn't tell. You know Willow." She drums her hands on the side of my bed. "Now, up. Stop stalling."

"I can't."

"You can and you will. We're going to see Barbara Cook."

"The singer?" I ask.

"No, the bag lady. Of course Barbara Cook the singer. Her one-woman show is in previews at the Ambassador. We're going to second-act the matinee."

"I don't know," I say, draping myself consumptively off the side of the bed.

Paula puts her hands on her hips, never a good sign. "Don't make me climb up that ladder in heels."

"We haven't second-acted since that time we got kicked out of *Sunday in the Park with George*."

"Please. That was *ages* ago."

I glance at the window. So much sunshine. Do I risk being seen?

"I don't think so."

Paula stomps her tiny foot in frustration. "What is going on? Ever since you left Juilliard you've been so distant. You don't return my calls. You don't come see my shows." She sniffs back her emotion. "Don't you want to be friends anymore?"

"Of course I do."

"Then why won't you come?"

I look at my old friend, her moonbeam skin so pale it's as if she'd bleed milk. Keeping a secret from her is almost physically painful.

Okay, maybe if I wear a hat.

. . .

The key to successful second-acting is to blend in with the intermission crowd, which isn't easy when one of you is wearing a battered Sinatra fedora and the other resembles a well-fed canary. It's even more difficult when one of you is ranting about the faculty of the finest drama school in the country.

"I've lost nine goddamned pounds," Paula says, "and *still* they're on my ass to lose weight, which, considering the size of my ass, is a lot of ground to cover." She fans herself with her *Playbill*, which is actually from *Starlight Express*, but the ad on the back is the same. "I've done everything I can, positively *everything*—taking those ridiculous pills, eating that wretched soup—and all it did was turn me into a jittering, farting madwoman. I tell you, Edward, there's just no pleasing them. And now, with *The Music Man?* canceled and Marcus so depressed, I find dieting nearly impossible."

"What?" I say. "You canceled *The Music Man?*"

"Didn't I tell you? It just *imploded*. There are only two actors left who are even speaking to Marcus. I feel so sorry for him. He never should have tried to direct." She shakes her head with pity. "If he could just find a role worthy of his talent."

The nutty scent of a hot-pretzel vendor wafts by. "C'mon," she says. "Let's go in before I accost that pretzel man."

As the rest of the audience returns to their seats, we see that we're in luck, having our choice of empty rows in the back of the orchestra. While I'm glad to have my pick of seats, it also makes me mad. The choo-choo musical is selling out, but you can't fill a theater to see a Broadway legend, the woman who originated the role of Marian in

The Music Man thirty years ago, the woman who sang the E flat above high C in "Glitter and Be Gay" eight times a week in the original production of *Candide*.

Candide. Of course. As we slip into a pair of seats on the aisle, I pull Doug's postcard out of my pocket. It's not like I carry it around with me everywhere; it just so happens that Doug got home last night and I'm going out to Jersey City tonight.

I look at the card.

> *P.S. Have you read?* ▬▬▬▬▬ *Made me think of you.*

That must be it. *Candide*'s a perfect book for a cruise—short, funny, and full of traveling. And I'd like to think I'm a Candide-like figure, a plucky innocent making his way in this less than the best of all possible worlds.

I'm imagining the look of delight on Doug's face ("Man, how did you guess? Now take off my clothes with your teeth") when a voice behind us says:

"Can I see your tickets, please?"

Busted. *Damn*. It must be the fedora.

I turn to face the usher, ready to play "I thought you had the tickets" with Paula.

"Gotcha!" Mrs. Fiamma says, laughing like a lawn mower that won't start.

"Wh-what are you doing here?"

"I wanted to see Barbara Cook, too." She gives me a little punch in the shoulder. "Enjoy the show."

She waddles away as the lights dim.

The matinee audience applauds arthritically as Barbara Cook enters. She's a large blonde going on sixty, wearing an outfit that makes her look like a sequined washing machine. But she exudes an irresistible farm-girl friendliness, as if she were about to milk the piano.

"Now, you've gotta be about twelve years old to sing this song," she says, a hint of honeysuckle in her accent. "But I first performed it in the City Center revival of Rodgers and Hammerstein's *Carousel* back in 19"—she makes a joke of covering her mouth with her hand—"so you'll just have to use your imagination."

She clears her throat, tosses her head, and begins to sing:

> *His name is Mister Snow,*
> *And an upstanding man is he . . .*

In an instant the years and pounds vanish. Without so much as a change in lighting, Cook transforms herself into a not-so-sharp lass in love with a herring fisherman, her clear, unencumbered soprano shining like the morning sun. Even though she has an operatic technique, there's nothing fruity or fussy about her sound. It's a voice you could imagine hearing through a screen door on a summer night—that is, assuming you had a freakishly talented neighbor.

Her performance is a revelation. I've always thought of this song as a silly throwaway, but Cook finds wit and warmth where I didn't think it possible. When she complains about Mister Snow's clothes smelling of fish the audience laughs as if they'd never heard it before, even though many of them are old enough to have heard it the first time. Then, as if reaching a clearing in the woods, she sings the chorus, drinking in the word *home* like it was springwater, sharing a vision of happiness so sublime I don't want the song ever to end. It's sheer theater magic—no laser light show, no flying scenery—just an actor with words and melody.

It's like going to heaven.

The magic moments keep coming, songs that are miniature dramas: the frantic "Vanilla Ice Cream" from *She Loves Me* topped with a high B like it's nothing; the heartbreaking "Losing My Mind" from *Follies*, a song that always makes me think of Doug.

> *I want you so,*
> *It's like I'm losing my mind . . .*

Cook pours a lifetime of struggle and disappointment into the number—a stalled career, a failed marriage, depression, alcoholism, obesity—it's all there for us to see. She opens her heart to the audience, saying, *Come on in; it'll be less lonely if we share this pain,* and I realize she's doing the exact opposite of what the faculty wanted me to do at Juilliard. Acting in a play is like living in a terrarium—it looks like nature, but it isn't. There's a glass wall separating you from the real world. With her diamond-sharp voice, Cook cuts an audience-sized hole in that wall until it's just her and us and the music.

A holy trinity.

Paula and I applaud with abandon, our arms stretching for Cook in a hug that can't possibly reach, our hands cymbaling together, refusing to let up until she does an encore. And, strangely enough, I find myself thinking about Hung. Not in an I-want-you-so-it's-like-I'm-losing-my-mind way, but because he would so love this. Unreservedly. Enthusiastically. Homosexually.

"Fuck 'em," Paula says.

"What?"

"The faculty. Fuck 'em." She gestures at Cook as she leaves the stage. "Look at her. Who gives a shit if she's fat? Look at what she can *do*. She doesn't let it stop her. It's like Marcus says—if you're an artist, create art. Don't sit around waiting for someone to give you permission."

Cook reenters and heads for the bend of the piano. Instead of stopping there, however, she places her microphone on the lid and crosses down to the apron of the stage. A murmur runs through the crowd as some of us realize what she's about to do, that she's going to sing her encore without a mike. As the pianist plays an intro, Cook's friendly face spreads into a wide smile, as if to say, *Let me show you how we did it in the old days,* and I feel a shimmer of excitement. I've never heard an unamplified voice in a Broadway theater.

She sings "Till There Was You."

Paula grips my hand in hers, her mouth disappearing into a taut, narrow line, her eyes welling. Cook's voice rings throughout the auditorium, entirely audible even on the softest notes. She sings directly to us, simultaneously blessing us while offering a prayer of thanks. We are the *you* of the title. The fact that there's no mike makes it that much more personal.

There was love all around
But I never heard it singing . . .

And suddenly it's the summer I'm fourteen, and I'm singing those words, harmonizing with the Marian, a senior who went off to study at the New England Conservatory of Music. Every night, when I came out for my curtain call, the audience sounded like a sonic boom, a wave of energy so strong I vowed right then and there that I would make my life in the theater.

I wish I could always feel the way I did during the curtain call of my high school musical.

Paula and I exit the theater in silence, only to be assaulted by the blaring of horns, the city asserting its ruthless authority. I look east on Forty-ninth Street and see a wall of traffic. Broadway is completely stuck, immobile. Cars fill the intersection, blocking the westbound Forty-ninth Street traffic. Across Broadway sits a trapped ambulance, its siren wailing for the life it can't save.

There's someone in that ambulance, I think. A person in crisis, hanging on to life by a thread. Someone like Eddie Sanders.

And no one's doing a damn thing about it.

Horns bray. Drivers shake their fists and scream. And still the siren wails and wails.

"We've got to help," I say.

"What can we do?" Paula asks. "It's a parking lot."

I look out at the sea of vehicles, each with no more than a foot between them. "We'll get them each to move a little," I say.

"What?"

"Baby steps," I say. "We do enough of those and pretty soon we've gotten somewhere."

Paula's mouth spreads into a full curtain-up-light-the-lights smile, as if to say, *Welcome back, Edward; we've missed you.*

I step out into traffic, zigzagging through the cars to the other side of Broadway, Paula clacking behind me. I tap on the window of the first car blocking the intersection.

"We need to clear a space for this ambulance," I say. "Would you back up about six inches? We'll tell you when to stop."

To my surprise the driver doesn't hesitate; nor does the next one or the next. By getting the cars at the front of the intersection to creep forward and the ones at the rear to inch back, we're able, car by car by car, to clear a space. A couple of Latino guys crossing the street see what we're doing and join in, speeding up the process. I feel my spirits lift higher and higher as Broadway opens up before us, Moses parting the Red Sea. We're actually making this happen. In a city of strangers.

Within minutes the ambulance crosses Broadway. Paula and I hug each other, high-five the Latino guys, and wave triumphantly at the driver as he passes. Some onlookers even applaud.

Then I notice a man standing on the corner, watching. He's a good-looking guy, clean-cut in a wholesome Mormon way: hair cut above the ears, white dress shirt, tan trench coat. The kind of guy you'd imagine would have a soap opera name like Tanner or Blake.

His eyes lock with mine in that unmistakably laser-focused way that gay men do. For the briefest of moments we see each other. Really see each other. An EGG moment. Then I glance down at his feet and see that he's wearing snub-nosed black Oxford shoes with white socks.

Cop shoes.

Thirty-three

Okay, maybe I'm being paranoid. That can happen at my age. Perfectly normal people can suddenly turn schizophrenic in their early twenties. Just like that.

Great. I'm either mentally ill or going to jail.

I turn and begin walking down Forty-ninth Street.

"Where are you going?" Paula asks.

I have no idea. I'm just hoping that a meteorite will enter the earth's atmosphere and crash into this Tanner or Blake person, knocking him unconscious while I figure out what to do next.

I speed up, Paula straggling behind me.

Then I hear bells. Playing "There's No Business Like Show Business."

The sound comes from a small stone church with a banner reading ST. MALACHY'S CATHOLIC CHURCH. THE ACTORS' CHAPEL. The Actors' Chapel? I must have passed it a thousand times and never noticed, having been too preoccupied looking at the Eugene O'Neill across the street.

A church. I can seek sanctuary. Assuming churches still do that.

I peer over my shoulder and see the fed gaining on me. "Edward, slow down," Paula says.

The steps of the church are just a few feet away.

"Edward!"

Paula grabs my sleeve.

I turn and there he is. Hair Above His Ears and White Socks. He furrows his brow.

"Excuse me," he says, "are you . . ."

He pauses, just to toy with me, like Javert in *Les Misérables*. Sadistic bastard. I square my shoulders, determined to admit who I am with all the resolve of Jean Valjean. Except I won't screech it on a high B natural.

". . . the Party Monster?"

I hear someone who sounds just like me say, "Uh, yes."

He hands me his Barbara Cook *Playbill* and asks for an autograph.

After he's gone, I slump on the stone steps, burying my sweaty face in my sweaty palms. "I thought for sure that was it," I mutter.

"What are you talking about?" Paula says. "What's wrong?"

I have to tell her. I don't want to, but I can't keep it in anymore.

"Let's go inside where it's cool," I say. And where she can't yell.

Two hours later my arm is still sore from where Paula punched me. Repeatedly. I've never known her to be violent, but then again, I've never implicated her in a federal crime before.

So I'm particularly happy to see Doug, and not just because he's wearing a pair of sweatpants without the cumbersome bother of underwear.

As always, there's something of the satyr about him, like he's about to perch on a tree stump and play pan-pipes. I wouldn't be surprised to find a pair of horns hidden in his cowlicky hair. He wears a shell choker around his neck, and a tank top reading IT'S BETTER IN THE BAHAMAS. With his umbered skin he looks like he's been bronzed as a keepsake.

He grips me by the shoulders. "Man, it's good to see you."

Whatever weirdness there was between us last fall seems to have melted away like the winter frost. I come in, stepping past a scorched spot on the living room carpet. Doug explains that they had a coming-home party and Napalm set the couch on fire. Then, grabbing a six-pack of Bud tallboys from the fridge, we head down the hall to his room.

We've just reached the door when Vernon appears.

"Yo, Junior," he says to Doug. "That Zebra chick is on the phone."

"Zee-ba," Doug says.

"Whatever she is, she wants to talk about the gig at the Waldorf."

Doug hands me the six. "Make yourself comfortable. I'll be right back."

"Tell her I say hi."

Doug's bedroom is decorated in Early Squalor. There's a mattress on the floor, a stereo, two guitars, and a beat-up TV with an antenna encased in tinfoil. A few posters of Bruce decorate the dingy walls, and I'm struck again by how much he and Doug look alike—if you squint. The room smells like Doug, a musky scent that instantly makes me harder than the *New York Times* crossword puzzle.

I crack open a tallboy and look around.

Doug keeps his belongings in a wall unit fashioned from stolen milk crates, although his books and albums are on a shelf made of bricks and boards. I kneel down, resisting the urge to sniff his clothes, and instead try to solve the Mystery of the Smudged Postcard. On the shelf sit a bunch of nonfiction books on rock 'n' roll, a rhyming dictionary, a couple of "*Doonesbury*" collections, and some titles I don't know: *The Dharma Bums. Howl. Naked Lunch. The Electric Kool-Aid Acid Test.* I pull out a tattered copy of one book I do know: John Knowles's *A Separate Peace.*

I open it and see that it says, *Property of Wallingford High School English Department.*

Because I took honors English throughout high school, I didn't read *A Separate Peace* until the summer after I graduated. That was when Paula and I worked as singing waiters at the Jersey shore. We lived above an ice-cream parlor in a rickety apartment with crooked floors, and I found a weathered paperback copy on the bookshelf next to the couch you sank into like quicksand. I read it in one long day on the beach, lingering under the lowering sun, lost in the fierce friendship of its prep school protagonists. As a result, I can't think of *A Separate Peace* without hearing waves and feeling the salt sting of the ocean breeze, remembering my own separate peace when life seemed so full of possibility, that magic time after I got the money to pay for Juilliard and before it all went horribly, horribly wrong. Paula and I would sit on the roof at night, singing "Our Time" from Sondheim's *Merrily We Roll Along*, harmonizing about the worlds we'd change and the worlds we'd win, and being the names in tomorrow's papers.

It never occurred to me that name would be the Party Monster.

It gives me a jolt to know Doug has a copy, because the book reminded me of him when I read it, though I couldn't decide who was who. If you read it as a tale of sublimated homosexual desire then, of course, I'm the bookish, brooding Gene, so tormented by his infatuation for the carefree, charismatic Phineas that he wants to destroy him. Yet, in a way, I'm also Doug's Phineas, enticing him to break the shackles of conformity and express himself.

What's more, I also stole my copy.

But is this the book that reminded him of me? I pull the postcard out of my pocket. It's got too many letters to fit.

I rise as Doug clomps through the door. "Ziba said to give you this," he says, then tickles me under my chin. A shiver crosses my cheeks and down my neck, making the hair on my arms stand on end.

"So you're okay with our plan?"

"Sure," he says, cracking open a tallboy. "I'm just bummed the Almost Shah's not coming."

"How's the rest of the band feel?"

"They don't care about him."

"No, I mean about pretending to be the E Street Band."

He takes a sip, wiping his mouth with the back of his hand. "They weren't sure until I told 'em how much we're making."

I'm about to instruct Doug in act two of his Bruce impersonation when he looks down at my hands. "Hey, that's the postcard I sent," he says.

"Yeah, it's been driving me crazy for three months." I hand it to him.

He reads it, giving a shy smile when he gets to the end. "I guess I wrote this next to the pool."

"So?" I say. "What was it you read?"

He turns and retrieves a paperback from his night-stand, or I should say the milk crate that serves as his nightstand. He holds the book up for me to see.

It's *On the Road* by Jack Kerouac.

I take back the postcard. "Well, in answer to your question, no, I haven't read it."

Doug flops onto the mattress and props himself up against the wall. "Oh, man, you've gotta. It's like Kerouac sat down and wrote a book especially for me. Everything I think and dream about and believe—it's all in there."

I sit on the edge of the mattress. "So why did it make you think of me?"

He leans forward, his eyes ablaze. " 'Cuz it's all about people who wanna get out there and live. Who aren't gonna sit around watchin' TV until they're dead."

He sees me. Really sees who I am. The person I'm struggling to hold on to. "Is that what I'm like?"

"Are you kidding?" he snorts. "When your dad told you he wouldn't pay for Juilliard, most people woulda just laid down and died, but you said, 'Hell, no,' and did whatever you had to. And it worked."

"Yeah, I got kicked out."

"And still you went out and did something."

"Please. I got kids to dance at bar mitzvahs."

"It beats flippin' burgers," he says, "or workin' in some office. Shit, my dad's driven a Tastykake truck for twenty years. Whose dream is that?" He hands me the book. "Take it."

I thumb through the worn pages, which are full of un-derlines and margin notes. "But this is your copy."

He smiles. "Eddie, if it wasn't for you, I wouldn't have had the guts to get up onstage and sing. And now look what I'm doin'. I know this Almost Bruce thing is kinda dorky, but with the money I'm earning from Ziba's party, I can record my own album. My own fuckin' album. I've been writing songs like crazy; they just keep comin' to me."

He reaches for his guitar. "Here's somethin' I've been workin' on." He tunes the strings, then gives a little cough.

"It's not done yet."

My face is a mask of eager anticipation. *Dear Saint Jude, please don't let it suck.*

He plays the intro, his long fingers working the neck while his other hand strums and beats time on the body. Some say that a guitar is shaped like a woman, but, as Doug's hand slides up and down the neck, I realize just how much it resembles a penis.

Funny, that.

Doug starts to sing, not in the tonsillitis tone of Almost Bruce, but as himself, a clear, cloudless sound:

Beer-spinned nights with parasites who tell me what I
  wanna hear,
When the morning comes there's just the crumbs from a
  midnight rocketeer.
In the light of day there's just no way to say what I
  wanna say.
I feel the thirst, but I fear the worst and I've got to get
  away.

I put my soul on the shelf,
Then nine to five to stay alive.
Put my soul on the shelf

Get on the road
And I'm running from myself.

He stops and looks up. "Whaddya think?"

His eyes are so blue—like bits of sky.

"I love it," I say. And I mean it.

"Really?"

"Absolutely. The melody's great and the lyrics are smart and honest. It's a real step forward."

"You don't think it's too derivative?"

"Not at all." And I love that he used the word *derivative* in a sentence.

Doug reaches into his guitar case and retrieves a baggie of pot. "C'mon," he says, grinning like a randy stable boy, "let's get wasted."

A friend with weed is a friend indeed.

We talk and talk and talk late into the night, devouring each other's company omnivorously, not only running over what he needs to do in our plan to trap Chad (Doug's concerns about acting lessening with each beer), but also musing about music and theater, of the things we've seen and the great things we've yet to do. I tell him my sordid tale, relishing his laughter (I love making him laugh) and welcoming his sympathy. He tells me about his (numerous) shipboard romances, and I share with him my disastrous crush on Chad, which he listens to without a trace of discomfort.

I study him as we talk, the veins in his neck pulsing, the muscles in the softballs at his shoulder rippling under his skin, and I want to inhale him, absorbing his effortlessly cocky essence into my bloodstream and letting him course through my veins, exhaling him, then repeating the process over and over, breathing him in and out twenty-four hours a day.

"Y'know," he says after we're fully toasted, "I'm not lak thiss wid anyhbuddy elss."

Me, neither.

We stumble to 7-Eleven and make the doobie-ous decision to buy Pillsbury chocolate-chip-cookie dough, frozen fried chicken, and Fritos. We microwave the chicken and eat the cookie dough raw, then return to his room and collapse onto the mattress, which bobs like a life raft on storm-tossed seas.

I wake up feeling like the Marx Brothers tried to perform brain surgery. My mouth is sandpaper dry, and there's a vise on my sinuses. The sun burns brown behind the roller shades, casting the room in a dull, dingy light. As I come to, I realize that my head is resting on Doug's calf, the hair on his leg tickling my face. We're sleeping head-to-foot, the accepted slumber-party position from adolescence, because nothing can dull the libido like the notoriously noxious stench of teenaged boy feet.

Maybe it's because I woke up this way. If I had been awake, I never would presume to reach over and touch his calf, but since it happened unconsciously, somehow this feels permissible to me. The muscles are long and fibrous, and they undulate beneath my hand. Barely awake and moving on instinct, I reach up to just above his knee to feel his thigh.

Doug stirs and my heart elevators to my throat. I remain motionless, my hand gently cupping the chunk of muscle, which is hard to the touch, even though he's relaxed. My breath stills, as if to compensate for the percussion solo of my heart. Then, at tai chi speed, I slide my hand up his thigh. I don't know why I'm so emboldened, but it feels like such a natural thing to do, so inevitable.

I'm halfway up when I feel Doug's hand on top of my own, his long fingers like tentacles.

He's awake.

He's awake. He's awake. He's awake. My nerves are rubber bands, stretched to the point of snapping.

Rather than swat me away with disgust, he gently moves my hand.

Back to his calf.

That's right, back to his calf.

The message is clear: *Not so fast*. Or *Not yet*. Or *Not now*. Okay, maybe the message isn't clear, but it's not *Get away from me, you fag*, so I'm encouraged enough to try again. Portioning his body in my mind like a butcher, I make a tactical maneuver, lifting my hand off his calf and placing it directly on his upper thigh. No creeping up this time, no fondling. Just lay it right there.

And, once again, he moves my hand.

To his lower thigh.

We repeat the pattern. I place my hand on the inside of his thigh, he moves it to the outside. It's like some exotic Balinese hand dance, a conversation without words. The tension is almost excruciating. Then slowly, almost imperceptibly, I move my hand back to his groin and his thighs part, an invitation to continue.

I reach up and rest my hand on the mound of his crotch.

For more than three years I have been waiting for this moment. I've seen Doug hard before, during a rather frantic three-way with Kelly in high school, and I've touched a few other guys (okay, two), but nothing prepares me for the thick tube of flesh straining the fabric of his sweatpants. If it were a fish, you'd be proud to have caught it.

Meanwhile, my own erection throbs, a tangible reminder that blood pulses through my veins, that I am alive.

I grope the spongy mass, then reach up with my other hand to undo the drawstring of his sweatpants, Doug's dick flopping against his belly with an audible *thwack*. I grip his cock in my hand, truly astonished. My thumb and pointer finger can barely touch. Later, when I relive this moment for about the gazillionth time, I will note that this is the same width as my wrist. Granted, I have dainty, delicate wrists, but still.

Apparently the ancient Greeks disdained large penises because they thought they represented a lack of self-control. I can see their point. When it comes to large penises, I certainly don't have any self-control.

Neither does Doug. In one swift move he throws aside the blanket, grabs me by the back of the neck, and thrusts my head against his crotch, his hard-on nearly putting out my eye.

"Ow."

"Sorry."

He needs to register this thing, like a gun.

I regain my bearings and attempt to take him in my mouth, but his cock is like a Russian novel—long, hard, and impossible to swallow. Still, I'm full of longing. Unfortunately, I am also full of cheap beer and raw cookie dough. And am the kind of person who gags on a tongue depressor.

Do not throw up, I think to myself. Nothing kills a romantic mood quicker than emptying the contents of your stomach onto your lover's penis. I take a breather, working Doug's dick with both hands like I'm trying to make fire. He arches his back, moaning, and I revel in the sheer voltage of making him happy. There is no place else on earth I would rather be, nothing I would rather be doing. No one I would rather be doing. I just wish I were better at it, and I instantly regret not having practiced on smaller, less important penises.

I'm just diving in again when I hear voices in the hallway, followed by a banging on the door.

Thirty-four

It's my worst nightmare. Okay, not my worst nightmare—that's still the one about being chased by an angry mob, falling off a cliff, and hanging on by the tips of my fingers; but this . . . this is *Bowers v. Hardwick*. The feds come bursting into the room, guns drawn, hollering in that military bark to put our hands up where they can see them.

At least, that's what I imagine will happen as Doug and I struggle to untangle ourselves. Because the Supreme Court said it's okay for the government to barge into the homes of American citizens and arrest them for consensual sexual acts.

What actually happens is that the door flies open and our friends tumble into the room like circus clowns exiting a Volkswagen.

Paula. Marcus. Natie. Willow. Ziba. Hung.

"Dear Lord!"

"Shit."

"Oops."

"Sorry."

"My God, you were right."

"You owe me ten bucks."

Doug fumbles to pull up his sweatpants. "What the fuck . . . ?"

Ziba hands Hung her purse and reclines on the edge of the bed like a Siamese cat. "Sorry to interrupt, darlings, but we had to talk to you."

I cover my lap with a pillow.

"Paula's had the most *mah*velous idea," Ziba says.

Paula plops down next to Ziba like they're at a pajama party and she's going to paint her toenails. "Well, I couldn't have figured it out without you."

"Still . . ."

Willow joins me on my side, followed by Hung diving on top of us, shouting, "Everybody on the bed!"

"Hey, watch your hands," Doug says.

Hung giggles. "Sorry. I thought that was your arm."

Paula and Ziba scooch in to make room for Marcus and Natie. Everyone's here except Kelly, who's got a Sunday matinee. I glance over at Doug to see how he's reacting, but it's tough to get a read. He's pulled his knees up to his chin, his baby blues flitting from person to person to see how *they're* reacting. Luckily, no one seems the least bit concerned, as if Doug and I being lovers were a foregone conclusion.

Dear God, please let it be a foregone conclusion.

"Well," Paula says, "it all started when you didn't come see *Earnest*." ("In the beginning there was the word. And the word was wordy.") "And it was abundantly clear to me something was *terribly, terribly* wrong. After all, we are the age when people can suddenly turn schizophrenic. Anyway, my first inclination after you told me what you'd done, rage and betrayal aside, was that you had to go to the SEC right away. But Natie made me realize that our best chance of keeping us all out of jail is to make sure the authorities understand who the real villain is."

"Wall Street," Marcus says, jabbing a finger in the air. "You're a pawn of the capitalist system."

"A willing pawn," Paula says, laying a tiny hand on his knee. "And a rather stupid one, I might add, but a pawn nonetheless. However, I had a few reservations about your plan, so we consulted Ziba. . . ."

"And me," Hung says. "And Willow."

Willow looks up from the copy of *On the Road*. "What?"

"We consulted you," Natie says.

"About what?"

"Never mind."

"Anyway," Paula says, "once we realized that the Almost Shah declined an invitation to Ziba's cousin's party, we saw an opportunity."

"To do what?" I ask.

Marcus smiles, something you rarely see. "To send your friend Chad to jail."

We work out the details crowded into a booth at a diner, because that's where you go in Jersey to work out details. Our new and improved plan is still risky, close to insane, but I feel fizzy and effervescent. I have the best friends in the world, a glimmer of hope for the future, and I'm wearing down the resistance of the man I love.

As we walk back, however, Doug pulls me aside and says, "Listen, man, I can't do this."

"But we still need you," I say. "The plan won't work without you."

"No, not that." He looks down, addressing a crack in the sidewalk. "I mean . . . well, y'know. I don't know what got into me." He runs his hand through his messy hair and looks away, as if the answer lay in the empty lot across the street. "I musta been really wasted."

"This morning?"

My head is going to explode. Right here, right now, my brain all over the Jersey City street. Once again he's led me on, practically telling me I'm his soul mate, even doing the little Balinese hand dance under the sheets until I nearly ruptured my tonsils and now he rejects me? I can't take it anymore. It's thoughtless. And unkind. Cruel, even.

"At least have the decency to look me in the face," I say, sounding more like a Lana Turner movie than I intended.

He looks up, his eyes wet and blue, like the Caribbean.

"I'm sorry," he says.

"Here we are," trills Hung as he throws open the door of his Chelsea apartment, "home sweet homo."

The room is the same curio cabinet as before, with the exception of a padded table in the center of the room. "What's that?" I ask as I dump my bag on the floor.

Hung makes a sweeping, someday-all-this-will-be-yours gesture. "That, my friend, is the best thing that ever happened to my sex life. Men who wouldn't spit on me if I were on fire will get naked when I tell them I need to give free massages to get licensed."

"You're going to be a masseuse?"

"Ucch, no," he says, shuddering. "Who wants to touch all those wrinkly people with sciatica?" He pats the table. "I got this baby from a guy I dated who moved to Minnesota or Mississippi or something." He notices a pile of deep purple fabric. "Oh! This is for you. I was going to wrap them, but as long as you're here . . ." He hands me the fabric, which is soft, like sweatpants. "It's on account of throwing your jeans out the window."

I unfold it and see that it is sweatpants, but not like any I've seen. They're structured like actual pants, with belt loops and pockets and cuffs.

"It's an idea I had," he says. "You know how everybody always changes into their sweatpants when they get home? Well, these are regular trousers you can wear to work, but they're made out of sweatpants material." He smiles. "I call them Swousers."

I hold them against myself. "Thanks."

"Of course, most men wouldn't wear purple. I made those especially for you. Go ahead; try them on."

Once again I slip out of my pants. "I really appreciate your letting me crash here," I say. "Now that we've got a plan, I don't want to risk getting arrested."

"*Whell*, you certainly couldn't stay with Doug, the cad. Those confused straight guys will drive you nuts."

At the sound of his name, a wave of hurt crashes over me.

"Oh, I'm sorry," Hung says. "I didn't—"

"What's wrong with me?" I say, standing in my underwear. "Why do I always fall for guys I can't have?" I lean against the table, covering myself with the purple pants.

Hung hops up next to me. "I used to be the same way," he says, patting my knee. "I thought maybe I was afraid of sex, or of being gay. So I only fell for guys who were unattainable, like the defensive linemen at the University of Texas. But I got over it."

"How?"

"I started getting laid." He gives me a look you could

spread on toast. "Trust me," he purrs, walking his finger up my arm, "once you have sex with someone from the tribe, you'll forget all about those amateurs."

He really is awfully cute, with his compact little gymnast body. It's just that every time he opens his mouth, rhinestones fall out.

"But how do you do it?"

In an instant he's a Puerto Rican girl on the subway, eyebrow cocked, lips pursed. "Girl, you are remedial."

"No, I mean, aren't you scared?"

He shakes his head. "Effie, we all got pain."

"I'm serious. How do you know what's safe? Or who's safe?"

He puts his hand on my shoulder. "Honey, I've got two words for you: Con. Dom."

I laugh. *I've got two words for you* is our high school joke, back when we were Play People instead of Theatuh People. He must have picked it up from Ziba. He's one of us. It feels good to have a gay friend.

"But condoms can break," I say.

He shrugs. "There's always mutual masturbation."

"That's not sex."

He puts his chin on my shoulder and whispers in my ear, his breath hot on my neck: "Obviously you've never done it with me."

Hung.

Thirty-five

We use a condom. And it doesn't break. So we use some more. Then nestle like puppies until we wake up and do it again.

Having sex isn't a major accomplishment—it requires neither brains nor talent—but anyone who's gone without can understand why I brim with a blue-ribbon happiness. For the entire day I can't stop smiling, even when Hung brings me to a planning meeting for ACT UP, the political action group that's formed out of frustration with the Gay Men's Health Crisis. Just last week, over two hundred of its members demonstrated on Wall Street to protest the exorbitant cost of AIDS drugs. I can't risk getting arrested at their next demonstration—a bit of guerrilla theater to be performed on the steps of the General Post Office for an audience of people filing last-minute tax returns (and the media who do stories about them)—but their courage emboldens me as I prepare for my own guerrilla theater.

The following night I call Chad at home and get his machine.

"Hey, Chad, it's Edward. Listen, *you can't tell this to*

anyone, but my Persian friend, Ziba, the one who's friends with *the prince who would be the shah of Iran*? Well, Ziba's throwing a party for her cousin from *Switzerland*, and she mentioned that His Majesty is looking to raise some capital for the resistance movement. So she was wondering whether you'd be willing to meet His Highness before the party star—"

There's a click on the phone as I hear Chad's voice say, "Edward? Edward?"

"Oh, hi."

"Heeeey," he says, all buddy-buddy. "Sorry I didn't pick up. I just stepped out of the shower."

Cock tease.

"What's this about the shah?"

The following days are full of preshow activity—rehearsals, rewrites, costume fittings. Each of us has a part to play except Kelly, who has to be at *Starlight*. It's so much like rehearsing a play, it almost makes me forget I'm wanted by the feds, although maybe I'm just relaxed because I'm getting laid twice a day. The fact that my carnal relations aren't complicated by operatic emotions ("It's friendsex," Hung says) keeps me focused on the task at hand.

On the morning of Good Friday, I go to a pay phone and call the SEC, hoping that the day works out better for me than it did for our Lord and Savior. After getting lost in a voice-mail labyrinth, I finally speak to a human, who puts me through to another.

"Mead Hunter," the human says.

"Hi, my name is Edward Zanni. I've been out of town, and I've just discovered I have a subpoena to appear."

"Hang on. How do you spell that?"

"Subpoena. S-u-b-p-o-e—"

"No, your name."

"Oh. Edward Zanni. Z-a-n-n-i."

There's a pause.

"The Party Monster?"

"Guilty," I say, immediately regretting the choice of word.

In the background I hear him tapping on a keyboard. "Well, it says here you were supposed to volunteer information last month."

"I'm really sorry. Like I said, I was out of town."

"You were supposed to come in."

"But I hadn't even gotten the subpoena yet."

Perhaps Reagan's right. Maybe government is the problem.

"You need to come in right away."

"Well, I was wondering if you'd be willing to meet me. You see, tomorrow afternoon I'm going to have proof that Chad Severson of Sharp, Thornton, and Wiley traded on inside information."

"Interesting," he says in a way that indicates it isn't. "Why don't you come in now and we'll talk about it? We can send a car around for you."

"No, no, I can't. I won't have the proof until tomorrow."

"That's okay. We can—"

"You don't understand. Chad is leaving the country tomorrow night. For Switzerland. You have to meet me at the Waldorf to stop him. I think he's been giving information to Rich Whiteman."

Silence.

"The Texas millionaire?"

"Yes."

There's another pause. More tapping.

"Can you hold for a moment?"

He goes away for a long time, and I wonder if he's keeping me on the phone just so he can trace the call, and at any minute a police car will come screeching up and officers will jump out with guns drawn: *Edward Zanni, you're under arrest.*

Finally I hear his voice on the line.

"Okay," he says, "what time do you want to meet?"

The morning of our sting, Hung and I have wake-up sex and shower; then he heads over to the Waldorf to do Willow's and Paula's hair and makeup while I throw on a T-shirt and jeans to run some last-minute errands.

When I stop back at Hung's apartment, the phone is ringing.

"Hello?"

"Thank God you're there," Natie says. "We forgot to bring your suit."

"What? Where are you?"

"At the Waldorf. Willow and I both had so much stuff to carry, and she thought I had it and I thought she had it. . . ."

"Can't you go back and get it?"

"There's too much to do here. Ziba's going crazy. You know how nervous these Persians make her."

"Fine. I've got a pair of khakis. They're dirty, but—"

"No, no, no. You've gotta go to the apartment. The tape recorder is in the garment bag with the suit."

"Shit."

"Don't worry. I was just there. There's no one watchin' the place."

How can he know that? The whole point of undercover surveillance is to be *undercover.* I immediately assess my options: 1) Find something to wear at Hung's. That fits. And doesn't make me look like a Mardi Gras float. Then buy a new tape recorder on the way. With no money or credit.

Okay, never mind. Option 2) Sneak into my apartment and pray that the SEC has better things to do on the day before Easter.

Just in case, I disguise myself with Etienne Zazou's fright wig and glasses.

My beating heart provides a sound track all the way to Hell's Kitchen. Even though Mead Hunter is scheduled to meet me at the Waldorf at 5:45, he sounded skeptical, like he thought I was up to no good. Not that I blame him. But I couldn't risk meeting him without proof of Chad's crimes.

This is my last chance to get it.

As I turn onto my street, I scan the parked cars for . . . for what? Guys with binoculars and earpieces? Every do-rag-wearing guy with a boom box on his shoulder is an undercover agent, every kid playing in the street an informant. I'm losing my mind. I walk toward my building, freakishly conspicuous in Etienne's dandelion wig and Elton John sunglasses. If I don't get nabbed by the feds, I'm going to get gay-bashed.

My heart a jackhammer, I slip in the front door and head up the steep and very narrow stairway to the fourth floor, my footsteps echoing as I ascend, my hands sprouting stigmata of sweat.

All's clear. Respiration resumes, though perspiration continues. I take off the wig and glasses.

I unlock the door with a deafening *thunk, thunk, thunk* and go inside. My Brooks Brothers garment bag is draped over Sweeney Todd's Chair of Death. I unzip it to make sure everything's there. Shoes, socks, shirt, jacket, pants, tie, belt. Plus my tape recorder, which I take out of the bag to test.

I'm just about to press record when there's a knock at the door.

My heart ricochets out of my ears. What am I going to do? What am I going to do?

There's another knock.

I'm going to die of a heart attack; that's what I'm going to do.

A bass voice says, "Anybody home?"

Damn this suit. It's brought me nothing but trouble from the start. *Okay, think. Hide. There's a sensible idea. Where?* This is a one-bedroom apartment with inadequate storage. *Damn.* The fire escape. I could hide on the fire escape. I could escape, too; that's what it's for. Except that the window's jammed. Natie and I never called about it because we're living here illegally.

Just then I hear the *thunk, thunk, thunk* of a key in the locks. Except the door was already unlocked. Which means I'm locked in. Trapped. Now what?

The person on the other side of the door tries the handle, grunts, and does the locks again.

Thunk.

Thunk.

Thunk.

The door swings open and there's a large bull of a man, breathing heavily. His eyes bug out at the sight of me, Stromboli right before he throws Pinocchio in a cage.

"You live here?" he says.

Say no. Say, "No hablo inglés." Say "Fuck you," kick him in the nuts; then run for your life.

"Yes," I say.

Stupid. Stupid. Stupid.

He advances toward me. In a moment that combines the fight-or-flight response into one colossally awkward move, I thrust the garment bag at him, slowing his progress just enough to squeeze past and tear out the door.

Unfortunately, I don't see that there's a toolbox on the floor. Actually, that's not true. I do see it, but only after I've turned around to see what made me fall flat on my face. Dazed, I scramble to my feet, looking around for the tape recorder I dropped. I see it by the stairwell and am just reaching for it when the bull comes charging out of the door after me. He, too, trips over the toolbox, but manages to break his fall by colliding into me, sending my body hurtling backward, my foot grazing the tape recorder. He grabs me by the shirt with a thick, hairy hand.

"You Edward Zanni?" he shouts, pinning me against the railing. I glance over my shoulder and see the sheer, vertiginous drop to the floor.

"Please don't hurt me," I say. "I'll go peacefully." I can feel his breath on my neck. He's sweating and needs a shave.

Using his free hand, the bull pushes aside his jacket. Oh, God, he's going to pull a gun on me. I'm going to die right here. I can see the headline in the *New York Post*: PARTY'S OVER FOR PARTY MONSTER.

He reaches into his pocket, pulls out a slip of paper, gives it an aggressive lick, and sticks it on my forehead.

"There," he says, letting me go and stomping over to the door.

I yank the paper off my face. It's a notice of eviction.

The bull takes out a drill and begins changing the locks. I reach down and retrieve my tape recorder.

"Can I at least get my suit?" I say.

The bull glowers at me over his shoulder. "No."

Like the song says, it's a helluva town.

I shuffle down the stairs, trying to puzzle out how I'm going to find an outfit suitable for entrapment. I'm so lost in thought that I don't notice the Chevy parked in front of the building. That is, until two guys with haircuts above their ears get out, clean-cut in a wholesome, Mormon kind of way.

"Edward Zanni," the driver says, flashing a badge, "you're—"

Gone, that's what I am.

I tear down the street, glancing over my shoulder to see one guy chasing after me on foot, the other pulling out in the Chevy. I dart into traffic on Ninth Avenue, zigzagging around the southbound cars as they screech to a halt, then head east on the westbound Forty-ninth so the Chevy can't follow me.

I chug like an engine as I pump my arms and legs, past the Eugene O'Neill and the Actors' Chapel, still not knowing whether churches grant sanctuary. As I zip across the street, I see that I haven't lost the other agent. The Waldorf is at least seven or eight blocks away. I've got to figure something else out.

I round the corner past the Ambassador where Barbara Cook is playing, grateful that the show hasn't let out yet so there are fewer people on the street.

That's it, I think. *I can find sanctuary in the theater.* Pushing myself even harder, I race up Eighth Avenue to Fiftieth Street, then head straight for the Gershwin.

Luckily, the house manager knows me. "Justpicking-somethingup," I say, bounding up the escalator. With any luck the agent will run past the theater. As I reach the auditorium level, I can hear the strains of "I Am the Starlight," the "Climb Ev'ry Mountain" moment when Poppa, the old steam engine, inspires Rusty, the young one.

I pop in the door that leads backstage. Luckily I'm familiar with the Gershwin's Escher-like layout, its labyrinthine hallways equipped with traffic mirrors at every corner so the freewheeling cast can see one another coming.

Kelly's playing cards in the men's dressing room when I come flopping in, a heaving, sweaty mess.

"Edward!"

"Hide me, hide me, hide me."

"What? Why aren't you—"

"No time to explain," I say, grabbing at the rack of spare costumes. "What can I wear?"

"Here, put this on." She hands me what appears to be a dump truck with legs, and I instantly recognize it as the spare costume for Dustin, the roly-poly hopper car who always reminds me of Mrs. Fiamma. I stick the tape recorder down the front of my jeans, which is easier said than done because they're a little tight, and step into the costume, which reeks like an old basement.

I had no idea a Broadway costume would smell so bad. This show really does stink.

"It's perfect," Kelly says, "because he's disguised in this scene." She grabs a mesh hood and Velcroes it to the hard hat.

"What size shoe do you wear?" she asks.

"Nine."

She grabs a pair of skates. "Close enough." As she ties them for me I catch sight of myself in the mirror. I look like a mobile beekeeper. "C'mon," she says, "let's get you in the wings where it's dark."

This is a true friend. I barge in backstage at a Broadway show demanding to be hidden and Kelly doesn't say boo, kiss my ass, nothing. She just leaps into action, unconditionally, unhesitatingly. Look up *loyal* in the dictionary and there's a picture of Kelly. On roller skates.

I follow her up a flight of stairs, walking on my toe stops and hanging on to the banister with two hands, the way I've seen the cast do. The costume must weigh thirty or forty pounds. It's like carrying around a dead second-grader.

The actors are gathered in the wings, ready for the final race. Through the scrim of the mesh hood I see the real Dustin chatting with the girl who plays Dinah. I try to back into a corner, which is not easy when you're half-blind and on wheels.

"Rusty and Dustin stand by," the stage manager says.

I feel someone nudge me. "You ready?"

"I'm sorry?" I say, leaning to hear better. Onstage, sirens wail.

"That *shmatte* on your head givin' you trouble?"

"What?"

Someone takes my hand and places it on the loop on the back of a costume. "C'mon, follow me."

"But—"

"Rusty and Dustin go," the stage manager says.

As I feel myself lurch forward, I hear a voice behind me say, "What the fu . . . ?"

Suddenly the ground disappears and I'm sliding down the slope to the floor, rolling across the stage, and then back up again. And because the Dustin costume is a fat suit, I'm basically skating from the knees down. It's like being wheeled around in a box. A soggy, smelly box. Rusty whirls down the bowl again toward center stage, comes to an abrupt stop, and I smash into him, nearly taking us both down.

"What's wrong with you?" he hisses. "Are you high?"

I've dreamed of performing on Broadway ever since I was nine, when I sang "Where Is Love?" in a school talent show. I've imagined this moment countless times. Perhaps it goes without saying this isn't what I had in mind.

Then, just as abruptly, we're off. Through a tunnel, up a bridge, around corners, down a bridge, through the bowl, into the audience, back onto the stage, Kong flying in and out, the Teeter-Totter teetering and tottering, lights flashing, music blaring, sirens wailing. It's like being inside a pinball machine.

I never thought I'd say this, but thank God I've seen so many performances of *Starlight Express*.

I'm beginning to get the hang of it when I feel the Velcro at my temples loosen and the mesh *shmatte* slips over my eyes. I now have two choices: I can either continue being led around and skate blind, or I can let go of Rusty and pull the hood off so I can see.

I choose to see.

And what I see are federal agents waiting for me in the wings, flanked by a pair of uniformed cops. I need to get to the other side of the stage, so I turn around and skate up the Teeter-Totter, narrowly avoiding the actors heading down.

"Sorry, 'scuse me, pardon me . . ."

Once I'm up on the third level, I whip around the corner to take the Front-of-House Bridge to the other side. But no one's supposed to be here. The gate is coming down; the bridge is rising.

And I'm going thirty miles an hour.

I duck under the gate and fly into the air.

Thirty-six

The audience gasps. I'm hanging thirty feet above the stage by the tips of my fingers.

Okay, this is my worst nightmare.

I try to gain more of a grip but there's nothing to grab onto. The surface is Plexiglas. My hands are sweating. And I've got shoulder pads the size of car batteries.

Saint Jude, I think, *if you save me, I'll do whatever you want, I promise. I'll go to Mass every day. I'll become a priest. Thy kingdom come, thy will be done, on earth as it is in heaven. Just don't let me die onstage in a show by Andrew Lloyd Webber.*

Suddenly time seems to slow and I feel as if I'm no longer in my body, like I'm outside watching myself summon every bit of strength I have, pulling, pulling, pulling myself up.

Nothing doing. I'm carrying a dead second-grader.

I need leverage. My only choice is to let go with my left hand and grab the railing. The orchestra continues sawing away because it's on the fourth floor by the men's room and obviously hasn't gotten the message yet.

I count to three.

One.

Two.

Three.

Okay, I'll count to three one more time.

One.

T . . . Oh, fuck it.

I let go with my left hand. The audience screams. The orchestra stops. My whole right arm shakes. I can't hold on. I'm going to fall to the stage and become a quadriplegic typing with a pencil attached to my head.

You know how, when you're faced with death, your whole life is supposed to pass before your eyes? It really happens. I read somewhere that this is your brain's way of finding a solution to the problem, as if it were flipping through a file cabinet in your head for information. As I hang by my sweaty fingertips, I see the kids on the school bus in the third grade, the ones who called me Edward Fanny and held their noses as I went past, even though I explained to them the proper Italian pronunciation of my name and how it rhymes with Bonnie (after which they simply called me Bonnie Zanni, accompanied by mincing, effeminate gestures). Then I see the time in junior high that I panicked while climbing the rope in gym and the teacher—the teacher—called me a fag. I see my mother saying good-bye, shutting the shade in my room so I wouldn't watch her car pull away, which I did anyway. I see the time in high school that Paula and I got mugged while in line at the TKTS booth and nobody did anything about it. I see myself running out of my house telling my father to call me when Dagmar is dead. I see me having a nervous breakdown at my Juilliard audition.

Nothing in my experience can help me here. My entire life has been misspent. I've been on the wrong track. In the space of a millisecond I resolve that, should I survive, I will dedicate my life to something more meaningful than my own ambition.

And then I feel the railing.

I currently weigh 155 pounds, perhaps closer to 160 since I stopped working as a party motivator. Okay, maybe 165. And the costume must weigh at least 30 pounds. So it's not unreasonable to think that I am pulling up somewhere in the neighborhood of 200 pounds using my right arm. And I'm left-handed. That would be like a pairs skater lifting a quarterback above his head.

Like a mother whose child is trapped under a car, I somehow summon the strength to lift myself up just enough to wedge my chin onto the bridge. With a samurai scream, I let go with my right hand and grab the railing, inch-by-inching my body onto the bridge. Once my shoulders clear it's pretty fast, like a baby exiting the birth canal.

The audience goes nuts, cheering, screaming, stomping. I stagger to my feet and feel the bridge lowering into place. The gate raises and I skate to the other side.

It is my first Broadway ovation. God, I hope it's not my last.

I sail down the Teeter-Totter, my heart pounding in every cell of my body. Never have I felt so alive. I am one with the universe. I am the starlight.

I am so out of here.

Sliding past the cheering cast on the stage, I zip onto the stage-right audience ramp, wave to the crowd, and jump off the ramp, adding a sprained ankle to my dislocated shoulders. Then I am out the door and into the lobby. I stumble down what feels like a thousand steps, tumble out of the theater and into the street.

I hear a police siren.

Thank God I have the presence of mind to head east on a westbound street, so the car can't follow me. Adrenaline soaring, I skate down Fifty-first Street, past the Nowhere subway station, *Cats*, Radio City, Rockefeller Center, St. Patrick's, and finally through the revolving door of the Waldorf equals Astoria.

Two parties compete for attention on opposite sides of the Park Avenue lobby, neither of which would welcome a roller-skating choo-choo, so I'm relieved when I see Natie.

"What the—"

"C'MON!" I shout, grabbing him by the hand and dragging him to the elevators.

"Where have you—"

"I don't have time to explain. I need you to get questioned by the police."

"What?"

The elevator doors open and I push him in. "Here, put this on," I say, peeling off the costume.

"Why?"

"The cops'll be here any second to arrest me, and I've got to meet Chad." I plop down on the floor and untie my skates, the costume bunching around my thighs. "You've got to be me."

"I don't wanna get arrested."

"You have to stall them," I say, yanking off my skates. "You owe me."

"What? After all I've done for you?"

"You mean done *to* me. If it wasn't for you, I wouldn't be in this mess."

He gives a marsupial sniff. "Is that how you really feel?"

"Yes." I step out of the costume.

"Okay." He shrugs, then bends down to take the outfit in his hands. "Jeez, this thing smells like a zoo."

I arrive on the eighteenth floor looking like I was fished out of the East River. In the marble rotunda stand Ziba and Hung, both dressed in Party Planner Black.

"What happened to you?" Hung says.

"Where's Willow?" I pant.

"She's with Paula and Marcus."

"Get her. She needs to fill in for Natie."

A shadow of worry crosses Ziba's face. "What happened to Nathan?"

"He's filling in for me."

"Then who are you being?"

"Myself."

"What?"

Hung returns with Willow, who is nearly unrecognizable with her raven wig and tan makeup, so much so that she could have played Mrs. Almost Shah, had the role not already been cast.

"Wow," Willow says, her eyes widening at the sight of me. "Talk about a sweater."

I take her by the shoulders. "Will, I need you to fill in for Natie and keep an eye out for the feds."

"But I'm supposed to escort Marcus and Paula."

"They've already got a bodyguard. That's enough."

The fact is, Marcus and Paula never really needed Willow to escort them. As gifted an actress as she is, we didn't want to assign her to any essential task. But Willow's a loyal friend, so we found her a role in our sting operation. Because that's what friends do.

I quickly explain what's happened to Natie and that she

needs to patrol the lobby for wholesome Mormony-looking men with haircuts above their ears. It's an extra precaution, but I have to be certain I connect with the feds when I bring Chad down to the lobby after getting his confession.

If I get his confession.

Ziba turns to me. "Where's the tape recorder?"

I pull it out of my jeans, click it on, and stick it back in.

"And here I thought you were happy to see me," Hung says.

I arrive downstairs just in time to see the back end of a train being dragged out of the lobby by two uniformed policemen. I smooth my hair and shake out my sweaty shirt. Judging from the age of the partygoers darting in and out of the ballrooms, there seem to be dueling bash mitzvahs going on, and I wonder if either is a *La Vie de la Fête* event. I miss being *La Vie de la Fête*.

I'm craning my neck to get a better look at the rococo interior of the south ballroom when a voice behind me says:

"What are *you* doing here?"

I turn around.

No. This cannot be happening to me. I must have done something awful in a past life (like been the Aztec priest who ripped the heart out of all those people) to deserve this.

"Lizzie," I say in the tone of someone who just got socks for Christmas. With severed feet in them.

"Fuck you, fuckwad," she says. "It's your fault I hafta go to therapy." She glances at her companion, a bovine creature with that sausage-y look prepubescent girls sometimes get before they sprout boobs. She wears an aquamarine dress with a large white satin bow, making her resemble a gift box from Tiffany. "No offense, Marcy."

Lizzie sneers at me. "I'm gonna tell the management to

throw your ass out." She starts to march away and I reach for her.

"Wait—"

"DON'T TOUCH ME!"

Several people in the lobby look up like prairie dogs.

"Okay, okay," I say, holding up my hands. "Listen, if you keep quiet I, uh . . . I've got a secret for you. I'm on my way upstairs to meet someone very important."

Lizzie tugs indecorously on the sleeves of her taffeta dress, a pair of paper lanterns. "Who?"

"If I tell you, you can't tell anyone. Promise?"

"Yeah, yeah. Who is it?"

"Bruce Springsteen."

"BRUCE SPRINGSTEEN!" Marcy screams.

More prairie dogs.

"Shh, shh."

"Oh, my God, oh, my God," Marcy says, flapping her hands in front of her face in that inexplicable way Miss America does when she wins. "I'm freaking out, I am freak. Ing. Out." She pulls an inhaler out of her purse.

"She loves Bruce Springsteen," Lizzie says, patting her friend's back. "When he got married, she was out of school for a week."

"Was not."

"Was too."

"I had mono."

I see Chad stroll through the revolving door.

"He's rehearsing upstairs," I say. "If you calm down, you can watch."

They grab each other's arms and jump up and down. Then, like two chimps, they start picking at each other, fixing each other's hair and outfits.

Chad spies me from the bottom of the stairs and gives

a politician's wave—friendly, but not too effusive, yet it still makes me swoon. As he trots up the stairs like he's the homecoming king, I remind myself that he's helping to bankroll the Moral Majority.

He shakes my hand, clapping me on the shoulder with the other. "It's great to see you, man."

Prick. Slimeball. Sleaze.

"You, too!"

And the Tony Award for Best Leading Actor in an Entrapment goes to . . . Edward Zanni.

"Sorry about how I look," I say. "I got locked out of my apartment." I'm supposedly introducing him to the former crown prince of Iran and I'm apologizing.

"You always look great," he says, winking.

Fuckwad.

I introduce him to our dates, the psycho stalker and the neurotic bed wetter.

"Lizzie's dad is Shel Sniderman," I say, "the TV producer."

"Oh, of course," Chad says, smiling and nodding.

Liar. Phony. Jerk.

"Do you work with Bruce?" Lizzie asks.

"Bruce?" Chad says, giving me a look like, *The shah's name is Bruce?*

As I lead them to the elevator, I explain that Springsteen is performing at a party being thrown by my friend Ziba, and it's okay to watch him rehearse as long as we stay out of the way.

Way out of the way.

Ziba's waiting for us on the eighteenth floor. I make introductions, Chad looking at her the way men always do,

Lizzie acting timid and giggly, providing a welcome change from her usual behavior as the miniature Lucrezia Borgia.

We head down the hall to the Starlight Roof.

Hung stands in front of the door flanked by a black-clad bodyguard, one of the two remaining cast members of *The Music Man?* still speaking to Marcus. Hung puts a finger to his lips and lets us in.

With its two-story windows offering a panoramic view of Midtown, the Art Deco room evokes an Astaire-Rogers fantasy; that is, if a man in a headband and a sleeveless T-shirt muscled his way onto the scene.

Chad looks as excited as a little boy seeing Superman, and I immediately appreciate the wisdom of having Almost Bruce open for the Almost Shah, "Blinded by the Light" acting as an aural aperitif. Just as Barbara Cook convinced us she was a not-too-sharp lass in love with a fisherman, the power of suggestion leads Chad to believe he's watching a rock 'n' roll legend. After this excitement, he should believe he's meeting royalty.

I look at Doug gripping the mike in his hand, his bicep bunching, and it makes me want to swing from a trellis and sing "Hopelessly Devoted to You."

There's just no getting over him.

We stay for "Born to Run"; then Ziba summons us into the hall, leaving Lizzie and Marcy inside.

"That was fucking amazing," Chad says. "Do you know what people would pay to see that?"

Usually a $2 cover charge.

"Come," Ziba says, glancing at her watch. "We mustn't keep His Majesty waiting."

We line up outside the elevator, clearing our throats

and smoothing our clothes. The bell rings, the door opens, and a bodyguard appears, followed by a gorgeous couple looking poised and imperial.

It's not Marcus and Paula.

"Your Majesty," Ziba croaks, her voice breaking like a bar mitzvah boy. "I thought you weren't coming."

It's a good thing I already stink. That way, no one will notice if I wet my pants.

The couple smiles at her, yet still look like they belong on postage stamps: Mr. Almost Shah, with his hawklike profile; Mrs. Almost Shah, with her feline beauty. They each kiss Ziba on both cheeks; then the prince says, "We weren't, but we heard that Bruce Springsteen is going to play. Is it true?"

"Uh, yes, but the party doesn't actually start until—"

The next elevator rings.

I widen my eyes at her, the Internationally Recognized Signal for "Get the real Almost Royalty out of here before the fake ones show up."

The doors open.

"Actuallyhe'srehearsingdownthehallway," Ziba says. "Wouldyouliketoseehim?"

"Oh, yes," replies the princess. "We love the Boss."

Behind them, a Juilliard-trained bodyguard appears. I give a frantic wave to signal him back into the elevator.

The princess stops and stares at me. "Are you all right?"

I regard my flailing arm. "Palsy," I say.

The royal couple passes.

"Should we go with them?" Chad whispers.

"No!" I say. "I mean, that's not the prince."

"It's not?"

"That's the prince's brother. The Almost Almost Shah."

Ziba returns, as does the elevator. This time the guard peeks his head out like a bird in a cuckoo clock.

I give a quick beckoning gesture with my arm.

"You really ought to get that checked," Chad says.

I stifle my arm as Marcus and Paula appear, looking poised and imperial. While they don't actually resemble their real-life counterparts—no one would put Marcus's mottled face on a stamp, and Paula's well-fed figure suggests the princess has been inflated with an air hose—I'm struck by how they've captured the self-possessed air of people they've never met. Marcus finally gets to play a king and Paula a leading lady. They seem to roll toward us as if on casters.

We repeat our earlier scene, except this time Ziba makes introductions; then we retire to the Palm Room for our meeting, the bodyguard preening so Chad can see he's packing heat. Chad and Ziba sit opposite Marcus and Paula while I remain standing just over Chad's shoulder to record him with my crotch.

"Mr. Severson," Marcus says, "you are aware of the political crisis in Iran?"

Chad gives a genial smile. "Somewhat."

"So you understand the need to fight the fascist clerical regime that corrupts our ancient heritage?"

"Of course."

"The resistance forces in our homeland need as much funding as possible," Marcus says. "We have resources. But what we need are more opportunities to grow those resources. Quickly."

"I see."

"May we speak frankly?"

Chad nods.

Marcus acknowledges Paula. "My wife and I have access to great amounts of information, valuable information. But it's only valuable if we can use it." Marcus gives a papal wave toward me. "This young man leads me to believe you could serve such a role for our cause."

"I would be honored, Your Majesty," Chad says.

"Excellent. All our banking is done in Switzerland. We trust that's not a problem?"

"Not at all. I quite like Switzerland." I can't be certain, but I believe his mouth hints at a smile.

Marcus sits back in his chair. "Perhaps you could tell us a bit about your experience with these matters."

Chad shifts in his seat. "I'm afraid that information is confidential."

Marcus glowers. " 'How all occasions do inform against me . . .' "

Paula lays a hand on his arm, preventing him from performing act four, scene four of *Hamlet*. "Mr. Severson," she says in a jasmine-scented tone, "we appreciate your discretion, but we need to work with someone we can trust. Some indication of your experience would help."

Chad hesitates, so Marcus seizes his opportunity.

In peace there's nothing so becomes a man
As modest stillness and humility:

I know this speech.

But when the blast of war blows in our ears,
Then imitate the action of the tiger;

What is it?

Stiffen the sinews, summon up the blood

Shit. It's *Henry V.* If someone doesn't stop him, he'll launch right into "God for Harry, England, and Saint George."

Chad clears his throat. "Your Majesty, I'd love to help, but there are limits to what—"

Marcus snorts, an angry bull.

> *Why, man, the Ayatollah bestrides the narrow*
> *   world*
> *Like a Colossus, and we petty men*
> *Walk under his huge legs and peep about*
> *To find ourselves dishonourable graves.*

He leans in to Chad, his charcoal eyes aflame.

> *Men at some time are masters of their fates:*
> *The fault, Mr. Severson, is not in our stars,*
> *But in ourselves, that we are underlings.*

I glance at Chad, worried that he'll recognize the sudden segue into *Julius Caesar.* But he's mesmerized, a rat about to be squeezed to death by a boa constrictor.

> *The Ayatollah. Why should his name be sounded more*
> *   than mine?*
> *Write them together, mine is as fair a name;*
> *Sound them, it doth become the mouth as well;*
> *Weigh them, it is as heavy; conjure with 'em,*
> *Reza Palahvi will start a spirit as soon as Ayotallah*
> *   Khomeini.*
> *Upon what meat does this Ayatollah feed,*
> *That he is grown so great?*

Marcus rises and looks at Chad as if he were shit on his shoes.

Oh, the shame. Iran has lost the breed of noble bloods.

He holds out his hand for Paula, who looks just as stunned as Chad. This wasn't how we rehearsed it. But I've got to admit, it's quite a performance.

Without another word, Marcus and Paula head for the door.

"Your Majesty," Chad says.

They turn.

"Maybe there are a few things I could tell you. . . ."

Chad smiles phosphorescently as we ride down in the elevator. "That's what it's fucking about," he says. "I'll scratch your ass, you scratch mine." He adjusts his crotch. "Just thinkin' about all that money gets me hard."

I look at my watch—6:06 Edward Standard Time. Which means it's exactly 5:55. Which means someone with a haircut above his ears is waiting for me downstairs. Which means Chad's going to jail.

But no one approaches as we pass through the lobby. Nor are there any uniformed cops. What's more, Willow's disappeared.

I stall, stopping in the center of the room to make small talk.

"So," I say, "how about a drink to celebrate?"

"I wish I could," Chad says. "I've gotta go."

"Come on. Just one drink."

"Sorry, no time."

"But you've got plenty of time. Your flight doesn't leave for hours."

"Still, I want to get there in . . ." He pauses. "How'd you know I'm going away?"

"Uh . . . you told me."

His eyes narrow. "I didn't tell anyone."

Apparently, I, too, am royal. A royal fuckup.

Chad looks around, then takes me by the elbow. "How about taking a ride?"

Having grown up Italian in New Jersey, these are words I never wanted to hear.

Chad walks me outside, where a black limo waits. I've never been in a limousine before. Under other circumstances this would be quite exciting. The driver opens the door for us and we climb in.

I briefly consider jumping out the other side, but Chad grabs me by the shoulder and thrusts his other arm around me.

"What are you—"

"C'mon," he says, groping my chest, "you know you want to."

The car slides into traffic as I slide across the seat, and Chad slides his hands down my thighs. "I've seen how you've been looking at me all these months. Well, now's your chance."

I squirm underneath him as he reaches for my groin, which is currently taping our conversation.

"What the fuck . . . ?" He knocks on my crotch. "I knew it!"

I try to push him off while he tears at my pants.

"Give it to me, you son of a bitch!"

"No!"

We wrestle on the seat, all arms and knees. The car turns a corner and Chad grasps my throat, choking me.

"Lemme have it, lemme have it."

I beat on his back with my fists. I'm drowning. I can't breathe. I reach up and yank on his hair.

Chad screams.

The limo stops and I thrust the door open, tumbling into the middle of Fifty-second Street. Horns blare. Tires screech. The taxi behind us comes within inches of smashing into us. As I scramble to get up, Chad leaps out after me, snatching me by the shirt collar.

"FBI! FREEZE!"

I look up, and there's Willow, surrounded by two armed members of the Coup d'État Group.

Thirty-seven

Chad and I raise our hands.

"Don't shoot," he says.

Willow advances toward us. Given her assertive stride, I see immediately that she's used Ziba as her inspiration, an effect compounded by her dark wig and tan makeup. "Chad Severson, you're under arrest for the crime of insider trading." Her voice is officious, almost masculine. She's such a terrific actress.

"You have the right to remain silent. Anything you say or do can be held against you in a court of law."

I'm not sure the FBI administers Miranda rights, but it's a convincing performance.

Willow hesitates, flicking a panicked peek at me, the Internationally Recognized Signal for "Line . . . ?"

Having been arrested a couple of times, I know the rest, but I can't think of any way to communicate through expression or gesture that Chad has the right to an attorney.

Flop sweat dews Willow's forehead. She glances down the street to see if help is on the way, but traffic is backed up because we're blocking a lane. She turns to Chad again. "Did I mention you have the right to remain silent?"

Chad narrows his eyes. "Where did you say you're from?"

"The FBI," she says, squaring her shoulders. A single tan droplet hangs from her eyebrow.

Chad looks over her shoulder at the armed actors.

"What department?" he says.

Willow's impassive face betrays nothing, but I can almost hear the gears cranking in her brain, and I pray that living with Natie has taught her something about securities fraud.

"The SEC."

Phew.

Chad slowly rests one of his upraised hands on the roof of the limo. "And what's that stand for?"

He knows.

He knows. He knows. He knows. Every nerve in my body vibrates, a thousand tiny tap dancers climbing the stairs of my spinal cord.

Willow swallows.

"The Saudi Electric Company."

In a flash I feel Chad's hand on my neck, hurtling me toward the limo.

"Get in!" he shouts.

"No," Willow cries, grabbing my arm. Our two gunmen come rushing forward while Chad and Willow pull on me like a wishbone. With his free hand Chad tries to reach down my pants, but my jeans are too tight. Even as I struggle to preserve the only evidence that will keep me out of jail, I resolve to start dieting. I feel Chad's hard hand pressing against the soft of my belly, the tips of his fingers gripping the edge of the recorder, inching it toward my waistband, closer and closer until . . .

Sirens.

I look up and see the flashing red lights of two approaching squad cars. They pull up cockeyed, blocking traffic. A pair of uniformed officers jumps out of each and duck behind their open doors, guns drawn. "Put down the weapons," one of them shouts.

The two members of the Coup d'État Group throw down their guns, throw up their hands, and try not to throw up their lunch.

"Everybody down on the ground," the cop shouts.

All five of us fall to our knees as the passenger door of the first squad car opens, unleashing the most powerful weapon of all.

"There," Lizzie screams, pointing an accusatory finger at Chad. "There's the man who touched me!"

Judging from the unsavory characters already gathered in the booking area, I'm sure the offices of the Seventeenth Precinct are accustomed to disorderly outbursts. But I'm not sure they've ever experienced the sheer volume of a roomful of hollering theater people, many of whom have voice and speech training from the finest drama school in the country.

"I don't have to tell you anything, you fascist."

"Sniderman. As in Shel Sniderman, the TV producer."

"I understand it's legal procedure, but I have five hundred guests waiting at the Waldorf."

"It's a name, not an adjective. Capital H."

"It's all *frightfully* complicated. You see, back in September there was this bar mitzvah. . . ."

"Grab. The -owski is silent."

"That's right. The former crown prince of Iran. Now may I call my lawyer?"

Across the room I see Natie enter dressed as Dustin the hopper car, accompanied by the fed who chased me on foot. He's followed by Kelly, pale as linen next to an officer in blue. A rumpled man with a face like tapioca pudding steps forward. He looks like an ulcer in a suit.

"Okay, everybody quiet down, quiet down," he says. "I'm Detective Joe Polsky of the New York City Police Department, and this here"—he indicates the federal agent with the hair cut above his ears—"is Mead Hunter of the Securities and Exchange Commission. And you people win the prize for the strangest case of the year."

Some of the members of Almost Bruce applaud.

"Shaddap," Detective Polsky snaps. "We're gonna figure out what the hell's going on, and we're gonna do it in an orderly fashion." He looks at Willow. "Since you were our arresting officer, why don't you start?"

"Well, I was sitting in the lobby," Willow says. "Actually, I was kind of pacing because I was worried about Nathan— that's him over there dressed as a dump truck—he's just too gentle a soul to keep in custody, and it made me realize that I had feelings for him."

"You do?" Natie says.

"Yes," Willow replies. "Even though you're gay."

"I keep telling you, I'm not gay."

"Then how'd you get the ushering job?"

"Can we get on with this?" Detective Polsky says.

"Of course," Willow says. "So then it was like, wham, sell the kittens, see who's on the phone."

"Sell the kittens?" the detective says.

"Yeah. It's an expression."

Detective Polsky frowns. "No, it's not."

"Really? I thought . . . Well, anyway, I start thinking to myself that if Nathan wasn't there because the feds thought he was Edward, then there was no reason for the feds to come back to get Edward because he was already with them. Except he wasn't; he was upstairs, taping Chad."

Willow-to-English Translation: Since the feds thought they had Edward Zanni in custody, there was no need to keep their appointment at the Waldorf=Astoria.

"And," she continued, "that gave me, like, y'know, brrr. So I went upstairs to warn Edward but he'd just left, so we all came downstairs again and there he was getting into a limo, and I figured, 'That can't be good,' and I was like, 'Follow that limo,' which sounded dumb but it worked, didn't it?"

The detective studies her face. "I have no idea what you're talking about." He turns to me. "Who are you?"

"Edward Zanni."

The intake sergeant hands the detective a sheet of paper. "He's got a record."

"Lemme see," Detective Polsky says. "Theft of a . . . what's this say?"

"A Buddha, sir," the officer says. "Actually, a lot of them were involved in that. But the charges were dropped. More recently there was an arrest for disorderly conduct outside the Delacorte Theater in Central Park."

"A flagrant violation of our First Amendment rights," shouts Marcus.

"These kids are all crooks," Chad says.

"And who are you?" asks Detective Polsky.

"Chad Severson of Sharp, Thornton, and Wiley, and I'm not saying anything without my lawyer."

"Good," the detective says. "That'll save time." He turns to me. "So where's this tape?"

"Down my pants, sir."

"I see. Would you mind producing it?"

I reach into my jeans and pull out the tape recorder.

"He's a thief," Chad cries. "And a liar. And an—"

"I thought you weren't talking without your lawyer," Detective Polsky says.

"I'm not."

"Then shut up and listen." He points to me. "You with the sweaty shirt. Go ahead, turn it on."

I press play:

I'VE GOT TO BE WHERE MY SPIRIT CAN RUN FREE
GOT TO FIND MY C—

"Guess I need to rewind," I say, which I do, making me sound like the mayor of Munchkin City. The *plink-plink* of piano disappears and a few Munchkin voices can be heard. I stop the tape and hit play.

There's Chad's voice.

"Information is the oxygen of our modern age," he says. "Do you know who said that, Your Majesty? Ronald fuh . . . uh, Reagan. So I don't care what the law says; when I found out that Hibbert and Howard was being acquired, I had to trade on that information."

I click off the tape.

Chad wipes the sweat off his face. "I can explain."

Detective Polsky nods to a uniformed officer. "I think you'd better."

The officer is just reaching for Chad when, from behind the crowd, a voice cries, "OUTTA MY WAY, YOU VERMIN! WHERE IS SHE? WHERE'S MY BABY?"

"MOMMY!" Lizzie shouts, breaking away from a weary social worker.

"Lizzie, what happened to you?" Judith says, checking her daughter for bruises.

Lizzie points to Chad. "He touched me!"

My last view of Chad is of his improbably handsome face being pummeled by a beaded clutch bag.

Thirty-eight

I pace around the Lincoln Center fountain as if it were a clock, the Met at twelve, Alice Tully Hall at three, the State Theater at nine. Beyond the plaza stands Juilliard at two, Fordham at ten, and, just past six, Little Liberty, the replica of the Statue of Liberty that rises improbably above the rooftops, which is appropriate because I'm tired, poor, and yearning to breathe free.

It's been a long month.

I fingered Chad, who fingered Rich Whiteman, who, in turn, went on *The 700 Club* to say he was a victim of a militant homosexual conspiracy. ("Oh, goody," Hung said. "I'll get started on the uniform.") The *New York Times* revealed that Chad was actually a community college dropout from Scranton, Pennsylvania, while the *New York Post* called me "the Juilliard Jackal." As a result, Sandra has started getting requests for me at parties again, which I gladly accept, particularly since she fired Dagmar for hitting on too many customers. She even apologized for calling me a con man in the paper and gave me a raise.

But the sweetest victory of all was one little line in the *Wall Street Journal*:

Edward Zanni, a Juilliard drama student on a leave of absence, provided a great service to the business community when he used his acting skills to expose a nest of vipers.

My father read that.

I look at the Mickey Mouse watch I bought myself at FAO Schwarz—2:53 Edward Standard Time—which means it's 2:53. Enough already with trying to fool myself. It never worked, anyway. I make a silent prayer to Saint Jude, take one last gulp of spring air, and shamble around the corner with the slow, heavy tread of an astronaut landing on the moon.

As I pass through the glass doors leading into the finest drama school in the country, I watch a passel of enthusiastic students laughing, talking, talking, laughing. I feel older and tougher by comparison. Surely none of them has a probation officer.

Even the building feels weird to me, so familiar and so foreign at the same time, as if I were a ghost, and I'm glad I chose to wear what I did. I debated whether my Swousers and an ACT UP T-shirt were too distracting for an audition, but I like how they make me feel: these pants are the most comfortable I've ever owned, and the shirt makes me feel strong, reminding me that I want to act up as well as act.

Life is too short not to act up.

I go into the rehearsal studio where Marian Seldes and the faculty are waiting.

"My little bird," she says, pointing like God creating Adam. "Welcome back."

"Hi," I say, giving a little wave.

She steadies her eagle eyes on me. "I see from the papers you took my advice. Though I must say this wasn't the kind of adventure I had in mind."

"Me neither."

She clasps her hands together as if in prayer. "So, what do you have prepared for us today?"

I've prepared Ronnie's monologue from *The House of Blue Leaves*, all about how he's going to prove to everybody he's not a loser by blowing up the pope. It's funny and angry and weird, and I think I do it much better than Ben Stiller. But, as I open my mouth to announce it, the words get caught in my throat. Over the last year I've played Eddie Sanders, Eddie Zander, Etienne Zazou, a bicycle messenger, a pizza delivery guy, a rabbi, and a crazy man with a colander on his head. That's eight roles, nine if you include faking a brain tumor. I just want to be Edward Zanni.

It's the role I was born to play.

"I'm sorry," I say. "At this point I don't think I can say anyone else's words but my own."

Marian Seldes murmurs something to the rest of the faculty, who murmur back in their murmury way. "Go ahead, then," she says.

I don't mean to, but I tell them everything—about Almost Bruce and the Almost Shah. About being the Life of the Party and the Party Monster. About Eddie Sanders and Eddie Zander.

Most important, I tell them about the Attack of the Theater People. If this were a play instead of a monologue I'd give them each a curtain call:

Natie—who managed to look as innocent as Paula and got off scot-free, although he did get thrown out of the funeral of a retired insurance salesman named Wilbur Branch.

Willow—who is . . . well, still Willow. And dating Natie.

Paula—who, by all accounts, did an amazing job at the agent presentations. And got no offers.

Marcus—who will star in the Coup d'État's production of *Macbeth*. Directed by Paula.

Ziba—who has gone from partying with Persians to planning Persian parties. And working as Sandra's much-needed assistant.

Kelly—who, because of me, got fired from *Starlight Express*. But is already down to the final callback for a role on *As the World Turns*.

Doug—who called me to complain he's being stalked by two junior high girls. I told him that's the price of fame.

Hung—who went off to Akron for the summer, leaving me with a sweet (and completely legal) sublet. With a massage table.

Everyone should have at least eight friends. One for each day of the week, and a spare in case someone gets sick.

Finally I say, "I haven't seen much of the world yet, but, in a way, it's come to me. I mean, if the Cossacks hadn't held pogroms across Russia, which sent millions of Jews to New York City, which can now sustain a bash mitzvah industry, I wouldn't have brought down the biggest supporter of the Moral Majority. And if Lyndon Johnson hadn't lied about an attack on U.S. ships in the Gulf of Tonkin, propelling the U.S. into a war we couldn't win in Vietnam, I wouldn't have had anal sex for the first time—using a condom, of course, because some unknown person in Africa probably got bitten by a chimp and caught a fatal virus. And if Oliver North hadn't sold weapons to Iran to fund the contras, forcing Nicaraguans to flee to Miami, where a vacationing Fran Nudelman poached the chambermaid from the Sheraton because she was impressed with the way she scrubbed a tub, I wouldn't have a baby brother and sister." (Named Al Junior and Alana, by the way. Don't get me started on the names.)

"I guess what I'm trying to say is that if all the world's a stage, I want to play my part, even if it's in a shiny shirt and tight pants. Years from now, when someone says to me, 'What did you do in the fight against AIDS?' I don't want to answer, 'I got a cheap apartment.' "

I look at Marian Seldes. "So I'd like to say thanks. If I hadn't gotten kicked out of here, none of this would have happened. And I'm glad it did."

Edward.

I pick up my messenger bag and head for the door, when I hear Marian Seldes say, "Will you wait a moment, please?"

I turn and see the faculty murmuring among themselves. Finally Marian Seldes rises. "My little bird," she says, "this rarely happens, but we'd like to invite you to return to Juilliard."

Time stands still. In that moment I sense everything—the hum of fluorescent lighting, the scuff marks on the floor, the smell of an airless room, the dryness in my mouth. "Really?"

She beams. "What you did just now is exactly what we've been looking for from you. For once, Edward, you gave us truth instead of a *performance*." She splays her quill-like fingers in a Fosse-esque manner, but the effect's all wrong.

Medea! The Musical.

And that's when I realize it. I don't *want* to pretend the

audience isn't there. I want to invite them in, connect with them. I want to hear them laughing, feel them listening, move them.

"Thanks," I say. "But Juilliard isn't 'jazz hands' enough for me."

It's an exit line, and I'm the one who exits.

Cast of Characters

Being a writer ain't as lonely as it sounds. I get so much support from my old friends, as well as all those new ones from around the world who write me via MarcAcito.com, My Space, or Facebook. I'm also grateful to my real parents: artist Megan Garcia and entertainer Chase Acito, for inspiring me to make dreams a reality; and my literary parents: agent Edward Hibbert, for being a Jewish mother when he is neither, and editor Gerry Howard, for providing the kind of strict fathering that won't let me verb a noun.

Thanks so much to all the people I bugged for research: BoBo Wilson, Mikey Long, Greg Dalvito, and James Kern for answering my stupid financial questions; Officer Jason Walters and Officer Vincent Glenn for being my go-to guys for police procedures; David Stone, Susan Sampliner, and Tony Galde for allowing me to tour the Gershwin Theater; Jason Headley, Karl Rohde, and Rob Peacock for trying to explain football to me; and Scott Waldman of the Waldorf=Astoria, whom I lied to when I said I was throwing a party for two hundred. Other important details came from Willard Crosby, Margot Hartley, Courtenay Hameister, James Rae, Peter Carlin, Deb Sheldon, James Lowther,

Steve Walters, Susan Branch, Dennis Hensley, and the guy from the SEC who asked me not to use his name.

My everlasting gratitude goes to the Early Intervention Editing Team of playwright Cynthia Whitcomb and novelist Eve Yohalem, who read and reread, counseled, and cajoled over marathon meals and phone calls, as well as one perilous mule ride up a mountain. They make my writing better, and my job a joy.

Finally, add together everything I've said above, take out the mule, and you can begin to understand the contribution Floyd Sklaver has made to my life. In a world of detours and stop signs, Mr. Absolutely is a succession of green lights.